SAVING SUMMER

SUZY RYAN

Saving Summer

by Suzy Ryan

Published by Warrior Publishing

Print ISBN: 979-8-9881366-0-6

Ebook ISBN: 979-8-9881366-1-3

Copyright © 2023 by Suzy Ryan. All rights reserved.

All song lyrics within used by permission of their respective artists or their estates.

Formatted for Publication by Ben Wolf (www.benwolf.com/editing-services/)

Cover Design by Damonza (www.damonza.com)

Available in print and ebook format on amazon.com.
Contact Suzy Ryan directly at savingsummersuzyryan@gmail.com for signed
copies and to schedule author appearances and speaking events.

Printed in the United States of America.

*Saving Summer is dedicated to and written for
Bart Bradford and Jack Munday.*

*Shakespeare said it best: "Good night, sweet prince,
and flights of angels sing thee to thy rest!"*

You both are missed every day on this earth!

"In the midst of winter, I found there was, within me, an invincible summer.

And that makes me happy. For it says that no matter how hard the world pushes against me, within me, there's something stronger—something better, pushing right back."

—Albert Camus

6·17·23

Dear Susan —

Thank you for your Pi Phi support. Your loving encouragement means the world.

God bless you!

♥ Suzy Ryan

CONTENTS

PART I

1. The Accident   3
2. Georgie and Marvin   17
3. Life Without Dad   27
4. Life With Georgie   39
5. Braxton Arrives   49
6. The Deception   63
7. Tricked Again   73
8. The Rental House   83
9. Disneyland   95
10. The Ranch House   107
11. Junior High   119
12. The Diary   135
13. Greg   149
14. Bubbles   163
15. The Dairy Freeze   175

PART II

16. The Getaway   191
17. The Sighting   205
18. Prom   215
19. English Class   227
20. Jay's Place   239
21. Meg   255
22. Homecoming   271
23. Goodbye   283
24. The Sweet Prince   295
25. Jay   307
26. The University of Kansas   313
    Epilogue   327

    Acknowledgments   329
    About the Author   331

PART I

CHAPTER 1

THE ACCIDENT

September 1977
Sophomore Year
Edgerton, Kansas

I tried so hard to be perfect. By the time our grandfather clock clanged seven chimes, I'd already taken the steps two at a time. Once Mom stomped her foot on the floor to summon me to the top level, I knew better than to dilly-dally.

"Man!" I bounced my fingertips off my bangs, catching my breath as I hightailed it to the glass-top table. "I only finished half of my scary algebra problems." I sniffed the air and smoothed out my napkin. "Yum! I'm starving from cross-country." I wolfed down a quick bite of meatloaf. "After running the two-mile loop today, I high-fived Coach and fell on my back. I laughed so hard I thought I'd broken two ribs."

Silence hung over the table. Mom stared at me without blinking, her eyes flat and cold. *Oh, no! That's what she does before saying something mean.* My sister and brother were careful not to make eye contact.

Mom turned to my stepfather. "Doc, Summer's talking too much again. She's always talking. And making fun of me."

How's acting silly in front of Coach making fun of Mom? I creased the napkin between my knees. *Why's she always on my back?* I scratched my burning-hot ears.

"Don't bull up and look ugly, Summer. I'm the one who should be upset." Mom's irritated brow froze into place. "Who do you think you are, anyway? Hiding downstairs like that. Making me do all the work alone in the kitchen tonight."

What? Before dinner, I peeled the potatoes, made a salad, and set the table, complaining to Mom about math. She'd nodded, saying, "It was hard for me, too. Just go downstairs and do your homework. I'll finish this." And now, she said that I didn't even help?

Mom kicked me under the table with the pointed toe of her boot, jolting me back to the present. "It's not fair. You're at school more than you're home."

No one said a word. I slunk down in my seat, forcing my head low. Mom tilted sideways and focused on Doc.

"Another vodka?" he asked, pointing to the bottle on the table. His face was already purple from the alcohol. She nodded as the early autumn wind rustled outside the open sliding glass door.

Across the countryside, the coyotes ran with muffled howls. *I'd rather be anywhere but here.* Our red brick house sat on seventeen acres of pasture, just two miles north of Edgerton, Kansas.

"I've stocked the liquor cabinet to get us through an early snowstorm," Mom said to Doc with glee.

Perched at the head of the table with his knee bent, Doc rocked back and forth in his chair. "I'll fill your glass." He poured vodka into Mom's tumbler and then wormed his way out of his seat for cigarettes. Lighting one, he inhaled hard, blowing out a smoggy stink before cracking his knees as he sat again.

"Today, I cobbled your pooch's hip back in place again for the umpteenth time. With my new surgical adhesive glue, it should last four months," Doc said as he leaned forward to snatch the over-sized aquamarine ashtray. "Miss Pooh's been on her deathbed longer than Franco of Spain."

Who's Franco of Spain? I wish I could ask him.

On her lap, Mom's snowy white poodle sat in her usual spot with her butt up against the front of Mom. Ten years before, the dog was a present from her parents after she'd divorced Dad.

4

"Miss Pooh, quit being a hoe, trying to hump Bubbles when you think I'm not looking," Mom said in a baby-talk voice. She glanced at my Chihuahua-beagle mix sitting at my little brother's feet. Mom lifted her squirming pet, pulling the dog's nose beside hers.

"Miss Pooh's toenails match your pretty polish," I said, pointing at her paws. "With cross-country, I've been too wiped to paint mine. I hope my new boyfriend doesn't notice."

"The basketball player?" Mom asked while stroking her dog's fur with blank eyes. "He notices. Mark my words."

"Really?" I skimmed my pinky finger over my bare nails.

Mom adjusted her poodle's custom-knit sweater, turned to Doc, and lifted her chin. "You've taken wonderful care of my baby all these years."

"It's a good thing you remarried Doc," I said without thinking before I scarfed down a clump of meatloaf. "If you'd had to pay those vet bills, they'd cost you a fortune."

"That's absurd," Doc grumbled in his three-pack-a-day smoker voice.

Why do I say whatever pops into my head?

Mom opened her eyes so wide they overtook her face. She shifted Miss Pooh higher on her lap to contort her body near mine. "How dumb can you be and still breathe? You better learn to control that diarrhea of the mouth, or you'll pay." As she raised her hand to flip me off, poop from Miss Pooh's butt smeared her frilly top. "You stupid dog. You ruined my new blouse." Mom tossed her poodle onto the floor and wiped her shirt with her napkin. "Oh, it's just a little dirt, precious one." Mom lifted Miss Pooh back to the table. She licked Mom's face.

With downcast eyes, I smothered a piece of hamburger in ketchup. "I don't ... I think ... I mean ... I don't know why I said that." *Mom's right. I do talk too much, but now, I can't speak at all.* I stopped eating.

"Braxton!" Doc turned toward my brother, who was fiddling with his dinner. "That spoiled dog's fat as a pig. Human food is detrimental to canines," he said, pointing with his fork. "I'll whip you if I catch you feeding Bubbles."

Leave Braxton alone. I fought tears.

My eight-year-old brother remained motionless except for the slight quiver rippling the right corner of his lip. Having inherited Mom's wide, toothy smile and Doc's large, ice-blue eyes, he was the perfection of their best features. His unruly, straight brown hair covered his scrunched-up forehead, touching his extra-long dark eyelashes as his tall, lean body slumped over the side of his chair to conceal the mushy meatloaf Bubbles was eating.

From that moment, Braxton's eyes fixated on his water goblet, and my sister, Katie, stared straight ahead. She wasn't Doc's daughter, and neither was I—only Braxton was his. My siblings were technically my half-sister and half-brother—same mother but different fathers—but I never considered them anything but family.

Bubbles wiggled closer to Braxton's leg.

"Son! Your dinner's hanging out of that mangy mutt's mouth!" Leaning sideways in the diamond-backed chair, Doc cuffed Braxton's head. "Stop fretting about that dog."

Katie looked cross-eyed at the floor. Her dad's genes gave her a fuller and curvier figure than my slender one, making guys worship her. A dark-eyed, dark-haired stunner, she resembled an Italian princess. Without a sound, she disappeared downstairs.

Braxton's cheeks spiked as pink as Bubble's tongue. "I'm the one feeding my dog," I said, bursting up from the table and clearing five plates in one sweep, stacking them in the dishwasher with expert accuracy. Glasses and silverware followed. *Maybe cleaning will make Mom forgive me for talking too much.*

Doc tightened his high forehead, shaking his head. His slicked-back dark hair didn't move. He pushed up his sleeves over his long arms, towering his six-three form over me.

I held out my hand without thinking. "Let's go, Braxtie. We'll take Bubbles downstairs."

"If you had half a brain," Mom snapped, "you'd sit your fat ass down."

What? I stared at my New Balance shoes. *I don't have a fat ass. I've got a sprinter's ass.*

I released Braxton's fingers.

"Don't be thinking you'll be getting off scot-free." Mom waved her hand at me. "Doc told me what you did while I was at Mother and Daddy's."

Great! Now what? "Braxtie, take Bubbles without me." I massaged my unpolished nails in my brother's cowlick and fanned my fingers through his thick, overgrown hair before dropping back into my seat. "I'll be downstairs later."

Braxton hugged my waist before he launched himself to the floor and nestled Bubbles under his arm, vanishing out of the room.

"Yesterday, Summer came home late and left the kitchen a mess." Doc wagged his finger. "And robbed money from my change bowl."

"Listen to me, Summer!" Mom's two vodka straights slurred her speech. "You make me sick." Her voice slowed. "I'm really off you."

That's nothing new. If I'm not doing everything Mom wants, she's "off of me." I turned to Doc. "Remember?" I lowered my eyes. "You told me to take lunch money." *But I've been stealing your quarters for the eight months since you've been back home. I'd die of starvation if I didn't.*

"Don't be condescending." He pivoted toward me, swooping up Miss Pooh and cleaning the goop out of her eyes. "It doesn't become you." Doc was a superior veterinarian but a lousy stepfather.

"S-sorry." *What's condescending?* My thick high school track sweatshirt itched against the dried sweat from practice.

"Summer, stop sassing Doc. You're not the boss." Mom swiveled around and took another swig of her cocktail. "Now, why were you late yesterday?"

"Because I had no ride home from cross-country. Dad said he'd start looking for a car, so I'll have—"

Mom shook her shoulder-length blonde hair that framed her face. "I don't want to hear about your father." Mom bad-mouthed Dad with adjectives that would make a drug dealer blush. And Doc could match her f-bomb for f-bomb. Mom's disgust for my dad was my Achilles' heel, and she knew it. Her large, round, aqua-gray eyes looked through me. "Nobody asked you to be a runner. No one cares how you get home."

"Somebody to Love," Queen's song from earlier on the radio, played in my mind.

"Always worried about yourself, Summer."

Mom just described herself.

"I didn't raise a selfish daughter." Mom's voice had a musical quality. "Why'd you ask Doc for money? You could've made lunch if you were that hungry."

We never have any food, and I refuse to take a large grocery bag for a lunch pail anymore. My eyes darted from Mom to Doc.

"You're being malevolent." A crush of conceit curved Doc's swarthy face as he spoke. "And playing your mother like a Stradivarius." At his last syllable, he swung his arms in my direction and imitated strumming a violin.

"Summer's always been a problem," Mom said as she glared at me. The beveled glass light fixture above the table spotlighted her angular face. "Get your lazy, pathetic fifteen-year-old ass off that chair and finish the kitchen."

I sprang up, scraped crumbs from the countertop, and turned on the garbage disposal. *Mom's ready to blow. I'll follow my sister's advice: "Don't let her bother you."*

Mom flipped her hand in my direction, turning toward Doc. "Don't worry! I'll get rid of Summer."

Perfect. Then I'll finally get downstairs.

Doc nodded and touched his temples, snorting a long, gurgling breath. "That's a start," he said, pushing away from the table and turning his back on Mom.

"Doc, sit here," Mom said in a flirty tone. Patting the chair beside her, she fingered the turquoise and silver stone necklace around her neck. "Look! I found these slacks on sale." With a flowing motion, her hands slid along her shapely legs, clad in vibrant, pink leather pants.

Grunting as he stood, Doc shook his shoulders and waltzed to the sliding glass door. "I'm leaving for the clinic."

"I'll get my purse," Mom said, her smile fading, "and go with you." Her fuchsia fingernails tapped the glass-top table. *Rat-a-tat-tat.*

Doc slid open the slider and left without looking back. His cowboy boots clapped across the porch pavement as his frame faded into the darkness.

Mom hurried to the door. The stench of dried horse manure wafted in while she scurried out. "Doc?"

Her call was answered only by the chirping crickets. If Doc heard, he didn't respond. No one else would, either. The nearest neighbor around the bend from our country ranch estate was an older lady who sold us fresh eggs. She might as well have been a world away.

With expert timing to dodge Mom, Katie crossed the kitchen, passed the built-in telephone table, and opened the utility room door to the garage. Full-on makeup made her look older than her seventeen years.

Scrambling behind her, I hauled open the heavy wooden garage door as white smoke swirled from Doc's two-tone black-and-gray truck speeding down the driveway. Meeting Katie at her Maverick, I slung my chin through her driver's side window. "I'll be toast if you go."

"I won't put up with Mom's crap, and neither should you. Get in!" She motioned to the passenger's side. "And get out of this nutso house. You can't change her, so stop trying."

"I can't, Katie. Mom needs me." I thumped my right foot on the cement floor, staring at my royal blue running shoes. "What if she hurts herself? I can't bear it. You know what happens after she drinks. That's when the drugs start."

"That's why I'm in the car."

"Why can't I be like you? Why does Mom have this weird sway over me? It's like I'm some hamster spinning on its wheel."

Katie squinted her eyes and turned on the ignition. "Since you were little, Summer, I've never understood a word you've said."

"But what about Braxton?" I clucked my tongue. "What'll he do?"

"I'm not going to be around once Mom comes out yellin' that psycho Doc's gone again. He's at his clinic more than he's home. Not that I care. I'm outta here." Katie jerked her car into reverse and zoomed out of the garage. Then, slamming on the brakes, she jammed the vehicle into drive, crunching gravel under her tires as her car's silhouette disappeared down the long driveway.

I shut the garage door and raced into the house, intersecting Mom, who was meandering back through the patio entrance. The moon's reflection boomeranged off the sliding glass door, back-lighting her wilted hair and black-smudged eyes. Sorrow lined her mouth into a lost little girl's pout. "I'm heartbroken."

"Let's play cards. It'll make you feel better." *Why do I feel responsible for Mom's problems?* "You're a knockout," I said, smiling at her. "Don't let Doc treat you that way."

Her face drooped, making her look older than her thirty-six years. "That means nothing. You just don't get it, do you? It's your fault. If you were nicer, he wouldn't leave."

Mom shuffled through the phone desk. Then, spotting Doc's filterless brand of cigarettes, she slid one out, crinkling the cellophane package. I backed up against the wall and hovered near the grandfather clock, resting my hand on the smooth, metal downstairs doorknob.

"Where in the hell do you think you're going?" Mom thrust out her lower lip and folded the matchbook, making a scratching sound. A spark of fire lit her cigarette. She took a drag. "You put Doc on trial. Go Windex the glass slider." With her finger, Mom removed a spec of tobacco from the tip of her tongue.

"I will."

"You bet your ass you will."

I returned to the kitchen for the cleaner and sprayed the glass door. Distracted by the starlit sky, I prayed, "Help me." *If I start crying now, I'll never stop.*

"Hurry up! You're always daydreaming," Mom yelled as she sat back at the table. "Do everything ass-backward."

I wiped the glass door, got on my hands and knees, and scrubbed the tile floor. After my high-mileage cross-country practice, my quads screamed in agony as I stood up and sprayed the matching countertop. *Maybe that'll please her.*

"I didn't mean to cause Doc to go." I tossed the flimsy generic paper towels in the trash, returning to the downstairs door.

"Well, you did."

"Sorry." I leaned forward on my aching legs, resting my hands on the antique clock. "I know you love him."

"You know jack. Since you started cross country a month ago, you haven't done dick around here."

She forgot that I'd just cleaned that filthy floor. "I'm exhausted,

Mom." *Why didn't I leave with Katie?* I cracked my neck and straggled back to her. "Can't I just go do my homework? I'm on my last ounce of energy."

"That's too damn bad. You're just like your father." She blew a smoke ring into my face. It evaporated as she stubbed the barely smoked cigarette in the clay ashtray. She immediately lit another. "Pigheaded. Running all those miles. I'll tell you what's going to happen." I cringed as Mom's face butted up against mine. Tight as a tick and reeking of alcohol, she sprinkled droplets of spit on me. The fiery amber at the end of her cigarette glowed between her yellow fingers. "Your legs will look just like your dad's hideous ones."

She's always making fun of my muscular legs. I closed my eyes.

"Cross me, and I'll destroy you." Mom's voice shuddered through her teeth. "I'm writing you out of the will, so don't plan on any of my money."

Mom changed her will more often than the Kansas weather.

"And good luck getting any cash from your tight-ass father. He still has the first dime he ever made, just like you. You're both so materialistic. Are you ever going to learn that things are just things?"

I sucked in a deep breath and backed away from her. For every second I held it, I felt sorrier for myself. "Y-you mean things like my birthday presents you took away after I made a mistake and then didn't talk to me for weeks?" I smacked my palms on my legs, leaving hand marks on my thighs. "You mean things like the lunch money you promised but never gave me and then made me go hungry?"

Before I could duck, Mom chucked the massive ashtray over-flowing with smashed butts across the table. *Clunk!* Her bullseye struck my right leg. The force flopped me to the ground like a rag doll. "*Ow!* My knee!" I couldn't move.

Mom fluttered over to me. "Look what you made me do," she shrieked. Her cigarette's burning glow mocked me.

Unpinning myself from the floor, I clung to the bare edge of the table and forced myself into a squat position, wiping the sharp, brittle pieces off my leg. Then I hobbled through the pottery shards and shuffled to the hall. "It's not my fault Doc left," I yelled back to

Mom before clobbering the downstairs door. "I didn't remarry him!" *It sucks that Mom's making me so angry.* I wrung my hands, trying to control myself.

"Not so high and mighty now that you're hysterical, are you, Summer?"

"I'll live with Dad!" I cried.

"Over my dead body!" Mom screeched. "He never even wanted you. He just didn't want to be drafted." Her tone changed to a checkmate calm. A line of victory stretched across her lips. "He only likes you because you're a runner."

Her words were a corset of wasps, stinging my stomach. My swollen right knee buckled, but I used the door as a crutch to steady myself. "You think you're sad because Doc left? Well, I'm sad, too!" I screamed. "Sad you treat me like scum. Sad you're my mother. Sad you cut me down." Badmouthing Dad had played the one string she knew would unravel me, but I batted it back to her. "Dad's the only one who loves me!"

"Stop! I can't handle it, Summer Michelle!" Mom fled toward the fireplace, bumping into the blue suede couch where she'd slept off her previous night's hangover. She paused for a moment, turning around toward me. "I'm fragile. Don't pick on me."

"You're the one who's picking on me!" Sorrow suspended over Mom's face, but I couldn't put the toothpaste back into the tube. "Just be normal. Be like other moms!" *What's wrong with me? I'm screaming just like her?*

"Don't tell me what to do. Doc's right about you." Mom snapped her fingers three times with wild eyes. "All your school and track accomplishments mean nothing. No one even cares," she said with a tight-lipped, emphatic nod.

My shoulders sagged against the downstairs door. "I just wanted to do my homework." Whimpers choked my voice. "I try and try. But it's never enough. And now I feel terrible." Air wheezed between my lips. "That we're saying mean things. Let's not ruin the night."

"It's ruined. And you're the one saying mean things, hurting my feelings." She put her fingertips over her eyes. "Ugh! I can't stand the sight of you."

"All I want is to get along." My stomach gurgled like I was going to throw up.

"We'll never get along." Mom's voice was far away. "Never have and never will. Tsk-tsk. We're too much alike."

I shifted side to side. My pulse pounded in my ears. "We can get along. I know we can."

She looked away.

I skidded on my good knee next to her. "Give me another chance."

"I'll never forgive you," she whispered, and then skittered to the kitchen and dialed the powder blue phone. "Hello!" Her charlatan's voice sang into the receiver. "How's Zoe?"

I pulled at my hair. "I can't. Can't. Argue like this week after week anymore."

"Summer's rotten to the core," Mom said into the receiver. "Your Zoe's so different." She swung the phone cord in front of her while talking to Zoe's mom. Zoe was a classmate who continually played tricks on me. Her latest was sneaking dog food into my hot lunch. Our moms were friends. We weren't.

Like a rash, hatred for my mother spread over me as I picked a long, light brown strand of hair off my sweatshirt and wobbled away. *Why didn't I just keep my mouth shut? When am I ever going to learn?*

On the orange-and-brown sectional downstairs, Braxton and Bubbles were fast asleep. I tucked the matching flecked quilt around my brother and fluffed Bubbles' fur, gulping the damp-smelling air between my crying hiccups.

Not wanting to wake up Braxton, I locked myself in the bathroom just in time to dry heave. Over the sink, I wailed guttural moans. I met my reflection in the mirror. My mouth opened and closed again. *You're going to be okay. Mom won't make you crazy.*

Since blood covered my right leg, I got toilet paper and wiped my knee.

But Mom doesn't love me. She's supposed to, so it must be me. I'm tired, and I didn't finish my math. I slammed my head against the wall.

"Mom, I wish you were dead!"

After an hour of sobbing, a faint voice came from the other side of the door. "Honey, open up. Sit with me. I'm lonely. So, so lonely. I have nobody. What would I do without you? I don't think I'd even be here."

I inched open the door, poking out my nose from the bathroom. A fiery heat burned deep beneath my eyes.

"You're a fabulous daughter." Meeting Mom's doting eyes that had sunk deep into her sockets, I inhaled her smoky breath. "I love you so much!"

What's wrong with me, wanting Mom dead?

I splashed water on my face, grabbed my homework, and followed Mom upstairs. In our house of mirrors, she'd cycled from a sloshed drunk to a needy addict. My mother would pop sleeping pills like candy but wouldn't be mean or ignore me anymore.

Mom elevated herself into a sitting position above the desk and chatted on the phone with Zoe's mom.

I sat at the kitchen table with my algebra worksheet. *If I concentrate, I'll finish.*

Static vibrations popped as the record player's needle began to play Elvis's "Moody Blue." The King's familiar, soothing voice crooned from the circling turntable until the record finished. *Click!* Since Mom only stacked one 45, surface noise cackled once the needle hit the single again, and Elvis repeated the same song.

> *Well, it's hard to be a gambler*
> *Bettin' on the number*
> *That changes every time*
> *Well, you think you're gonna win*
> *Think she's givin' in*

Mom held the phone on her shoulder while resting her feet on the desk chair. When her lively chatter switched to dead silence, I swiveled my eyes around to her. *Crash!* The receiver slid off Mom's arm, twisting the phone cord as it swung behind her and knocked against the glass slider.

Thud! In slow motion, Mom's body free-fell through the air past the desk chair and face-planted without any break in her fall onto the same kitchen tile I'd earlier cleaned.

The tick-tock of the grandfather clock shattered the sickening stillness.

I charged to Mom, flipped her over, and in one movement, scooped up her head and cradled it in my lap. Ruby-red, ketchup-like blood slowly poured out of Mom's mouth and nose. Her eyes never opened.

I've got to call Zoe's mom! Dragging my mother, I scooted my butt over to the dangling telephone. Once my fingers touched the cord, I pulled the receiver to me. *But how will I dial? What'll I do with Mom?*

I started to weep. I tried to hold her with one hand and stretch my other toward the desk, but it was too high. I gingerly placed Mom's head on the ground, stood up, and speed-dialed Zoe's mom. "I think Mom's dead. She's bleeding all over the floor. Please hurry!"

"Don't worry," she assured me. "I'm on my way."

I hung up the phone and held Mom's head on my lap again. Days before, in health class, I learned that when people pass out, they may swallow their tongue. I fished under Mom's teeth with my pointer finger until I found it. *What do I do with this slippery, wet thing now?* It slid out of my hand, leaving a warm, sticky substance all over my fingers.

As Elvis's voice repeated, "Moody Blue," I kissed Mom's cool, gray forehead and milky-white cheeks. While I rocked her motionless body on my tender knee, the grandfather clock began to chime. *I'm covered in blood.* The antique clock chimed again.

It's all my fault.

The clock chimed a third time.

Why did I wish Mom dead? I didn't mean it!

Something like thin ice cracked under heavy footsteps. I heard my voice shout toward the sliding glass door. The spinning kitchen went black.

CHAPTER 2

GEORGIE AND MARVIN

June 1967
Overland Park, Kansas

"Mommy, Mommy!" I screamed. "Don't be mad! I don't want to die!"

"Wake up, Summer." Katie shook me. "You're having that same ol' nightmare."

I rubbed the sleep out of my four-year-old eyes with one hand and latched onto my six-year-old sister's shoulder with the other. "They're fighting again." I kicked off the covers. "I think it woke me up."

"Stop touching me," Katie mumbled. "It's fiery hot." Her short pixie cut fell thick over her ears, not a hair out of place.

My nightshirt stuck to my tummy and pulled at the seams. "We got to help!" I sprang from our double bed and crawled over my sister, landing with a thump on the floor.

"Stay out of it." Katie rolled onto her side. "Go back to bed."

"How can you sleep?" I stood by the door with my hands on my hips and stringy, light-blonde tangles matted to my head. "Listen to them."

Katie waved me away and pulled the top sheet over her head. I spun around and charged down the hall beneath the rumbling attic fan, squishing the olive-green carpet between my toes.

Not one to ever go slow, I barreled over the top of the stairs and tripped down the first step. With the help of the railing, I peeled myself upright and lifted my head toward Katie's and my room. Even if our parents always fought, at least I had my sister.

She and I had friends in the neighborhood. Every day at 3:07 p.m. sharp, we met them at the ice cream truck that circled the street. I couldn't wait to start kindergarten in the fall. Katie had learned so much in school, and I didn't want to be left behind. She said the ice cream man was a "Pied Piper." I didn't know what that meant, but I couldn't wait to find out.

Most days, we never had any money for a frozen treat, but we always had the time to play in our friends' yards of fresh-cut grass, drink water out of their garden hoses, and stay outside by ourselves until dark.

I started down the stairs, releasing the railing for speed. Without warning, my feet slid out from under me. I lost my balance, tumbled over the stairs, and skidded to a stop at the kitchen door. Daddy stood by the oven, his hand resting on the handle. A haze of gray, icky-smelling smoke hung below the lights. Blood covered Daddy's face.

I popped up and bolted toward him. Seeing me out of the corner of his eye, he hollered, "Summer! Out of the kitchen. There's glass. You'll get cut."

Daddy met me where the linoleum became carpet. Mom followed him, and their yelling continued. Earlier in the night, I'd put on Katie's doll shirt. It was too tight and split as I waved my hands over my head. *They don't know I'm here.*

"Stop! Please. Daddy's bleeding." My chest squeezed.

Mom screamed words that I couldn't say, or she'd wash my mouth out with soap. "Watch it, or I'll throw another glass," she said before slapping Daddy. Blood flew into the air. "My daddy warned me that you were just a country-bumpkin hick." Mom raised her head in defiance. "But he let me marry you anyway, Marvin. Daddy always gives me what I want."

"Your father only capitulated to you, spoiling you because your mother couldn't get pregnant and have children."

"You're such a know-it-all jerk."

My grandparents adopted Mom as a newborn. She said she hit

the jackpot when her parents chose her because they wanted a tall, blonde, musical daughter. I never understood how they knew what Mom would become, but I knew better than to ask. My grandparents named her Georgina—my great-aunt's name—and called her Georgie for short.

"Don't fight!" I hollered while jumping up and down, tugging Mom's shiny shirt. With one swoop, she flung me out of the way. I dove for Daddy's bare ankle and hung on for dear life. Maybe he would look down, lift me up, and stop yelling.

"We can't afford an air conditioner, much less a horse," Daddy shouted, ignoring me. He wiped the blood off his face with his shirt. "Grow up, Georgie."

Mom said more bad words. "You're so cheap, you squeak." With bulging eyes, she circled him. "So, my father bought me my palomino."

Daddy's cheek started bleeding again. "We can't afford to board your horse." His voice sounded grumpy. I pressed my face into the back of his knee. His leg hair tickled my chin.

"Mother and Daddy said ... "

"Piss on them."

"You didn't think that when Daddy bought this house. Paid off your university loans." She fluttered her cigarette in his face. "Mother warned me that you weren't well-bred enough for me."

"Oh, Georgie, your mother said that Katie's dad wasn't good enough for you, either."

My sister and I had no clue that Katie's dad was Mom's high school boyfriend, Troy. After Mom divorced Troy, she sped off in her Chevy Impala to college, where she met Marvin, my dad. Mom left Katie behind for my grandparents to raise.

"Stop!" I clung to my father's leg. "Daddy's hurt!"

Mom ignored me, pointing her finger at my dad. "It's all your fault I failed that miserable prerequisite class. Otherwise, my father would've never taken away my gorgeous '61 robin's-egg blue convertible."

Daddy gave a sideways smile but didn't make eye contact.

"That's the only reason I married you." Mom blew smoke toward him. "You had to know, Marvin, that I never even loved you. And that I was too good for you, anyway. That's what everyone said."

Daddy bit his thumbnail and spit it on the floor. "It's time to grow up, Georgie. Be a mom." I repositioned my face away from his leg hair. "Be home with Summer instead of hanging out at that barn."

"What," Mom said, taking another drag of her cigarette and putting her hand by her ear, "in the world are you talking about?"

"Leaving Summer alone when Katie's at school." Daddy's eyes watered. "What kind of mother does that, Georgie?"

"How dare you, Marvin. And what kind of name is Marvin anyway? Who names their son that?" Mom puffed her cigarette. "Well, Marvin, I never did such a thing. You're the one who left Summer alone." Mom set her cigarette in the ashtray. "Believe you, me. Breathe that lie, and I'll mutilate you."

"Daddy!" I tugged on the bottom of his shorts. *They're mad at me.* I'd never forget their words, even if I didn't understand what they meant.

"You're a manipulative storyteller, Georgie. Hear what you want. Believe your own lies. You could convince the Pope that Jesus was a sinner." Daddy stepped backward from Mom, tilted his head, and started to say something but stopped. "You're charismatic, all right. I'll give you that, Georgie."

"Who do you think you are?" Mom closed her eyes. Sparkly blue eyeshadow covered her eyelids. "Don't you dare talk to me like that—big football and track star. Ha! You're nothing without my daddy." Mom's words ran together before she snorted with a laugh. "Who do you think pulled strings to get you that bank job, Marvin?"

Daddy stared straight ahead and loudly cleared his throat. Suddenly, spit flew out his mouth and sailed through the air, going splat on Mom's face. The saliva landed under her eye and slid in slow motion down her face.

Knotting up her fancy blouse, Mom wiped off the drool and picked up her cigarette burning in the ashtray. With heavy eyelids, she took a long drag, held her breath, and blew smoke rings over the white coffee table where the night before, Katie and I drank pickle juice, pretending it was alcohol, all the while chewing candy cigarettes.

"Tomorrow, Katie and I leave for my parents' house. We'll be out of here before sunrise. Mother was right. You're as common as cornbread. We should've never let you adopt Katie."

Mom glided toward Daddy, arching like a cat before she passed him, and singed her cigarette into the side of his neck. He bent underneath her, lifted me from the floor, and carried me to my room. I buried my head in his chest and sniffed the burnt-flesh stink, grabbing his spiky flat top hair with my red hands.

Once I got in bed, my sister pretended to be asleep. "Daddy was bleeding." I found my fluffy, beige stuffed doggie and scooted close to Katie. "Lots of blood."

"Don't worry about it."

"But I do, Katie." I pulled on her arm. "I'm writing to God. All by myself. I stole your paper. Does God hear? Is He air?"

"How would I know?"

"Are you mad I watched you make letters? Copied you?"

"You talk a lot, Summer. Go to sleep."

"Thanks for snuggling, Katie."

"I didn't know we were."

I tucked my doggie under my chin, put my bloody thumb in my mouth, and sucked off the sweet-salty taste.

After I woke up and had breakfast, Daddy drove four hours to Grammy and Grandpa's dairy farm. He didn't turn off the car until he circled by the barns. Then, he scooped me out of the front seat and set me down on the dirt driveway.

"When I was a kid, if something was broken, we never called a repairman—even for the outhouse. Instead, we were the repair-men." He sighed as his eyes traveled around the property. "I wish I could repair what's broken now." Daddy forced a smile and rustled my uncombed hair. "I've got to get back to Overland Park. I know you'll be a good girl, Summer, until I return."

A sugary spice aroma greeted me the following morning as I cracked one eye open. I bounded out of bed to the small, tidy

SUZY RYAN

kitchen and stuffed three of Grammy's hot, melt-in-your-mouth cinnamon rolls down in record time. After we ate, Grammy and I made our way to the brown barn to scatter the chicken's pellets and feed the calves with a liquid grain goop that smelled good enough to eat.

There was a schedule on the farm, so at midday, I played in the dirt by Grammy's side while she tended her acre garden until we picked blackberries growing on the fence. That night during dinner, I ate almost the whole carton of cottage cheese and four of Grammy's sweet homemade rolls.

"A girl needs a lot of food to grow strong," Grandpa said, trooping to the silver tin barn to milk the cows. He showed me how to place suctions on the cows' pink teats as they chewed grain. Once Grandpa got all the milk for the night, he sterilized everything, making it smell clean.

When we returned to the house, we devoured Grammy's homemade blackberry pie. I pulled off the crust, eating it first. *I like it best.* The sweet flakes of butter and sugar felt grainy against the fruit. "Over the weekend, I'll teach you to make a cinnamon and sugar crust," Grammy said.

I skipped around the kitchen, waving my hands.

The next morning, Grammy washed the clothes. First, she added soap and water to the big white round tub, making them swish back and forth. Then she cranked each one through two long, round squeezer things, making them stiff and flat. *It's so much more work than Mom's washing machine at home.* Jumping into action, I helped Grammy string the clothes across the porch because she had no dryer.

That evening before dinner, we sat under the willow tree, splitting pea pods, nibbling on sweet radishes, and eating slices of American cheese. To entertain my grandparents, I did cartwheels, giggling as the spiky grass tickled my bare feet.

Days later, Sunday rolled around, so Grammy, Grandpa, and I put on dress-up clothes and crammed into their old gray truck, and drove for what seemed like days on empty, gravel roads until a small white church with a large cross under a bell tower appeared out of nowhere. Beneath the cross, a red door opened wide and welcomed us.

"Let's go, tiny peanut." Grammy smiled, grabbing my hand. I hopped out of the truck, and we sailed up the stairs into the church. I waved wildly at Grammy's friends, who nodded at us.

We rounded the corner to the basement stairs in a quick minute, and Grammy pointed to an entrance. "I'll take you to Sunday school down there, and then we'll meet in the big church."

"I can do it myself." I broke free from Grammy's grip, charged to the bottom of the steps and swung the door open. The smell of liquid paste filled the classroom as I sat at the oversized, wobbly wooden table.

During story time, the teacher held up a paper doll cutout of Jesus and taught that He was God and He loved us. Once she placed Jesus on the flannel board, He seemed to come alive in his baggy bathrobe and knowing smile. Jesus was my instant friend with His unusually long hair and outstretched hands. After I scribbled my Jesus puzzle picture, I painted the backs with tacky paste and pounded them on the thick cardboard. The excess glue stuck my fingers together.

When class was over, I brought my masterpiece to my grandparents, sliding like an Olympic ice skater across the lemony-waxed wooden floor in my black patent leather shoes. Grammy hugged me under the big wooden cross that clung to the wall. "You're spunky, Summer. I'll say that." She had a cheerful voice but sad blue eyes. "Grandpa and I are happy you're here."

On the way home from church, Grammy talked about Daddy. "Did you know your dad, aunt, and uncle milked the cows before school?" She smiled above my head. "Together, they rode bareback to a one-room schoolhouse, tied up our old mare, and then rode her home at the end of the day."

"Tell me more, Grammy. I love hearing about Daddy!"

"In the ninth grade, your dad transferred to a nearby larger town with a football and track team. He wanted to earn a college scholarship."

Grandpa interrupted her. "From her garden, your grammy sold bushels of produce and used her fresh farm eggs to cover your dad's high school room and board."

Grammy smiled and patted his arm. "After four years, he left for Fort Hays State University. He did it! Marvin finally got that track and football scholarship he worked so hard for."

"And an academic one, too," Grandpa added.

Snuggled safely in the truck between Grammy and Grandpa, I wanted to be just like Daddy. I thought about Katie. She couldn't be having as much fun. I wanted to visit Grandmother Mema and Grandfather's house, but for some reason, I never did.

My month-long visit to my grandparents' farm seemed like a day when a 1962 Ford Falcon drove into the long, dirt driveway. I missed Daddy but not Mom. She wasn't around much. Once Daddy got out of his car, I vaulted into his arms, sniffing his smoky cologne smell and running my hands through his flat top hair.

We ate lunch with Grammy and Grandpa. Then we took off for Overland Park, but he didn't say much. "Daddy, why aren't you talking? Are you mad? Did I do something?"

"Oh, no, Summer. You didn't do anything. You are such a good little girl." He touched his eye. "I just want to hear about your time at the farm."

"You don't have to talk, Daddy." I put my hand on his strong shoulder. "I'll talk for the two of us."

"You do that. Tell me all about your visit."

With barely a breath, I summarized my stay at his parents' house day-by-day and week-by-week. "Since you weren't here, Daddy, I had to ask Grandpa what happens if I forget to breathe. He told me God would make sure I always remembered." I bent my legs under me, facing him. "And every Sunday, we went to church. Why does Jesus only wear an old robe? Even though it's white, I colored it rainbow colors outside the lines. Do you think Jesus cares?" *Something's wrong with Daddy. He isn't answering my questions. He isn't even trying.*

When I paused to catch my breath, he swallowed. "Summer, I've got something to tell you." He stayed quiet for a long time.

"Daddy, did you forget what you were going to say?"

With an effort, he turned to me and said, "Your mother and I are getting a divorce."

"That's okay, Daddy." I nodded. "I'll live with you."

"I wish you could." His head dropped. "Divorced children

always live with their mothers." I pressed my hands over my ears to block out the happy hum of his car engine.

"No, Daddy, I must live with you." Out his window, a field of amber wheat waved stalks of grain. I tugged on his sleeve. "Who'll take care of me?"

He didn't answer.

Staring at the car's ceiling, I blinked twice. My nose itched, and my teeth chattered as I touched the tiny dimples denting my chin. I looked up as long as I could, trying to stop the tears from sliding down my face. Finally, they dripped over my cheeks and lips, leaving a salty taste in my mouth. *Daddy always tells me I'm one tough customer.* Scooting to the edge of the seat, I wrapped my bony arms around my knees and cried harder.

"I wish you could live with me, Summer. But you have to live with your mom. There's nothing I can do." He clamped his hands on the steering wheel and stared at the road. "I would take you if there was any other ... "

"Daddy! Daddy, please don't leave me with her. She scares me."

It was the last time I called my father "Daddy."

CHAPTER 3

LIFE WITHOUT DAD

June 1967 – October 1967
Overland Park, Kansas

Little Summer's Diary
Der God,
R u ter? I r 5. Kat r 7
🖤 *Sum*

"W e're here." Dad turned into the driveway and shut off the car. "Even though your mom and I are getting divorced, Summer, I'll still see you."

"And Grammy, too?" Bouncing on the front seat, I opened my door. "Gotta go potty. Bye, bye, Dad." I dashed out of the car into the house and passed Mom talking on the phone. She didn't make eye contact, so I ran upstairs.

By the time I opened the bathroom door, tinkle rushed down my legs. Pulling off my damp clothes, I used them to mop up the mess and shoved them deep under the sink.

Leaning out the bathroom door, I waved at Mom. She was drinking coffee and still yakking on the telephone, so she didn't see me. I raced to my room. Katie was on our bed, writing in a notebook.

"Eww!" Katie screamed. "Put something on!"

"I'm gonna!" I pulled my clothes out of the dresser, tugged them over my legs, and hopped on the bright orange silky bedspread. Fluffy beige-and-brown ears brushed against my leg. "I'm glad to see my stuffed doggy." I hid him under my shirt. "Mom said if I took him out of our room, she'd hide him." I peered over Katie's shoulder. "I missed you. Did you miss me? Did you have fun? I had fun."

"All I did was homework."

"You're still doing it. I wanna do homework." My hands flipped up and down. "Do you like school? I'll like school."

"You'll hate it." Katie blinked against the orange light shining through our window. "You can't talk so much."

I started kindergarten in a month and couldn't wait to be like my sister.

"You smell." Katie sniffed my arm. "Need a bath."

"I'll take one tonight. Will you help me get the soap out of my hair? Dad always did that."

"If I'm not too tired. Grandmother Mema made me write cursive the entire vacation. Said I needed the practice to start second grade." She frowned. "And for the hour I've been home, that's what I've been doing."

"Can you share paper? I can't do cursive, but I can practice regular letters."

Katie tore a piece from her spiral notebook. "Here. Take this, too." She dug through a stack of books, pens, pencils, and crayons near the new Barbie until she found the felt-tip markers and handed me one.

"You always get stuff from Grandmother Mema. Did she send me some?"

Katie colored her letters. "You didn't live with her like me."

"Why didn't I live with her?"

"You weren't born yet." She stopped and looked up. "Don't you know anything?"

"I know I want your old Barbie." I stood up on our bed. "Can I? Pleeaase?"

"You're so loud." Katie handed me her doll. "If you're not rough, you can borrow her. And don't be getting into my new things. I can always tell."

"Oh, I won't, Katie." I hugged the blonde doll who looked like Mom. "I love her so much. Thanks." I held my newfound treasure while using our bed like a trampoline.

"You're wild." Katie grabbed her crunched papers. "Stop, and I'll play Barbies."

"You will?" I flung myself on Katie. "I love you."

"Stop touching me, or I won't."

My stomach growled as I rolled over to my side of the bed, making my shirt stick to my skin. "My tummy hurts. Let's eat after we play." I patted my belly button. "Dad forgot to stop for dinner."

"Just don't think about it."

At least I have a new doll.

Breathless and smelling like Grammy's garden, Mom entered the room and circled our bed like a spinning jack. "Bob's coming over with his Jaguar. I told him to stay home on this July scorcher, but he wouldn't listen."

"Who's Bob?" I asked.

"Never mind. You and Katie need to pretend you're asleep." Her eyes darted back and forth through the blowing bright orange curtains. "Understand?"

I nodded yes. *I'll be a good girl even though I don't.*

"I'm afraid I might have written a check I can't cash." Katie and I looked at each other in confusion. "Quick, get under the covers." She lifted them high. "I don't care if outside is as light as your bedspread."

I snuggled my stuffed doggie under my arm and dove under Katie's new presents. *I'm wide awake.*

The next thing I knew, it was morning. I questioned Mom about Bob. Her mouth made a strange smile while she showed me a pearl ring he'd given her.

Even though all of Dad's things were gone, he rang the bell the following weekend.

When I opened the door, he stared at the sky. "I know you turned five at the farm, but we're going to celebrate your birthday at the French Market Carnival." Dad tried to sound excited. "I'll be in the car."

Ten minutes later, we all piled in his Ford. Once Dad backed out of the driveway, Mom asked, "Where's the child support check?"

"It's not due till Monday." Dad grimaced. "Two days."

"So flawless playing bridge." Mom's voice got louder as the car lurched up the hill. "But too tight to play the stock market like Daddy told you. Then you'd have some real money."

"Georgie!" Dad slammed on the brakes. "If you're pissy now, just wait. I'm deducting Summer's tennis shoes I bought from your monthly check."

"What? Why you son of ... " Mom's fingertips flicked the passenger side door handle, cracking open the door like she would jump. "You wouldn't dare."

"You don't scare me." Dad swerved the car to a stop on the side of the road. "Shut that!"

"I'll say you pushed me."

"Everyone would know that's hooey. Just like thinking I can bring the money early. I have to scrape together every penny of your child support." He hit his hands on the steering wheel. "You've taken me to the cleaners, Georgie. I'm in a tiny apartment, paying your mortgage and my rent. I need another paycheck. I get paid Monday. It wouldn't have cleared the bank if I'd brought it today. Bounced sky-high."

"You're such a smart aleck."

I started to say something. Katie put her finger over her lips.

Dad started driving again.

Mom lit a cigarette, and I sneezed from the stinging in my nose.

"We don't have to celebrate my birthday," I yelled. Mom and Dad's words whacked me like I was a birthday piñata.

I started full-day kindergarten with little chairs, tiny desks, and daily snacks a month later. My favorite was Friday's Show and Tell. During my turn, I stood on my tiptoes before the class. Everyone listened. After school, Katie and I trekked through a neighborhood, turned the corner, and ran down the hill to our unlocked, empty house. It was always open. Mom was with Bob.

While watching *Batman*, I smothered butter on pieces of bread until the loaf was gone. Then *Dark Shadows* played on TV.

"Katie!" I screamed. "That bad man scares me! Let's go outside until it gets dark."

"Butter's for adults, Summer," Mom scolded when she finally got home. "And you ate all the bread again. I have no money. If your cheap father would give me any, I'd buy more food."

How do you have enough to buy boxes of clothes every week?

I couldn't find any bread the following day after school, so while *Batman* played in the background, I dug through the edges of the family room chair for money for the popsicle man. Digging my knees into the carpet, I squeezed my arm through the side crease of the wooden chair. Seconds later, a thin, metal object met my pinky finger, so I yanked my hand out from under the cushion.

"What are you doing?" Katie asked after appearing in the living room.

"I'm hungry." I rubbed my tummy and held up the coin. "I want a banana pop."

She shook her head. "That's not enough."

"I know." I hurled myself to the floor and started sobbing.

"Stop your tantrum. You've been crying since Dad left." The ice cream truck's familiar jingle of joy sounded on our street. "Grandmother Mema gave me money."

"Enough for a banana bomb pop?" I clasped my hands in glee. "Batman can wait!"

"Meet me outside. But I won't buy one if you make a scene."

"I won't!" I yelled before she ambled upstairs for spare change. "And I won't steal money from your secret hiding spot either!"

No time later, Katie appeared outside, bought the popsicle, and handed me the cold, fruity treat. Tearing off the wrapper, I chomped off the top with my teeth. The banana taste melted in my mouth and slid down my throat, giving me a brain freeze. *My tummy feels happy inside.*

On the way home from school the next day, my stomach growled. Katie opened our front door. I elbowed her to get inside first.

Mom was home. "Girls, I'm too thin for my work clothes."

Weeks before, Mom started a job as a department store model

and even had her picture in the newspaper. "I've got to gain weight." With her dog, Miss Pooh, under her arm, Mom rushed us out the door to the car. "We're going to a new food place where you drive through," Mom said, glancing in the rearview mirror. Her poodle's head hung out her open window, making the dog's curly hair blow in the wind.

Ten minutes later, Mom turned into a restaurant with a big yellow arch and ordered at a side window. Right away, a worker handed Mom a straw and a large paper cup.

She leaned over the back seat. "Wipe that look off your face, Summer. I'd buy one for you if I got more child support. I need the calories to model. And after what you girls did to my figure giving birth, it's surprising that that high-end store hired me, even though I'll never make it to New York's fashion runway, where I'm told I belong." She slurped down the last drop of the milkshake, took off the lid, and let Miss Pooh lick the cup clean.

"Quit staring, Summer. Why can't you be like Katie? She's never hungry."

The following morning, I woke up to Mom hollering, "Out of bed! It's a Saturday sizzler. No breakfast. Get your asses in the car. Now! I was supposed to be at the barn twenty minutes ago."

Katie and I flew down the stairs and jumped into the car, shutting the door just as Mom sped her white Bonneville coupe up the hill. Thirty-five minutes later, we arrived in Edgerton, where Mom boarded her palomino, Conquistador. Once we arrived, she said nothing while she rolled down the windows, slammed the door, and headed to the barn. We knew the rules: Don't leave the car for any reason.

Hours dragged on in the September sun until I couldn't hold it anymore, so I broke for the bushes near the apple tree. "Don't sneak away again," Katie warned when I returned to the car. "Mom'll spank you."

"But I had to go potty." I leaned over, holding my waist. "I'm dying of hunger, and I'm so thirsty I can't swallow."

"Just don't think about it." In her blue jeans, brown boots, and sleeveless white cotton shirt, Katie pretended to drive the red steering wheel.

"Look, Katie! Right above the yellow apples." I pointed to the fruit tree. "It's the Bat Signal."

"You're blind, Summer." She shook her finger. "And Mom'll beat you with her big brush if you pick apples from that tree."

I hung half of my body out the window, dreaming of food, water, and *Clifford the Big Red Dog*, the story my kindergarten teacher read to the class. It was my first book. Mom had no time to read, and Grandmother Mema only read to my sister.

"Katie, are you hungry?" My clammy skin stuck to the red vinyl car interior, even with my spandex shorts and crop top. "For apples?"

"Forget about them." My sister turned her head to the back seat, snapping her fingers three times. "Mind me, Summer."

"You sound like Mom. I'll get the Bat Phone." I pretended to make a telephone call. "Batman's coming to the rescue."

No sooner were the words off my tongue than the barn owner's wife swung open my car door, dragging my bare toes through the dirt. Slightly overweight with ratted strawberry blonde hair, she wore a lime green headband that matched her eyeshadow, making her sea-green eyes and painted brows look even more friendly. "Now, y'all girls," she said with a Southern drawl, her bright orange lipstick sticking her lips together, "get on out of that balmy car. Not on my watch. No, you'll not roast another second there."

I stood beside the barn lady's flowery, flowing blouse, but Katie sat fixed in the front seat.

"You remember me, Miss Sugar?"

Katie didn't move. I pleaded with my eyes. Mom blamed Katie and me if anyone took pity on us.

"Y'all's mom won't be getting all hot-n-bothered. I'll tell Georgie I made you."

Katie inched toward Miss Sugar.

"Come now, or you'll be wilting like a flower on prom night."

Katie and I formed a single line, following like newborn ducklings behind Miss Sugar. When she opened the tack room door, the arctic blast of frigid air gave me chills from my dried sweat. The rich, polished leather smell welcomed us as she let us choose a bottle of soda. Katie opted for a Welch's grape, and I picked an orange Fanta. Waves of terror rippled through me that I'd chosen wrong. *I better pick the perfect flavor. I'll never have another chance.* Once the liquid bubbled down my dry, tight throat and the soda swirled with satisfaction in my belly, I sighed. I'd chosen right.

"There now. You two don't look so withered." Miss Sugar offered us peanuts. I gobbled mine down. Katie shook her head, so Miss Sugar gave me hers. "And here's a basket of sunshine." Miss Sugar handed me a paper sack full of yellow apples. I hugged her waist.

"At least you don't have to ride your mom's horse today, Summer." Miss Sugar stroked my hair. "That's something to thank the good Lord for."

A month before, Mom forced me to ride Conquistador. He bucked me off, and I'd gotten cuts and bruises all over my body, so Miss Sugar had bathed me in her tub. It took a couple of weeks, but my injuries healed, leaving me with a healthy fear of horses.

"There's Mom." I pointed to the indoor arena and moved away from Miss Sugar. Mom pouted, shaking her fist. I stiffened.

Opening the tack room door, Mom warned, "You better not have begged for those sodas or—"

"Miss S ... S ... Sugar said—"

"Don't bumble, Summer!"

I dropped my shoulders forward and bent my head low.

"They all sure did not, Georgie!" Miss Sugar interrupted. "I forced them into this pothole. Didn't mean to upset you. It was all my idea."

"They were fine in the car and didn't need a thing." Mom opened a bottle of soda. "I'm just bugged. Summer's dad's playing dirty. Deducting my child support for a bunch of crap he bought her." Mom stopped mid-sentence. "So, I'm calling him every day."

Dad only deducted money for my tennis shoes.

Miss Sugar tilted her head. "You're what?"

"I'm calling at midnight and hanging up once he answers." A triumphant delight shone in Mom's eyes. "I might just tell him that his ex-wife was almost a Playboy bunny. They wanted to hire me, but since Daddy found out, he said that over his dead body would any daughter of his be one."

Later in the car, Mom let loose. "You humiliated me, asking for soda. And I'm sure it wasn't Katie's fault."

My sister shot me a fake smile. Mom rested one arm across the front driver's seat, turned her head to the back, and swung her fist. I shrunk myself small on the car floorboard, wishing Miss Sugar were my mom.

"You better behave, or you won't go trick-or-treating on Saturday," Mom warned.

When we got home, she sent me straight to bed. The next day after school, Katie and I rushed home to play outside before it got dark. We enjoyed an hour before the neighbor kids' parents called them inside for the night. Even though Mom wasn't home, that was our signal to go indoors. Without saying a word, Katie and I dangled our arms over the couch, clamped our elbows along the back cushion, and pressed our noses against the cool windowpane.

If headlights appeared on our street, we cheered, "There she is!" But once those car lights passed, we waited for more lights, and more lights, and more before finally falling asleep. *Even if Mom's not like other moms, it's scary being home alone.*

Late in the night, Mom shook me awake on the couch. "Why's every single damned light in the whole house on and the TV blaring full blast? If you want to trick-or-treat tomorrow, Summer, you better get your ass in bed."

She didn't have to ask me twice.

One day later, Mom appeared in the bathroom where I was applying her old makeup for Halloween. "Doc's coming in a couple of minutes, so hurry, or I'll be late for my date."

I nodded but had so many questions. "What's it mean to go on a date? Do you date somewhere special? Who's Doc? And what happened to Bob?"

"That's not important, Summer. The babysitter's here." She tapped the mirror. "You're slow as molasses."

"I'm ready." I swooped off the bathroom countertop. *Do I dare ask about food?* I shifted from my left foot to my right. When we had babysitters, Mom treated us to TV dinners. "Can I have one of those yummy chicken pot pies? I'll eat so, so fast. I promise I will."

"Forget it." Mom snapped her fingers. "You took too long to get ready." Mom shrugged. "You should've gone faster."

"It's okay." I clicked my top and bottom teeth together. "I'm not hungry."

"Good girl." She grabbed my shoulders, poking me in the back toward the front door. Katie and the teenage babysitter stood there with an unfamiliar man.

"Georgie! You're more lovely than I remember."

"Hello." Mom smiled, showing all her teeth. "The kids are just leaving."

I put my peacoat over Mom's sparkly dress. Katie tied Mom's scarf to the straps an hour before so the makeshift Halloween outfit wouldn't fall off. Katie stood straight and tall in the boots and jeans she wore to the barn. Mom never bought us real costumes. We didn't care; we were just thankful to go trick-or-treating. I fingered the beads on Mom's gown. *I'm pretty like her.*

"You look like a clown," Katie teased, handing me a large grocery bag. Even though the teenage babysitter was getting paid, Katie was in charge. Mom didn't seem to notice. Katie looked older in Mom's makeup. Remembering my reflection in the bathroom mirror, she was right. *I look like the Joker from Batman.*

A warm rain like a hymn from Grammy's church fell on Katie, the babysitter, and me as we clomped into the inky-black night. We turned right and headed down the street. Mom and Doc turned left up the hill. From trick-or-treating at the first house, I stuffed the candy bar in my mouth, and a milk chocolate nutty taste filled my stomach. The next home was our friend's place. Katie rang the doorbell. Cathy opened the door, holding her life-size doll, and handed us three giant Snicker bars.

"Wow! Thanks!" Once Cathy shut the door, I turned to Katie. "She's nice."

"She's a spoiled rotten brat," Katie mumbled, "with all those doll clothes."

"You sound like Mom."

Katie ignored me.

House after house, we got candy until Katie's bag was full, but mine barely had any. I'd eaten most of it. My stomach didn't feel right, and I had to go to the bathroom. The sprinkling rain had turned into a steady downpour. While a car passed, a splash of chilly water sprayed over me. I wiped away my dripping hair just as my paper sack tore in two, scattering my candy on the pavement. I started wailing. "Look, Katie." I held up the two brown pieces. "What'll I do?"

"There's hardly anything in it." Katie kicked water near me. "Don't whine. It's just a bag."

I threw myself on the pavement in the pouring rain, sprawling myself over the gutter grate. Rivers of water washed my remaining goodies down the drain. That's when a rush of lukewarm liquid ran down my legs. I sucked my hair into my mouth. *Why am I so upset? Katie always shares her candy.*

"Quit throwing a hissy fit, Summer. And stop chewing your hair." Katie put her hands on her hips. "What if it freezes like last winter?"

I spit out my soggy hair. "My bag's messed up, and my candy's all gone." Tears covered my cheeks. Katie wadded up my ripped paper sack, took my hand, and hauled me to my feet. Then, she dragged my cold, soaked body up the hill. As the rainy, potty mixture sloshed in my new squeaking tennis shoes, a crack of thunder shamed me.

Why am I always crying?

When we got home, I heaved my drenched dress and soaked underwear under the sink and climbed into the tub. My scrawny body and bloated belly shook with goosebumps. I squeezed Prell shampoo into my hair, lathering it and making clean-smelling bubbles tower atop my head. The babysitter talked on the phone while Katie sneaked into the bathroom and threw three potatoes sprouting long white things into the bathtub. Soap-suds dripped down my face.

"Watch out, Summer. If those touch you, they'll eat your skin."

"I'm afraid, Katie." She disappeared. "Come back. The bubbles sting my eyes."

Katie reappeared. "You're such a baby. I was just teasing." She had a tall, light-green plastic cup in her hand. She tossed the rotten vegetables in the trash, filling the cup with warm water. "Here." She poured the soothing liquid over my head. "That'll get the soap out."

I hiccupped between gulps of air.

"I won't tell Mom you went number one on yourself if you don't tell that I threw potatoes at you."

"I won't. I didn't tell when you said the vacuum would suck me into the bag if I didn't do your chores."

Katie didn't answer. She'd already left.

I dried myself off and climbed into the empty bed, putting my thumb in my mouth. I sucked with such force that the white bubbled scab formed from years of sucking peeled off. I rested my beige doggie in the space between my head and neck, curling up into the fetal position.

"Are you there, God? Do you always wear that same old white bathrobe? Thanks for answering the Bat Phone and sending Miss Sugar."

CHAPTER 4

LIFE WITH GEORGIE

November 1967
Overland Park, Kansas

Little Summer's Diary
Der God,
I now 6. Katie is 8.
♥ *Sum*

I jolted awake with my face smooshed into the green pillowcase. I dabbed my glued-shut eye with my pinky fingernail and scratched the itchy crust from inside its corner. "Katie!" I yelled before pushing myself up on my elbows. "Where are you?" I blinked against the autumn sun shining through my window, but Katie wasn't there. She was in her room.

Mom had moved me to the smaller bedroom near the bathroom two days before. "You're in first grade and too old to have accidents every waking night," she had said.

On my first solo evening, the bad man from *Dark Shadows* blocked the door to the bathroom. Maybe it was my imagination, but he seemed real enough for me to wet the bed instead of trying to slip past him. Miraculously, my soiled sheets had dried by bedtime, so Mom never found out.

The next morning with my head still heavy from sleep, I stretched my arms to the sky. *Maybe I held it this time.* I patted the sheets around my legs. *Dry! I've got to go potty before it's too late.* The bathroom door closed. *Katie! I can't hold it any longer.* I hoisted myself out of bed and tiptoed to Mom's room. *Do I dare use hers?* Sleeping with her hand fanned over her face, Mom didn't move as I passed her bed and raced to the restroom. She jostled but didn't wake up.

I made it just in time to avoid a mishap, flushed the toilet, and used the Zest soap to wash my hands. A strong, clean smell filled my nose as I sped back to my room and dove into bed. From under the mattress, I pulled out the Jesus picture I'd colored at Grammy's church and traced the light around His heart. "Are you still wearing that old-fashioned, baggy bathrobe?" I giggled. "It must need a good washing like my dirty sheets."

Ten minutes later, Katie tilted her head into my bedroom. "I heard you hollering, and now you're laughing. You're so emotional." Katie shrugged her shoulders. "Mom wants you." Katie's dark brown hair sat in a thick ponytail near the top of her head. "Don't make her wait. She's not happy. Someone woke her up." Katie pointed at me before handing me a rubber band. "Mom needs to fix your hair."

"I don't like that." I flung the tan elastic back at her. "It hurts."

"Don't complain." Katie picked it up and returned it to me. "She'll pull harder."

"Summer," Mom yelled from her room. "Get in here. And I mean now."

With lightning speed, I hurried out of bed and jerked on my white turtleneck, red plaid skirt, and matching red vest, hiding the Jesus picture under my bed. Then, I grabbed my saddle shoes, white tights and ran to Mom. Almost every day, my teacher complimented my school outfit. "My girls are the best dressed in town." Mom bragged to Miss Sugar.

"Sit on the floor by the bed so I can put your hair in a ponytail." I covered my mouth with my hands, but my shoulders shook as I situated my back against her king mattress. "*Humph!* What's so funny, Summer?"

"I'm wondering why God's always wearing the same thing. Do you think it's a bathrobe?"

"You sound dumb as a post asking such a stupid question." Mom never moved from her reclining position in bed but extended her arms to cram the stiff brush into my scalp, tearing the bristles through my sleep-tangled hair. Using the rubber band, she pulled my thin hair into a tight ponytail, stretching my eyes and making them water. "Quit wiggling. You sure didn't get Katie's hair. Yours is so straggly."

"Thanks for doing mine," I said. *Mom expects me to be thankful.*

"Go watch TV." I scrammed down the stairs and turned the knob to one of our three snow-spotted channels. A commercial later, Mom blocked the television. "Why, you lazy little thing. Why're you watching this?"

"You said to." Mom was addicted to soap operas but got annoyed when I watched cartoons. Dad said Mom was a "do as I say, not as I do," type of mom. An alarm sounded inside my head. "I mean, I don't know. I won't watch." *I better not talk back.*

"You're damned right you won't." She punched off the television, and all the dots blurred into one center black spot and then disappeared. "And you drank all the milk again. So, I have to ask your tightwad father for more money." I backed up from Mom. "I don't like your look. Do you think your dad loves you? He didn't even want you. Do you understand?"

"Yes, Mom." I lied. "I'm s-sorry."

"You think you're smart like him" Her fingers formed a clawing motion by her ears. "Don't you?"

What should I say? The last time she got angry before school, she made me stay home, so *I'll just keep quiet.*

"Answer me. Now!"

"No, Mom." *She doesn't like Dad.* "I'm not smart like him." *That's the answer she wants.*

"But you love your father more. You always beg to visit him. You can tell me." She grabbed my chin, rotating it front and center. Her stale breath blasted up my nose. *Mom needs to brush her teeth.* "Answer me, Summer Michelle. Hell will freeze over before I let you go to school if you don't."

"He ... he ... he ... " The words stuck on my tongue. *Dad just married a kind-hearted woman, but I better not say that.* "He has lots of food."

"After all, I've done for you." She wagged her finger. "This is how you repay me?"

I tried to hug her. "I'm sorry," I begged. "I won't do it again!" She pushed me away.

"I'm going to knock your head off." Mom was stone-faced when the swinging started. I lunged sideways away from her hand. "Your stingy dad's going straight to hell. Do you hear me? And you don't like me! It's not right, I say. Not right!"

"I like you." *Why won't she listen?* I slapped my head. "It's all my fault."

"Yes, it is." Mom rocked back and forth. "You've ruined the day just like you ruin everything." She spun around and started up the stairs.

"You're just like your dad. You'll never amount to a thing." She stopped on the first stair and turned back. Her bottom lip hung down in a pout. "Clean the garbage disposal before school. I'm going back to bed. It'll take me a long time to get over how you treated me."

Mom stomped upstairs and slammed her bedroom door. I shuffled to the kitchen sink and stuck my hand down the broken garbage disposal, pulling out the slimy food and throwing it in the trash.

A bottle of baby aspirin sat on the kitchen windowsill.

The fizzy orange tablets taste like candy. *Maybe I should eat them all.*

I easily opened the childproof bottle, breathing in the fruity scent. Over the sink, a beam of sunlight warmed my face through the window. The light around Jesus's heart from my church picture flashed in my mind. I put the cap back on the aspirin.

Once I cleared out the gunk, there was no soap to wash my hands. I didn't want to return to Mom's room, so I rinsed them, causing the sink to fill with brown water. *All that work didn't even fix the disposal.*

"Mom said time for school," Katie ordered when she appeared in the kitchen. "But go straight to her room after you get home."

Head down, I kicked the carpet and followed Katie out the

front door. A sharp pulse beat in the middle of my head. I stroked the tender part of my scalp before shutting the front door behind Katie.

"You smell awful, Summer."

The chilly November air made me shudder while I sniffed my hands. *They're worse than ever.*

"Mom got angry. I was watching TV. But she told me to." I burst out crying. "She made me clean the disposal, and there wasn't any soap to wash my hands."

"Why didn't you use the bathroom near your new room?"

"I don't know." I cried harder.

"Don't be such a baby."

"But why does she tell me to do something and then get mad when I do it?" I yanked some hair strands out of my ponytail and then stuffed my smelly hand into my pocket. "My head hurts."

"Don't let Mom bother you." We turned left up the hill toward school. "That's just the way she is."

Random wings of hair fluttered in the wind. "Is this all there is, Katie?" I blinked, shielding my eyes from the sun with my clean hand. My sister stared at me as if I were from Mars. "There has to be more."

"More than what, Summer?"

"More than what's going on right here. Right now. More to the world. More to life."

"What are you even talking about?" She squinted her eyes. "I don't understand you. Never have. Where do you get your strange thoughts?"

"I don't know. They just come. They do. God must know. I talk to Him. Even write Him sometimes."

"You're always babbling like someone's there when you're alone in your room."

"I'm asking God questions." I walked backward in front of her up the hill. "Like, why's Mom grumpy all the time?"

Katie didn't answer. "Here, let me loosen your ponytail." She reached forward and adjusted my hair.

"I love you, Katie."

"Say that at school, and I'll kick you."

Once we got to our red brick, single-story elementary school,

Katie and I passed the office and split ways. She turned right to her third-grade class, and I turned left for my first-grade one.

After rushing into the bathroom to wash my hands, I tore down the hall and into my classroom just before my teacher shut the door. The crayon smell made me forget about the morning. Miss Stiglic's ratted dark brown hair high on her head nodded as she examined me from head to toe. "Another outstanding outfit, Summer." She wore bright, colorful clothes, big gold-hooped earrings, and a cheerful smile. "You are lucky to have such a generous mother."

"Yes, I am," I said.

On the first day of school, Miss Stiglic told the students, "If you're going to fall through the cracks in my class, you'll have to wiggle through my fingers first." I didn't know what she meant, just like she didn't understand about Mom, but every chance I got, I hovered around Miss Stiglic's desk just to be near her.

I took my seat in the straight rows of desks and started the worksheet coloring project. My head still ached, but I finished in record time. Since I watched over Katie's shoulder while she did homework, I was always ahead of my class.

When Miss Stiglic asked for volunteers, I popped in my seat like popcorn and waved my hand like a flag. *Call on me! Call on me!* Every time I got the answer right, I sat straighter in my seat. *I'll answer just one more question.* But that was never enough.

"Miss Peppy, Summer," Miss Stiglic said, "I see you brandishing your hand like a sword. You could teach the class, but let's give the other kids a chance."

I heard Mom's voice. "Stop talking! No one cares what you're saying."

I tried to let another student answer the following question and even squeezed my hand between my legs, but it broke free and swung even higher.

Before I knew it, it was lunchtime. Mom hadn't given me money, and I was afraid to ask. For kids with no lunch, the cafeteria handed us a milk carton and a peanut butter and jelly sandwich, sending us to recess early. I downed the cold, rich milk but didn't take the sandwich. Instead, I raced out to the field. *I don't want anyone to think we're poor.*

"I want Summer on my team," shouted the freckle-faced boy playing soccer. "She's faster than all of us." The field's sweet, fresh-cut grass aroma followed me as I chased the ball.

Breathing hard after recess, I returned to the classroom. My legs throbbed from the exercise, but I was ready to learn.

We took a math test as soon as the students filed back to their seats. Math was easy for me, so I sprang out of my seat once Miss Stiglic asked for a volunteer to answer her question. A flash of irritation passed through her eyes; it was Mom's "you talk too much" look. Tears poured down my face, so I put my head on my desk.

"Why's Summer crying?" asked the freckle-faced soccer boy.

"Summer and I will figure that out later." Miss Stiglic moved on to the next subject. When afternoon recess arrived and every student had left, I was still sniffling but lifted my head.

"You're going to be okay." Miss Stiglic caressed my shaking shoulders. "Your eyes show sorrow, but your spirit screams resilience."

I stared at my fingers. *I don't know what resilience means, but she's the best teacher in the whole wide world.*

"I wish you could answer all the questions."

"No, I talk too much." I looked up and tightened my ponytail.

"That's not it, Summer. But I do need to give other students a turn. Do you understand?"

"Yes."

"Would you like some of my shoestring potato sticks?"

"I'm not hungry." I lied. *It feels like I haven't eaten in a week.*

"Oh, just have a few. We'll share." She pulled a small chair to my desk and, with a *whoosh*, opened the can. Dumping an enormous amount on my napkin, she motioned for me to eat. I popped a handful through my lips. The salt and grease taste swirled in my mouth, taking away the emptiness in my stomach. I dried my tears. "Eat the rest and get a drink out of the fountain. Then we'll get the kids at recess. For today's PE, we're going to play Red Rover."

"My favorite." I bent back my head, capturing the napkin's every single crumb.

Once I got a drink, Miss Stiglic and I gathered the class on the field to play Red Rover. The students formed two lines and linked arms on opposite sides. She told the freckle-faced soccer boy to choose someone from my team to break through the chain of his line of students. He shouted, "Red Rover, Red Rover, send Summer right over."

I jumped up and down and scampered toward the boy. As I sprinted across the field, I forgot about the morning and barreled through his linked arms.

Soon after, I skipped home and rushed upstairs, knocking on Mom's bedroom door.

"Start with rubbing my back, Summer. I've been in bed all day because of you."

The doorbell rang. Katie appeared by Mom's bed. "Some neighbor kids are waiting at the front door for Summer to play."

"I'll do better, Mom." I massaged faster. *I don't want my friends to leave.*

"Don't even think about going outside. Now that you've done my back and legs, rub my arms and neck."

My mind faded to black.

The following Monday, a mist hovered over Katie and me as we trudged up the hill to school. My peacoat kept me warm until two buttons popped off. I complained to Katie.

"Stop hanging on my shoulder, Summer."

I shuffled into class, put my head down, and started crying.

"Why's Summer crying again?" the freckle-faced soccer boy asked. Not wanting to make a scene, I forced my head up and finished the worksheet.

"Summer, stay in at recess." When the other kids had left, Miss Stiglic asked, "Why are you in tears?"

"They started this morning. The buttons popped off my coat."

"That's an easy fix. Let me sew them on for you, and then you can scoot out to recess."

Later that day, Katie pulled me into the school office instead of walking home. She wanted to buy tickets for our school's fundraiser to win a basket full of toys. The night before, Mom had gotten home late, so Katie had dragged the kitchen chair to the fridge. "We're borrowing Mom's modeling money. She'll thank us because of all the prizes we'll get." She'd nabbed Mom's hidden stash of cash on top of the fridge.

Holding the wad of money, Katie and I waited in line to buy

our tickets when Mom suddenly appeared. *She never comes to school.* I yanked Katie's arm, pointing as Mom charged toward us.

"You girls are getting the brush," Mom yelled once we finally got into the car. She stuffed the stolen loot back into her purse. "And if you steal from me again, I'll kill you."

Katie was up first. Before her spanking, she ran into her bedroom. I followed her. She put on five pairs of underwear under her pants.

"That's cheating, Katie. We deserve a spanking, taking Mom's money like that."

"Who cares? Add the layers of underwear, Summer. Then it won't hurt," Katie said before she left her bedroom. "Mom never notices anyway."

When Katie returned, she couldn't hide her delight. "I wanted to laugh."

"Summer!" Mom shrieked, so I took off running downstairs.

"Why did I ever have kids?" Mom forced me to lay across her lap and raised the brush high in the air. Her five whacks licked like flames. I jumped up and rubbed my backside. "Summer, you're nobody's fool, so tell me if Katie's going to do something stupid like that again."

"Yes, Mom." I lied. *I'll never tell on Katie.*

A week later, Katie and I roamed the neighborhood. Cathy, the next-door neighbor girl with the yummy Halloween candy, shouted across the street, "Your mom never wears any clothes."

She's right. Mom strutted around the house in her bra and underwear without closing the curtains. Calm as a cucumber, Katie marched over face-to-face with Cathy, ripped off her glasses, shattered them on the sidewalk, and ground the glass into the cement with her shoe's heel. Katie crossed the street again and hollered, "At least my mom doesn't wear Pilgrim clothes."

After school the following day, Katie stopped me at the front door. "Cathy's going to get it for badmouthing, Mom. We're taking her doll clothes."

"But Katie, you already crushed her glasses." I crossed my arms. "And she's right. Mom doesn't wear clothes. Stealing Cathy's doll clothes is wrong."

"No." Katie stuck out her chest. "It's payback."

47

My sister pointed to Cathy's driveway. "No cars." Minutes later, Katie and I sneaked over to her house, lifted the garage door, and stormed down the stairs to the basement. A playroom filled with wall-to-wall doll clothes hung on racks, displayed as if they were for a real girl. The Play-Doh smell reminded me of Grammy's Jesus.

I squeezed my eyes shut from the image of His face and followed Katie. In less than a minute, Katie and I swiped armfuls of the outfits, bolted out of the garage, and pulled down the door behind us. As we raced back to our house, hauling the stolen items, Cathy's mom's car cruised slowly past us down the hill. With the window rolled up, our friend sat in the front seat. Her eyes grew gigantic, and her mouth opened wide as she pointed at us.

"Katie! We're busted!" We threw the contraband on the ground and disappeared safely through our front door.

The next Saturday at noon, Cathy's mom rang our doorbell. "Is Georgie home?"

"She's in bed," Katie answered.

"Please tell her we need to talk."

Katie looked at the ceiling and scratched her head before heading up the stairs to Mom's bedroom. "Cathy's mom's here. She's waiting downstairs."

"The large one?" Mom sleepily asked Katie. "With the husband who's always flirting with me?" My hands touched all over my face.

Mom hobbled down the stairs and yawned, facing Cathy's mom at the front door. "Your girls need better supervision, Georgie." Cathy's mom inched closer to Mom. "They're always home alone. Last week they stole Cathy's doll clothes."

"My girls would never steal your daughter's trashy things." Mom straightened her hunched body and raised her raspy voice. "Your daughter's a spoiled rotten, lying little bitch." Cathy's mom backed away from the door. As she rushed down our front steps, Mom yelled, "No one in the neighborhood likes you anyway."

"Mom!" The tip of my tongue beat against the roof of my mouth. "We did steal her doll clothes."

"Quit clucking that mouth of yours, Summer, or it'll be the beginning of the end for you. I'll ship you off to Timbuktu. And don't think I won't."

CHAPTER 5

BRAXTON ARRIVES

July 1968 – April 1969
Overland Park, Kansas

Little Summer's Diary
Dear God,
Do you live inside a cloud? I am 7. Katie is 9.
💜 Sum.

"Summer, you're a fabulous daughter. So, I'm giving you a fabulous birthday." Mom pointed to the ivory marble coffee table piled high with colorful, wrapped boxes. "Those are your birthday presents."

"For me?" I ran over and examined them. "I can't wait!"

"I'm off to get you one more thing."

I hope it's a shake from that yellow arch place.

Mom jingled her keys toward the unattended electric skillet, bubbling with chicken fried steak and gravy. "Your birthday dinner's simmering."

Mom rarely cooked, but if she did, it was homemade heaven. "Thank you. It smells yummy." I zoomed over to hug her. The roasted meat aroma followed me. "I love you!"

After Mom left, I called Dad like I did every day. He said happy birthday and told me he wished he could celebrate with me.

Once I got off the phone, Katie appeared with the telephone book. "Let's prank people." She flipped through the thick, white pages, finding a random number, and dialed it. "Is your fridge running?" she asked when the person answered. "Then why don't you go catch it?"

I fell flat from laughing. "Come on, Summer. Let's ding dong ditch."

Katie and I charged out of the house. Three doors down, a woman who had just delivered her second child had taped a piece of paper over the doorbell. "Baby sleeping. Do not ring."

Katie rolled her eyes and hit the bell three times.

Minutes later, I barged through our front door with an out-of-breath Katie close behind and headed straight to the rectangular coffee table. I placed my fingers through my birthday presents' curly-cue crimped ribbons. "Open them." Katie leaned over me. "Mom won't mind."

I popped my thumb knuckles. "Won't she kill me?"

My sister shook her head. "It's your birthday. And we always open one present on Christmas Eve."

"You're right. Mom won't care." I held up the hot pink box. "Especially if I just open one."

By the time Mom returned, I'd opened every gift and sat in a sea of shredded wrapping paper. Mom's face went blotchy red. "You selfish thing." She took a box of unwrapped clothes and slammed it on my head. "Ungrateful little girl. I'm losing my livid mind, trying to give you a nice birthday. And this's how you repay me?"

My tongue stuck to the roof of my mouth. Words wouldn't form. "K-Katie told me I could." I buried my face in Mom's tummy. "Please don't be angry." Mom pushed me away. "I'm such a bad girl. I'll get the brush."

"Don't try to butter me up." Mom turned her back on me. "You'll get the brush when I'm damned well good and ready. And you won't touch your birthday bicycle for years. Cathy's mom's hiding it in her garage." *Wait? She doesn't like Cathy's mom.*

After three weeks of rubbing Mom's arms, neck, and feet, I

finally earned back my neon purple banana seat bike and cycled to the bottom of the hill. Honeysuckle grew near the storm grate where I'd thrown the trick-or-treating tantrum years before. Inhaling the fruity lemon scent, I raced back up the street. My tingly legs pounded the pedals while sparkly purple and white handlebar streamers flew in the wind. *I'm strong. I'm happy. I'm free.*

Mom found me in the garage. "Because of that birthday stunt you pulled, you're not going to Mother and Daddy's with Katie."

I hate making mistakes. Mom uses them against me. But Grandmother Mema always only wants Katie to visit. Still, I blurted out, "Please, let me go."

"You're too hard for them, and remind them of your father." Mom glared at me without blinking. "They hate him. It's all his fault."

"Can I go to Dad's then?"

"Always looking for the best deal, aren't you?" She lowered her brows. "You'll stay with me."

Twenty-four hours later, Katie dragged her bag downstairs to my waiting grandparents without saying goodbye.

Early the following morning, Mom tapped her foot by the front door. "Let's go!" she shouted as I trailed the well-worn path to her Bonneville. She held up her two-year-old dog. "Hello, little one. It's time for your beauty appointment." Miss Pooh licked Mom's face before she snuggled her poodle in her lap underneath the steering wheel. "And then it's time for mine." Setting her chin, Mom turned to me. "We're going to the hair salon after dropping Miss Pooh at the groomer. It's in the vet's office. Don't be a problem."

I nodded.

"Roll the windows up. I'm turning on the air." Swirls of cigarette smoke filling the car made me gag, so I positioned my nose on the air conditioner's vent, inhaling the cool breeze.

When we parked the car, Mom put out her cigarette and applied her frosted peachy-pink lipstick. "Carry Miss Pooh." She handed her to me. "My back aches." *Mom's body always hurts.*

Chirp! The bell dinged as we stepped onto the off-white speckled floor. I sneezed from the disinfectant odor. "Georgie, you're an exquisite beauty. Your phenomenal outfit looks like one of Elvis's pizzazzy backup singers." *Doc's words are friendly, but his face's grouchy.*

Mom's animated eyes glowed. "Oh, this old thing?" She flitted her hand across her waist. "I just pulled it out of the closet." That was a lie. She bought it yesterday from The Jones Store Company, where she'd dragged me for two hours instead of letting me play with friends. When I had to go to the bathroom, Mom stomped her foot. "You always have to tinkle. Don't be a pansy. Hold it."

But I couldn't, so I held myself with both hands, prancing in place.

"Okay." She clucked in disgust. "Go!" I'd leaked through my shorts by the time I found the bathroom. The wet fabric rubbed me raw. Mom's voice brought me back to the combined groomer and veterinary office.

"We're off to the beauty shop." Mom playfully shook her shoulders at Doc.

"Your hair already looks professionally styled."

What? Her hair's flat with no poof.

"Sweet pea, Summer, right?" Doc squatted, cracking his knees. "What an enchanting stunner."

I followed Mom to the car. "What's a stunner?"

"Never mind." I shut my car door just as Mom's face leaned into mine. "You're too smart to be stupid, Summer."

"I like Doc, Mom."

"You bet your ass you do."

I nodded faster.

While the stylist pulled strands of Mom's hair through a cap to make her hair blonder, I roamed the shopping center, peeking into the large Woolworth's window. At the counter, a waitress served vanilla ice cream. *I'll ask Mom for money.*

When I returned to the beauty shop, I strolled past Mom and thumbed through a magazine. Soon after, I shuffled back to her chair. The strong bleach odor was gone. So was Mom.

"Georgie left." The beautician frowned as she cut another woman's hair. "Ten minutes ago."

The hairdresser called the house, and Mom came back. "I didn't even know Summer was gone." Mom flipped her hands high and tilted her head. "I had to pick up Miss Pooh."

She pulled me aside. "Don't breathe a word of this to Doc." She snapped her fingers at me. "Once we get home, if you clean your room spick and span and don't do a half-ass job, I'll call a babysitter."

"Oh, goodie!" I cheered. "I love to—"

"Can you ever for just one-second shut that mouth of yours?" Her thick brows almost touched.

I hunched over with my eyes on the ground.

"Don't be so moody." Mom prodded me toward the car. Doc was there.

The babysitter wasn't available, so shackled to Mom and Doc at a late-night horse show, I counted each sixty-second minute. *I wish my stomach would stop growling.*

"Ugh! Is that you, Summer? You've got such a hollow leg."

Mom's always crabby when I'm hungry.

Katie was still gone seven days later, so Mom and I dropped Miss Pooh off at the groomer/vet's office. Doc wasn't there. Mom's lower lip puffed out. She didn't speak all the way to the beauty shop but complained about Doc as soon as she sank into the hairdresser's chair. I waited until they were deep in conversation and glanced over my shoulder before swinging Woolworth's door open. The tinkling bell welcomed me.

Sitting straight and high at Woolworth's counter, the giant Coca-Cola sign and greasy french fry aroma made me swing my legs in delight even though they didn't touch the black-and-white diamond square floor. I spun a circle in the red chair and pulled twenty-six cents from my jean shorts. It weighed a guilty ton before I plopped the change on the tan countertop.

I'd stolen it from Mom's orange-and-pink leather purse earlier in the morning. *The trick's not to get caught.* A heavyset waitress appeared with a pencil in her cinnamon-brown hair and a pad in her ring-clad hand. She returned my smile, lighting up her yellow-green eyes while taking my ice cream order.

Soon after, she set a fluffy swirl of ice cream before me. The July sun filtered through the wide windows and warmed the counter. Digging a heap of creamy joy out of the chilled silver cup, I plunked the sloppy spoonful into my mouth, savoring the silky-smooth texture. "Mmmm!"

For Mom's hair appointment the following week, I stole another quarter plus a penny for tax. Certain Mom was in the hairdresser's chair; I darted to the drugstore for the tall, milky, cool treat. I timed Mom's hair appointment with five minutes to spare, and she found me waiting by her salon chair.

Before we got home, we stopped by to pick up Miss Pooh. Doc was at the counter. "I can't wait for tonight." Mom looked at me. "My Summer's so happy to see you." She elbowed me. "Right?"

My shoulders sagged. "Yes." *I never said that.*

"Summer's worked like a dog. Katie took the best deal with my parents."

Sheesh! That's what she says about me when I go to Dad's. As we headed home, Mom smacked her wad of Wrigley's gum. Earlier that morning, she'd slapped me for chewing a piece with my mouth open. Every pop of Mom's spearmint gum seemed to stab my head. I stretched my hands over my scalp. "Ouch! Ouch!" I yelled without thinking.

"What the hell's wrong with you?" Mom rolled down her window, tossing out her gum and other trash. "Stop pulling on your head, or I'll knock it off."

After dropping off her dog the next week, Mom and I got back into the car and headed to the beauty salon. Halfway through my Woolworth's routine, I swiveled my stool back and forth, crunching crackers between spoonfuls of ice cream. "Summer Michelle?" Hearing my full name, I coughed up the saltines. "You robbing little bitch." With her blonde, ratted hair curling down her side part, she shadowed over me, yanking me off the spinning seat.

With a plastic smile for the waitress, Mom hauled me off the floor with one motion. "Who do you think you are?"

The pity on the waitress's face ached more than my bruised arm. *It's the same look Miss Stiglic gives me if I cry.*

"You better not be pulling that stealing and sneaking around crap for Doc." I staggered alongside Mom, trying to keep up. "Before Doc and I leave, you're getting it with the brush."

We got to the car, and I started crying. "I'm sor—"

"Stop talking. Children should be seen, not heard. You're grounded for the rest of the summer. I'm sick of you." Mom clicked the back of Grandmother Mema's massive diamond ring on the steering wheel and started her Bonneville. "When we get home, call your father."

That night after I got the brush, Dad's black 1965 Ford Mustang roared into the driveway. I was Cinderella; he was my Prince Charming.

A week later, Dad dropped me off at home, and Mom and I drove the two hours to my grandparents' small Kansas town. "Grandmother Mema's widow's peak and high cheekbones give her such an old-fashioned elegance, don't you think?" Mom asked as we trudged up the long, winding staircase.

Out of breath, I nodded. *I don't understand, but I'll try not to ask too many questions.*

"You know Grandfather made his fortune in the Kansas coal mines. He's a savvy boss. All his men are terrified to death of him." We found our room and put our bags on our luggage racks near our matching twin beds.

Five minutes later, roaming through their wood-shingled mansion, Mom pointed out the classic rich mahogany pieces, expensive cherry four-poster beds, and elaborate marble-top tables. She explained what relatives previously owned the antiques. I could have listened all day. It was such a change from her usual up-and-down behavior. "Mother and Daddy even have central air." She kissed my forehead. "No more sweating because we only can afford the attic fan."

The following day, the aroma of Grandfather's sizzling bacon drew me downstairs. After devouring breakfast, I spied the scrum-delicious-looking carrot bars. The cinnamon-pumpkin smell stole my willpower, forcing me to slice row after row of gooey goodness. I smacked my lips in pleasure.

"What happened to the sheet cake?" Grandmother Mema asked at dinner, peering at me over her glasses that had slid down her nose.

"S-sorry. I don't know why I'm hungry all the time."

"That's fine," she said, "but get your elbows off the table and make sure you cut your meat correctly." She bunched up her lips. "And don't pluck off one or two grapes from the rest. I evenly snip them in groups of five or six, so once you touch a grape, take the cluster."

"I finished my milk." Katie squealed with her empty glass on her head. Everyone clapped. "I'm a bear!"

How does drinking milk make Katie a bear?

The next night, cooking by taste and without a recipe in his spacious kitchen, the scent of Grandfather's masterpiece ribs and twice-baked potatoes filled the house. I drizzled Grandfather's homemade buttermilk ranch dressing over homegrown tomatoes on my iceberg salad.

Without checking if it was too hot, I shoveled a forkful of potato into my mouth, burning my tongue. I didn't want to fuss, so I swished milk around my cheeks and downed the rest of the glass. I knew better than to say I was a bear.

After dinner, I grabbed a toothpick to get the meat out of my teeth. "Toothpicks are repulsive manners." His right eye twitched. "And not to be used at the table."

Why are they here, then?

My tongue was still raw when the sun sneaked through my window the following morning. I burst out of bed, ate a quick breakfast, and dashed outside the seven-bedroom, seven-and-a-half-bath house. Grandmother Mema had told me geraniums grew in the windowsills under the thick shutters. Trying to find more red flowers, I took off running, following the mint-scented bubbling brook that landscaped the property through the green grass and trimmed bushes.

When Katie marched across the cherry-wood brick deck that connected the house to the resort-like pool, I ran so fast that I almost knocked her down. Multiple red-liquid hummingbird feeders swung in the air as the zippy birds played tag.

Once I slathered on baby oil over my Hawaiian Tropic sunscreen that Grandmother Mema made me use, I begged Katie to swim with me before cannonballing into the pool.

"You smell like a coconut. And we can't make waves because Grandmother Mema has to kick her two hundred daily flutter kicks." Katie splashed me in the face. "But you wouldn't know. You're never invited. They only want me."

Tears filled my eyes as I swam away with erratic zigzags, slapping the water. After I got to the other side, away from our grandmother, I circled back, dog-paddling over to my sister. "That's not nice, Katie!"

In her oversized pink sunglasses and matching lipstick, Mom chain-smoked cigarettes deckside in a chaise lounge, her peroxide blonde hair ratted to perfection. In a split second, she swooped near Katie and lowered her voice so Grandmother Mema couldn't hear. "You may be the queen bee here," Mom said. "But you don't have to be a bitch."

I love Mom so much. She stood up for me.

The following day, instead of swimming, Mom said she was going shopping once she and Grandfather finished their coffee. Katie, Grandmother Mema, and I hit the pool. I swam over to Katie's raft, but she pulled my hair. Diving underwater, I moved like a dolphin along the bottom, so Grandmother Mema wouldn't hear me crying.

"Summer's having another tizzy fit," Katie yelled across the pool. "She's such a baby."

Katie's raft was beside me the next time I came up for a breath. "Grandmother Mema's through with her kicks. We can play. I don't know why I teased you."

"That's all right, Katie." Hopping on her raft, we held hands and made a seesaw out of the floaty until Mom shrieked, "Get out of the pool, Summer!"

She's supposed to be at the mall. I dove under the raft. *Maybe she'll think I didn't hear.* Whenever I came up for a breath, I barely lifted my head out of the water, ignoring her shouting my name. *I hope she doesn't pull me out by my fingernails.*

Mom finally left, so I hung on the side of Katie's raft, almost flipping it over.

"Here Mom comes again, Summer," Katie said, floating away. Mom motioned me to the side of the pool. I sat on the steps and shivered. *What have I done now?*

"I never even got to go shopping. Daddy told me you'd better be more ladylike." Mom loomed over me. "You're wearing Mother out. Stop talking so much, or we have to leave. Now go upstairs. And start acting like Katie."

"I will." I fled inside. A cool blast from the air conditioner made me even colder. When I got to my room, I stripped off my suit and placed it in the tub. I didn't want to get in more trouble by leaving wet clothes on the fancy bed.

Holding my breath to stop the tears, I pulled the tags off the colorful shorts outfit Mom had laid out and dressed in it. Opening the closet door, I hurled myself on the thick carpet the color of Miss Pooh and closed the door behind me. The itchy top tickled my skin, and the pool's chlorine burned my eyes. Even if it was time for *Speed Racer*, I didn't want to watch Grandmother Mema's twenty-eight unspotted TV channels. I crawled through the dark, squeezing myself through the boxes, clothes, and shoes. *Why can't I be Katie?* The closet door opened. I froze.

A creamy, fresh brown face bent down and leaned near me. "I thought I heard something." My grandparents' maid, Cora, crawled back to me until we came eyelash to eyelash. "Why, Summer, honey, why's you in here for? You just dry your ol' eyes and come on down and help me iron in the basement. I could use the company."

"You won't get mad if I talk? Mom says I talk her ear off. She says I could talk to a wall." I sniffled as Cora pulled me out of the closet and dried my eyes with her apron. "Mom said the wall would be so sick of me that it would answer just to make me go away."

"Heavens to Betsy." She put her hand to her heart. "You're too beloved for words. Come with me, Summer." She held my hand, and we walked past the third-floor laundry chute, circling to the back staircase.

Once we arrived on the main floor, we went by the kitchen's dirty clothes chute, crossed the hall, took the steps down to the basement, passed the bathroom only Cora used, and then turned the corner to the laundry room.

"Yesterday, I dropped my towel from the third floor and raced down both sets of stairs to see if I could beat it to the basement." I pointed to the floor's laundry basket overflowing with clothes. "The towel got there before I did."

Cora laughed out loud. "Yessiree, that's the final stop for the house's dirty clothes." She smoothed out a white sheet on her ironing board while I hung over the back of the couch.

I swung my arms back and forth. "Do you think God lives in the clouds?"

"That's right, honey. Somewhere up in the heavens." She nodded. "Good question."

"That's what I thought." I put my chin in my hands. "Do you think the wind blows God from place to place? Or does He fly?"

"I can see God flying on the wings of the wind. Yes, I can."

"I knew it." I clapped my hands together. "I just knew it."

Cora smiled and started the next sheet, carefully laying it across the ironing board.

"Why does Grandmother Mema make me say dinner instead of supper, regurgitate instead of throwing up, tinkle instead of pee, and grunt instead of poop? I can say the others, but to say grunt is just too gross."

As Cora glided the iron across the sheet, she belted out a high-pitched howl of laughter.

I can't believe she wants to listen. I better not talk too much. "Did you know Mom when she was little?"

"Oh, yes! The prettiest girl in her class. Everyone loved your mama! And always the best dressed, too. She took the three-hour train uptown to the Country Club Plaza and shipped her clothes back home. Then, after wearing those outfits that spoke to your soul, she'd drop them where they landed, and I was happy as a clam to wash, press, and return them to her closet."

I put my hand over my heart. "Grandmother Mema doesn't give me clothes, but she gave me a Bible, and there was a picture of Jesus with a light above His head. I was glad He wasn't wearing that old white bathrobe anymore. Instead, he wore a red Batman-looking cape and belt over His cream nightdress. But if it's cold in the clouds, He'll be freeeeeezing. *Brrrrr!*" I grabbed my shoulders and twisted back and forth.

Cora put her iron down and touched my nose with her soft finger. "I love hearing your precious chatter. Don't let anyone tell you that you talk too much."

"Can I always hang out with you?"

"Anytime." She started ironing again. "Do you ever read the Bible, Summer?"

"I tried. The words were hard, and then Mom got even meaner." I held my breath. I never told anyone about Mom. It was God's and my secret. I put my hand over my mouth. "M-Mom's not m ... m ... "

"Your secret's safe with me, honey."

I blew out a breath. "Is it hard to iron all those sheets?"

"Not really."

"I love the bed in my room. The sheets feel so tight, and the covers so cozy."

"I'm glad, Summer. There's nothing like being secure under heavy blankets. That's like God's love, I think."

I leaned over and kissed her cheek. Her eyes were all misty.

Around the corner, Mom's voice boomed. "Summer? I heard you all the while I was coming down the basement stairs. Time for dinner." Mom appeared in the laundry room. "Cora! Summer's watching you iron just like I used to." Mom rushed to the maid and hugged her. "Oh, how I miss you, Cora."

"You were such a sweet little girl—just like Summer. I loved listening to your questions, too."

"You were the only one who had time to answer them." Mom licked her lips. "Mother was too busy with bridge club, PEO, and Junior League."

"I couldn't have loved you more if I'd birthed you myself."

"I love you, too, Cora." Mom took my hand. Her eyes had pink around the edges. "Mother and Daddy are waiting for us to eat, Summer. We need to go."

Getting out of earshot of Cora, Mom stopped. "It's never been right, my parents buying Katie more presents than you. So I shouldn't be surprised they're taking her on a Hawaiian cruise and haven't invited you. I'm just disgusted." Mom pounded her heel, making her bronze-powdered cheeks shake. "It's wrong. I'll make it up to you."

"I just want you, Mom." I touched her cheek. Tears filled her eyes.

Once we returned home, Mom complained to Cathy's mom on the phone. As she hung up, she said, "I can't stand that you weren't invited. Go to your father's. It's all his fault, anyway."

After I spent the last two weeks of August with Dad, he dropped me off back home.

Mom and Doc were drinking coffee at the breakfast table when I opened the front door. "We're married," Mom said before wrapping her arm around Doc's neck and giving him a smoochy kiss.

I put my thumb in my mouth even though I only sucked it at night.

"Summer, say hi to your new stepfather."

"Hello, Doc."

On the last day of September, Katie returned from Hawaii. My sister talked nonstop about glass-bottom boats, coconuts, and cruise ships. "Instead of going to school, I heard Don Ho sing 'Tiny Bubbles' on a sandy beach at a pink hotel."

At the end of the week, I followed Katie into her room. "In Hawaii, I overheard Grandmother Mema talking to Grandfather, but you can't tell." Since Katie had gotten home, Mom turned her head away if my sister spoke.

"I won't tell." I sat on her bed. "If you let me wear your new clothes with the big flowers on them."

"You can have my puka shell necklace instead." She handed it to me.

"Thanks so much. I love it." I put it on. "What did Grandma Mema say?"

"Even though Mom's so skinny, she's going to have a baby. But you better not tell you know she's pregnant."

"My lips are sealed."

"The baby's coming around your birthday." Katie crossed her arms. "But you don't even know where babies come from." In the blink of an eye, Katie sailed my stuffed doggie across the room.

Hopping off the bed, I rescued my toy animal, snuggling him in my arms. "Since you've been home, you've been angry all the time." Face to face with Katie, I whispered, "The baby's my birthday present."

When Katie and I arrived home from school six months later, Grandmother Mema opened the door. "We're going to dinner and the movies," she said. "Your mother is in labor. And that's no April Fool's joke."

I took the stairs two at a time to change into my best outfit and wore it while Grandmother Mema treated us to dinner and Disney's *101 Dalmatians* in Overland Park's Glendale Theater.

Before we took our maroon theater chairs, I put the change Grandmother Mema gave me into the soda dispenser. The paper cup flipped upright with a sudden pop, and chilled cherry cola filled my glass. I opened the vending machine door and clutched my drink, guzzling down every smidgen of the sugary, liquid cola. Although full after eating my steak, baked potato, and chocolate pudding with whipped cream on top, I always had room for more, so I was thankful that Grandmother Mema handed me a tub of buttered popcorn.

Spellbound by the film with the spotted dogs, I closed my eyes as a familiar woman tried to steal the puppies. *She's just like Mom!* I sucked my thumb for the rest of the movie.

Returning home, Grandmother Mema told Katie that Braxton was born, so my sister rushed upstairs and told me. Then we moved my clothes back into her bedroom. "It's just like the 'Twilight Bark,'" I fell back on Katie's pillowy bed. "Grandmother Mema telling you, Katie, you telling me, and me telling Dad when I see him tomorrow."

When we were supposed to be sleeping an hour later, Katie asked, "Are you awake, Summer?"

"Sorta." I loved my baby brother already for returning me to my sister's double bed.

"I'm glad you're in my room again." Katie was crying. Katie never cried.

CHAPTER 6

THE DECEPTION

April 1969 – May 1970
Overland Park, Kansas

Little Summer's Diary
Dear God,
Your hair is so long for a boy. I'm almost 8. Katie is 10. Braxton is a newborn
baby.
💜 Sum

"Don't you dare open it, Summer!" Katie ordered as our
babysitter pounded the front door and sobbed on the steps.
"I'm the boss if Mom and Doc are gone."

"Why're you the boss?" I screamed. "I can't take the doorbell
ringing anymore." I put my fingers in my ears.

Mom called the mousey high school girl the day before to
watch Katie and me. She and Doc had been gone since sunrise,
and when they returned just before sunset, Mom rescued the
weeping babysitter. "You've done it now." She snatched off her
sunglasses and glared. Her eyelids never closed. "You just became
the babysitter, Katie. For your brother, too. He'll be home soon,
and then, get ready to work your ass off."

63

"I can't wait to help with Braxton," I said.

"Quit yammering, Summer. Your sister's a cruel bitch."

Once Mom returned home from the hospital, I expected to meet Braxton, but instead, Katie told me that he was born prematurely and needed extra doctors. Day after day, I wandered home from school disappointed until one day, I hopped like a bunny through our overgrown lawn's X that a jokester neighbor had cut with his lawnmower. The front yard's fresh-cut smell followed me as I barged through the door.

Forcing myself to slow down, I inched into my old room. *Braxton!* He was asleep in the crib. I got my stuffed doggie and tucked it under his arm. His eyes opened. Staring back at me were mirrors of Grandmother Mema's pool when the summer sun shone through the water.

That night slipping into Katie's bed, I traced the white headboard with the square cutouts, touching the teal wall behind it. "I love your room, Katie." I turned off the white poodle lamp and snuggled under the pink bedspread with the white polka dots. "I was lonely all by myself."

"I'm wiggling my foot faster if you don't stop talking," Katie warned. I accidentally rolled into her. "Get back on your side." She pushed me over to the edge of the bed.

I reached for my stuffed doggie, but Braxton had him. It didn't matter. I was safe in my sister's room. The scary man from *Dark Shadows* disappeared. Katie must have been glad I stopped wetting the bed because she didn't cry anymore. "Katie, does Doc scare you?"

"Go to sleep." She wiggled her foot so fast the bed shook.

I stayed clear of Doc. He whistled if he wasn't drinking and cussed when he was. He and Mom were either spitting mad or lovey-dovey. For some reason, Doc called Katie "Hayseed" and made her help at his clinic. He never called me "Sweat Pea" again. He only complained that I was always moving.

Doc tried to take Katie to the horse show the following Sunday instead of Mom. "If you take Katie and not me," Mom screamed, "I won't just choke your neck. I'll break it."

Mom and Doc drove away ten minutes later, so Katie and I took turns carrying Braxton to the dime store. While I held him,

Katie swiped a bag of Jolly Ranchers, hiding them under her shirt. She gave me the sour apple ones. I stuffed them in my pocket and, one by one, dissolved five in my mouth. The sweet and sour taste made my lips smack together.

The whole family, minus Braxton, who stayed with Doc's sister at her house, drove to the American Royal Arabian Horse Show the next Sunday. "Breakfast, my ass!" Mom complained as Doc handed her a box of cookies. "I need caffeine before sunrise."

Once Doc parked, we stopped by the hospitality booth. Mom slurped her coffee, and I devoured two extra-large, sticky glazed donuts. My stomach expanded, heavy with the fried dough. Mom wouldn't let us open the cookies, much less get any other food, so throughout the day, I returned for more.

On my way back to the arena, a pack of boys tried to get me to come into a horse stall to play. I hid from them, finding another way back to the ring just in time to watch Katie win second place with Conquistador in Western Pleasure. The hours dragged by before Mom placed third. Ready to go even before I devoured the first two donuts, I finally climbed into the truck fourteen hours and four more donuts later. Katie whined and stomped her feet behind me.

"There, Doc! All over town, gas's thirty-six cents a gallon." Mom's voice pulled me out of peaceful sleep. "But at that corner, it's only twenty."

"Across the street, Georgie, it's eighteen," Doc said. "It must be the gas wars again for it to be that cheap."

I tried to go back to sleep, but the car swerved violently and stopped.

"Summer!" Mom pounced on me. "Get up! All you do is sleep." *Why does she care?*

Bright and early the next morning, Miss Stiglic reviewed our second-grade end-of-the-year activities. The hair on my arms stuck out with excitement. "We've already had our school play." Her eyes rested on me. "You, students, did a stellar job." Right after Braxton was born, I got a part holding a sign that said, "My name is seven, and I rhyme with heaven." I asked Mom to attend and scanned the audience for her. She wasn't there.

"Remember," Miss Stiglic continued, "Open House is this

Thursday. It was great to meet your parents during the fall for Back to School, but now I look forward to showing them how well you're doing this spring."

Braxton was over a month old, so I thought Mom would come. I wanted her to hear Miss Stiglic praise me and show off my schoolwork. But she was a no-show, so I dashed to school early Friday morning to hide the papers I'd displayed on my desk.

Dad wanted to attend, but I didn't invite him. I thought Mom might come if she knew Dad wouldn't be there. I didn't rat out that she'd bailed. If I talked to Dad about Mom, he listened slowly, wrinkling his eyes in frustration. *I love Dad's attention, but I wish he and Mom could be friends.*

Mom didn't miss much with my Open House sunflower wall-hanging project. My papers were all A's, but I ran into a ditch with my creative ability. During the class craft, I sniffled, wiping away tears because the glue stuck to my fingers and the yellow yarn wouldn't stay on the canvas backdrop. Then, with the patience of Job, Miss Stiglic helped me paste the decoration on my project. "Why are you always on the verge of crying, Summer?" She slightly lifted both of her shoulders at once. "You can tell me."

"I just miss my dad."

"I'm sure you do. It's hard if your parents are divorced. It forces you to play both ends against the middle."

I don't know what she means. I sobbed harder.

"I worry with your constant tears, something's wrong at home."

Like turning off a water faucet, I stopped crying. *I won't tell her about Mom. I'll be a good girl.*

"I'm fine. I am." I nodded my head and held up my work of art.

She stared at me. "Summer, I'm going to help you curb your emotional outbursts."

Seven days later, Miss Stiglic reminded the class, "Tomorrow's Field Day. Make sure to invite your parents."

It was my all-time favorite school activity. Twenty-four never-ending hours crawled by until I entered every race I could. Inhaling the delicious fruit fragrance of the pink crabapple blossoms hanging from the nearby tree, I stepped up to the fifty-yard-dash starting line, straining my neck for Mom. She wasn't there, but in his light tan suit, Dad was. He stood close enough to touch. The wind blew his brown hair, covering the top rim of his aviator sunglasses.

"Go!" The fifty-yard dash starter hollered to the crowd of girls. I put my head down, destroying my competition. My feet barely touched the grass. Thirty minutes later, the hundred-yard dash was the same. To complete the day, I cruised to win my final two events, the standing long jump and the high jump.

While waiting for the awards ceremony, Dad talked to the other parents as the kids enjoyed Twister, a new game where players contorted in all different positions. Katie and her new friend ran over to play. He was nice and helped me up after we all dropped with laughter onto the blanket-sized game board.

Finally, Miss Stiglic shuffled students to the playground shade with our backs against the red brick gym building as she called the winners up for awards. I puffed out my chest and galloped toward Dad with my haul of paper ribbons. He held out his arms as I splattered my awards into his open hands.

At the end of the week, our school was out for summer. Skipping through the doors, the students sang, "No more pencils. No more books. No more teachers' dirty looks." But I already missed Miss Stiglic. Hers were nothing but kind looks.

The weather turned humid and hot, signaling the Fourth of July was near. The summer holiday was my favorite until Katie blew the seat off my treasured neon white, sparkly banana seat bike with firecrackers from America's birthday party. I tried to ride the bicycle without a seat and wailed like a toddler while Mom junked it in the trash. "For Pete's sake, I'm damned if I do and damned if I don't," Mom said when I complained. "I never get a break from you two." Mom twisted my arm. "Don't throw a fit. It's just a bike."

"Georgie, need help with the girls?" Doc suggested, his eyes enlarging unnaturally.

"I'm at my wit's end," Mom complained. "I was just too young for kids."

Doc whipped us both—Katie for breaking my bike and me for crying about it. He balanced a cigarette between his lips as he unbuckled his enormous sterling silver belt buckle with the thick, roped gold trim. I gagged on his noxious oily aftershave mist as his brown snake of a strap slashed across my legs, back, and butt. His cigarette had burned so long that the ashes dropped to the floor.

In our model-like new clothes, Katie and I trudged up the hill for the first day of school six weeks later. When I arrived, it was like seeing a long-lost friend. I turned right to third grade, and Katie took the stairs to the new upstairs addition for fifth. By some act of God, I had Miss Stiglic for a combo second/third-grade class. Entering her familiar room with the crayon scent, I was home.

"We picked kids for this class who could thrive without needing much of the teacher's time," she encouraged. "It's going to be a magnificent year." Three years in a row of Miss Stiglic was like winning the carnival cakewalk.

Success in school seemed to forge a "Big Summer" side of my personality, just as making mistakes created a "Little Summer" one. Fashioned by Dad's belief that I was confident, capable, and would succeed with hard work, Big Summer thrived in the school's learning environment, and Little Summer, who was scared of her own shadow, was only too happy to get a break from Mom's mood swings.

Third grade sailed by as I gained more control over my unpredictable crying. I didn't want to disappoint Miss Stiglic. She'd chosen me especially to be in her class. Sometimes still, Little Summer materialized if Mom dropped me off late. I hobbled through the door, defeated, putting my head on my desk. The freckle-faced soccer boy chattered, "Summer's at it again."

Miss Stiglic brushed her hands over my back, so I stopped sobbing.

She believes in me.

The crisp smell of autumn seemed to turn the leaves the color of Halloween. I couldn't wait to dress up. Katie was celebrating with our grandparents. For some reason, Mom told me I couldn't trick-or-treat. It was like the year before when I wanted to watch *Rudolph the Red-Nosed Reindeer.* It only came on television once during Christmas.

"You're so strong-willed." Mom clicked off the television knob. "All you do is sit in front of that damned TV." That's the moment I learned not to act like I wanted something; it would be taken, and I would be left in the "Land of Misfit Toys."

Even though our porch light was off, Halloween-costumed kids rang our doorbell for treats. Mom didn't buy any, so without saying a word, I crashed into bed early and dreamed that Rudolf the Red-Nosed Reindeer and I ate red frosted, green sprinkle sugar cookies, and he told me I'd do something meaningful with my life.

Crash! I sat up in bed. *Bang! Crash!* I fell to the floor, dusted myself off, and fled by my sleeping brother's bedroom downstairs. Mom was choking Doc from behind.

While I tried to separate them, she started choking me. *What's wrong with my mom?* Doc flung the receiver off the wall and called Dad.

Ten minutes later, my father whisked me into his Mustang. My stepmother, a strawberry brunette with short hair and brown doe-like eyes, met us at the door. "Are you hungry?"

I nodded.

She warmed up a slice of pineapple upside-down cake, filling the kitchen with a heavenly brown-sugar aroma, and then covered the dessert with a scoop of Cool Whip. Swallowing the tangy-sweet topping, I forgot about my sore neck. Dad paced the floor.

"You're such a trooper," Dad said. "Such a trooper. Playing the hand you're dealt." He sat down, watching me finish my dessert. "Summer, I want you to know something." He paused for a long time, finally putting his hand on my shoulder. "You're the only good thing Georgie's ever done in her entire life."

What do I say to that?

Maybe Dad snapped from the previous night, but before he dropped me off for school in the morning, he said, "I want you to know that I adopted Katie when she was two, right before you were born." His news made me feel important.

Mom always said I had difficulty keeping my mouth shut, and she was right. I couldn't wait for Katie to get home from our grandparents. Right after she dropped her bag on our polka-dot bedspread, I let the cat out of the bag.

"Your mouth's always running, Summer Michelle. You're going to get it now. Katie told me your news." Mom's lips disappeared. "Doc! Doc! Summer needs the belt."

While I was at Dad's the following weekend, he told me Mom was adopted. Once Dad dropped me off at my house, I rushed up the stairs and leaked my juicy secret to Katie. Doc punished me again. When Dad told me Santa Claus wasn't real a month later, I kept my mouth shut.

Before I knew it, spring had sprung, displaying beautiful buds with shadows of pink in our school's crabapple trees, making way for the hot summer ahead. The week school was out, a dental hygienist spoke to our class. Mom never took me to the dentist, and Dad never asked about it. At the front of the class, a woman in a white uniform held up treats, asking for two volunteers. I was all about competition and food, so with my hand raised, I jumped up and down, getting one of the two lucky spots to brush my teeth and chew a red piece of candy. *It's Willy Wonka's Golden Ticket.* Once I got to the bathroom, I scrubbed them longer than my competition. *I'll win this contest and get a piece of candy to boot.*

After returning to class from my brushing bonanza, my rival sat criss-cross applesauce in a class semicircle. At the same time, we chewed the red sticky tablet. Her smile showed minimal pink. My pearly whites were bright red, matching the crimson shame rippling across my face.

"And even with Summer being in the bathroom so much longer," the freckle-face boy yelled. *Maybe the floor will open and suck me underground.*

On my sprint home, I didn't look for Katie, talk to anyone, or care about the steamy weather. Instead, I flew through the door, anxious to get upstairs to Mom's bathroom. Her toothpaste would remove my humiliation. The front room was empty, but voices sounded from the top floor. I marched upstairs and down the hall. The attic fan hummed over me before I turned toward Mom's bedroom. Katie was with a boy. Fully clothed, they rolled around on Mom's king-sized bed.

I stood at the door. *Something's not right.* I blinked my eyes and scratched the inside of my ear, turning to leave.

"Summer! You know me. We played that Twister game together," the older boy said. "I'd dance with a lampshade on my head to know you better." He waved me over to him. "You're puppet-sized. I've been watching you. You're Katie's pretty and smart sister—the athletic one. You always win all those Field Day races. Your legs are sporty. Like nothing I've ever seen."

Katie's with me, so everything will be fine. He seems so excited to see me. And it'd be rude to leave after all his compliments. I lingered by the thick, high wooden headboard. Katie and the boy were sitting on Mom's flowered bedspread. The boy reached out past Katie and leaned over to touch my legs. "They're so muscular. And so far out."

I'm thankful he doesn't notice the red gunk on my teeth.

I dropped my eyes in embarrassment, touching my calves. *Mom tells me my legs are ugly, but Katie's friend likes them.* I lifted my head. The boy's pants were unzipped.

Where's his underwear? Where's Katie?

His thing was sticking straight up. It was much bigger than Braxton's. I didn't know what it was called, but I'd seen Braxton's thing when I changed his diaper.

My eyes spiked wide. "You can touch it. It's all right. It is." He nodded. His eyes were friendly, and his voice was calm. He took my hand. "Here, rub it. It's nice and smooth."

I sat on the bed and played with his toy-like thing. Its soft surface bounced back when I pushed it down. I held it down on the colorful bedspread and took my hand off it. It popped straight up. I gasped.

Suddenly, he grabbed my shorts. His face had a strange smile. I sprang off the bed for the door.

I'm eight years old and not a baby. He's going to hurt me.

He jerked me back to the bed, and before I knew it, he was moving on top of me. I tried to force him off, but he was too strong. I tried to squirm away, but he was too heavy. The unusual feeling was confusing, like something I wasn't supposed to do. I traveled outside my body, viewing the scene from the ceiling.

As quick as he started, he stopped. I rushed off the bed for the bathroom toilet. Once the tinkle came out, a flaming force ignited between my legs with such fire it scorched my insides. My right leg jiggled. I tried to hold my knee down and make it stop. It shook more.

What just happened? It's all my fault. I'm stupid, just like Mom says.

I collapsed on the cool bathroom tile. My tongue tasted blood. Even though I was awake, I couldn't move.

"Are you there, God?" I lugged myself off the floor and read-justed my stretched-out shorts and underwear that hung off me. "I'm freezing."

I returned to Mom's bed. The boy was gone, and I couldn't find Katie or anyone else.

I made some toast, bathed, and scoured myself with a Zest-covered washcloth until my skin hurt. After scrubbing my teeth and removing all the red, I studied the image in the mirror. My eyeballs had no emotion. They were like Cathy's doll's eyes.

I limped to bed even though it was still light. *If only I'd left when Katie did.* Even though I'd stopped sucking my thumb, I put it back into my mouth and closed my eyes, trying to forget the failure of the flowered bedspread.

Hours passed, but I couldn't sleep. Finally, my sister slipped into bed. "Katie? Is that you?"

"Go back to sleep, Summer."

"I can't sleep. I've got to ask you something." I scooted myself up on my pillow. "Why did you leave me alone with that older boy?"

"In Mom's room?"

"Uh-huh."

"He likes you. He's always talking about you. He's harmless. Why?"

"It was hard after you left."

"Wait until you're my age. That's when things really get hard."

I drifted back to my side of the bed and cried without making noise.

That night I dreamed I had a math test and couldn't remember any multiplication tables. I flunked it and woke up soaking wet.

I'll never tell anyone what happened on Mom's flowered bedspread. Ever!

CHAPTER 7

TRICKED AGAIN

August 1970 – April 1972
Overland Park, Kansas

Little Summer's Diary
Dear God,
I can't stop crying. I'm 8. Katie is 10. Baby Braxton 1.
 Sum

"I hate my birthday. And being twenty-nine." Mom barricaded herself in her room. "I'm older than Methuselah." She wailed from behind the locked door. Katie and I looked at each other and shrugged.

"Watch your brother," Mom ordered.

Earlier in the morning, Doc inspected a horse named Montez for Mom's present. When she lost it about her age, Doc slammed the door in her face.

Twenty-four hours later, Mom appeared in Braxton's room. "Is Doc home yet?" Mom asked as Katie fed our brother a bottle. My sister shook her head. "What if we can't celebrate our year anniversary?"

Mom leaned over the front of Braxton and peeked out the

73

window, tapping the pane. "Doc's right. You two haven't done jack around here." She shook her head in Katie's face.

"What about Braxton?" I blurted out. "We take care of him, don't we?" Katie handed him to me to burp.

"If I weren't so upset about Doc, Summer, I'd get the brush." I wiped milk dribbles off Braxton's chin with my finger.

"Watch yourself! You better start caring about me getting old."

The front door creaked. "Doc's home!" Mom pushed Braxton and me out of the way and rushed downstairs.

"I overheard Mom on the phone, Katie." I glanced over at her as I patted Braxton's back. "Doc's going to train and show Arabian cutting horses. It's when the horse keeps the cow from the herd or something like that. No Western—"

"No Western pleasure anymore. I know, Summer. Doc already told me." Katie wrestled on the cowboy boots that Doc had bought her. "You've got too big of a mouth for him to tell you."

"You don't have to be so snotty." With my sleeve, I wiped Braxton's runny nose. "If you can't say something nice . . . You know how the saying goes."

~

"Happy birthday to me! I can't believe they did it!" Mom hung up the receiver and rushed upstairs to find Doc. "Mother and Daddy felt so bad that I cried all day after turning twenty-nine last year that they bought me land for my thirtieth. What a present—seventeen acres near Sugar's place."

"That's magnanimous, Georgie, but what about my vet clinic in Overland Park?"

"We have to build a barn. Let's build a clinic, too!" Mom clapped her hands. "You wanted to train horses. Now you can. Then decide which you like better."

At the end of the week, my grandparents picked up my sister and flew out of KCI to New York to catch their Bermuda cruise ship. They'd planned another vacation and were only taking Katie again. Once they drove away for their two-week trip, Mom didn't look me in the eye. "I can't say a word, Summer, after their birthday present."

Three days later, Mom woke me up at sunrise. "Get up! I need you to watch Braxton at the American Royal Cutting Horse Show." She heaved the covers off my bed. "And don't you dare whine."

Mom complained my sixteen-month-old brother didn't talk much and wasn't doing the same things Katie and I had done at his age. "At this rate, Braxon's not going to be potty-trained until kindergarten," Mom said before we pulled up to the horse show.

To entertain my brother, I found a fold-out chair by the stalls. Mom and Doc weren't showing a horse; they were meeting Doc's potential horse-training client, Mr. Swagger. Once we got situated on the seat, I started singing "Old Mr. Frog, Sitting on a Log," bouncing Braxton on my lap. Then, when the part came, "And he jumped in the water," I swung him upside down. Braxton burst out laughing like the Pillsbury Doughboy, making his crystal blue eyes crinkle around the edges.

"At least we're out of earshot of Mom," I said to my brother, giddy with pleasure. "She gets so crabby if we make noise." He smiled.

Starting to get hungry, I hauled Braxton to the indoor arena where Mom and Doc sat with the hefty, not a muscle in his body, Mr. Swagger. I tapped Mom on the shoulder. She jerked the Oreos that Doc had bought from his hands, frisbeed them to me, and then shooed me away. The intense cocoa aroma made my mouth water while pulling apart the chocolate discs from the creamy white insides. I scooped a finger full onto Braxton's tongue and then polished off the entire box one by one, giving Braxton part of each cookie. At the end of the night, Mom asked for the rest of them. "Braxton ate them all." I lied.

On the way home from the horse show, Braxton fell asleep.

It was quiet until Mom demanded, "Why aren't you making love to me anymore?"

I stared at my shoelaces. *Doc must not be kissing Mom.*

"Georgie, you drank too much today."

"I'm not stupid, Doc. You're in someone else's bed. Not under my flower bedspread."

Mom's flower bedspread? She's talking about my mistake with the older boy. I put my hand over my mouth and sucked my thumb, tipping my head back to stop the tears. *The flower bedspread must be what married people do. I'm not married. Maybe that's why it hurt so much. I wish I could ask someone.*

When we were almost home, Braxton startled awake. Mom's comment must have rattled Doc. "Stop those cranky, counterfeit tears," he yelled at Braxton as he tried to tear Braxton's brown-eared, beige stuffed animal out of his hands. Braxton hunkered down on his doggie, refusing to let it go. The tussle continued, but finally, Doc wrestled it from his tiny hands, tossing it out the window. Braxton held out his arms and feet, waving them in the air, and sobbed for his favorite toy.

"No!" I shouted. "That's Braxton's." Doc's eyes flashed as dark as the black highway before he struck me. "That was his," I whimpered, touching my stinging face. Heavy tears rolled down Braxton's cheeks.

"Mom!" I screamed from the backseat. "Braxton's cuddly doggie!"

Mom said nothing. Instead, she turned to Doc and said, "I finalized plans for the barn and your clinic. They'll be finished by spring."

By September, the Edgerton property had a large pond. By October, it had a split-rail fence. By November, it had an outside shed in the pasture, and by December, the ground was broken on the twenty-stall horse barn and Doc's vet practice. Mom intended to build a house on the land but said, "I won't have the money till the cows come home."

Doc moved Mom's palomino, Conquistador, and Montez, her new bay Arabian, a birthday present from the year before, from Miss Sugar's place to the outside shed. "Once the barn's finished, they'll move inside for protection from the weather," Mom said.

From the moment Mom owned the property, we spent every Saturday there unless she had a hair appointment. Then Doc and Katie went to the barn together while I stayed with Mom to babysit Braxton.

For Christmas, Doc bought Yahtzee for Katie, Montez's spirited younger brother. She squealed with delight while she rode him. "I never want to hear a blip about you selling that horse." Mom pointed her finger at Katie.

Doc agreed. "That nervous nelly's a perfect sidestepping beauty for your equestrian prowess. He'll live to be thirty if you take good care of him."

I didn't share Katie's unconditional love of horses. I enjoyed riding a well-trained one like Montez, but after getting bucked off Conquistador in kindergarten, you couldn't pay me a million dollars to ride Yahtzee.

By late March, the turquoise barn with six skylights and storage rafters towered on the property. Doc used a private section of the building for his vet clinic.

The next Saturday, Mom woke me from a deep sleep. "For your brother's birthday, you two are going to the barn with Doc and Katie. And that's no April Fool's joke." Mom flung the covers off me. "I'm leaving for the beauty shop. Watch Katie. I think she's been sneaking cigarettes."

Shortly afterward, the four of us arrived at our new barn. As luck would have it, Katie and I got the green light to ride the horses while Doc saddled Champ, Braxton's birthday present, a former show gelding with a black body and even blacker mane and tail. Doc and two-year-old Braxton rode him together, brightening Braxton's face while they trotted around the property.

Katie saddled our horses within a hot second and put a full-pinched bit bridle on my horse: the older, fully broken Montez. She used a bitless hackamore bridle on Yahtzee.

"Come on, Summer." Katie's face illuminated with promise as she clucked her tongue. "Let's go swim the horses."

"Just don't make me ride your skittish horse or use that flimsy bridle with mine."

Yahtzee whipped around toward the pond, so I chased my sister on Montez. Katie cackled louder with Yahtzee's every crow-hopping step, weaving through the budding violet trees and blowing brisk breeze. While I kept an iron grip on the saddle horn, holding Montez for dear life, I plunged behind Katie and Yahtzee into the pond packed with murky-smelling water. Shimmering rays from the day's last gasp of glowy light shined on my sister as I lifted my legs high, winging above the stirrups.

"Hold on, Summer," Katie hollered back, her voice barely audible in the wind.

Once the horses trotted out to dry land, Montez shook, spraying water from his body like a sprinkler. Yahtzee broke into a canter toward the barn, and Montez and I followed. When we arrived at the stables, we dragged off the wet saddles and hung them on the oversized meat hooks Doc used for makeshift saddle holders. Then, rubbing down the horses, we returned them to their stalls with oat grain, hay, and fresh water.

"*Woo hoo!* Summer!" Katie shut the wide barn doors. "Best day ever!"

"For me, too, Katie!" Let's run to the truck. Those black clouds look like a storm's coming."

With rain spitting on us, Doc drove his truck back home. After we pulled into the driveway, I dashed through the front door. Mom cornered me alone in my room as I put on a sweatshirt.

"Summer, Katie's too young for cigarettes." Mom got in my face. "She's smoking? Tell the truth."

I knew the truth. My sixth-grade sister was smoking. Being a fourth grader, I never wanted to disobey, but Katie continually bumped against the boundaries.

"Oh, honey." Mom purred with genuine concern, "Doc and I know she is."

Then why ask me?

"We're worried," Mom continued. "Be a good sister, and tell me."

As soon as Doc and Mom married, Katie started smoking—and shoplifting. Stashed under our bed was a 500-piece box of Bazooka bubblegum from the dime store. I kept silent, dancing back and forth. "I gotta go. Mom."

Mom barged into the bathroom after me. "You've got a good read on people." The weight of Mom's concern fell on me. "I need to know."

I forced my face blank. I wanted to help, but I couldn't squeal on Katie. Working with Mom was like expecting food in our empty fridge.

"I promise she'll never know. Doc and I just want to help if she's smoking. Be a good sister, now, Summer." Mom smiled with her eyes.

I want to do the right thing. Tell the truth. But can I trust Mom? "Huh. Um. I don't know."

Concern filled Mom's face. "If you care about her, you'll tell. You're not a liar. You're better than that."

I lie all the time. I'm not better than that. But I want to be.

"Um, yeah, for Katie's own good, I'll admit she smok—"

"What? Doc!" Mom's smile gnarled into a straight line. "I was right. Katie's been smoking. I knew it. Summer just blabbed."

"You said you wouldn't tell. Said she wouldn't be in trouble."

"That's too damned bad. I'm livid." Mom bobbed her head up and down and shoved me away. "She'll pay."

Why did I tell Mom? The day's ruined! Why didn't I keep my big, fat mouth shut? I'll never tell Mom anything again.

Doc flew by us, taking three stairs at a time, thundering down the hall and into Braxton's room, where Katie was just getting ready to change his diaper. I trailed Doc as he yanked my sister down the stairs by her hair and flung her into the kitchen chair. Katie didn't say a word. Sitting straight and tall with lifeless eyes, not a hair on her head moved. I hovered beside her.

"Here's the little bitch." Mom struck a match and started smoking. "Let's see you do your thing, little missy." Mom handed Katie her cigarette. "You're going to smoke the whole carton. Then we'll see how much you like it."

The heavy smokers mocked Katie as Mom said, "Not such hot stuff now, are we?" They forced her to puff one filterless cigarette after another while acrid smoke filled the small kitchen. Katie didn't shed a tear.

In a flash, a rip-snorting rain cloud split apart with ear-deafening thunderclaps, and seconds later, lightning cracked. "Please, let me stop," Katie finally broke, wilting into herself. "I don't want to smoke any more." The fumes caught in her throat, and she coughed herself hoarse,

"Stop making Katie smoke." A dizziness overtook me, so I threw myself at the foot of Katie's chair, sprawling myself over her legs.

Mom and Doc, I wish you'd go away and never come back.

"Why won't you let me stop?" Katie cried to the adults who stood over the crumpled eleven-year-old.

With her long, matted hair plastered around her forehead, Katie's dilated pupils shifted side to side. Dots of perspiration swelled on her face. She flopped her head back and forth. Her legs clamped over the kitchen chair, anchored for support as rain pelted against the kitchen windows. With every boom of thunder, Katie crouched in the chair.

Braxton appeared around the corner with his faded-green thermal blanket wrapped around his shoulders and thumb in his mouth. My head slumped over him; he reeked with a rotten smell. I checked his pants. Yellow-soaked balls of tinted brown made his disposable plastic diaper droop. I peeled myself off the floor, tucked him under my arm, and carried him up the stairs for a clean one. I hoped he'd eaten but couldn't be sure.

When Braxton and I returned, I brought Katie a roll of toilet paper. Mom and Doc were gone. "This's all my fault." I got on my knees next to her. "Mom said you wouldn't get in trouble." My voice strangled out the words. "I'm s-sorry. I'll never tell on you again."

Katie's lifeless body seemed to come alive. With the toilet paper, she wiped her tears and blew her nose. Her shaking hands drew me close. The odor of stale smoke on her breath made me gag. "Doc's an SOB." She released my face and rocked forward off the chair.

Looking like a hundred-year-old lady, Katie padded out of the kitchen, grabbing the stair railing. She tugged herself upstairs with the handrail, one step at a time, and then pinballed down the hall, disappearing through our bedroom door.

Five minutes later, I tiptoed into our room with Braxton in my arms; Katie was asleep. The bed smelled like cigarettes. With my clothes on, I snuggled Braxton next to her and dropped next to him. "Happy birthday, little brother."

On the heels of Katie's punishment, Doc sought me out after school. "Does Katie swear?"

"Oh, yes." I chirped like a birdie. "She swears all the time."

"Get your sister." His eyes bugged out, and his body shivered in anticipation.

Oh, no! Didn't I learn anything from telling on Katie? So why didn't I lie?

I played dumb, scratching my elbows and looking at my fingers.

"Katie does swear. But it's because the neighborhood kids test each other to see if someone is telling the truth by asking, 'Do you swear on the Bible?' Doc had already undone his belt and staged it for the first lash. "Katie's swearing on the Bible to prove she's telling the truth. Is that wrong?" It was true about the neighborhood kids' swearing test, but it was also true that my sister swore like a trucker.

I held my breath. Doc had beaten me for less. "What does it even mean to swear anyway?"

Doc, the man who hurled hourly f-bombs, straightened his silver belt buckle and weaved his brown belt back through the loops of his jeans. Sweet relief rolled over me. Stunned, he sat on the same kitchen chair where, days before, Katie hacked down a pack of cigarettes. I marched up the stairs to my room, gathered all my spare change, and sailed down the stairs, laying out the peace offering before Doc.

"What's this?"

"It's for not spanking Katie."

Doc's eyes misted. "Keep your money."

I pushed it closer to him. "No, it's yours." I zoomed back up the stairs to the safety of Katie's and my room.

CHAPTER 8

THE RENTAL HOUSE

April 1972 – August 1972
Edgerton, Kansas

Little Summer's Diary
Dear God,
I got Katie in trouble. I'm almost 10. Katie is almost 12.
Baby Braxton is 2.
🩶 *Sum*

"Summer!" Mom yelled from inside the front door. "Get your ass into this house right now."

I raced up the front steps.

"What did Katie say after school?"

"I never saw her."

"They must've pulled her out before it was over." Mom shook her head. "The school office called. What was I going to say? No to Mother and Daddy?"

I tilted my head in confusion.

"Katie's staying with them until further notice." Mom gulped a mouthful of coffee. "They called and didn't let me get a word in edge-wise."

What? What'll I do without my sister?

I blinked rapidly, collapsing near the marble coffee table where Katie and I sat the night before, putting Bugles corn chips on our fingers. We pretended the crispy cone-like snacks were manicured nails and ate them one by one off our fingers.

"Get up! This isn't about you." Mom hauled me to my feet. "Very convenient that Katie called Mother and Daddy just in time to get out of packing. *Humph!* She knows that I never made her smoke." Mom mumbled to herself. "She'll rue the day she crossed me."

I coughed from the image of Katie puffing cigarettes.

"Quit coughing. We're packing this place. Even though it wasn't on the market, a friend of Mr. Swagger's bought it. He's got high, mucky-muck, filthy rich friends. So, we're moving to an Edgerton rental three days from now and starting to build our new ranch house." Mom extended her arm in a sweeping motion. "We've got to box up everything."

"What about finishing fourth grade?" I stopped breathing. "And Dad?"

"You think I care about your pathetic father? He's so stupid he didn't even know I hid our divorce papers in his glove box. He found them on the way to his parents' farm."

What's she talking about?

"And don't plan on calling him every day. It's long-distance, and your dad's too tight for more child support. So, he'll have to pick you up to talk to you. I won't drive you."

With the back of my hand, I wiped my eyes. Mom dragged me over to a stack of dishes. "Here. Wrap Grandmother's china in this newspaper. But be careful. It's priceless."

Mom's voice softened. "You'll like being closer to our new ranch property. And watching the house being built." Mom took a deep drag of her cigarette. "You'll pass by it on the bus to school from our rental." Mom could make getting the flu sound fun.

"Can I at least go say goodbye to Miss Stiglic?"

"Don't always be so worried about yourself." Mom blew smoke in my face. "And get that chip off your shoulder."

She grabbed the phone and started dialing while I ran upstairs, flicking my shoulder with my fingers. *I better brush that chip thing off.*

"Where do you think you're going?"

"Braxtie's crying," I shouted from the top of the stairs, "and so am I!" As I stepped into his room, I shouted louder, "My head's about to explode, too."

"Sum! Sum!" Braxton cooed.

I bent over Braxton's crib. He didn't say much at two but understood what I said. I tousled his brown hair. Rays of sun radiated through his window, drying my tears. I swung him out of his crib and hoisted him on my hip. He was like another arm. Sniffing his bottom, I opened the box of disposable diapers. It was empty.

I put my brother on the floor and got on my hands and knees, grabbing a diaper from my secret stash behind his dresser and getting a whiff of the fresh baby aroma. I always had spares for when Mom forgot to buy them. Lifting Braxton in the air, I started singing. "Baxton, Braxton, bo Braxton, Banana-fanna fo Faxton. Me-mi-mo Maxton. Braxton."

After I changed his diaper, I slid a piece of Katie's pink bubble gum out of my pocket, chomping down the sugary, chewy texture. *At least Braxtie will be with me in Edgerton.*

When I returned with my brother, Mom complained to Cathy's mom. They'd become fast friends. Mom made even her enemies like her. "And I'm gonna lose my entire trust fund inheritance, and Katie, too, if I discipline that spoiled rotten brat again."

Let them take the trust fund thing, but don't let them take my sister!

"Katie always gets her way." Mom squawked into the receiver. "That lying, little bitch. Mother says she's worried about her."

Moments after Mom hung up, she nipped my back and handed me Grandmother Mema's china to wrap. "It's all Katie's fault you're forced to pack all this and can't go to school. She's giving you the short end of the stick. She always does."

Mom was either mad at Katie or me. The last weekend I spent with Dad, Mom made sure I overheard her tell Cathy's mom that I was lazy because Katie had to work while I was gone. I cleaned for days just to get Mom to talk to me again.

"Mark my words." Mom tapped a cigarette on the table and then spun it in her hand before putting the filter into her mouth. "This's the nail in Katie's coffin," she said, lighting it and sucking in the smoke until her lips wrinkled. After she blew out the fumes, she continued, "She'll pay."

Days later on a snowy April morning without Katie, we moved to our Edgerton rental place. From the stuffed car, I waved to the only home I'd ever known. The previous night it snowed and sprinkled a powdery coat on the house, making it twinkle farewell from the front yard. I twisted my head to keep my eyes focused on our tree for as long as possible before it disappeared from the back window. "Uh oh!" I shouted when we reached the top of the hill. "I forgot my Jesus picture."

Doc didn't stop. Mom didn't say a word until she leaned over the back seat. "Don't let it slip what Doc did last night, Summer." Mom grasped my chin. "To anyone!"

To compete with the unseasonable snow the night before, Doc manufactured his own storm. Drunk off his butt and swearing like a sailor, his screaming woke me from a deep, dreamless sleep. Dazed and confused, I dashed down two staircases to the basement. The hall dripped with bloodlike brandy, trickling streaks across the white walls. Dark cherry alcohol glass shards littered the hardwood stairs. Mom was nowhere to be found.

Out of the blue, Doc's shadow appeared on the basement stairwell. He smashed another bottle. An airborne glass chip cut me on the cheek. The air fumed with a flowery smell as I touched my face. It was wet. When I wiped the blood with my shirt, it turned red.

As I wondered what to do, Doc aimed his orange-tipped cowboy boot and started kicking doors. I counted: 1. The basement door. I ran up the stairs after him. 2. The kitchen door. I followed him to the family room. 3. The TV cabinet door. I escaped to the bathroom and splashed water on my smudged face; the cut was minor. We had no bandages, so I took a wad of toilet paper and made it stick on my face like Dad did after he cut himself shaving. I hid the rest of the night in Braxton's room, climbing into the twin bed next to his crib. With Katie gone, our room was a ghost town. Before I knew it, I was asleep.

By morning, Mom appeared, and she and Doc were like honeymooners. *What are the people who bought our house going to think?*

At least Mr. Swagger's hired hands didn't mention the mess

when they arrived bright and early and started hauling our furniture to their truck.

"Do you think the movers will find my Jesus picture?" I asked Mom. "Last night, I slept in Braxton's room and forgot to grab it from under my mattress."

"You'll be lucky to have a bed tonight, Summer." She rolled her eyes. "They can only worry about big items."

No one uttered another word for thirty-five minutes until a sign read Edgerton City Limit.

"We're here," Mom finally said as we drove by Skelly's Gas Station. "The relator said this small town with no streetlights rolls up its sidewalks every night at 8:00 p.m."

How do they do that?

Doc stopped the packed car in our driveway next to the elementary school. "Here's the two-bedroom, one-bath, single-story house," Mom said. "When Katie comes home, you'll share a bedroom. Braxton's in the front room."

At least we're within walking distance of school.

After four never-ending days of being Mom's personal servant and unpacking every box, I begged, "Please! Can I go to school now?"

Mom shook her head. "You can go when Katie returns." I wanted to confront her about the promise that I'd ride the bus and watch the building of our new ranch house, but it didn't seem to matter.

At least I have Braxton.

I hoisted him on my hip. "You hide in plain sight, little brother." I stacked Grandmother Mema's china while eavesdropping on Mom's telephone conversation in the dinky, narrow corridor-like kitchen.

"Tomorrow, then." She smiled wide. Mom thrived on the thrill of buying and selling, and by her giddy expression, she was in full sales mode. "Yes, he's a gelding. A two-year-old chestnut." That night after Mom and Doc fell asleep, I sneaked out of bed to call Katie. After talking to my sister, I climbed back into bed and pretended to snooze. *I'll not stay silent and watch Mom sell Katie's horse.*

Double-checking that everyone was still sleeping, I put on my tennis shoes, covered up Braxton, and grabbed the front doorknob.

The rusty hinges of our rental house squeaked as I shut the door. *Great! I'll be in trouble before I'm even out of the yard.* I paused, tapping my fingernails against my teeth.

No light clicked on, so I tiptoed across the driveway. The chalky, full April moon was my accomplice as it illuminated the dark sky, guiding my way. I thanked the heavens and started running, inhaling the sweet jasmine that hung in the air. The two miles to our barn straight up Highway 56 never winded me. I turned right on Four Corners Road, sailed over the two railroad tracks, and was at Yahtzee's stall in less than thirty minutes.

"Be easy on me. I'm not Katie. But I'll do my best to get you to Miss Sugar's place."

I glided the hackamore bridle over the chestnut's head. Montez whinnied. *Oh, how I wish I were riding you.* I swished spit in my desert-dry mouth to focus on something besides the taste of fear.

Running my finger along the worn leather seat, I couldn't use the saddle; it'd be too heavy to carry back to the house. *It's bareback all the way, Yahtzee.* I gently led him out of the barn, put on the weightless bridle, and snatched the mane above his shoulder bone, flinging myself onto his back. With his crow hopping, I almost slid off his sleek coat. "I can't do this," I whimpered. "I'm scared!"

Katie's glassy-eyed dread as she smoked those cigarettes gave me inner strength. I tattled to Mom. Yahtzee's sold. *It's all my fault, I have to disobey my mother, but I never have before—until now. She'll kill me.*

I clucked *go* to Yahtzee and trotted across the barn entrance, turning right and clomping down the driveway. I hung a left back onto Four Corners Road when the horse broke into a gallop, his hoofs pounding too close to the wayside of the street. I yanked the reins. He settled down into a canter. Katie warned me that a horse could tell if you're afraid.

"I'm not afraid. I'm not afraid ... " I repeated. *I don't feel like I'm going to fall off anymore.* I turned right on the gravel road before the first railroad track. Only another mile to Miss Sugar's ranch. I hadn't told her I was coming but remembered her words, "I always keep a spare stall open in case you need a fast getaway."

Coyotes howled as her property came into view. *I miss Overland Park.* Shrinking back onto Yahtzee's muscular back, he sensed my terror, skittering close to the ditch. "I'm not afraid! I'm not afraid!" I relaxed my stiff neck and straightened my back. "Oh, God, I'm so afraid." I jerked the reins into my stomach. "Whoa!" Yahtzee sidestepped with zigzagging fervor. "We're almost there, boy," I chattered. "We can do this." Patting his warm flesh over his pronounced muscles, I sank into his neck, empowered by helping Katie.

"Good boy," I coaxed. "Thank you for going easy on me." He steadied himself, so I kept talking. "Once I get to the barn, I can run back home. That's easy. The hard part's almost over. We can do this, and then Katie can keep you."

The barn emerged as Yahtzee, and I passed the big yellow-apple tree. I swooped off Katie's horse, led him to the barn, and swung the door open, turning on the lights near the tack room.

Tying Yahtzee up to the grooming post, I found a bucket of water and filled it for him to drink. He sucked down most of it and slobbered the cool remains on my hand when I stroked his velvety muzzle.

"Yay, Yahtzee!" I tickled his nose, leading him to the empty stall and shutting him in for the night. He lifted his head goodbye after I took off his bridle. I sandwiched it under my right arm, turning off the lights and closing the barn door behind me.

A lamp flashed in the house, so I hid behind the apple tree, holding my shaking knees. Soon after, the barn lit up like a Christmas tree.

Sprinting as if I were a 100-yard-dash Olympian, I started down Miss Sugar's lane and never looked up until I got to the rental house. I hopscotched up the driveway.

Sneaking back through the front door, I dropped the hackamore by Braxton sleeping in his crib. "You're brave, Summer," a voice whispered to my heart. I collapsed onto the bed that I hoped Katie and I would soon share.

Early the following morning, the sweetness of satisfying sleep drugged me until Mom stormed into my bedroom and slapped me, crunching my teeth together.

Instead of the nightmare that I'd forgotten to study for a test, in my peaceful slumber, I'd dreamt that I'd stashed Yahtzee at Miss Sugar's barn to prevent Mom from selling him.

Stealing Yahtzee was only a dream? It seemed so real!

Mom's bugged-out eyes with dark circles met mine. "You've got balls of steel, Summer, phoning Katie at Mother and Daddy's, telling her that we sold Yahtzee."

I inhaled Mom's coffee breath, curling up into a ball for protection.

"Hope you're happy. Daddy called this morning. Said selfish Katie gets to keep her horse." Mom shook my arm until she seemed to pull it out of the socket. "She'll be home the day after tomorrow."

Mom looked at the door, set back on her heels, and whipped her head toward me. "What kind of stupid are you? Thinking I wouldn't get wind of you telling Katie. Stop digging into places you don't belong. Doc'll be right in to make sure you don't pull this stunt again." On the way out of my bedroom, Mom burst into tears, crying so loud that the whole block heard her.

Why do I feel worse for Mom than I do for myself?

By the time Doc's belt marks stopped burning, Katie arrived at our rental house. Mom wouldn't look at her. It didn't matter. All Katie wanted was to ride Yahtzee. After we got to the barn, a glorious gleam of gladness spread across my sister's face. That night alone in our double bed with the worn-out mattress that made us sink together into the middle, I asked. "Why did you come back after Mom and Doc made you smoke all those cigarettes?"

With her nonchalant attitude, Katie bent her face near mine. Moonlight cascaded through our small bedroom window, high-lighting her olive complexion and thick, dark hair. "You're my sister, Summer. Where else would I go?"

"I missed you so much and feel terrible telling Mom that you were smoking."

"It wasn't your fault. She tricked you. Somehow you let me keep Yahtzee." She smiled. "I'm the older sister and supposed to take care of you. But you take care of me."

"You've been taking care of me since I can remember. And always sharing your stuff."

"You can have some of the new school supplies Grandmother Mema bought."

"Thanks, Katie! I don't want to start school without you, and it will make it so much easier with Grandmother Mema's things to—"

"If you don't stop talking, I'll start wiggling my foot."

With that, we went to sleep.

The following morning, Katie and I got up early. I danced in the doorway. "Hurry, Katie." I pulled her arm. "We'll be late."

Mom stayed home with Braxton while Katie and I trooped to school. Together we found the office, and they gave us directions to our classes. Katie turned left to her sixth-grade class, and I charged right to my fourth-grade one. I passed the cafeteria. The cinnamon breakfast French toast smell made my empty stomach cramp.

My fourth-grade teacher, Mrs. Larson, with her long nose, tight bun, and doughy body, wasn't Miss Stiglic. Everything Mrs. Larson tried to teach me, I already knew. I didn't try to be a know-it-all and should have kept my hand down, but my desire for attention overruled my common sense. *Pick me! Pick me!* My bouncing body screamed. Mrs. Larson had little patience for my attention-seeking shenanigans.

Two weeks into my new school, she stood up from her desk on a hot and humid April day. "Summer, you're leaning back in your chair." Her lips turned downward. "Come with me." I didn't know I was leaning back in my chair, but many students were, and one boy was still sprawled, face flat across his desk. *I won't argue.*

I followed my teacher to the hall and slumped into the secluded desk Mrs. Larson reserved for bad kids. I'd never been in trouble at school. I was one blink away from sucking my thumb. Sobs escaped from my mouth as Mrs. Larson hung a sign around my neck that read: "I'm an example of sitting in a chair." Then, for some reason, she handed me a box of milk. I tried to take a sip but spit it up.

The rest of the afternoon, older kids came by and howled with hilarity. "Look at the new girl. She's showing us the right way to sit in a chair."

I'd long since dried my tears and joined the party, making fun of myself. "Yes, I'm showing everyone how to sit properly." A pen and scrap paper were on the desk, so I wrote, "I love my dad."

Hours later, exhausted from appearing unconcerned, I found Katie and shuffled out the double doors. "I saw you in the hall,"

Katie said without looking at me. "That Mrs. Larson's a nasty one. You can tell by the dirty looks she gives students."

When I got home, I told my mother. She sided with Mrs. Larson and had Doc whip me.

I'll be okay, I thought after each blow of his belt. *They'll not beat me. I'll make my life count.*

That night I had another dream: *I'm looking up at a pencil-thin, tall lady. It's Mom. She's staring straight ahead. A breathtaking-looking man I know to be Jesus is standing next to me.*

One by one, I take large, small, and tiny cans out of my pockets and show them to Him. He nods as I drop them at his feet. As I do this, I grow taller and taller until I pass Mom's height. Jesus smiles. "Well done!"

Mrs. Larson smiled at me the next day, but her cheerless eyes gave her away. After that, she never made another student go out in the hall or wear that sign even though students still leaned back in their chairs, but not me—no, never again.

Right before summer, Katie and I shuffled out of the school's double doors. Our saddle shoes squeaked on the waxed and polished floor. On the way home, wispy and puffy clouds formed high in the sky from a quick-moving spring storm. The dark breeze exchanged the clean air scent for a storm smell.

All at once, Danna, a neighbor girl, rushed up to us, out of breath. "Georgie's screaming at your dad! Things are breaking."

"Come on, Katie." I seized her arm. "Let's go help."

She wrenched her arm away. "Who cares, anyway?"

Racing after Danna, I called back to my sister, "I'll see you at home."

When I peeked through the front window, Grandmother Mema's demolished china covered the kitchen floor, and Mom was just revving up for more. I slipped into the house to rescue Braxton from his crib. Mom and Doc didn't notice. "Why you, Mother ... Who's your little whore now?" She picked up another priceless plate.

"Georgie, you're hallucinating." Doc ducked while she aimed the next piece of china at his head. It exploded on the wall, looking like a valuable mosaic until it splattered on the floor.

"I know you're screwing that sleazy bitch." Mom didn't wait for an answer. Instead, one by one, she threw the cabinet full of water glasses at Doc. "What's her name? Can't hide your slut from me, Doc."

I flew back to Katie. "It's horrible. At least I got Braxton." I bounced him on my back. "Danna's mom told us to come to her house."

For thirty minutes, we played in Danna's yard until the cussing stopped. When I swung open the front door, a sliver of sunlight peeked in behind me, casting a cloud of glass dust over Doc and Mom as they embraced in the sea of destroyed dishes. She'd shattered every single plate, bowl, and glass. Mom pulled away from Doc and handed me the broom. "Get Katie and clean this up."

I brushed the hair out of my eyes. The crisis was over, but there would be another. Our new ranch house in the country wouldn't change Mom and Doc; it would just give them more acreage and a private stage for their broken relationship.

CHAPTER 9

DISNEYLAND

August 1972 – October 1972
Edgerton, Kansas and Anaheim, California

Little Summer's Diary
Dear God,
I love my dad. I am 10. Katie is 12. Baby Braxton is 3.
 Sum

C *rack!* Doc's horsewhip just missed snapping my toes. I jumped
back, bumping into the side of our turquoise barn. "There's
no mystery in making animals obey." He flipped up the brim of his
cowboy hat, stroked the length of his whip, and nodded his forehead. "I'll win that elusive purse money in California, yet."

A natural horseman, Doc demanded his Arabian pupil perform
on cue. Since Mr. Swagger wasn't around to watch him train his
prized horse, Doc dropped his whip and slammed a two-by-four
between the animal's ears. I shrank back at the clunking sound but
said nothing.

Soon after, the third Monday in August rolled around, and
school started again. Katie took a bus to junior high, and instead of

my sister keeping me company on my way to my fifth-grade class-room, the cafeteria's grilled French toast aroma did. I'd have given all my summer birthday presents for just one bite.

Although I didn't want to get out of bed the following Saturday, the whole family arrived at our new property at 8:00 a.m. sharp. I spent the day sweeping up the construction mess of our contemporary home, starting in the great room with its large picture windows that outlined the front of the house and ending in the bathrooms with their different colored matching marble toilets and tubs.

Months before, Mom helped the architect with the ranch house blueprints, and now, she supervised its building. Ahead of her time with a visionary open floor plan, she created one large area, including a kitchen, dining room, and living room with an island near the elevated telephone desk beside the backdoor slider. Since a phone was already in the barn, we were used to the street's party line. If you picked up the receiver in the great room, you might hear another person's conversation. When Mom got sick of waiting for the telephone because a neighbor was using it, she'd yell, "Get off, bitch!"

While I was helping Mom, Braxton roamed the property unsu-pervised. Doc made Katie ride the new customer's wild stallion as he rode Mr. Swagger's gelding to train him for the horseshow. After my sister got bucked off the crazed male, Doc snorted with plea-sure. "Hayseed, you're younger than me, and your bones will heal faster." Bruised and bleeding, Katie got back on the sleek stud. A steady *tlot, tlot, tlot* sounded throughout the property.

One week turned into two, and two turned into three until the last Saturday in September sizzled burning hot. Still, Mom dressed herself to the nines with her frosted hair ratted to perfection and makeup perfectly applied. She entertained Mr. Swagger and his band of buddies as they encircled her, listening to the animated stories of her contributions to the design of the ranch house. When Mr. Swagger's wife didn't show up earlier, Mom complained that she'd stopped coming to the barn. "She thinks I'm too friendly with her husband."

Once Doc started riding Mr. Swagger's Arabian around the indoor arena, Mom and the group of men moved near the door to

Doc's clinic for a better view. He still had his practice but was increasingly transitioning away from his vet business to training horses.

"Doc sure knows his craft," Mr. Swagger complimented. The client and his entourage nodded their heads in agreement. Although they glanced at the expensive cutting horse, they secretly ogled Mom. They couldn't resist her halter top tied in a knot under her overflowing cleavage that highlighted her tanned, flat stomach. At the same time that she captivated them with yet another story, a tiny, stealthy mouse inched up Mom's skin-tight, hip-hugger jeans. It happened before I could warn her.

By the time the bulge of the creature's outline had crept up to Mom's thigh, she'd started shrieking and ripping off her pants for her astonished audience. When her foot was finally free, a baby mouse plopped from the top of her collapsed jeans on the barn's floor. Panting and wheezing in her panties, Mom blushed. "There was a mouse. D-did you see it?" Mom eyed the men, nodding her head. "Did anyone see it?"

None of them said anything at the striptease show except Mr. Swagger, who stared along with the other men with their mouths wide open, gaping at Mom's pink lace undies. "No, Georgie." His eyes had stars in them. "We didn't see a thing." The smile never left his face.

"I saw it, Mom." I jumped up and down. "I saw the mouse. I did."

As Mom hitched back up her pants, the men hit each other's backs. Mr. Swagger and the boys couldn't wipe off their smirks.

"I love you so much, Summer. If you hadn't seen the mouse"— Mom pointed to all the men—"everyone would think I was nutty."

I stood on my tippy-toes. Her praise made me tall.

The following Saturday, before Mom left for her hair appointment, she said, "Doc's spoiling Katie rotten. Letting her ride Yahtzee all the time." She plucked the skin on her neck. "I can't stand her. Tell me what happens at the barn." Mom slammed the front door on the way out.

"Hayseed! Sweet Pea! Five minutes and we leave for the barn." Doc whistled. "Get your brother, and let's go."

Doc always called Katie Hayseed, but he'd only called me

Sweet Pea when we first met. At the sound of my nickname, goose pimples appeared from his unexpected attention.

"I ... I will." Grabbing crackers, I stuffed a sleeve in a grocery sack. Then I found an open box of Pampers and dumped a bunch in the large brown bag. Even though my brother was three and a half, he still needed diapers. Five minutes later, we crammed into Doc's black truck. "Sit next to me, Summer," Doc suggested, but Katie slipped through the open truck door by Doc. Braxton squeezed between us.

When we got to the barn, Braxton roamed the property, leading his horse, Champ, around the pond and letting him drink. Katie and I got right to work feeding, watering, and haying the horses, breathing in the hay's fresh fall fragrance.

"Doc, we finished the last of our hay," Katie yelled out the barn door. "We need what Summer, you and I bailed a couple of days ago from the rafters." I itched the scratches all over my legs and arms.

My sister and I returned to our chores, getting on each side of the five-gallon bucket to carry the water to the stalls. Next, we dragged the hay to the middle of the barn, cutting the wires and dividing it into flakes—two in the morning and two in the evening. "Katie, how'd we ever bail hay? Even if we lift it together, it's too heavy."

With our morning chores finished, I checked on Braxton.

"Sweet Pea," Doc called as he rode Mr. Swagger's Arabian in the front pen. He was trying to perfect his cutting horse strategy where a horse singled out a cow for the competition, not allowing it back into the herd. "I need a calf." Doc stopped the animal. "Go run back and forth in front of my horse."

"Sure thing!" I sprinted through the gate so that Doc wouldn't slap me. A couple of weekends before, when he thought Katie lied about exercising the new client's stud, he yanked her hair and launched her across the barn. Once she stood up, he kicked her in the back. She landed on her nose.

After being the cow for ten minutes, I was so winded that my head collapsed on my chest, and I had to sit until my breathing returned to normal. Katie brushed Yahtzee, feeding him a sugar cube, hoping to ride him, but Doc made her exercise the new client's stud so long that the autumn sun disappeared. *At least Mom won't be mad at Katie.*

My tired, sore body begged for food as the grueling day ended. I'd eaten all the crackers I'd brought for Braxton; he and Katie never seemed to care about food. My sister and I repeated the morning routine like we did every night, getting right to work feeding, watering, and haying the horses.

"Doc," Katie called out while he brought Mr. Swagger's horse into the barn, "remember we need another hay bale."

Doc whistled. "Get over here, Sweet Pea." I shut off the water and tried to manage the five-gallon bucket solo, teetering side to side, splashing water on my legs. "Just leave it," Doc said as he stood by the built-in wooden ladder. I jogged over to him.

He hoisted me gently to the first step. "Go push off three bales from the top of the rafters." In a frenzy, I knocked the hay to the barn's dirt floor and lowered myself to the ladder.

On the way down, Doc's fingers tickled me under the arm while he guided me to the ground floor. As a reflex, I yelped.

Suddenly, Katie bumped Doc from behind, knocking him off balance. When he regained his footing, he punched Katie in the face, sending her sailing across the dirt. I raced to help her, and we made eye contact but kept our mouths shut.

Katie and I finished feeding the horses. "You're an enigma, Hayseed. You know better." Doc spit on the barn's dirt floor. "Next time, you'll get the belt, too." Doc kicked his boot through the saliva. "Remember, I don't miss anything." He headed to the door. "And am ubiquitous. I can appear anywhere at any time."

I hovered around Katie. "You okay?" I tried to wipe the blood off her split lip.

She intercepted my hand. "I'm fine. Don't open Pandora's Box."

"What's that?"

She lifted her shoulders and walked away.

As September changed to October, Mom spent every second selling Katie and me on the adventure of riding to California in the back of the truck. Doc was showing Mr. Swagger's Arabian at the upcoming Long Beach Cutting Horse Show.

I didn't want to miss a day of fifth grade, much less a whole week, but Mom guaranteed we'd spend one day at Disneyland, so I changed my mind. At 6:00 every Sunday night, if Mom was in a good mood, we'd watch *The Wonderful World of Disney*. Katie didn't care a whit about Mickey Mouse but was happy to get out of school. Braxton stayed with Doc's sister.

The week before we left for California flew by, and the next thing I knew, Doc and Mom were settled in the truck's cab. Katie and I were in the back of its bed. The stars were night lights as I fell fast asleep. By the time I woke up, a reddish canopy covered the horizon. Before long, the skyline knitted together a burnt-orange oval, a deposit of hope to come. With each mile, the sky elongated its image with patches of magenta and stripes of tangerine. It followed the truck, inching higher and higher, eventually disappearing into a white light of warmth.

Once we stopped for a late lunch, my arms and legs had turned golden brown, and my thin hair tangled into a stringy, straggly mess. Long after daylight ended, Katie and I were still bouncing around the back of the truck's unforgiving bed with gas fumes for ventilation. I grumbled to Mom when we finally stopped for dinner as I crammed down my food. "My head's woozy, and my body hurts."

"What planet are you from eating so fast? You're going to make yourself sick." Mom lit a cigarette and pointed to the truck bed. "Just zip up your sleeping bag and keep your mouth shut. Everyone and their brother would love your deal. Riding back there."

We piled back into the Ford, and I rolled back and forth over the truck's bed for hours in the jittering air. Then, finally, for what seemed like a million headlights later, we stopped for the night. "Doc, why wouldn't you make reservations? For the horse and us?" Mom's voice spiked with panic. "What's wrong with you?"

After an hour of searching, Doc finally found a shabby place to board the horse and a cheap inn for the night. Katie complained her thick hair was knotty, so I knew I was in trouble. Her sturdy mane quickly detangled, but as much as I tried, the comb stopped halfway down mine.

"It's a rat's nest," Mom said. "Just go to bed and worry about it tomorrow." We all shared a room, but with Doc's never-ending snoring, I snatched my blanket and escaped into the bathtub to sleep.

When I woke up in the morning, I tried again to get a comb through my hair. "What'll I do?" I whined to Mom. "My hair's just awful. Do you have a rubber band?"

"Stop worrying about your hair. Nobody cares."

Over breakfast, Mom and Doc fought about money, and she stole our tip from the restaurant table. "Don't look at me cross-eyed, Summer." She pocketed the coins. "Doc won't give me any."

What's wrong with Doc? I frowned. *Or is Mom telling the truth?*

On the second day of driving at 8:00 p.m., we hit Needles, California. After all day in the back of the truck, the dry, suffo-cating heat produced a dusty grit film all over my skin. Sunshine in the daytime was my friend, but the enemy of the night spooked me. I hid crouched in my sleeping bag from the hot, windy dark-ness and the vehicles that seemed to eyeball me as their blinding headlights passed our truck and trailer.

An hour later, I scooted on my butt over to Katie. "I can't stand being in the back of this truck anymore. I'm going to beg Mom to let us sit with her. Then maybe she'll stop for dinner. We didn't even get to have lunch."

"I wouldn't." Katie shook her head.

I touched my stomach. "But I can feel all my ribs. And what about my hair." I used my fingers to try to smooth it out. The greasy, matted strands stuck straight out as if I'd been electrocuted. "Where will we sleep tonight? Where's the horse going to stay? When're we going to eat? Aren't you ever hungry?"

"Not really. I like my stomach empty."

I glanced at the front of the cab and raised my fist.

"Don't do it, Summer," Katie said without emotion. "She'll freak out."

"I know." I pounded on the truck's back slider. "I know!"

With her finger, Mom motioned for me to keep quiet.

I pounded harder.

She cracked the glass enough for cold air to blast my face. Bugs smeared the dashboard window. Elvis's "Patch It Up" played on the radio. "What do you want? I'm missing my song."

"Can't we please sit up with you? The last gas station said it was 110." I burst into tears. "It's a different kind of hot here, and I'm so thirsty I'm gonna die. Maybe the horse needs a drink, too."

"Well, I'll be damned. It's a dry heat. That horse's fine, and so are you." Mom's arm slid off the backrest, and she nuzzled Miss Pooh under her chin. "Don't make me sorry I brought you." She thumped the window shut.

Katie didn't have to say, "I told you so."

I slumped down and counted the stars in the sky. By number twenty-four, I fell asleep. We must have checked the horse into the show's fairgrounds. I don't remember. The following day, I woke up in a motel bed. We didn't stay in Anaheim. Instead, we stayed in the next town over. I felt better when I showered and put on my new striped fuchsia-and-white shorts outfit. "I thought we weren't allowed to wear white after Labor Day?" I questioned Mom and fidgeted with the fringe at the bottom of my shorts.

"This is Southern California, baby." Mom readjusted the straps on my shirt. "Wear all the white you want."

I pulled my poncho over my outfit in case it got cold. Katie took one look at my hair and handed me her comb. I ripped out hunks, but at last, it was tangle-free. Mom pointed to my shawl. "You don't need that. Let's hustle to the truck."

Peeling it over my head, I threw it on the hotel bed.

Disneyland, here I come.

On our way to breakfast, we drove past rows and rows of orange groves. "Welcome to the home of Mickey Mouse," the sign said before we stopped to eat. The young blonde waitress counted menus and seated us on the outside patio. I hung back by massive green vines, sniffing the sweet-scented lavender flowers. *I can't believe it's October, and I'm eating in the sunshine.*

At the table, a fresh fruit platter waited. The California grapefruits tasted like Kansas oranges, and the California oranges tasted like liquid sugar. I gawked at the tall trees with green fans sticking out the top. *Are those supposed to be leaves? Southern California trees are so skinny.*

"Should we check the weather, Mom? Make sure it's not going to rain. And that today's a good day for Disneyland." I played with my napkin.

"People don't check the weather in California like we do in Kansas." Mom pointed at the clear, blue sky. "It's paradise every day here"

I didn't want to annoy Mom and blow my chance for Disneyland, so I put my napkin in my lap and asked no more questions. Mom gave me the once-over. "You ready?" I nodded but kept prying bits of my napkin loose, silently begging Mom not to change her mind.

She didn't.

Since we'd arrived in Southern California, Mom let Katie and me ride in the cab. Ten eye-popping, jittery minutes later, I bolted out of the truck into a Disneyland cartoon character's parking lot sign. "There seems like as many cars as in all of Kansas, Mom."

After standing in line at the little dollhouses to buy our tickets, we finally set foot through Disneyland's entrance. I skipped under the brick arch at the same time a train whistled and a clock clanged above me. "Whoopee!" I said with a tickle in my throat.

The street of my dreams emerged before me. With different facades of vivid and multicolored candy shops and restaurants, the confectioner's aroma of salt-water taffy and caramel apples whipped my head side to side as we strolled down Main Street, USA. Cartoon characters I'd only seen on TV held out their arms for a hug while jolly people singing in colorful clothes swept every speck of trash from the street. The lemonade and popcorn vendors wore such happy smiles that I stepped closer to see if they were real as enormous, shiny horses pulled carriages through the park's cool breeze and warm sunshine.

Mom flung her arm around me, leading the group to the Matterhorn Bobsleds. Doc bent his head and pinched the bridge of his nose, refusing to talk. With her hip, Mom whacked him in the butt. "Don't act so ugly, Doc. I promised the girls Disneyland." She kneed the back of his legs as she moved past him in line.

"I'll go on this one, Georgie, and that's it."

I held my breath and picked at my fingernails. Mom said nothing. After the rollercoaster, Doc ditched us.

"Good riddance!" Mom shooed him away with the palms of her hands. "Let's get some of that buttery popcorn popping." Mom sniffed her nose in the air like a little girl. "And that's not margarine." After getting our salty treat, we sat in the roundabout near the Walt and Mickey statues.

"Let's ride every ride we can, girls." Once we licked the oily coating off our lips, we wasted no time. Mom and I took Disneyland by storm.

"Get on the stick, Katie," Mom ordered when she refused to keep up. "Don't ruin It's a Small World for Summer. We're just about to get on the boat."

Dragging Katie along to the next attraction, I gushed, "Mom, I loved that last ride so much. "

"You were fun to watch, Summer, but it's a wonder your neck didn't twist off. You spun your head around so many times."

After that, we charged through the happiest place on earth, enjoying the E-ticket rides of The Monorail, Autopia Cars, Submarine Voyage, and The Haunted Mansion until our ticket books were empty. With the backdrop of make-believe, it was a front-row seat to the best day of my ten years. Strolling by the steamboats hand in hand, I imagined Mom kissing the top of my head as peaceful swans swam by the park's man-made river's edge. "My first trip to California was in high school. Mother and Daddy tried to make me forget about Troy, Katie's dad." Mom laughed so loud that the woman passing us smiled. "It didn't work." Mom looked like a movie star. "That's all she wrote, girls. Let's go find Doc."

Mom and I linked arms, twirling toward the exit. Katie followed behind. Doc sat drinking orange juice under the Coca-Cola sign at an outdoor cafe near the end of Main Street. "You two look like two peas in a pod."

"And you look like you've been drinking."

He huffed out his chest and trailed us to the exit.

Like Cinderella's coach turning into a pumpkin, everything switched once we passed the ticket dollhouses. My glass slippers reverted to sandals before Mom jammed me in the neck. "Summer, quit twiddling your thumbs and get moving," Mom screeched like the Disneyland train whistle. "Just be thankful you got to go."

With tears in my eyes, I blew Mickey Mouse a kiss goodbye. Fifteen minutes of walking found us front and center of the truck. I squished in between Katie and Mom in the front seat. Driving out of the parking lot, Doc accelerated toward the exit. My eyes wouldn't stay open. My head fell backward from exhaustion.

Mom's elbow rammed me. "Summer, stop sleeping!"

I squealed in pain, and my head rolled back into blackness. No matter how often Mom jabbed me, I couldn't keep my eyes open. *Why's Mom waking me up?* I wanted my Disneyland Mom back. My eyes closed for good.

Bright and early the following day, we arrived at the horse show. By the end of the day, Doc placed second in the cutting horse competition, winning hefty prize money. That night when we returned to the motel, we packed for home. Twenty-four hours later, Katie and I waited by the truck. "You girls are getting on my nerves." Mom pointed to the pickup bed. "You're back there."

"Georgie's right," Doc chimed in after her. "Who cares if Californians think we Kansans pick bugs out of our teeth."

A creepy guy hovered near our car during our gas stop before the long trip home. Doc and Mom didn't notice, but I warned Katie, "Stay away from him. He looks like a sleazeball druggie. He's even barefoot." I reminded Katie again about the sketchy guy before I rushed to the bathroom.

After we'd been flying down the freeway ten miles, Katie flailed her arms and legs inside her sleeping bag.

"What's wrong, Katie?" I wailed as my hair knotted in the wind. I couldn't see my sister's face, but her jerking motions became more and more pronounced. A wave of terror seized me. "Katie?" I rocked her body, which had just gone still. Then, pouncing on her, I peered into her sleeping bag. "You've just gotta be okay! Just gotta!"

From the flimsy bedroll came her frail, muffled voice. "I took pills from that scuzzy guy at the gas station." Her hands clawed the air. Tinkling bells sounded in my head.

"Help!" I hammered on the back window, sobbing for Mom to open it. She ignored me, so I banged harder. "Help! Please!"

"Just kidding!" Katie slipped her head out of her sleeping bag with a wicked grin. It was the first time she'd smiled the whole trip.

"Oh, Katie!" I launched myself over her. "Don't scare me like that again. I don't want to ever be without you." I snuggled in my threadbare blanket against the hard bed of the truck and didn't stop weeping until the lights of Las Vegas appeared on the horizon.

CHAPTER 10

THE RANCH HOUSE

August 1973 – August 1974
Edgerton, Kansas

Little Summer's Diary
Dear God,
Here's my poem: "Like is when it's in your mind. Love is when it goes to your heart."
I'm 11. Katie's 13. Braxton 4.
 Sum

The school bus door flung wide open. "Hello, kiddos. Hurry! Skedaddle on up here." The driver talked as fast as she chewed her gum. In a groggy daze, I boarded the bus behind Katie. "I don't wait for anyone." The strawberry blonde, slightly overweight woman in her zip-up pantsuit had a friendly smile but a lead foot. She took off like a rocket, pinning me to the back of my seat. After school, the same bus driver whisked us home.

Days before I started sixth grade and Katie eighth, we moved into our decorated-to-the-tee ranch house that smelled like a department store.

"Better catch your bus in the morning," Mom warned. "You'll pay if I have to drive you."

At 6:30 a.m. on the dot, with toast wrapped like a present in a paper towel, I burst out the ranch house's front door. The bus's horn blared while it blew past our house. A mile up our street, the vehicle picked up the neighbor kids and barreled back down the hill for Katie and me.

The first two months of school were warm, turning cooler as summer changed into autumn with half-red and half-green leaves intermingled on the trees. By the second week of November, the trees had no leaves at all, but the cooler weather forged a rigid resolve to make the bus instead of waking up Mom.

In the third week of November, I hit a snag. Putting on my boots, I crunched something under my big toe. I cringed, ripping off my footwear—out jumped a cricket. After jamming the boot back on, I grabbed my books, ran upstairs, and through the door just in time to see the bus's taillights disappear toward school.

Katie was still asleep when I woke up a hungover Mom.

"You girls are too old for this cattywampus bull! I'm not your taxi." Mom drove us the four miles to school in her robe as I picked fuzz off my wool skirt.

"I need coffee." She floored the engine to what seemed like a hundred MPH. The car fishtailed. Mom glared at me in the rearview mirror. "Because of you, I didn't get my caffeine. Summer, do you hear me?"

Why's she blaming only me?

As Highway 56 widened into Main Street's four lanes, Mom nearly sideswiped a blue sedan, forcing it over the curb and onto the grass. "How's it even possible for a car to go that slow?" Mom sped away, never looking back. "Dumb ol' woman should learn how to drive."

"Mom, stop!" I said without thinking. I swiveled my head back to the median to see if the lady was okay.

"I'll do no such thing. It wasn't my fault."

I didn't know if it was for the woman in the car or me, but I kicked off my boots and started crying. A smooshed cricket and seven more of his jumping brothers fell out. "Eww!" Katie yelled.

"That's gross! Did those crickets come out of the holes in your boots?"

"What? You've destroyed another pair of shoes, Summer?" Mom banged the steering wheel. "No wonder! You stomp around like a bull in a china shop." She looked over at Katie. "Your sister's never ever worn out one pair of shoes."

I rolled my right ankle. It popped. By the time I'd cracked my other ankle, my neck, and all my fingers, Mom pulled up near the school's bus lane.

I sat sentry still.

"Get out now and run the rest of the way. If you're late, too bad. Maybe tomorrow, you'll make damn sure to catch the bus. I've got to take back roads home, so the cops don't find me in case that woman got my license plate."

Stepping on the sidewalk, I scraped cricket guts off my boots.

"You're always bugged about something, Summer," Mom hollered before she drove away.

Throughout the year after Doc's remarkable showing in Orange County, he gained more and more customers, spending less time on his vet practice. Every weekend, Cadillacs filled the long, gravel, circular driveway. Doc's wealthy clients gawked as he rode their well-behaved horses. Doc never allowed Katie and me to touch the animals within eyeshot of their owners, but if they weren't around, Katie joyfully trained the wild ones, and I reluctantly exercised the broken ones.

After Katie and I had done our morning chores, Doc pulled us aside. "You girls need to clean the stalls—all twenty."

Katie and I staggered under pitchforks while shoveling the heavy horse muck into the manure spreader, but when we got it loaded, Katie started the tractor. Then, in the seat together, Katie and I blasted out of the barn as fast as the ancient jalopy would go, breathing in the fertilizer odor as we distributed the droppings throughout the pasture.

Once we finished, we ran to the house and sneaked downstairs to our bedrooms.

Boom! Boom! Boom! The ceiling reverberated. If Mom wanted Katie or me, she banged her heel or a broom on the top floor. My sister and I scampered up the stairs to the oversized great room with rustic brown beams below the vaulted white ceiling.

Mom shriveled up her nose. "You girls need to make dinner." For the winter, Mom splurged on a half side of beef. "There'll be six of us. Don't make something lousy—make spaghetti." I fought a smile. That's all Katie and I knew how to make. "Feed Braxton and get him out of the way downstairs."

After Mom thumped the sliding glass door shut, I reached for her brand-new china. "I'll set the table, Katie. And I'll use that pumpkin pie-smelling candle Grandmother Mema bought for a centerpiece."

Katie nodded and ran scalding water over the package to thaw the meat she'd just grabbed from the garage freezer, peeling it off in layers. While she struggled to get the ground beef out of the plastic crevices, I chopped onion. When my eyes started to water, I poured oil into a large skillet and tossed the hacked pieces into the pan, inhaling the roasted onion scent.

"I hope I got all the plastic out," Katie said, adding chunks of meat with the browned onions. Finally, she added tomato sauce, garlic salt, and boiled and drained pasta, then splashed it into the gigantic skillet to complete the main course.

Slicing off a slab of soft butter, I slathered it on the sourdough bread and sprinkled it with garlic salt, wrapping it in aluminum foil before flinging it into the oven. As the baking bread's garlic aroma permeated the kitchen, Katie transported our masterpiece meal to the table.

Crack! Clap! Crash! There was a terrific explosive noise. I turned my head from the oven. Katie's hand gripped only the pan's handle. It'd snapped, breaking off from the skillet. Leaked spaghetti juice covered the overturned pan. Doc's clients' dinner splattered onto the grimy kitchen floor.

"Quick! Before they come up from the barn," Katie ordered. "Put the spaghetti back into the pan. They'll never know the difference. We won't tell."

"I haven't told on you since that smoking thing." I shuddered at the memory, thankful that the swearing incident with Doc fizzled before Katie got whipped. "No, I'm not telling. I don't want Mom to call us every name in the book."

Katie gathered the spaghetti in the pan, putting the lid back on. No one said a word about the handleless serving container. Instead, they all ate spaghetti, iceberg salad, and garlic bread, praising the delicious meal.

Katie remained emotionless over the food. Even the Robin, I was by my Batman's side.

As soon as Katie and I cleaned the kitchen, we disappeared downstairs. *Boom! Boom! Boom!* I raced back upstairs. Katie stayed in her room.

"I've got a bone to pick with you." Mom gave me the stink-eye. *Does she know about the spaghetti?*

"Your chin should be dragging the ground. I'm so embarrassed. Dinner was good, but you forgot to light the table's candle. It's low-class to display one with an unlit wick. Now make a pot of coffee. You know how I need my caffeine."

The Dynamic Duo's secret is safe.

Wasting no time, I opened the coffee pot and dumped the stale grounds into the trash. Wet, black particles clung to the side of the bagless can. I filled the machine with water and rinsed the filter. Once I popped it back in place, I opened the coffee and added twelve heaping spoonfuls. The rich nutty aroma made me wonder why I didn't like it. Mom sure did. She drank pot after pot all day and all night long.

I plugged in the percolator like I'd done a thousand times as heavy raindrops started pounding the roof. Then, without making eye contact with Mom for fear of more work, I split down the stairs. My footsteps sounded in unison with the rain.

In the middle of the night, like a kitty with its ears back, Katie sprang on me. Turning on my side to make room for my sister in my twin bed, I pulled the red, white, and blue bedspread around her ears. "The thunder woke ... woke ... "

Even though she was thirteen, she cried like an infant. After smoking the pack of cigarettes, Katie crumbled at the first hint of thunder. With my blanket, I wiped the sweat off her face. "Why ... why ... aren't you scared, Summer?"

A supernatural crash of light lit up the sky outside my window, illuminating the eyelet rods holding my matching red, white, and blue curtains.

"I'm just in awe of the storm's strength." Gratitude replaced fear in Katie's eyes. In an attempt to distract her, I touched my bangs. "I guess I had way too much strength with those scissors. Remember? When I cut my hair in the first grade?"

"Yes. You gave yourself bangs." Katie found her voice. "But you only had one jagged piece of hair down the middle of your forehead."

We laughed together. "I looked so dorky." With my palm, I bumped my forehead.

Katie fell asleep first. Her chest moved up and down in unison with her gentle breathing. I watched her until I couldn't keep my eyes open and then enjoyed the best night's sleep since our rental house.

"What the hell's Katie doing here?" Mom shouted in the morning. "Get out of bed! You're painting the fence all day. The snow comes next weekend. If you start now, you can finish all seventeen acres by tonight. Kansas weather decides what we do around here, so get your lazy asses moving!"

Two hours later, fancy client cars started parading down the driveway. Doc whistled for us, so we dropped our brushes in the can and ran to the barn.

"Go enjoy the warm weather." Doc's client's unexpected arrival rescued us from our painting prison. Mom and Doc didn't like people to see how much we worked.

"Let's ride." Katie poked her head out of Yahtzee's stall. "Bareback. Swim the horses in the pond. They'll love it."

"You don't have to ask me twice." I forgot all about the paint and brushes we'd left by the fence. "We caught a break. We're not Mom's slaves today." Katie nodded in agreement. "Even though it's the last day of November, it feels like Southern California weather."

On Montez, I followed Katie and Yahtzee to the pond, trotting by Doc. "Lean upon the horse's neckbone now, Summer. Do that, will you?" He taunted in front of his customers. "You'll like it—it'll feel so g-good." Chuckling broke out in Doc's circle of wannabe cowboys as they hee-hawed in unison. Montez cantered up to Yahtzee.

Doc's making fun of me, but what in the world is he talking about?

After we rode, Katie and I made a swing from the Horse Walker, finding a two-by-four without nails and looping the chains into the wood. Usually, Braxton was off looking for butterflies, but my brother appeared once Katie flipped on the electric Horse Walker that automatically made horses go around in a circle. He and I hopped on the makeshift swing, sailing back and forth through the air. Although Katie didn't join our party for two, she couldn't hide her satisfaction. Braxton's toothy grin made me hoot and holler to see him so jolly.

"Stop that racket," Mom yelled from the house. "Or you'll go back to painting the fence."

The last blast of warm weather disappeared the following day, and December arrived. Kansas's ever-changing climate's air smelled of snow. I turned into a popsicle while slogging down the driveway to the bus. After school, Doc didn't make us ride the training horses. I gave Katie a thumbs-up. It would be an easy night; I could start my homework, eat a quick dinner, and get to bed early.

Doc and Mom hijacked my plans when they loaded us in the truck. We drove through the recent light snow flurries the mile and a half to Miss Sugar's barn. She wasn't there, but the two horses Mom and Doc wanted Katie and me to ride back to our barn were. I wasn't excited about being their "horse trailer," but the one they usually pulled behind their truck had a flat tire. There was nothing to eat at Miss Sugar's place except coffee. I tried to choke down a cupful with a ton of cream and sugar, but I bolted outside and spat out the bitter, milky liquid, leaving a stale aftertaste.

Katie and I mounted horses we'd never ridden. Under the lights, the sprinkle of precipitation had turned into a slanting, spitting snowstorm. Katie smiled wide, but I scowled even wider. After being outside for two seconds, I missed the soothing warmth of Miss Sugar's barn heater.

As if Mom could read my thoughts, she appeared. "Get that mule-headed look off your face, Summer, *because* I said so." Mom pronounced it *be-cawse*, holding the last syllable for effect. "You need to practice keeping up with Katie's natural equestrian seat."

With chattering teeth, I nodded yes, but my face still said no.

I hate being cold. I rubbed my bare hands over my thin jacket and followed Katie single file as the moisture turned into a steady stream of sleet and ice underneath a layer of powder and frost. My horse's shoes slipped when a gust of wind almost blew me off him. *What if the snow makes drifts?*

After we hung a right, snaking around the corner of Miss Sugar's property, we turned directly into the hissing air and swaying trees. I stayed flat on the animal, keeping Katie in sight until we passed a house chimney, puffing gray haze. The warm wood-fired smoke saturated the back of my nose, reminding me that I hadn't eaten. *I hate being hungry.*

Katie was no longer in view.

The wind whipped snow in my face. *This's too much.* I slumped over the horse's neck. *Why does Mom always want more than I can give and then get mad that I can't give it?* I hung on to the saddle horn while tears froze on my cheeks.

In a flash, strings of white light tinged with violet edges crackled through the sky. Can there even be lightning in a snowstorm? *Katie! She's not too far ahead.* I made the animal go faster and turned left onto our street, chasing my sister.

When I finally arrived at the barn, I swung my right leg over the saddle and dropped to the ground. My numb feet burned on impact. "I hate riding."

"And I hate lightning." Katie put away my horse.

I followed her up to the house. "I loved the lightning. It was angry. Like I was at Mom." I slid open the slider. "And it made me see you."

Mom, Doc, and Braxton weren't home, so Katie and I ate cornflakes for dinner. I ate five bowls for Katie's one, and then we made a game out of cleaning the kitchen, agreeing to kiss a boy if we didn't finish the dishes in under five minutes.

"I'll kiss Jay," I told Katie as she washed the bowls with the cheap dishwashing detergent that refused to bubble. "He's so cute with his dimples and dark hair. Today, we made sissy scratches on our arms, rubbing off the skin with erasers." I raised my forearms. "See?"

"That's weird." Katie washed another bowl, handing it to me to dry. "Jay won't work. It sounds like you like him. You've got to swear to kiss someone you don't."

I made a face and dried another bowl without rinsing it. Washing them with a sudsless, watery detergent worked in our favor because Mom wouldn't let us rinse the dishes anyway. "Water's too expensive, and we can't afford to haul any more this month," Mom had told us the day before. "You two girls are wasting too much. Draining our water tank dry. Pretty soon, you'll have to quit taking showers."

Katie and I had turned to each other and mouthed, "Gross."

After finishing the kitchen, we headed back to the barn to feed, water, and hay the horses. Once Katie turned on the barn lights, twenty hulking, dark gray rats hopped through the air and scampered for cover, but not before their bulky, fat tails and yellow clacking teeth made me jump on Katie's back. "Rats scare the heebie-jeebies out of me, but at least they're not in the house."

"Haven't you heard them in our garage water storage?" Katie pushed me off her back. "And in the walls?"

"What? In the water we drink?" I tapped my teeth, pretending to bite all my fingernails. "Is that what I hear when I get up to go to the bathroom at night?"

"Yes." Katie was unfazed. "Every night at the same time."

I bent over and pretended to throw up. "The rats don't wake me up. But the banging of Mom and Doc's headboard in the middle of the night does," I said. "Their room's above mine." Katie put her hands on her knees and spit up.

After school on Friday, I did cartwheels in the front yard; it was my weekend with Dad. Even though I loved my brother and sister, I treasured the forty-minute drive with my father all by myself to his house.

"Mom gave me a new notebook for school." I bragged, leaping into his car with my overnight bag. I never expected Dad to like Mom, but I kept trying.

"Watch your mom's things. They're the gifts that keep taking."

I tilted my head in confusion.

"They've got strings attached, Summer."

Does he mean like Braxton's toy butterfly my brother pulls around with a string?

Mile after mile, Dad munched a bag of carrots down to the stem, holding them like a cigarette while he quizzed me about current events, book characters, and geographical locations. I didn't know the answers. At school, I was distracted by our house's chaos but memorized the material to get A's without understanding the concepts.

"I think the carrots not only kicked my smoking habit but prevented me from getting a cold this year."

"Mom thought she had pneumonia," I said, pronouncing it with a *p* sound.

"If you don't know how to pronounce a word, Summer, look it up in a dictionary. That way, you'll get it correct."

I nodded my head in agreement. *I can't even get the first letters right to find the word, much less find a dictionary at our house.*

Dad continued, explaining Neil Armstrong's moon landing.

Great! I actually know about this. "Yes, Dad!" I tucked my leg under my body, turning to him. "I learned one side of the moon was black from Mom's *Dark Side of the Moon* album." Then I added with extra enthusiasm, "I bet because Pink Floyd's got so much money, he'll take a tropical vacation to the South Pole."

Before we arrived at his house, Dad lectured me about the planets and the equator. Being a man with a razor-sharp engineer's mind, his daughter's apparent lack of knowledge puzzled him.

He stopped asking me questions. I missed his attention, so I told him about Mom's latest alarming behavior. "After she ran the woman off the road on the way to school, she made me chase Doc with her to the bar. She had to take his keys because he got so drunk."

Dad shook his head. "How'd he get to the bar without his truck?"

"He rode his client's six-thousand-dollar horse." I started laughing and then paused. "Maybe I'll write a book about all the shocking things Mom does."

Dad drove into his garage and shut off the car. He turned to me and patted my knee. "What a good idea, Summer."

"But maybe it would make Mom feel funny. I love her and wouldn't want to hurt her. Or for her to be mad."

"Write your book, Summer," Dad encouraged with red-rimmed eyes. "Tell your story. It'll be a bestseller. Since you were born, your mom's given you nothing but a free trial of seppuku."

I massaged my lips together, not even trying to understand what that meant. "Maybe the book would make her nicer."

"The proof's in the pudding."

"What flavor's the pudding, Dad?"

After the weekend, on the way back to Mom's house, Dad said, "Some day, I want to climb Mount Everest in the Himalayas." He glanced at me and paused, wiping his lips. "You know it's a mountain, right, Summer?"

"Oh, yes, Dad. It's in Kansas. I know that!"

He couldn't speak.

Winter passed into spring, and then school ended. In mid-May, Katie and I started working in the cornfields. Katie drove Mom's white Cadillac convertible to the farm near Miss Sugar's barn. Earlier in the year, without Grandfather's permission, Mom traded his silver-blue Ford for her new Eldorado. "Don't you girls open your mouth about my car."

We didn't say a word when we drove with the top down to the field to detassel corn. Grandfather told Katie he'd pay her salary if she wouldn't take the job. She ignored him, hiking up and down the cornrows with the other teenage band of farm workers. Enjoying the earthy smell, I removed the tassels from the top of the corn plants and threw them on the ground. The supervisor explained that it was like bees pollinating the flowers.

Since workers were required to be twelve to get paid, I lied about my age. As a result, Katie and I each earned two hundred dollars. *At least I'll have lunch money to start seventh grade.*

After the long, exhausting two weeks of work, Katie found me in my room. "Let's drive to town and cruise Main." She jingled the keys in her hand. "Mom and Doc are gone with Braxton."

"What about no driver's license—or even a permit?"

"Who cares? Mom's always sending me on errands anyway. Let's go."

With the convertible's top-down, my head rolled back on the

white leather headrest. The bright star Dad said was a planet made me wonder about the Jesus picture from Grammy's church. *Does He know sometimes I hate my mother? Or that the last time Katie drove the convertible to the cornfield, Mom forced us to dump our garbage there because we don't have trash pickup?*

"Katie, remember a couple of months ago, Mom made us throw trash by Miss Sugar's field?"

"When I hit that car?"

"Yes, remind me how we got home."

"Miss Sugar took us."

A month later, junior high started. Before bed, I said goodnight to Mom. An annoying buzzing sound whizzed around her sitting at the kitchen table. "I'm nervous about school tomorrow."

She ignored me, placed her cigarette in the ashtray, and picked up the flyswatter. Then, with one slap, demolished the fly. Never looking up, she raised her cigarette to her lips, taking a long, slow drag. "Shut the back sliding door, Summer. Flies are getting in."

That night, I dreamt I showed up in my pajamas for the first day of school. Then, I got back to sleep, dreaming I forgot to go to class and flunked seventh grade.

CHAPTER 11

JUNIOR HIGH

August 1974 – May 1975
Edgerton, Kansas

Dear God,
Junior high starts tomorrow. I'm 12. Katie is 14. Braxton is 5.
♥ Sum

"I'm so tired I could fall asleep standing up." I hung on Katie's shoulder while we waited by the mailbox. A yellow streak appeared on the horizon.

Five minutes later, our favorite school bus driver slammed the brakes in front of our house.

"I only got four hours of sleep," I complained to my sister as we stepped up the vehicle's stairs. "I had nightmares all—"

"I'm in high school now and can't listen to your jabbering anymore." A girl motioned Katie to the back of the bus. I found a seat near the front.

Ten muggy minutes after the driver unloaded the high schoolers, the bus pulled into my junior high school's drop-off zone. My plaid shirt stuck to my back. *So much for my new school clothes.* The gold-and-blue buildings appeared before me. I tried to get off the bus, but the sweat cemented my legs to the seat.

Will I like seventh grade? Will I have friends? Will I miss Katie? I felt my blown-dry hair. Even though Mom said I was vain, I got up early and managed the perfect flip, but the weather had other plans. The mid-August heat wilted my hair into stringy strands of fuzz.

The next day, I conquered my beginning junior-high jitters and bolted off the bus to my first-period math class. Days of school turned into weeks, and weeks turned into months until one sky-blue October morning, a bright, amber-eyed girl burst through the door. Our teacher, Mr. Joseph, waved the new student toward an empty desk by mine. Instead of sitting there, she pretended to sit on my lap. Her bouncy brown hair touched my shoulder.

"Hello, Sunshine! I'm Lexie." She pointed to my Converse sneakers. "I'm dying to get a pair of those. When I try out for basketball, my dad said I could."

"Tryouts are in a couple of weeks." I shuffled my navy-blue shoes. "I want to be on the basketball team, too."

Mr. Joseph pushed his thick, black-rimmed glasses up his nose and cleared his throat.

Lexie popped out of my chair and scooted to the neighboring empty seat by me.

"Oops, well ... " She threw up her hands in the air. "I guess I got that wrong."

Mr. Joseph scratched his flat-top buzz cut. "*Well*, now, that *is* a deep subject," he said without blinking his bright blue, amused eyes.

"Surely, I'll do better tomorrow."

"Don't call me Shirley." Boys and girls burst out laughing, so he waited for them to stop. "All right. No more guffawing from the peanut gallery." He fought back a smile. "Class, this's Lexie. It appears she won't give us one minute of silence, and Summer will be her partner in crime."

I loved her at that moment.

"Thank you, Lexie, for finally getting to your correct seat." Mr. Joseph's students hung on his every word. Strict and supportive, they worked hard for him. He returned the favor, allowing the class to call his house for math tutoring.

I gave Lexie a thumbs-up.

After the bell rang, Lexie and I ambled to second-period social studies. At lunch, I saved her a seat. We picked up our conversation as if we'd never stopped. Humming a catchy tune, my new fast friend opened a bag of cheese puffs. "Want some?"

I took a handful of the cheesy crunch, which chased away my grumbling stomach. Unfortunately, I was out of money again. My cornfield-detasseling job only lasted four weeks of school lunches since I blew most of it at the Johnson County Fair weeks before school started. "You've got some of that orange stuff on your chin." I brushed it off. "Want more? I packed a double lunch today."

Grammy's God just gave me an early Christmas present.

After meeting Lexie, I was extra determined to make the morning bus. "Hello, Sunshine," Lexie greeted me the following Friday as we sailed into our algebra class.

"You two must be trying to break a gabfest record." Mr. Joseph nodded from his door as he welcomed the pupils. "Lexie, don't go to your old seat. That ship's sailed." He strutted across the room to an empty desk and tapped his index finger. "This's your new one."

Returning to the front of the room, Mr. Joseph sat on the edge of his desk and took off his glasses, wiping them on his white short-sleeved button-down shirt. "No more being the class chatterboxes," he chuckled, putting back on his glasses.

"Okay, Sunshine," Lexie said on our way to social studies. "Mr. Joseph needs to take a chill pill, but we both better join the basketball team."

When I got home that afternoon, I paced around my room. *I just can't stand it if I'm not on the b-ball team. I know I'll make it. But will Mom let me? I don't want Lexie to find another best friend.*

Later that night, I asked Mom.

"You've got some nerve. You're at that school every waking minute. You're still a cheerleader and already did that other sport."

"You mean volleyball?"

"Yes, that was enough! Picking you up ran me ragged." Mom

lit a cigarette, sucking in a breath. "You don't even want to be home," she said before she stubbed out the butt.

"Yes, I do." I lied. *She's right. I joined every school activity to get away from home.* "I'll do every chore to the max on the weekends." I pleaded with my eyes, blinking back tears.

"Stop always crying and shooting off your mouth." Mom lit another cigarette. "Then I may just let you."

One sleepless night later, I broke the news to Lexie. "I want to join the b-ball team, but Mom's not the taxi type." Eating a corndog and chips for lunch, I inhaled the deep-fried breaded aroma that hung over our lunchroom table. Before school, I'd stolen money from Mom's purse. "It doesn't look good."

"Dad'll take you home. Where do you live?"

"In the country, about four miles from school." I offered Lexie some chips. "For volleyball and cheerleading, Mom was either late or a no-show. And she gets pissed if another mom takes me home. So, I'm usually the last girl at practice. She just refuses to pick me up."

"Pick you up, my ass!" Lexie studied me. "She's riding your ass."

"Don't I know it?" I crunched chip after chip and finished off my cup of fruit cocktail. "She says she's easygoing."

"Right. And I can squeeze into size three jeans." Lexie's light laughter indented her upper lip. "You know you eat like a fat girl despite having a concave stomach." She rolled her eyes, "Don't worry. I won't hold that against you." She plopped a red Starburst in her mouth and handed me a pink one. "Look, I'm six miles from school, so you must be on the way home." Her eyes widened. "If not, I'll just make sure you are."

The next morning, I found Lexie before math class. "She said yes!" I did a cheerleading jump.

Lexie high-fived me.

"And she said if she's home, she'll try to pick me up."

"That sets you up to fail, doesn't it?"

"Uh-huh, but at least we'll be together."

The following Monday at 3:00, Lexie and I chatted non-stop as we dressed for basketball. I couldn't make a free throw during tryouts to save my life, but I could steal the ball. "You have one speed, Summer," Lexie praised before our wind sprints started again. "Fast! And you're great on defense."

"If only I could s-slow down," I said, taking a knee to regain my breath, "going for the layup. It bounces off the backboard halfway to center court." I stood up. "You need to teach me how you never miss a shot."

"I will, Summer. We're going to make the team, so we'll kick butt and take names later."

After practice, Mom was a no-show. Lexie's dad appeared in his Lincoln Mercury. "Come on, Sunshine. You're with me." We piled into her family's light green sedan. "You won't be the last one left today."

"Like I've been a thousand times before." I blubbered a sigh of relief. "Thanks!"

Lexie had her dad's toothy grin. With his athletic build and serious eyes, he commanded authority. Suddenly, he furrowed his eyebrows. "Some crazy driver's about to run us off the road."

Like a bat out of hell, Mom's white Cadillac blurred past his vehicle in the opposite direction near Miss Sugar's place, almost forcing us into the rockpile's edge. My mind clicked Mom's tight-lipped image into my brain. A choking cloud of exhaust stirred up a dust tornado in her wake.

Twisting my hair, I willed his sedan to go faster, calculating how long it would take Mom to get to school, find me gone, and catch the older car on her way back. Too close to call, but with Mom's need for speed, it didn't look good. The miles crept by.

Five farms later, Lexie's dad glanced in his rearview mirror and did a double take. "It's that white car again," he said in a husky voice. "Inching up on us."

Clocking an Indy 500 qualifying time, Mom blasted past us again on the narrow gravel road, pinging grit and grime on his Mercury. Her hypnotized-like eyes stared straight ahead.

"She almost rear-ended us!" Lexie's dad coughed. "Do you know that lunatic, Summer?"

Boom! His car backfired.

Motionless air filled the car. I stared across the road, twisting my hair harder. "No," I said. *I'm such a liar. Why's the lie off my tongue before I even know it? Mom'll be home by now. Maybe she parked in the garage and shut the door.* "Just let me off at the corner ... " I begged Lexie's dad.

Once he passed the mailbox, I closed my eyes and didn't open them until Mom's white Eldorado appeared before me; its engine fan churned as fast as my pulse. I thanked Lexie's dad, racing out of the car like my hair was on fire.

When I opened the slider, Mom held the blue receiver by her ear and shot me a disgusted look. "I hung up on Zoe's mom to go and get you, and you weren't even there. So don't ever ask me to pick you up again!" The echo of her cuss words followed me like an assassin across the room.

Swoosh! Click-click-click! "Hello, again!" Mom's telephone voice changed to nectar-nice. "I'm back to hear all about Zoe."

At least Lexie gets to sleep over tomorrow. But should I cancel? No, she's used to her mom's unstable house.

The following day during basketball practice, I couldn't concentrate. I counted the seconds before Lexie's dad dropped us off for our overnighter. Once we finally got home, Lexie and I headed straight for my bedroom.

After putting her overnight bag on the connecting white square nightstand, she sat on one of my twin beds with matching bedspreads. "Okay, Sunshine. We need to get this out on the table." She knocked on the single patriotic, star-dotted wallpapered wall behind her. "Your mom drives like Cruella de Vil."

I nodded my head.

"Dad knows she drove that white car. He's not mad. But don't ever lie to him again. He doesn't like it. So, take my advice and run with it."

"I will." I sniffled. "I don't know why I lied. I feel horrible throwing Mom under the bus like that. I never want to be her."

"Look, Sunshine. You lied because you're afraid of your mom. I'm afraid of mine, too. That's why I fled her house. After my parents divorced, with the number of men she paraded through the front door, you'd think she was running a homeless shelter." Lexie chuckled, sounding like her dad. "Maybe she was."

"I get it. Mom's done that, too." I pretended to gag. "I know you understand. That's why you're the only friend to ever spend the night." I scratched my shoulder and looked up at the ceiling. "I also want to tell you that ... that I'm stealing money from Mom."

"Of course you are." Lexie opened my red, white, and blue curtains; the last flash of the setting sun cast an orange glow over the room. "Since Georgie never gives you any, what else can you do?"

"Exactly! But I've just got to stop lying and stealing."

"You might have to scratch stealing off your list."

"You're right." I smiled halfway. "I love lists. I make them and then cross off the items." I waved one of them from my nightstand. "Sometimes, I even write the completed task I forgot and then check it off."

She laughed. "I do that same cross-off list thing." Lexie tapped her temple. "We must share a brain."

"Of course we do!" We got into our nightshirts and crashed into bed, chattering until we fell asleep.

Crash! Bang! Boom!

"What in the world?" Lexie rolled out of bed. "It's like *The Twilight Zone*. I'm back at Mom's."

"This isn't good, Lex." I glanced at my clock radio. "We've only been asleep thirty minutes." I stumbled out of bed. "I'm thankful you're here. Katie's gone. I hope Braxton didn't hear."

We sprinted upstairs as Doc smashed a plate of spaghetti over Mom. The angel-hair pasta sat like a hat on her head, and the tomato sauce streaked through her blonde hair. Doc disappeared down the hall, and I got a tea towel and cleaned up Mom. While the grandfather clocked dinged eleven times, Doc reappeared silently in the hallway. By his side, he held a black pistol.

This can't be happening.

Nobody said a word. I dropped the rag and clasped Mom and Lexie's hands. "Follow me!" We darted down the stairs and out the slider door.

Doc's footsteps sounded behind us as we circled the backyard to the horse pen near the barn's outdoor lights. Somewhere along our escape route, Mom cut her foot on broken glass.

"Watch your step, Lex. Mom's bleeding." With the full moon cloaked in a see-through cotton web, I yanked off my nightshirt and wrapped Mom's bloody foot, not even feeling the crisp November breeze. *Great! Now, I'm shirtless in front of Lexie.*

By the time we reached the driveway, Doc's truck was popping gravel down the lane. Soon after, Lexie and I helped Mom limp back home and into bed. When we returned to my room, I found another shirt and faced Lexie.

"Well, I'll say this." Lexie sat down on the bed and stared me straight in the eye. "This's like no other sleepover I've ever been to."

Somehow, I laughed. "Will your dad let you come back?"

"Are you kidding me? I'm not telling him." She shook her head. "Two months ago, he rescued me from my mom's house in the middle of the night."

"This's so embarrassing!"

"Don't be embarrassed." Lexie wrapped the bedspread around her shoulders and curled her toes under it.

"I still can't believe Doc had a gun," I said, massaging my arm. "Where'd he get it?"

"You'll never believe it."

"Try me."

"We keep a loaded gun under the towels in the linen closet."

"You're right. I don't believe it." Lexie covered her face with a pillow, muffling her laughter. "Pat yourself on the back for survival. Just don't bruise yourself."

We fell back into bed, and I buried my filthy feet under the warm blanket.

Once we woke up, Lexie's dad arrived to pick her up. Minutes after his light green sedan pulled out of our driveway, Mom hugged me. "What did I ever do to get such a fabulous daughter?"

"I'm just thankful I could help." I pointed to Mom's bruised cheek. "Doc's awful to do that." I squeezed Mom tight. "Does your foot need stitches?"

"Maybe, but I'm not getting them."

I licked my lips. "I need to tell Lexie I'm sorry she had to see Doc in action."

"Don't go blabbing about what happens here." Mom thrust her face in front of me. "You better be careful. She might not want to be your friend anymore."

The following Saturday, I spent the night with Lexie. "Mom doesn't want me to spill the beans about Doc and the gun."

"He's not the sharpest tool in the shed even if he is a vet, but mum's the word from me." Lexie and I were painting our finger-nails. "Who would believe it, anyway?"

"I'll spend the night at your house from now on." I painted a second coat on my nails and held up my fingers. "I love this lime green polish. I usually wear pink. I didn't know this color even existed."

Once I returned home, Mom slapped my hand. "You look like a whore with that green crap on your nails. Doc'll put a stop to that!"

Before Doc took off his belt, his puffy eyes bulged crisp blue. He set his lit cigarette in the large aqua clay ashtray and struck the belt all over my body. Boiling pain seared through me, but I didn't flinch, speak, or cry. After he finished, he picked the butt back up and took another drag. The stench of the smoke lodged up my nose.

The next day, just in time for school, my welts became beet-blue bruises. Experience from Doc's continual beatings taught me when changing for PE to wear pants and put on my PE uniform with my back to the wall; pulling it down to hide any evidence. At least Lexie wasn't in my class. *I don't want her to know I got whipped for wearing her green polish.*

Later that night, Katie and I were down by the barn door. "Let's ride horses,' she suggested.

"I'm too sore." I waved my hand over the back of my legs as Doc drove away. Katie flipped him off.

His truck's brake lights flashed red before he backed up, spin-ning his tires down the driveway. Then, leaving the door open and the engine running, Doc stormed toward us with a burning cigarette in his mouth and a pointed stocking cap on his head. He grabbed Katie by her thick mane, cracking her neck while swinging her to the dirt. I screamed. He got back into the truck and sped away.

For some reason, when Saturday rolled around, Mom and Katie took off for Grandmother Mema's house without Doc, Brax-ton, or me. I got up, and they were gone. I was supposed to spend the night at Lexie's, so I called her. "Can't sleep over. It sucks, but I've got to help Doc take care of Braxton." *At least she won't see my black-and-blue body.*

Doc heard me and charged out of his bedroom. The back of his hair stuck straight up. "Hey, Summer. How about you whipping up some eggs and bacon for breakfast?"

I nodded and placed the bacon in the skillet, taking a whiff of the sizzling fried aroma drifting throughout the kitchen. I made Doc two sunny-side-up eggs and served him at the glass-top table. He sopped up his toast dripping with butter in the runny egg yolks. Then, using the remaining egg juice for an ashtray, he stubbed out his cigarette butts, drowning them in the egg-and-ash mixture. Washing the dishes, I lost my appetite. Doc's belly shook within five minutes as he snored on the velvet burnt-orange recliner.

I'll never marry a man who snores.

While Doc napped away his egg breakfast, I worked on math, and Braxton roamed the property.

"Ow! Help! Summer!"

Shrieks from the barn rang through the open slider. I turned over the kitchen chair, scrambling out the door.

Playing in the tack room, Braxton hung himself by the lip on the meat hooks that displayed the saddles, shredding the inside of his mouth. Blood was everywhere. I took off my sweatshirt and made him hold it over his face while I led him to the Ford. "Wait in the truck. I'll wake up Doc."

In world record time, Doc was backing out of the driveway. I swung the door shut as he floored the vehicle to the emergency room. The truck's heater blew Braxton's red-and-white stocking cap string ties.

After Braxton's thirteen stitches for the inside of his jagged cut cheek, Doc stopped by the Dairy Freeze—a burger-and-ice cream joint without inside seating but with a customer counter for ordering. He left us in the truck and resurfaced from my favorite restaurant with only one chocolate soft-serve ice cream cone for Braxton. *Why didn't he buy one for me?*

Braxton took a bite and then offered it to me. I took a couple of licks of the light, creamy texture until a red swirl revealed Braxton's blood mixed in the brown ice cream. I gave it back to him, slunk down in my seat, and pulled my t-shirt over my head. *Mom's right. I'm selfish.* Then, in panicky shame from my desperation for food, I stretched my fingers around my neck and choked myself.

Dark spots appeared, and the air deflated out of my chest. A gentle voice said to my heart. "Stop! I love you." I removed my fingers from my throat. "Don't hurt yourself again."

Doc didn't notice. He was too busy backing into the Highway 56 tavern's parking lot stall. "I'll be right back."

"This's the bar where Mom followed Doc, Braxtie," I said. My brother tilted his neck in confusion, shivering in the December chill. "After she hid his keys."

"What do you think Mr. Swagger would do if he knew Doc rode his prized Arabian two miles down the highway?" I glanced out of the truck at the windowless building. "That's probably why Doc's horse training business ended. Good thing he's still a vet."

"If I had Doc's keys now, I'd start the truck." I rubbed Braxton's hands in mine. "But I don't, so we're going inside."

The stale stench made me sneeze as I cracked open the bar door. "Your kids are so cute, Dockey." An overweight, heavily painted woman with kind eyes motioned us to the bar and handed us colas. "But what happened to your boy's cheek? Looks like he's been in a bar fight."

Doc strutted toward us. "Let's go!"

I waved at the pretty lady, and Braxton and I trailed Doc to the truck. He weaved over the wrong side of the road all the way home.

Mom and Katie got home twenty-four hours later, but Braxton had already gone to bed. Katie didn't have to flaunt her ring with the twelve diamonds circling the large emerald, green stone Grandfather had given her; it was a blinking lighthouse. She also wore a diamond watch. Going straight to her room, she never looked at me.

"It's just the way it is." Mom lit a cigarette. "Zoe's mom told me your dad's the one who should buy your jewelry anyway."

Once again, winter turned to spring. The fragrance of soft lilacs and twittering bluebirds signaled the winds of change. After my first track practice, Lexie's dad brought me home. Although more for socializing than running, Lexie also ran track. Sore from the workout, I thanked her dad and hobbled into the house.

"Mom said Doc's gone. For good." Katie put on her sandals. "Mom's not here either."

"What?" I put my hand over my mouth. "What happened? What about his clinic? How'll he take care of the animals?"

"He rented a place in the next town over." She picked up her purse from the telephone desk. "I'm leaving."

"Wait! W-what about Braxton?" My words became breathless. "W-where's he?"

"Living with Doc."

I dropped onto the blue couch. "H-how do you know?"

"Mom told me before she left with Peter."

"Peter? Who's Peter?"

"Her new boyfriend."

"What? Was Mom two-timing Doc?"

"How would I know?" Katie opened the sliding glass door. "Who cares anyway."

Thank you, Grammy's God! Doc and his belt are gone. But Braxton's gone, too. And I never got to say goodbye to my little brother. I collapsed on the recliner.

Mom finally came home the following day, so I asked about Braxton. "W-when will I see him again?"

"It's not your business."

I dreamt I forgot to feed Braxton that night, and he died. I woke up to a blood-curdling scream—mine.

Careening her Eldorado into my junior high school parking lot at the end of April, Mom attended her first parent-teacher conference. Perfectly made up, she looked like a *Vogue* model in her gold-roped trimmed jeans and matching jacket. I'd never loved her so much.

She and I strode through campus as her platform heels clunked the sidewalk to Mr. Joseph's room. My chest puffed out with pride when I introduced Mom. "This's the math teacher whose house I call for help."

"What a fabulous man you must be, then." Mom locked her sea-blue eyes on his, not breaking her gaze as he motioned her to sit. "I was never good at math. That's why I became a runway model."

Despite his deadpan personality, Mr. Joseph grinned. "Take a load off your legs and sit by your savvy mother, Summer." He pointed to an empty chair. "Your daughter's wired tight, but the kicker is that I've never met a student who works harder. I wish I had a classroom full of Summers."

Mom spun toward me and flashed her cover girl smile. "My Summer's so smart. Always tries so hard. Gets all that determination from me. I wish her older sister were not so drab and more like us."

I wasn't about to tell Mr. Joseph that Mom flat-out lied. Katie's not drab, and I'm like Dad. When we got ready to leave, Mom gushed, "Well—"

"That *is* a deep subject." Mr. Joseph kept his tone even.

Mom laughed. "I could talk to you all day."

I looked over at her. "But you told me we were in a hurry."

She glared at me. Mr. Joseph's eyes lit up. I dropped my chin to my chest and itched my neck.

"Don't worry, Summer," my teacher said after Mom bolted the room. "One day, you'll have a Road to Damascus experience, and your mom will make more sense."

I didn't know what he meant, but I thanked him and raced after Mom. "Don't ever expect me to go to another school event again," she said with gritted teeth as she shut the car door. "Because if I do, I'll tell your precious teacher he's so ugly. I bet his wife won't even screw him."

Mr. Joseph's not ugly.

The following day, Lexie's dad brought me home from track. Since it rained during practice, I was soaking wet. Mom's car wasn't in the driveway, so she must be with her new love—Peter.

Opening the slider, I wandered downstairs to Katie's room. "Do you have a ponytail holder?" I pulled my soggy hair off my neck. "It's dripping."

"Get out of my room. Now!" Sprawled out on her yellow bedspread, she threw a pillow at me.

"Why're you so crabby, Katie? What did I do?"

"Just get out!" She tucked her knees under her colorless chin and started to whimper, barricading herself under her other pillow. "Wait till you're my age. Things are hard. Then you'll know how easy life is for you, little Summer. And all the stupid things you worry about."

"Why do you always say, 'Wait until you're my age?'" I stomped out of her room and into mine. *I'm only two years younger.* I wish I could call Lexie and ask her what's wrong with Katie. She always knows everything, but she's not home yet.

I tore out a piece of paper from my spiral notebook, found a pen, and clicked it two times. and began to write: "Dear Diary, What's wrong with my sister?" I paused. My eyes darted back and forth. I put down the writing utensil and tiptoed back into Katie's room. She'd crumpled herself into the fetal position.

"Are you okay?" I shuffled over to her and placed my hand on her spasming back. She hid under her covers. "You can tell me."

"It's nothing." She pivoted to a sitting position. "I'm just happy Doc's gone, that's all." She squeezed her eyes shut and then blinked them again, closing them halfway. "Even if there were something, I'd never tell."

"You know I won't tell, either." I folded my hands like a prayer.

"There's nothing to tell." She stared at the ceiling. "And I don't want to get into trouble. Or get anyone else in trouble." She pulled her thick hair off her neck. Tears trickled down her face. "It'd kill Mom. She'd kill Doc. It's my fault anyway. And it's over now, for good."

We were silent. I leaned on her nightstand with one finger over my lip and two under my chin, scrunching my forehead. *Doc? Constantly alone with Katie. Calling her Hayseed. Paying so much attention to her and so little to me. Calling me Sweet Pea that time getting the hay bales.*

"Doc!" I snapped my fingers. "You charged him in the barn when he tickled me." Katie cried harder. "He used to come to your room. In the middle of the night. He did."

Knees to her chest, Katie rocked back and forth and started wheezing.

I gasped. "Oh, Katie. You've been protecting me. I know you have."

She was quiet for a long time. "Doc said life would change if I told. I'd go to juvie."

"What?"

"You know, juvenile jail." She stared at me. "He started when I was seven, but he'll never touch me again." In a trance-like monotone, Katie sounded like him. "Your Mom won't believe you. She'll believe me. She always does."

I put my dukes up. "If Doc ever shows his face again, I'll rip his balls out—one at a time. If he even has any."

Katie unraveled her arms from her knees and sat up straight. She had her color back. "If he ever sets foot into my room again, I'll tell him to get the hell out."

"Oh, Katie!" I threw myself on her. We hugged.

"I'll get you that ponytail holder." The strength returned to her voice.

Back in my room, I paced by my twin beds. *Should I tell Mom about Doc? No! She'll make it Katie's fault. And after how she tortured her for smoking, I'll never tell Mom anything again.*

I shredded my diary entry and tossed the tiny pieces into the trashcan by my window. A taffy-stretched partial rainbow hung across the sky.

CHAPTER 12

THE DIARY

March 1976 – September 1977
Edgerton, Kansas

March 1, 1976

Dear Diary,

Hello! I decided to make you my diary. I'm reading Go Ask Alice *about a girl who does drugs and writes it all down. I'll NEVER do drugs. I'm 13. My sister Katie's 15. My brother Braxton's 6. I'm in the 8th grade and love track. Last year I went to Jr. Olympics and won 3 gold medals. I run till I dry-heave.*

My parents are divorced. When I'm with Dad, Mom's mad. When I'm with Mom, Dad's disappointed.

Mom and I don't get along. She won't come to my track meets. Dad comes to all my track meets. He says Mom's Greek to him (??). Mom says Dad's a tight-ass. I've never heard them say anything nice to each other. Lexie's my bestie. Jay told me he loved my jeans. They were Mom's. (We're the same size.) Jay's SO cute & makes me laugh. I kissed his cheek. He touched the spot and smiled.

March 19, 1976

Dear Diary,

Mom just left with Peter. They've been dating on and off for a year.

Peter's a dentist and last month gave me a crown and fourteen fillings. Mom told him to leave on the temporary crown, but he didn't listen or charge her.

I had to go to the dentist before I got braces (my teeth are crooked bad). A week ago, I got spacers (what a pain), and now my mouth is full of silver (bigger pain), but I want straight teeth.

I was afraid at first cuz if I got stranded on an island, how would I get them off? (feel silly now). Dad paid for mine. He didn't want to pay for Katie's (Mom took him to court.) He adopted her, but she never sees him.

March 21, 1976

Dear Diary,

It's 10:00 p.m. I'm in bed after watching Charlie's Angels. Katie wants me to call Mom at Peter's to know if she'll get caught sneaking out with her boyfriend. I said NO. Mom bought me a PERFECT graduation dress and platform shoes. She says I'm the smart one and Katie's the pretty one.

I just dragged myself to the phone & called Peter. Mom wasn't there. Is she with a new guy? She's been talking about Doc. Not DOC, the DOG again. Peter bought me running shoes and a silver "S" necklace. He's handsome for an old guy. And makes Mom nicer. I pray they get married.

March 24, 1976

Dear Diary,

I've had enough! I can't take it anymore! Mom's NOT going to make me cry. I should have kept my BIG FAT MOUTH shut, but she said something BAD about DAD. That PO'ed me (ALWAYS does). She sent me to my room for the night. NO Dinner. Grounded! At least Mom's back with Peter.

April 21, 1976

Dear Diary,

Peter took Katie, Mom, and me to see Elvis Presley. His music's still playing in my head. We ate at Houlihan's on the Plaza. Mom looked all glitzy for Elvis at Kemper Arena. Peter bought me a glossy program. I knew every song, word for word. The KING looked like he does on TV—a blue shirt, white jumpsuit, and big belt. All the women screamed for his scarves. I wanted to scream for one too. Then Elvis left the stage, and the speaker said, "Elvis has left the building. Thank you, and goodnight." I dreamed Elvis's plane landed on Highway 56, and Elvis rang my doorbell for help.

April 27, 1976

Dear Diary,

Katie stayed out all night with her boyfriend. Mom never came home. It's hard to be alone. At least I'm not at Zoe's. She's fake nice to my face but stabs me in the back. Mom says Zoe's jealous but to be her friend (only cuz she makes me stay there when she travels with Peter). I told Zoe about Mom not coming home at night. Zoe turned her head, so I pleaded for her to be my friend. Why did I do that? I started bawling like a baby & now feel like a space cadet. Mom says I'm too sensitive and a blabbermouth.

April 28, 1976

Dear Diary,

Mom wasn't home this morning. I had no money for my chorus field trip. We ate at the new McDonald's in the town over. I can't sing my way out of a paper bag, but I joined the group cuz I'd rather be at school than home. Zoe has a pretty voice. She asked me if I wanted some of her fries. I pretended not to be hungry.

May 1, 1976

Dear Diary,

Today was the WORST day of my life. Mom said my headaches might be a BRAIN TUMOR. Man, then, like a big boob, I started bawling and FREAKED OUT—I don't WANT to die. My headaches are terrible. WOW. They started when Mom & Dad were FIGHTING OVER ME. But this time, they're even WORSE! Gotta go. Mom's pounding on the floor.

May 14, 1976

Dear Diary,

Guess What? I MADE freshman CHEERLEADER for next year when I'm in high school. BUT I found out Jay smoked pot. I HATE drugs. I NEVER want to see him again. I whacked him HARD, and ran away.

May 23, 1976

Dear Diary,

Mom came to 8th-grade graduation even though she said she wouldn't if Dad did. I didn't trip or anything. Braxtie was there but didn't talk. I was SO happy to see him. He lives with Doc. We made a graduation cake.

I opened the box and poured it into the bowl with all the eggs and stuff

& used the mixer but tried to scoop up some batter with my fingers. They got stuck in the beaters, & it HURT so much that I yelled. Braxtie pulled out the plug. We looked at each other and cracked up. Mom got irritated.

May 24, 1976

Dear Diary,

I don't know what's wrong with me. When I see Jay talking to Zoe, I want to sock him in the stomach. Mom took me to her palm reader who told me I'd die young. I can't stop crying.

July 6, 1976

Dear Diary,

Last night, I spent the night with Lexie. There was a thunderstorm, and Lexie laughed when lightning lit up my braces headgear.

July 18, 1976. I'm 14

Dear Diary,

I've been at Dad's for ten WONDERFUL days. When I got home, Mom wouldn't talk to me. It's my birthday and special day no matter what— no one can take that away.

July 19, 1976

Dear Diary,

When I was at Dad's, I tried for days to get a hold of Mom, so I spaced out & called Peter. He said they'd broken up. I was so out to lunch that I sobbed. Not out loud, but I couldn't talk. And I can always talk. She wasn't home when Dad dropped me off. Hours later, she appeared from who knows where and blew a gasket. I apologized over and over and rubbed her back & legs & feet. "Rub harder," she screamed when I got tired. & rammed me with her leg. Then she kicked me in the head & said I made her look bad & screamed, "Get out! I can't stand your face." I left. Then she screamed for me to return. I didn't dare say she'd told me to leave. She made me dump my birthday presents on her floor.

July 20, 1976

Dear Diary,

Hallelujah! Peter and Mom are back together.

~

July 1976
Edgerton, Kansas

By the time my clock radio's alarm music blared, I'd already dressed and had a piece of toast. While I waited for Mom by the sliding glass door, I shifted from foot to foot.

"Windex that." She snapped her fingers as she strutted by in her off-the-shoulder shirt. "I'm almost ready."

I grabbed the cleaner, made the door sparkle, and dashed for the car. Twenty minutes of twirling my thumbs later, Mom was still a no-show. *Why didn't Dad take me to the track meet? Mom doesn't understand that it starts with or without me. And if I don't place first or second, I won't qualify for State. I should've run the thirty miles there myself.*

"I'll ride shotgun," Katie said out of nowhere. "Oh, you're already in the backseat."

Mom shut the driver's door and checked the rearview mirror. "Change your look, or you'll stay home."

I slinked behind Mom's seat and dug my fingernails into my thighs. "We ... we might be late."

"You won't run me." She tapped her nails on the dashboard. "It's all your father's fault, anyway."

How's being late his fault?

Forty minutes later, I shouted, "There's Dad." Pacing the parking lot, he motioned to us with his hand. Mom drove up to him and rolled down her window. A blast of summer's hot air circulated throughout the car.

My usually composed father gnashed his teeth and pointed to Mom's chest. "Summer was the fastest seed in the area, but her race is over. She missed it." Dad's lips barely moved. "Do you realize what you've done? You made her miss the Junior Olympic Regionals and squelched her chance to run the 220-yard dash at State. Her best race."

The air turned thick, and tiny black dots jiggled before my eyes. A mosquito flew through the open window, stinging my arm. An instant red bump swelled into a fiery itch.

"Humph! Why you dirty rotten—" *Rrrr, Rrrr, Rrrr.* Mom's familiar words were like a skipping record.

"I don't have time for this, Georgie." Dad waved me toward him. "I'm going to ask the race director if Summer can run alone and compare times."

I buried my head in my knees, and my shoulders shook so hard the car seat rocked. *Everything's against me today, but if anyone can fix this, Dad can.* Lifting my head, I flicked tears off my chin while Katie sat statue-still in the front seat.

"Let's go, Summer." Dad's tongue stuck out between his teeth as he opened the back door. "There will be no more mind control from Nurse Ratched. Not on my watch."

Standing by Dad, I sniffed my drippy nose and clicked my track spikes together.

"I can't believe you're real," Mom said before she left, leaving tread marks.

Somehow Dad finagled a solo 220-time trial, and I demolished the invisible competition. But it wasn't an anonymous competitor. I'd stolen a girl's spot who was on time and deserved to run. *I can't think about that.* I qualified for State in the 440-yard dash and 440 relay during my next two races.

"Thanks, Dad, for saving the day." He drove me home after the race. "But how'd you convince them to let me run?"

"It was easy, Summer." He glanced my way and smiled. "I just told them you're the fastest 220 runner in the state."

"Oh, Dad!" With wet eyes, I threw myself on his shoulder. "I love you!"

Seven days later, on a cloudless, humid Saturday with *Wizard of Oz* gusts of wind, it was showtime. Mom didn't drive me to the Kansas State Junior Olympic meet. Dad did. We got up at the crack of dawn to make the two-hour trek to be there early. The night before, I couldn't sleep.

Peter drove Mom, Katie, and Miss Pooh.

Mom stroked her poodle as Peter prepared to record the 220-yard dash with his impressive new handheld video camera. Even though my competition earned a faster seed time, she didn't stand a chance. *I'm not about to lose—Mom's in the stands.* With confetti in my stomach and Peter's soundless contraption filming, I ran the race of my life and set a 25.3-second state record.

"Way to utilize that intestinal fortitude, Summer." The approval in Dad's voice gave me an adrenaline high, but it didn't last long. *If I can win my 440, then I'll relax.* When I won that race, I needed another victory. *I'll get my relay team a medal.*

Wedged between Peter and Zoe's dad, Mom's white hip-hugger jeans, halter top trimmed with lace, and bigger-than-life personality drew a lot of attention. Zoe's mom said nothing, sitting by her husband. "Zoe sure looks like a runner," Mom said as she waved Miss Pooh's front paws goodbye at me. "And so do you."

Zoe and I both have long legs, but I'm faster.

For the 440 relay, I used every ounce of my speed and then some to inch out our second-place victory. Mom removed her large, white glasses when I brought my medal to the stands. "You're so fast, honey. I always thought your running was off the wall, but you really are good."

My insides bounced along to the Bee Gee's dance song booming over the loudspeakers as Mom talked to me in her Miss Pooh voice.

"Remember, you're staying with Zoe. Peter and I are off to Hawaii." Mom applied hot pink lipstick. "I'll see you in two weeks."

"Can't I just go home with Dad? Zoe's so two-faced."

"I came to your race, Summer. Just do it my way," Mom said before she and Peter drove away in his convertible Mercedes coupe.

I followed Zoe into her dad's truck. Her shiny blonde hair hung as if she'd just washed it with conditioner. My light brown hair was a stringy mop.

During the first thirteen days at Zoe's, we played cards, picked strawberries, and watched TV. She was climbing off the walls by the last night of my stay. At midnight when her sixteen-year-old brother, Todd, strolled in the door, Zoe suggested, "Hey, you guys, let's go for a joyride. Mom and Dad are asleep, and we'll only drive down the street."

"No, Zoe," I said, "You don't have a license. Your parents would kill you, and besides, I'm tired and want to go to bed."

"Aren't you just oodles of fun, Summer?" She crossed her arms. "You're such a chicken. Come on! Todd's driving anyway. Don't ruin everyone's fun by being fake. You can't be that much of a goody-goody that you're concerned about being gone ten minutes." She disappeared into the garage, calling, "I'll be waiting in Dad's truck."

Zoe's right. I'm always afraid of getting in trouble. Maybe I should be more carefree like her. And if Todd drives, what's the problem? He has his license.

When I arrived at the truck, Todd wasn't driving. Zoe was. "Get in, Summer." Zoe revved the engine.

She'll be so disappointed if I don't go.

"You're a great brother, Todd," Zoe said after I leaped into the Ford, and he closed the door.

Music blaring, we shot out of the driveway and started down the endless road. Since Zoe lived out in the country, blackness blanketed the horizon. *What fun! I'm glad I didn't mess up everyone's good time.*

I stretched my arms between Zoe and Todd, making my fingernails clink the back window. None of us wore seat belts. Zoe drove about forty-five miles per hour and then, with a maniacal laugh, made a sharp turn to the left.

"Wheeeeeee," Zoe squealed as gravel pinged like popcorn against the bottom of the vehicle. Zoe careened the truck through the rock pile by the side of the road and then overcompensated with a sharp right turn to navigate back to the center. Unfortunately, the vehicle swerved too far, blazing through another rock pile by the side of the road.

Pop! Bam! Pop! The gravel beat mercilessly against the bottom of the truck. Zoe abruptly turned left, and the truck's steering wheel spun like a carnival ride.

We spiraled from one gravel pile to the next. The car was out of control. Then, unexpectedly, Zoe began screaming and covered her face with her hands.

What? No one's driving! I tried to stop the circling Tilt-A-Whirl-like steering wheel. We'd not even been in the car for five minutes.

"Hit the brakes!" Todd hollered.

Time moved in slow motion once the wheels stuck into the right side pile of rocks, causing us to sail through the air, rolling the truck over and over. Being suspended in the dream-like atmosphere tangled our bodies like a deck of shuffled cards.

A floating sensation engulfed me. *Is this what it's like to die?*

A terrific crunching metal sound shattered my fog of confusion as we crashed upside down on the left bank of the ditch. I struggled to break free from the arms, legs, and glass that smothered me.

Todd stuck his arm out the broken window of the crashed truck and opened the passenger's door. We tumbled outside the tiny cab. The truck's shattered windshield and flattened cab looked like a trash compactor had compressed it. With one hand, Todd turned over the wreck. The pickup's wheels bounced right-side-up, crunching the gravel road.

"Todd! How'd you just turn that truck over?"

"I don't know, Summer! I just did."

Am I hurt? Is this for real? I patted myself all over—no blood—not even a scratch.

Just then, Zoe took off running.

"I'm going to kill myself! I'll be dead anyway when Dad finds out what happened."

Todd and I raced after her and found the nearest house to call the police.

It's a head-scratcher that none of you three died or even got hurt," one of the two officers marveled, "but the truck's totaled."

I stood in stunned silence. Somehow, God spared our lives.

The following morning, fresh from her vacation with Peter, Mom picked me up from Zoe's.

"I never should've gotten in that stupid truck." I cried all the way home. "I knew better. I'm so angry with myself!"

"You made a mistake, honey. It happens." Mom looked tired and broken down. "I'm just so thankful you weren't hurt. I'd be lost without you."

Once we got home, I ran to the barn phone and called Dad, telling him about the wreck. "Zoe's trouble," he choked out. "You shouldn't be spending the night with her."

"Mom makes me, but I swear I'll never sneak out again."

"I know you won't, Summer." The crackling static made it hard to hear. It took Dad so long to speak that I thought the phone had gone dead. "That grizzly bitch's such a sinner."

"What'd you say, Dad?"

"Oh, we had grisly fried chicken for dinner." He held his breath. "I don't have the heart to discipline you, Summer. You're always so hard on yourself."

September 14, 1976

Dear Diary,

I've been flirting with Greg. Zoe likes Jay. I HATE that. Zoe told everyone I was such a spaz during the truck crash.

January 2, 1977

Dear Diary,

I think you're like God. Always there. Warm and cozy, like the electric blanket Lexie gave me for Christmas. I remember Grammy's church said God created the trees, earth, & stuff. So God must be everywhere. Is He love? Maybe He's the air. I miss Grammy. I don't get to see her much and never stay with her anymore.

January 4, 1977

Dear Diary,

Mom got drunk off her butt and is lying about Peter. She hates him. If I had to choose Mom or Peter, I'd choose Peter. (NEVER TELL MOM).

New Year's resolutions:

    1. Don't cry or cuss

    2. Don't lie or steal

    3. Don't do drugs

    4. Make honor roll every time.

I did something so awful. Mom made me go to Zoe's, and we ate lunch at the Downtowner restaurant. I had no money, so I sneaked out without paying. I won't do that again! Tonight was just not my day.

January 15, 1977

Dear Diary,

Mom and I had a HORRIBLE fight. She's dating DOC again. She sent me downstairs without dinner. I tried to talk to her, but she cussed me out. Then she wanted me to stay up and talk. Only cuz no one else was home. Who cares anymore? Me.

January 31, 1977

Dear Diary,

Mom married the (*%@—I'm trying not to cuss) Doc again. I want her to be happy, but NOT with Doc. At least Braxtie will come home.

Doc gave me twenty dollars with a puke-fake look. If he whips me again, I'll tell Dad. And if he touches Katie again, I'll get the gun. I WILL.

February 22, 1977

Dear Diary,

Mom convinced me to go to the dance with Greg. He's good-looking & smart & a sophomore basketball star. Greg's dad's my math teacher and track coach & said I'm scatterbrained. That hurt my feelings.

Then he said my mouth goes faster than my brain. That made me laugh. Mom says Greg's better for me than Jay. But I still flirt with Jay. Am I OK?

April 6, 1977

Dear Diary,

I'm in bed listening to the Doobie Brothers' "Jesus Is Just Alright with Me." Track's going great, but everybody on the team wants me to lose. I hate all the girls rooting against me. I got 1st in the 220, 440, and 100. My 220 time was the fastest in the entire state. I even won the long jump. (I'd never jumped before). All my friends started drinking. Should I drink? For sure, not during track. Varsity cheerleading tryouts are Friday, and I'm scared—This is it: VARSITY. I haven't had headaches for a while. HURRAH.

May 2, 1977

Dear Diary,

I made VARSITY cheerleader! Only two girls in our sophomore class did. Katie was one of the two senior girls. Katie's the head cheerleader. The student body votes before the summer break. Mom and I had a long talk. She said she was sorry for not giving me money & to go get some from her purse. I found POT & pot papers and blue pills. I want to pull all my hair out. I'll NEVER do drugs. After school's out, I'm going to Dad's for two weeks! YAY!

~

July 1977
Edgerton, Kansas

Opening the ranch house slider, Mom wouldn't look me in the eye. "While you've been at your dickhead dad's, Katie and I painted the entire seventeen acres of fence." She turned her back. "Thanks to you, we had no help."

Why do I always have to paint the fence? Why am I always to blame?

Mom refused to speak to me until I cleaned the house from top to bottom, rubbed her feet, and pulled her toes. That got me off her crap list, so she let me drive to Chloe's house, even though I only had my permit.

The last time I was at Zoe's, she bragged about chugging beer and wine. "Ready to party, girls?"

"You're bombed, Zoe."

"And Chloe is, too," Zoe said. "Her parents are never home, so we started early."

Cute with curly brown hair and gray-green eyes, Chloe was Zoe's sidekick. Lexie arrived right behind me. Even though Zoe talked behind my back, she still tried to be my friend, so after she invited Lexie and me to Chloe's, we said yes. I never knew when Mom would drop me off at Zoe's house. *It's safer to be her friend than her enemy.*

"Todd bought us beer and strawberry wine. Let's guzzle!" Zoe said, pouring Lexie and me each a glass. *As long as I don't do drugs, drinking's okay.*

We tried to gulp the alcohol. "This tastes like crap," Lexie said as we spat our mouthfuls into the sink. "Do you have any saltines?"

Chloe got some crackers, and once we chewed a crunchy mouthful, the alcohol wasn't so bitter. I finally swished down a glassful of each. The room started spinning.

"It's time to cruise Main. Summer's driving," Zoe yelled before waltzing out the front door. "I can't. I just totaled my mom's Lincoln Continental."

"But I only have my permit." I scratched my thumbnail with

my bottom teeth. Zoe opened my passenger door and jumped in the car.

"Let's go."

Lexie and I looked at each other. "Let's just stay at Chloe's," I begged.

"Don't take your marbles and go home, Summer. You'll make everyone suffer."

What do I do? I strummed my fingers over my lips. *How can I say no?*

Against my better judgment, I agreed, and we piled into Mom's car, Zoe sitting up front and Lexie and Chloe in the back. Since my head felt heavy, I flipped it side to side, forcing myself to focus on the wavy Main Street yellow line that was usually straight. *Adults really shouldn't drink and drive.*

"Let's go off-road here." Zoe seized the wheel, jerking it toward the large vacant lot.

With the windows down and the warm summer air whirling through the car, Zoe turned up "Bohemian Rhapsody." We sang at the top of our lungs.

Zoe beat her fists on the dashboard. "Faster, Summer!"

"Okay! I'll floor it." The tires spun under the car. *Was that thunder? There's no storm.* A commanding voice shouted in my ear through the fuzz of my buzzed brain. "Stop! Stop the car!" *Who said that? Not the girls. Did I imagine it?* I slammed on the brakes.

Coughing from the gravel's smoky smell, I parked the car but didn't turn off the lights. We all burst out of the vehicle. The girls were so drunk they just kept singing Queen's song.

I didn't sing. I crept by the front of the car, inhaling the dust. The hazy headlights spotlighted the hazard. Inches in front of the hood, a basement-deep, Olympic-swimming pool-sized sinkhole awaited us if I had not stopped. My friends and I would have nose-dived into the twelve-foot pit with no barriers or warning and nothing to alert the danger ahead.

Numb, I tried to explain, but the girls didn't understand. I didn't understand. *Who told me to stop the car? God? If my friends had died or gotten hurt, how would I have lived with myself?*

September 16, 1977

 Dear Diary, I woke up in a cold, dark sweat. Last night I said horrible things before Mom passed out from vodka and drugs. She broke her fall with her face. The last thing I remember was her bloody head in my lap. I have no memory after that. Somehow I ended up in bed, but now I'm afraid to go upstairs. Maybe Mom's really hurt. Or dead. I don't know if I can tell my new boyfriend, Greg. He has such a perfect family. How could he understand? I've only let him see Mom's nice side. And Lexie's visiting her mom for the rest of the week. I would tell Jay, but he's dating Zoe.

CHAPTER 13

GREG

September 1977 – March 1978
Sophomore Year
Edgerton, Kansas

B y the time the ranch house's maroon autumn foliage flitted across the back patio, Mom's bruises from her face-first fall had turned from deep purple to pale yellow. She captured me by the shoulders when I opened the patio slider from school. "Let me have that blouse." She grabbed the bottom edge. "I need it to make a load. I never seem to get the laundry done around here."

My body whiplashed as she ripped the shirt off my back.

"I'm glad you're feeling better, Mom." *I don't even care if she's making me strip.* "You've got such a love-hate relationship with laundry. How many items do you have in the washer this time? Four?"

"And this makes five."

"Thanks for always keeping my clothes clean."

"You must look your best to keep that gorgeous basketball player's eyes only on you." I peeled off my socks and added them to her pile. "It's easy to get a guy but hard to keep him, Summer, so for the love of money, keep your nails painted if you want what's-his-name to stay interested."

"Greg. His name's Greg."

Although I still smiled at Jay in the hall, Greg and I became an instant item at the start of my sophomore year. A good-looking junior, hotshot basketball player, Greg was our school's honor student and golden boy. With long eyelashes and thick brown hair, his matching chocolate eyes and bushy eyebrows made girls take notice when he passed by.

Witty and clever, Greg's dad was my math teacher and track coach. Sweet and encouraging, Greg's mom made even washing the dishes fun. "Let's clean them by hand," she said with a giggle. "Then we can talk."

Greg was brilliant like my dad, and I wanted him and his family to be my destiny.

Since Greg seemed to have the perfect house, I only shared snippets of Mom and Doc's drama. I didn't want to scare him. Even so, he didn't freak out when I mentioned Mom's accident.

"I still don't remember all of it, Greg, but over a week ago, she had a bloody fall on the kitchen tile. I gotta get out of the ranch house. Mom's a manic mess, and Doc's a douchebag. And I'm stressed to the max."

"Other than that, how was the play, Mrs. Lincoln?" Greg and I laughed. Thankful I'd just finished a report on the sixteenth president, I finally got one of Greg's jokes. From the moment we started dating, it was a lot of pressure to pretend I understood his humor. "Just tell Georgie you crossed the Rubicon and won't deal with her trauma anymore."

"Exactly!" *I'm unsure what a Rubicon is, but I'm at the end of my rope.* "That's why I'm moving to Dad's."

Greg stroked his pointer finger over his chin. "You should live with my aunt and uncle instead." His brown eyes shined with confidence. "Remember what Shakespeare said: 'The quality of mercy is not strained,' so I'm offering you their house. Small-town Kansas takes care of its own."

I can't quote Shakespeare, but in our town's population of 2,000, living with Greg's relatives wouldn't be abnormal. Greg means his offer, and I'm thankful—but I've got a Dad.

Once I returned from school, I headed straight to the barn phone. "So, we're set." Dad's voice was unnaturally jubilant. "I'll enroll you tomorrow, and then you'll start school on the first of October."

"Thanks, Dad." I strummed my fingers on my cheeks. *I hope I can still be a cheerleader and on the track team.* "I'll have to have Lexie and Greg over all the time, even though it's an hour away."

"That'll be fine."

After I hung up, I rushed to the house, dropping my books on the telephone desk. "Hey, Braxtie." My brother sat at the kitchen table with Bubbles on his lap. I opened the fridge for a snack. "Look what I found." I waved the black olives under his nose before putting one on each of his fingers.

Mom appeared while I was finishing the can and swiped it out of my hand. "These are an expensive delicacy."

Once I got too hungry, some foods made me sick, but not the oily olives mushing together in my mouth; they coated my stomach with comfort.

Mom said, "I can't believe you."

I swallowed.

"Now that you've eaten me out of house and home, clean the fridge and toss out all the spoiled stuff." Mom swung open the door. The rotten things reeked. For some reason, she got angry when I ate the food, but then it went bad, so I had to throw it all away. "And pour out this sour milk."

I turned the carton upside down in the sink. The lumpy curdles disappeared down the drain.

"Even though I'm barely black and blue, I'm still achy and sore. I've got to get back to bed." Mom wobbled down the hall. "Come with me, Braxton." One by one, he popped the remaining olives into his mouth, lowered his eyes, and trailed behind her carrying Bubbles.

Today's not the day to tell Mom I'm leaving. At least at Dad's, I won't get in trouble for eating.

Five minutes later, Katie wandered upstairs. "Seems like you're never home." I rubbed my hands over my knees. "Mom's healing from her faceplant. She no longer looks like the walking dead. But man, I was a basketcase."

Jerking on her boots by the slider, Katie opened it. "Mom's always doing stupid stuff. Don't let it bother you."

"I'm trying ... "

My sister didn't respond. She'd already shut the door.

"Not to," I said into the air.

When I got home from school the next day, Braxton was nowhere in sight, and Mom was in bed. *After my run, I'll tell her I'm moving.* I laced my tennis shoes and sprinted down the long, gravel driveway. Out of nowhere, Braxton pedaled up beside me.

"Where are you going?" He stopped his bicycle. "Are you coming back?" Not much of an athlete, Braxton's lack of wind slumped him over the handlebars. I stopped and faced him.

"Braxtie, I'm just going for a jog. I didn't see you at the house."

"I've been down at the barn." He got off his bike and picked up a leaf that had started its transformation into harvest colors. "Then you came home. I ... I thought you were gone for good." Terror clouded his blue eyes.

I redid my ponytail that was slipping out of the holder. *How can I abandon Braxton?* A blast of warm air blew through my hair, carrying away my decision to leave the ranch house. *My brother needs me.* "I'm just getting a quick workout and then making dinner. I'm not going anywhere." I touched my eyes. "Stale bread and eggs make marvelous French toast, and you don't even need milk. How about that?"

Braxton nodded.

I lightly scratched his back. He stopped frowning. "I'm going to get you a professional sketchbook. You'll need one if you're going to be that famous architect." I feathered my hand through his cowlick. A slight glimmer of light pulsated through his face. "I can only imagine all the grand structures you'll create."

Braxton's cloudy eyes met mine as an orange, black-bordered butterfly appeared. "Look." I pointed over his head. "It's like a stained-glass church window or something, but the colors look fake. They're too bright."

"It's a Monarch butterfly."

"How'd you know?" I asked.

"We learned about them in school." He stretched his arm near the hovering butterfly. "I love them. They always find me. And follow me."

"I'd follow you, too." I tapped his nose. "You must be starving. Dad's getting me a car, so we'll go to the Dairy Freeze, but until then, French toast it is."

Braxton climbed onto his bike and rode toward the house. The cantaloupe-colored butterfly fluttered beside him.

I raced down the driveway, across the railroad tracks, and along the creek to my favorite countryside meadow. The forest dusk shimmered with a canopy of colored scenery, wafting a heavenly rosemary aroma. I bent down and snapped off an evergreen twig.

As I wiped the sticky substance onto my polyester athletic shorts, a white-tailed deer emerged before my eyes. My heart quickened. With a deliberate stare, he turned toward me before disappearing into the golden hues of the horizon. I picked up my pace and pushed my cardio to the brink. My breath skipped for air. *I don't know how I'll survive living with Mom, but I know I'll never leave my brother.*

Later that night, I called Dad. "I want to live with you, but I don't want to hurt Mom." I twisted the phone cord. "And I don't want to hurt you, either, but I just can't leave Braxton. Who'll help him with his homework? I can't do it, Dad. Sorry."

"Well, I guess I understand."

Am I making the right choice?

After saying our goodbyes, Dad hung up the phone. I rubbed my eyes. My mind tricked me into believing I was responsible for making my parents happy. As their only offspring, the older I got, the more their animosity for each other weighed on me. Greg's words replayed in my mind: "Your mom and dad pull you back and forth like you're the turkey wishbone."

I called Greg to tell him the good news. "Thanks for offering your aunt and uncle's house. I'm going to stick it out here. It has to get better."

Once I got home from school the following day, Mom started humming Elvis's "Always on My Mind" while making dinner. "My bruises are healed," she said. I clapped. The King brought out the best in my mother, making her happy as he sang to her. I did my math at the kitchen table as Braxton sketched a building beside me. Katie was MIA.

After Doc's return, if my sister wasn't spending the night with a girlfriend, she was with her boyfriend. Doc hadn't beaten either of us. Still, I watched him like a hawk, which wasn't much because he was seldom around, and if he was, he stayed upstairs.

At least Braxton's back.

As usual, Doc was pouring Mom straight vodka. We ate like one happy family until he abruptly left the table, vanishing along with the last of the warm weather. Chasing him to the slider door, Mom cupped her hands to his ear. I couldn't make out what she said, but I could've recited it by heart.

After she released him, she returned through the slider, flying past Braxton as he toted Bubbles to the fireplace. Mom stormed over to me, washing dishes. "You don't even like animals."

I faced my brother. "Braxtie, take Bubbles downstairs. I'll be there soon."

Not another fight this week. I just want to do homework. Tenth grade's so much more demanding.

"Don't pretend you care about that mongrel monster."

"Why do you say that, Mom?" My teeth clenched as I rinsed our plates. We finally got city water instead of having to haul it. "I love Bubbles."

"Animals have never liked you."

"That's not true." *She's picking on me because Doc left. I won't take the bait.*

"Don't you dare call me a liar, Summer Michelle." She forced her face near mine. "I'm your mother. Do you hear me? I gave birth to you. I own you. You'd be nothing without me." I closed my eyes, knowing her next words. I silently mouthed them with her. *"No one will ever love you. Even your dad doesn't."*

Before I could stop myself, I slammed the pan I was drying on the countertop. "Please stop drinking, so you'll be nice like normal moms."

Mom sprang from behind with panther-like agility and laced her cold fingers around my neck. I whipped my chin down and wrestled out from under her.

Did my mother just try to choke me?

"I'm done with you," Mom muttered, teetering before me. "You're crazy, just like your father."

I wheeled behind the kitchen island for a buffer. "Wait until everyone hears you choked me—especially Doc."

She believes what she's saying. But if Doc touches me, I'll tell Dad. I crumbled to my knees and beat my head with my fists. "That's not true. You just choked me. You're trying to make me go insane!"

A rustling noise made me crane my neck toward the fireplace. Braxton cowered in the corner with Bubbles's body soaking up his tears. I jumped up from the floor and hurried over to him, bending down face to face with my shaking brother. "Braxtie, you take Bubbles, go downstairs, and finish your beautiful building."

He never left. I can't believe he saw all that!

After Braxton shut the basement door, I sounded calmer than I felt. "I know it's difficult when Doc leaves. Just go to bed." I moved over to the kitchen table. "Or come sit with me." I patted the chair. "And play cards."

I can't believe I'm trying to comfort Mom. I should be running away instead.

Once Mom popped a couple of pills, chasing them down with vodka, she clicked "Suspicious Minds" on the turntable before tripping on the carpet and dropping into a kitchen chair. Lighting a cigarette, she blew out a thick fog of smoke.

I sneezed as a wet sensation licked my legs. *Dog kisses!* "Bubbles? How did you get the door open?" I scooped up his warm little body and draped him over my lap like a blanket, comforted by his dog smell. I turned my head. Braxton's shadow illuminated the stairwell.

I love you, little brother.

Mom's voice rounded my head back to her. "Don't plan on me forgiving you."

While Elvis's song looped on the record player, Mom and I sat in front of our large picture window. Twenty minutes later, the drugs kicked in like the crack of a whip, catapulting me to her good side.

She snatched the deck of playing cards used for a table centerpiece. *My homework won't get finished, and I'll be up late, but Mom'll be my best friend.*

My mother shuffled the deck, making a flawless bridge, evenly feathering the cards into each other, and shooshed them into a rectangular stack of cards. I yawned with my mouth closed. "Here. Shuffle and deal gin. Give me the extra card." Mom dotted her pointer finger over the glass-top table, gathering dinner crumbs.

"Why did I ever marry Doc again? I should have known he was a problem. What kind of man plays Hearts by passing the queen of spades and then leading with that suit?"

"I know you love him." I mimicked her perfect shuffle with Las Vegas authenticity and dealt the cards. "But I agree, it's a bummer when someone enjoys watching you squirm because you had to eat the queen of spades he just passed you."

"You're sharp, Summer." She organized her suits into a distinct fan, holding them with elegant fingers. "I mean it. You know exactly what I need. I'm so, so proud of you. You're smart. And strong."

"Thanks, Mom. That means the world."

"You're my world." She slurred and folded her cards with a clack. Her watery, bloodshot eyes elongated as she emphasized, "I adore you." Intoxicated with Mom's favor, my insecurity faded.

Just when I thought I couldn't take anymore, Mom gave me enough attention to keep me trying to please her. If I was not one hundred percent for Mom, she was one hundred percent against me. But even if I gave up everything, she still couldn't be consistently nice. *I should've moved to Dad's, but I'll never leave the ranch house. It's not only Braxton. It's Mom. Like it or not, she's my mother. And I don't know how not to need her.*

"I love you, Mom." I meant it.

"You're the most fabulous daughter in the whole world." She rocked in her chair. "I hope Greg's treating you right. If not, I'll get a hitman." She opened the crinkling wrapper and stuck the spearmint gum on her tongue. "I'm serious."

"I never doubted you weren't."

The days became shorter, marking the arrival of winter. After Mom's accident, I gave up trying to hide my home life from Greg or trying to remember what happened the night she fell. Over Thanksgiving break, he came over to watch *Saturday Night Live*.

"Summer, you're not just a firecracker. You're the whole fireworks display. As Fleetwood Mac sings, 'Everything you do makes me happy.'" Sprawled out on our downstairs orange sectional, his hands were behind his head. "You're sassy. A piece of work." He pulled me to him. "And I love it."

Braxton was usually downstairs, but he stayed away when Greg arrived.

Greg's stomach grumbled. "What do you have for snacks?"

Embarrassed at my house's lack of food, I dashed upstairs and found an old box of Cheez-It crackers and one lone Coca-Cola can hiding in Mom's closet. She'd be in a rage that I'd swiped them from her secret stash. *I can't think about it. Why does she hide food from me, anyway?*

I was saving money to hit a home run over Christmas break and make Greg my taco casserole topped with melted Velveeta cheese, but I couldn't pull off the win just yet.

With a fizzle, Greg popped open the aluminum tab. The carbonated liquid erupted over the opening. He quickly slurped down the overflow. "Why didn't you get one?"

"Oh, I'm not thirsty." I bobbed side to side. "You enjoy."

"These crackers are stale." He said as the basement filled with a cheesy snack aroma. Orange particles mixed with the cola stuck on his large, white teeth. *When I grow up, I'll have enough food to feed the whole neighborhood.*

Thanksgiving flew by. Christmas came and went, and New Year's Eve was over before I knew it. Greg and I spent all our free time together.

After the first of the year, the cheerleaders had to ride the boys' basketball bus for an away game. Waiting for the coach, Katie smiled at Greg. He slipped into her seat and put his arm around her. She'd turned her hair jet black and used spray tan all over her face and body. With her cheerleading uniform barely fitting over her big boobs, no player could take his eyes off her—Greg included. His lanky arms hovered too close to Katie's chest.

"Here comes Coach!" a player yelled. Greg bounced out of her seat.

I wasn't about to let the team see me sweat, but I raised my shoulders at Katie. She shook her feathered Farrah Fawcett shoulder-length hair and looked away.

Right before halftime, Katie refused to move for a girl from the opposing team who wanted to pass by. My sister continued our cheer, exaggerating her clapping hands close to the girl's face.

At halftime, Lexie came running. "A shot-putter-like girl's got Katie by the throat. This way!"

I sniffed the popcorn smell through the concession stand until I came front and center with Katie face up in a chokehold. I stroked my neck, remembering Mom's hands around it, and vaulted into a stance of power, putting up my dukes. "Don't hurt my sister," I shouted.

The sturdy girl, flanked by her hefty gal pals, released Katie, who flopped to the waxed floor like a limp noodle. Humor flashed in the aggressor's eyes as she balled up her fists and hit me square in the head, sending me airborne. I landed on my back, knocking the wind out of me. Greg's dad helped me up and then caught me when I almost passed out. I traced the large lump forming on my forehead but started cheering again since my breath had returned to normal and the dizziness had disappeared.

For the entire second half, I scanned the gym for the gang of girls. They'd split, but after the game, they reappeared and attempted to infiltrate our squad. The basketball team made a hedge of protection around the cheerleaders and escorted us to the bus.

Once we returned to the school parking lot, Katie and I got into her car.

I shook my head. "What's the deal with Greg?"

"Oh, he was just teasing." Katie started the car. "But those bitchy girls weren't. Thanks."

"Of course. We're sisters. You'd do the same for me." I pulled out the pockets of my royal blue letterman's jacket. They were empty. "I forgot your money." I'd been paying Katie fifteen cents each time she drove me to school.

"Keep it. Grandfather gave me his credit card." She shot me a smirk. "Are you hungry? Remember that red hair-pigtailed-girl commercial?"

"Yes! That new fast-food place with those delicious-looking square cheeseburgers?" I licked my lips. "But it's way back in Overland Park. And it's already 10:00 on a school night."

"My treat." Katie nodded. "Let's go."

"Ten-four!"

After the basketball game, something shifted between Greg and me. When the days turned longer, signaling spring was in the air, I tried to convince myself nothing had changed. He avoided me at school, and if he called, he barely spoke. "Is something wrong?" I asked.

"I don't know." His voice was flat. "I don't."

Why doesn't he show the same excitement? Especially when I'm trying to be the perfect girlfriend. If Greg acted interested, I was Strong Summer, but I turned into Weak Summer if he was distant. Even though it wasn't the same as Mom ignoring me, it felt like it.

A heavenly distraction from Greg's indifference came by way of Dad's bank. For $2,000, Dad and I rescued a 1973 Chevy Nova SS from his bank's repo lot. I convinced my father it was the car for me since it took the cheaper regular gas instead of unleaded. "Plus, the SS must stand for Summer Stevens. It's meant to be, Dad." He'd spring for half of the eighty-dollar monthly car payment, and I'd be responsible for the rest. He also issued me a credit card in my name with a two-hundred-dollar limit. I'd pay off the card balance every month to not incur any interest. I cherished my shabby Nova with the rusted-shut dilapidated hatchback.

Once I drove my sports car home, I confessed my Greg troubles to Mom. "I'm always begging Greg for a date. I'd rather not have a boyfriend than one who doesn't treat me right."

"Let's go shopping." Mom jangled her keys. She was a homing pigeon for finding the one valuable item in what she called a sea of crap. "You'll forget all about him."

I did until I got home. At that moment, even the on-sale caramel leather purse Mom bought wasn't enough to protect my heart after Greg called and refused to talk.

"Have I done something wrong?" I cracked my wrists. "Tell me. I'll change."

"No, you haven't." His voice hardened. "I don't know why. But I don't feel the same. I don't want to pull the rug out from under you, but I'm breaking up."

The next Saturday night, Katie hustled to town to cruise Main Street with some girlfriends—a typical high school weekend activity. I stayed home, sitting at the kitchen table, pining away for Greg with an instinctual knowledge that he and Katie were hooking up.

Headlights pulled into our driveway. It was Greg's green station wagon.

When the walkway to the sliding door crunched with two sets of footsteps, I concealed myself in the pitch-black restroom by the slider. I didn't see Greg, but Katie and his smooching was a megaphone. The grandfather clock ticked along as a musical accompaniment. Then once the slider shut and the stones crackled with one set of footsteps, I barged out of my hiding place. "How could you?"

"You two aren't even dating anymore."

"But you know I never wanted to break up." I rushed eye-to-eye with her. "You reek of alcohol. You're a skanky scumbag."

The following morning after waking up, I ran up the stairs and came face to face with a massive hickey on Katie's neck. *I've got to get out of this house.* I returned to my room and squeezed my keys into my jeans pocket. Doc was gone. Braxton was quiet, and Mom was hungover.

Before I left, Katie gawked in the open fridge, so I leaned over her back and whispered in her ear, "Eat! Eat! Eat! Fat! Fat! Fat!"

Katie whisked around with feline agility and clawed my neck, gashing the flesh with three extra-long scratches. They turned bone white, filling with scarlet blood. "What have you done?" I screeched. "My chest—it's all red and burns like a razor cut." A metallic scent filled my nose.

Not concerned about grabbing my driver's license, my fingers outlined the keys in my tight jeans back pocket. I escaped out to my waiting wheels. Swirling gray and black clouds foreshadowed the coming March storm that hung in the air. Trees bent in the windy gale as I barreled into the driver's seat of my Nova. I revved her 350 V-8 engine and gunned it through the popping gravel, plowing down our driveway, turning left on Four Corners Road, and rocketing over the two train tracks by our house.

I rolled through the stop sign, turning left on Highway 56. My Chevy complained as the engine lurched forward until the motor caught up with the floored gas pedal. Linda Ronstadt singing, "Desperado" drowned out the roar of my Nova's four-barrel Holley carb. "Preach it, Linda! I did let someone love me!" I wailed through the windows, screaming to no one. "And look where it got me. I'll never let anyone love me again."

After speeding down the highway for two miles, tears blinded me. An evil voice mocked, "Keep driving. You'll never be loved."

"No!" I belted out so loud that my ears rang. "I will be loved."

I skidded to a stop at Skelly's gas station and tried soaking up my tears with my bloody shirt, but my waterworks refused to end. "Jesus, help!" I collapsed over my steering wheel. "Make me stop crying. Take away Greg's power to hurt me."

As if a master puppeteer pulled the strings, I straightened my back into the driver's seat. I blinked. *My tears are gone.*

When I returned home, Katie apologized, and Greg called to say sorry. "I only want to be with you." His voice was tender. "I was such a fool to even look at another girl, much less Katie. Please give me another chance. We're meant to be together."

"It's over, Greg." My voice was firm. "Especially after you were with my sister." Katie and I never again mentioned her hooking up with Greg.

Later that night, Mom sat at the kitchen table, chain-smoking cigarettes, gulping vodka, and staring straight ahead. She tapped the twenty-dollar bill in unison to Gerry Rafferty's "Baker Street." Doc had slipped the cash under her ashtray before disappearing to his clinic. Her barren, scarecrow-thin face reminded me of a kitten —one that scratched. But unlike Katie's chest gashes that left scars I could see, Mom's wounds were invisible ones that I didn't even know I had.

CHAPTER 14

BUBBLES

March 1978 – April 1978
Sophomore Year
Edgerton, Kansas

"You'd be gorgeous if you got a nose job, Summer." Mom used her compact mirror to put on her lipliner. "Maybe getting your braces off tomorrow will not only have straightened those crooked teeth of yours but help your nose not look so big."

Is my nose big? I touched the tip of it.

"Remember, Katie's driving and getting hers off, too."

After two years of spacers, headgear, and adjustments, I slid my tongue over my smooth, thin, polished front teeth as Katie and I waltzed out of the Overland Park orthodontist's office. Unwrapping a piece of bubble gum, I popped it into my mouth. "Wanna piece? I can't believe I haven't chewed any for two years."

"Why not?" Katie questioned.

"Remember, the doctor said it'd wreck our braces."

"You always do what you're supposed to? I chewed gum the whole time."

That's why I got mine off early, and you got yours off late. "Look, Kate." I pointed to the sky. "The clouds are like cotton candy." Picking a dandelion, I took a deep breath of the fresh spring air and blew off the white, puffy top. The seeds twirled across the sidewalk like helicopters.

"Drop that stupid stem and get in the car." Then, in one sweeping motion, my sister flung my schoolbooks off her dashboard and screeched her tires out of the parking lot. "Don't put all your crap up there."

"What's with you? It's like your head's ready to blow off or something."

Katie didn't say two words until she braked at the traffic light, adjusted her rearview mirror, and positioned a contact lens in one eye. Then, when it turned green, she sped to the light ahead, putting in the other. "Now, I can read traffic signs."

Yikes! She couldn't before?

Once we got back to town, I reminded Katie that I needed to stop and get my picture taken. Our local newspaper, *The Gardner News*, wrote an article about me winning four gold medals at the Ottawa Track Relays and wanted to include a headshot.

"You always do this, have another errand. I should've made Mom drive you." Katie blasted REO Speedwagon. "Make it fast. I'm not waitin' long."

"I'll try." I pulled down my visor and opened its mirror to examine my teeth. "I want to show Mom my smile. Maybe she'll think my nose looks better."

"Tell her to buzz off and stop worrying about what she thinks."

On the way home from the photo, a midnight blue Corvette accelerated past us on Highway 56. "It's Mom and Braxton!"

Katie floored her Maverick and tailed Mom to the house, parking beside the new sports car.

"Katie, you're another Mario Andretti." I laughed out loud and hustled out of the vehicle. I ran my fingers over Mom's white leather seats and said, "Wow, Mom, it's a stick. I've always wanted to drive one since that old tractor. I bet it goes fast."

"Quit jawboning. Of course, it does." Mom thumbed her nose at Katie before she disappeared from view. "Your sister walks like she's got a corn cob up her butt."

"Don't say that." The blowing wind picked up the dirt and hit my calves like needles. *Achoo! Achoo! Achoo!* "She's been so crabby. I don't know what's up."

"She's not a very good girl."

"What do you mean?" Mom ignored me, so I pointed to my nose. "How do I look without braces?" I nodded enthusiastically.

She studied me. "You've got a nice smile, and your nose looks slightly better." She turned back toward the car. "Let's talk about my fabulous new purchase. You're just materialistic enough to enjoy it."

Me materialistic? That's you.

"Don't say one word that I traded in another of Daddy's cars." She swung her arms side to side. "Take it for a test drive."

"I want to." I rested my chin on my hand. "But I've got so much homework."

"Katie will take it if you won't."

If Katie's pattern held, she wasn't leaving her bedroom tonight except to sneak out with her boyfriend. "Well, I guess I better drive it, then." Mom threw me the keys, and I hollered, "Braxtie, jump in." Dark clouds twined and tangled, replacing the sunny weather as I tapped the T-Tops. "It looks like it might rain, so I won't open them."

"You're too smart to be stupid." The passion returned to Mom's voice.

"Here I go—driver's permit and all." Mom leaned across the open window while I pressed the clutch with my left foot and started the car. *Varoom.* The noise filled the driveway.

"Love that sound." I floored it again. "If it's not raining when I return, I'll wash it."

"Will you? I don't know how."

Of course, you know how to wash the car. You just pretend to be helpless.

Grounding the gears into reverse, I waved as I backed out of the driveway. The car sputtered into first gear down our lane, but I shifted like a racecar pro before turning right onto Highway 56. Once I popped Emmylou Harris into the eight-track player, music filled the car, so I sang with her breathy soprano voice.

"You sound just like that singer." With the engine's rumble, Braxton's voice vibrated with the RPMs.

I lightly slapped his knee as I shifted, holding the steering wheel with my right thigh. "That's how I know you love me, telling me I sound like Emmylou. Let's get a Dairy Freeze chocolate dip cone. I can taste the thin, crunchy chocolate already."

Once we got home, it started drizzling. We'd just missed the violent March thunderstorm. When we got downstairs, the pelting rain beat against the slider. "Well, Braxton, I caught a break from washing the car."

He sat on the couch sketching one of his architectural showpieces instead of doing his third-grade times tables. Bubbles slept between us. Unexpectedly, Mom appeared out of nowhere. "Your stark raving mad, Braxton, if you think you're getting away with drawing pictures instead of doing schoolwork. You better get your ass in gear, or I'm sending you to that military school in San Diego. I already have the brochure."

My brother's head hung low, and his mouth opened wide. "One day, you'll be sorry," he warned as his chin indented and his upper right lip quivered. Braxton's shoulders sagged against the couch, and his scuffed shoes kicked at the thick, orange carpet.

Mom mumbled something and fled the room.

"She doesn't mean it," I said as I did my math.

"But I do." Braxton used his ruler to measure the walls, his tongue resting on his bottom lip.

I scratched his back. Overwhelming love for him gripped me. "Who do you want for a friend? Tell me."

"Jack," he answered without looking up.

"What's he like?"

"Jack's the most popular kid in the third grade, but he doesn't know me." Braxton licked his lips, sketching his house, turning his paper sideways. "He's fast like you and kind to everyone. He's always chosen first for PE and makes the class laugh."

I leaned closer to Braxton. "How?"

Braxton stood up and cleared his throat: "Knock, knock."

"Who's there?"

"Anita."

"Anita who?"

"Anita go to the bathroom." Braxton sank backward into the sectional.

"Funny. Tell me more about Jack."

"Once on the playground, a boy was upset, so Jack spun

around, flipped in the air, and landed in front of him. Then he bowed. The boy started clapping."

"Impressive." I put down my math notebook and thumbed through Braxton's hair. "Get his number at school tomorrow. Then, I'll call his mom and invite him to the movies and dinner— just the three of us. I still have some of my Christmas money."

Braxton looked up. Hope spread across his face.

The next day, Braxton got Jack's number, and we planned an outing for the upcoming weekend. By the time Sunday rolled around, Braxton was so anxious that he pulled his arm hairs out one by one until we picked up Jack.

Sunny and enthusiastic, Jack's lean athletic frame swaggered out the front door. Not bound by gravity, he vaulted over his four-foot front-yard fence in one graceful motion. "I'm stoked to go to *Star Wars* and see the spaceships." His green eyes enlarged with his crooked smile. He got into my Nova's back seat, and my brother leapfrogged beside him.

"Braxton told me your super silly knock-knock joke."

Jack rapped Braxton on the shoulder. "Wanna learn how to fart with your arm?"

Braxton's beam-like eyes puffed out. "Sure."

Shaking his sandy blond hair, Jack cupped his hand under his armpit, partially raised his winged arm, and swung it three times down to his side. *Braaat! Braaat! Braaat!*

"It sounds like you passed gas, Jack." I held my nose, and we all had a belly laugh. "Braxton's right. You're hilarious."

Five minutes later, Braxton mimicked his new friend and made three-armpit fart noises. His face flushed as maroon as my car. "See, Summer. Jack's the same fun in class."

I gave Jack a thumbs-up.

Jack turned strangely quiet and wiggled in his seat. "I see who's unhappy and then try to make them happy."

Three knock-knock jokes and four farts series later, we smiled our way into Overland Park's Glendale theater parking lot.

Once Jack pulled open the door, I sniffed the air. "That kettle corn's killing me. Let's get a large tub." After the movie, we headed to Winstead's for dinner. Sitting in the mint green booths, we munched on hamburgers and fries.

All through the meal, Braxton sneaked glances at Jack.

"*Star Wars*'s my favorite, even for the third time," I said, handing them a dessert menu. "What'd you boys think?"

"It was groovy. No goofin' off in that movie. The best part was the space war with the fighter jets," Jack answered. "Maybe I'll be a pilot."

"Jack, with your upbeat personality, you can fly through the air without a plane," I said. His almond-shaped eyes magnified. "How about we share one of those ice cream mud pies for dessert?"

When we pulled up to Jack's house, he exited the car. "Thanks, Braxton. I had a swell time." Braxton moved to the front seat. Jack took two steps and turned back, a half-smile covering his face. "At recess tomorrow, I'll show you my new dance move." He swiveled his hips like Elvis, hopped over the fence, and disappeared through his front door.

Braxton bumped my elbow. "You're so boney." He let out a satisfied sigh. *If Braxton had a tail, he'd wag it.* Sweeping his hands over my knuckles, he said, "Thanks, my sweet, boney sister."

"Being with you and Jack was the best part of my day." I exhaled a deep breath. "Remember, we're returning to Winstead's to celebrate Mom and Doc's remarriage anniversary—even though it's over two months late—go figure. But nothing with them makes much sense."

Braxton closed his eyes.

"Let's not think about that now. It's all backroads home." I jingled the keys in the ignition. "Do you want to drive?" He jumped on my lap in the driver's seat. "I'll take that as a yes."

I worked the pedals, but my baby brother controlled the steering wheel. Once we took the shortcut to the ranch house, I turned on The Marshall Tucker Band's "Can't You See." Braxton and I sang all the way home.

A week later, the family filed through Winstead's. Mom's rainbow-colored linen outfit made a statement, and all the men checked her out. A hostess seated us in the same green booth where Braxton, Jack, and I had eaten. I wrapped my retainer in a napkin and complained. "My stomach's so hungry. It feels like it's eating itself."

Mom shook her head. **"She'll have the grilled cheese,"** Mom told the short waitress with the double chin. "She doesn't like hamburgers, but I'll have one and a glass of white wine."

Is Mom talking about me? Why does she lie? I love hamburgers. I rustled my napkin between my fingers, threw it on the table, and twirled my hair.

Once the waitress left, Mom's eyes shifted toward me. "You're a grown-ass girl. Stop being such an airhead."

Tears formed under my eyes.

"On my life, stop crying, or I'll give you something to cry about."

"I just have something in my eye."

"You need a shrink." The waitress reappeared with Mom's wine. "Doc and I are seeing one. If I can afford it, I'll take you." Her glass clinked against her teeth as she drank. "You're a wreck. That's why Bubbles is so nervous. Animals take after their owners."

"None of our dogs are nervous," I said, shaking my head.

"My Miss Pooh sure isn't nervous because I'm not sensitive like you. You don't quite have the discipline your dad brags about." The waitress filled our waters. "And that's a fact."

I kicked up my legs and bashed my toe into the table, making it shake.

"Summer, you're a load. Always have been. Even the waitress knows you are, right, Doc?"

"That's right, Georgie."

The waitress lowered her eyes.

My throat went dry. "I'm not a load," I whispered.

Mom drained her glass of wine and ordered another. The red-faced waitress left.

"Don't be so touchy. I'm the one who gets my feelings hurt because of how you treat me."

Why can she get her feelings hurt but not me?

"If you know what's good for you, you'll shut your mouth. I got sick of your dad, got rid of him, and I'm just about sick of you, too."

Just then, a melted cheese-and-beef fragrance filled the booth. The waitress balanced the sizzling cheeseburgers but forgot my grilled cheese. My eyes watered.

"You're always crying." Mom put her hands on her cheeks, making her eyes wrinkle. "You're almost sixteen."

Why am I always crying? I wish I knew.

"I'm okay." Without warning, the restaurant started to turn black. I couldn't keep my eyes open. I took a long drink of cold water, sucking on ice cubes. My lightheadedness passed.

Just then, the server brought my grilled cheese. "That fat waitress forgot my wine." Mom barked loud enough for the girl to hear.

I stared at the ceiling until the waitress left and scarfed down my lunch in world-record time. My stomach felt like I'd not eaten one bite. Once the waitress cleared my empty plate and napkins around it, I reached for my retainer. It was gone. *She must have tossed it in the trash.* I asked her about it, but she couldn't find it.

Great! Mom will make Dad cough up the two hundred and fifty dollars for a new one, and Dad will be disappointed. *I can't win for losing today.* In a last-ditch effort, I checked the floor for my retainer.

With the tip of his boot, Doc kicked Braxton under the table. "Eat all your cheeseburger." Braxton shredded his bun, not saying a word.

"Doc's right. The poor kids in Africa would kill for the food you're wasting." Mom motioned to the server. "Just pitch it."

On the way home, Katie fiddled with the safety pin in the missing buttonhole on her shirt. Even though the new-car smell hadn't worn off, Grandfather had already repossessed Mom's Corvette and bought her another sedan. She changed cars as often as her shoes. *I never know if today's the day Mom's sports car will disappear.*

While Doc drove home, Braxton sat by Mom in the passenger seat. Without a word, Katie took the safety pin and stabbed Braxton's neck. He swatted away the sting. I kicked Katie, so she smacked my foot. After five minutes, she stuck the pin deeper into Braxton's neck. He yelped. The blinking horizon lights illuminated his stooped head.

"Mom! Katie's hurting Braxton." *What in the world's wrong with my sister? And why doesn't my brother speak up?*

Mom spun to the back seat, snapping her fingers at me. "Stop lying about Katie. How dumb can you be, Summer, and still have a brain?" When Mom turned back around, Katie flipped me off.

I'm The Brady Bunch's Jan, but I don't hear, "Marcia ... Marcia ... Marcia." Instead, I hear, "Katie ... Katie ... Katie."

The following Tuesday, I sped home from track practice, turning right down the driveway. Katie's car was there. *Why's she home? I haven't seen her at school. Maybe that's what senior-year spring fever looks like.* I opened the slider. Moments moved in slow motion as the grandfather clock struck four times.

The air stood still. *How's this possible?* I tried to make sense of the scene before me. Huddled together at the kitchen table under a halo of haze, Katie, Mom, and Doc sat with a bong and a large pizza between them. Smoke hovered over the glass-top table while they wolfed down pepperoni slices. The burnt-plastic stench of the pot made me want to puke.

"Wh?" My dry lips tried to form words. "Wha?" I wiped my mouth. "What are you doing, Katie?"

She looked away.

Katie's doing drugs with Mom? And that sleazy creep, Doc? I can't get a breath. I tugged at my collar. *Braxton? He'd stayed home from school.*

"Put away the hard stuff. Summer's here." Mom cackled. "She's so uptight. We need to help her relax."

I swayed my head side to side as if I were reading a picture book. *Katie? You're my Batman. I'm your Robin. How can you do this?* I inched across the kitchen and headed downstairs. Bubbles slept by Braxton's feet. He was sketching another home he wanted to build.

"Hey, Braxtie." I forced a cheerful tone. "Are you hungry?"

"Yes, but Mom told me to stay downstairs." He rubbed his stomach. "I've been here all day."

"I'll find some food." I massaged his shoulder. "Be right back."

I rushed upstairs. Pink Floyd blared from the furniture-like speakers. I held my nose, so I wouldn't smell the blue-tinted smoke rolling over the table.

"Summer's so rigid. She only has two uptight brain cells to scrape together." Mom's glassy eyes followed me as I crammed a knife, a jar of peanut butter, and bread under my arm. "You think you're better than us, but some drugs might do you good."

"Georgie, you've flummoxed Summer."

Laughter erupted.

I gotta get to my brother.

"Okey dokey, Braxtie. I found food." I said as I dropped dinner on the low, square leather downstairs coffee table he used as a desk. "I'll make sandwiches and then do my homework."

As late afternoon became evening, Braxton fell asleep on the oversized couch. I tucked the throw blanket from the back of the sofa over his body and groped the wall, feeling my way up the stairs.

"Get rid of that judgmental attitude, Summer." Mom lit a cigarette. I bent low, digging my hands into my gaucho pants pockets.

"Not such hot stuff, getting your picture in the paper, are you now?"

Digesting her words, I raised my eyes and tipped my head toward Mom. Only she could use something positive against me. I didn't trust myself to speak. I was too tired to do my math, brush my teeth, or even care. I gave my mother a broken smile and stumbled downstairs, curling up on the sectional near Braxton and Bubbles.

Doc was gone before I left for school the next day, and when I got home, Mom pulled a rectangular baking pan out of the oven.

"Our dinner's ready, and I've made brownies for dessert," Mom said, not mentioning the day before.

I blinked my eyes. *Should I confront her?*

"Braxton's already had a bowl of cereal. Katie just got home." Mom stared above my head. Katie wouldn't make eye contact.

"You made my favorite meal? I love your company casserole. And no one's even visiting." *Maybe it's a peace offering.* I tossed my books on the telephone table. "I'll just go say hi to Braxtie and get Bubbles."

I returned with my dog in my arms, pulled out a chair, and plopped him over my footie socks. With dull-looking eyes, Katie sat by Mom. I breathed in the dish's bubbling tomato meat sauce, swirled together in the cream cheese and sour cream mixture, picking off a piece of melted cheddar cheese topping. *Why didn't she make me set the table or do any work?*

Mom glanced sideways at Katie just as I devoured a massive helping of the spicy main course. The scalding macaroni scorched the roof of my mouth. I put my fork down to let it cool.

At the table, Mom moved unevenly like a wind-up plastic toy. With unnatural gestures, she complained about taking donations earlier to the city's food bank. Katie stared at her plate. I scooted my chair back from the table. *Something's wrong.* I sloshed down some water and picked up a flimsy noodle, turning it over in my hand.

"You've overplayed your hand, Summer, if you think you're not eating." Mom heaped another forkful of the casserole into her mouth. "I worked too hard to make this."

"You know I love it." The food and water mixture gurgled in my gut. "I just ... I can't put my finger on it." I swung my "S" necklace back and forth, faster and faster. "It's ... I don't know."

"Why, you ungrateful little thing." Mom flung down her fork. "You give me anxiety. I can't do enough for you. You're never satisfied."

How's Mom's anxiety my fault? I ran to the bathroom.

Woof! Woof!

Bubbles? I raced back to the table and craned my neck for my dog. Bubbles lapped up my unfinished plate of food. Orange cheese juice dotted the fur around his mouth.

Gliding over to my dog, Mom used her Miss Pooh voice. "Isn't that good, now?"

"Why're you paying attention to Bubbles?" My voice pitched to an unnatural alto sound. My head felt too heavy for my shoulders. "I just read an Ann Landers column about a mom sneaking cut-up hair into her daughter's mashed potatoes." I turned to Katie and then to Bubbles as the blurry truth came into focus. "You put drugs in our dinner. Didn't you?"

"Only in the brownies and casserole." A confident line of victory painted Mom's lips. "It might help you not be so emotional."

What? Does she think by drugging me, she's doing me a favor?

As if on cue, a wobbly Bubbles circled the kitchen island. I snagged him and burrowed my face into his laid-back ears. "You're all right." I lifted his limp little body and wiped off remnants of the drug-laced dinner. His eyes got big.

"Go downstairs. And take that mutt of a dog. I don't want to see your face again."

Fine by me! I snuggled my dog in my arms. It was like a nightmare where you scream, but your voice makes no sound. *At least Braxton didn't eat any.*

That night I dreamt that I showed up to school naked.

When I returned from track the following afternoon, my dog wasn't at the slider to meet me. "Bubbles. Here, boy. Bubbles?"

Mom passed me with an armful of laundry. "Your dog ran away." She snapped her fingers. "Give me what you're wearing. I need a full load."

I never saw Bubbles again.

CHAPTER 15

THE DAIRY FREEZE

April 1978 – April 1979
Sophomore and Junior Year
Edgerton, Kansas and Gardner, Kansas

W hen I opened the ranch's sliding glass door during my school's open lunch period, I coughed from the now-familiar acidic pot smoke. The foul stench clung to my nose. A quacking mom and a confused Katie sat near a lit bong at the kitchen table.

With bulging, bloodshot eyes, Mom pointed at me. "There's Little Miss Perfect." A couple of pills dropped from her hand.

"Katie!" I pleaded. My sister didn't look.

"Don't look so shocked." Mom frowned and then burst out laughing. "You're the one who looks funny in that track shirt."

If Mom wasn't high all the time, she'd know I'm in my uniform because I have Regionals this afternoon. At least Braxton was safe at school.

I would have stayed there, too, but during my second period, the cafeteria's chocolate chip cookie aroma made me so hungry that I couldn't focus or concentrate. Since I had no money, I sped home as soon as the lunch bell buzzed, thankful for the high school's open campus lunch policy—until I stepped through the slider.

Since our great room included the kitchen, there was no place to hide, so with shaking hands, I ripped open the crackers. Stuffing the stale saltines in my mouth, I swallowed them with a mouthful of the polluted air, leaving a chalky taste on my tongue. I dropped the can of chicken noodle soup and the sleeve of crackers on the kitchen island and shut the slider. *I'm not hungry enough to eat around a stoned mother and sister.*

Later that night, when I returned home from my track meet, I devoured the chicken noodle soup. I'd won four gold medals, qualifying for the state finals.

No one was home but Braxton. Snuggled into a little ball on the downstairs sectional, his sleepy eyes met mine. I swabbed crusty flakes off his eyelashes and said, "Hey, why're you up so late?"

"Waiting for you."

I pulled the throw blanket over his wrinkled school clothes, folding it around his chest. "You can go night-night now." I tapped his nose with my pointer finger. "Tomorrow, I'm applying at the Dairy Freeze, so I'll bring double cheeseburgers and fries home."

He didn't answer. He was already asleep.

Once track practice finished the following day, I stopped by the Dairy Freeze on my way home. The April sun sizzled hot on my back as I filled out the application on the outside rickety blue picnic table. Even though they didn't pay minimum wage, food was free, so I seized the job when they hired me on the spot for $1.85 an hour. Minutes later, I started taking grilled hamburger and onion ring orders at the popular teenage hangout.

After a few hours, I zoomed home with the white takeout paper sack dotted with grease spots. A steely dark sky with a mustard-dried earthen fragrance met me at our back sliding glass door. So did Mom.

"How'd the pasture get mowed?" I asked, meeting her nose-to-nose. "I smell the cuttings."

"Oh, that fabulous Zoe's something else. She's the only one I can trust." Mom opened my sack, giving me a whiff of our Dairy Freeze dinner. She took a bite of one of the cheeseburgers. "You know we never get it mowed, but Zoe somehow did it. Where were you?" Mom chewed her sandwich, giving me no time to answer. "Doing something for yourself, I'm sure."

I ignored her. "How'd she do it?"

"Zoe hot-wired that tractor from the vacant property across the street." Mom smacked another mouthful of our meal. In the wilderness, the voice of a jackal's hoot sounded over the clatter of a train, sending a shudder through me as I followed Mom into the kitchen. "Zoe's a godsend."

"I was at the Dairy Freeze. Got a job there." I caught myself from the familiar falling sensation by grabbing the corner of the counter. "I work three days after school in the evening and one day on the weekend." I ate a handful of fries; their salty flavor steadied me.

"If you want to keep that job, you better start working around here." The kitchen light shined on Mom's frosted pink lipstick, smudging her front two teeth; her boozy breath fogged the space between us. "And I mean it."

"I'm sure you do."

"Don't talk back. Or I'll knock you across the room."

"Just tell me what you want." My eyes became heavy with sleep. School, track, and now working seemed overwhelming.

"Clean the kitchen and Windex the slider. You don't have another damn thing else to do."

The following day, Greg appeared at my order window while working at the Dairy Freeze. "Knock 'em dead at State this weekend. As luck would have it, I'll be there."

Once Greg had been with Katie, he'd lost his power over me. We weren't getting back together. Besides, I had my eye on another guy.

That guy turned up in my Dairy Freeze line the Saturday after the state track meet.

My pulse spiked high when Jay's muscular physique slanted over my order window. His warm eyes seemed to know my deepest secrets. Turning around to fill his large drink, I didn't have to look back to see his smile that indented his two symmetrical dimples.

Handing him his fizzing soda, he slowly sipped it, bending toward me. "Word on the street is you're an Amazon woman, Sum." He high-fived me, grabbing my hand in the middle of the air. "With your state medal haul."

"Winning my two gold made me so giddy that if I had a chandelier, I'd have swung on it."

"I'd have swung with you." A boyish grin formed on his face as he released my hand. "When do you get off work?"

"Four."

"Come over to my house and play catch?"

I tapped my chin. "What about Zoe?" I batted my eyelashes.

"We broke up." His gaze never left me. "And a little birdie told me you and Greg did, too."

"We did. But I can't come over. I'm spending the night at Lexie's." I rang up his order. "Anyway, you can't handle my spiral."

"Ah, but I'd love to try." He pressed his lips together. "I need your help to practice for the QB job this year." Another customer appeared behind Jay at my window. "You can be my private coach."

"Flattery will get you everywhere," I said as he paid me for his coke. "I'll swing by before heading to Lexie's after work."

"I was hoping."

"It's a date." I put his change on the counter and stared at his dark hair. "It's not really fair that your bangs look like you just had a hot oil treatment."

"Flattery will get you everywhere."

"You're such a wise ass."

"Ya got that right." He chuckled, putting his coins in his pocket as I motioned to my next customer.

Once I got off work, I hustled to Jay's place. We played catch for twenty minutes in front of his forest-green house with freshly painted white trim.

"You're a freakin' wide receiver." He spiked the ball in his front yard by the oak tree. "And you've got a mean spiral."

"Thanks to Dad. He also taught me to catch the football as if it were fragile." I mimicked loose fingers. "At first." I held up straight fingers. "It bounced off these."

Jay picked up the ball, held it above his head, and did a couple of pump fakes, practicing passing without releasing it. "This's too easy for you. Go down the street."

I ran by the outside dryer vent blowing a fresh, washed fragrance, and turned around to ready myself for his throw. But instead, Jay waved me farther down the road with the football high in his hand. Then, he disappeared through his front door.

I barged back into his house and found him smirking in the kitchen under a framed poem titled "Dreams" by Langston Hughes. "I'm going to whack you upside the head." I pointed to the picture frame. "And that graceful bird soaring in the purple sky won't be able to rescue you, either."

"Ya promise?"

I walloped him hard on the shoulder, and then we lost it with laughter, bending over and holding our stomachs.

"You tricked me. I believed you when you told me to keep going."

"Whatever." As he chortled his deep, gravelly bear laugh, his dark brown eyes crinkled with amusement, making his face's crystal-clear complexion shake. His broad shoulders and thin waist set off his well-built body. "Sorry, Sum. Running in the house like that —that was crummy of me."

"I've got your number. I've had it for a long time."

"You've been under my skin since elementary school." He lifted his eyebrows. "Not to mention the birthday parties."

We gave each other a knowing look.

Three years earlier, Mom dropped me off at Jay's house for his seventh-grade bash. The birthday boy led me to the basement to play Spin the Bottle. Jay was my first kiss, and I got a funny feeling when his underarm hair touched my bare shoulder. Minutes later, he had sequestered me in a corner, kissing me for five minutes before his dad yanked us apart. The warmth from his kiss had stayed on my lips long after I had gotten home.

Jay and I hadn't kissed again until his eighth-grade birthday party. That year, his parents drove their motorhome with twelve of his friends to Worlds of Fun, an amusement park an hour from home. Everyone enjoyed the starlit, moonless night until the park closed, and his parents chauffeured us home. Zoe and I were the last two. While Jay's dad was steering, Jay whispered to him, and he passed my Highway 56 turnoff and headed to Zoe's house.

As soon as she stepped one toe off the motorhome, Jay started kissing me and didn't stop the entire time driving to my house. The outside world blurred. Fifteen minutes flew by before Jay's mom,

Meg, with her soft brown eyes and short dark hair, pulled back the curtain that separated the front section from the back. Jay and I sat angelically nearby each other.

Now, two and a half years later, we stood face to face.

"You're trouble, Jay, with a capital T."

"Mom calls me uncouth. She'd say I hoodwinked, bamboozled you."

"You did." I raised my turned-over palms. "I'm not sure what uncouth means, but I'm sure she's right."

"She is. And this uncouth guy wants to know what you are doing tonight."

"Lexie and I are going into town." I tucked a stray strand of hair back into my ponytail. "Maybe I'll see you there."

"Be on the lookout for this uncouth football player because you can bet he will be looking for you."

"Whatever."

"Wait! That's my line."

I raised my eyebrows. Minutes later, he opened my car door, and I sped away. Before I got too far, I swiveled my head back toward his house. He was watching me.

Driving on air, I headed to Lexie's house to glam up. I couldn't wait to tell her about Jay. Over the years, the conversation she and I started in Mr. Joseph's seventh-grade math class became one long, run-on sentence. Lexie had grown into her large gold-brown eyes and wide smile, becoming even prettier. She could analyze a solution before most adults knew there was even a problem.

A couple of hours afterward, Lexie and I drove my car five miles back into town to cruise Main Street through our one-streetlight town. As soon as we turned onto the primary drag, Jay's silver Trans Am appeared next to my maroon Nova. Lexie rolled down the passenger side window.

"Follow me to Pizza Hut." He gunned his car ahead of us.

Lexie's and my unspoken understanding was that we'd hang together until a better deal came along. *Lexie knows Jay's my better deal.*

"You go with Jay," she said as I pulled into the restaurant. "Although no one wears seatbelts, you might consider them. Just kidding. Don't have too much fun." She shifted in her seat. "Dad's expecting us home by midnight. I'll leave the back door open—just let yourself in." She winked. "I won't wait up."

"Lex, I know why I love you so much." I left my car running, opened my door, and sprinted to Jay's car.

"Dang, girl! You look freakin' awesome! I've been buzzing Main for an hour looking for you. Let's book."

He rested his right hand on my fingers, which was tricky with a manual. He drove with his knees until he had to shift. "I'm sure glad I begged my dad to get me the stick. He calls me his 'little shit,' but he likes me to have a good time." He cracked a smile. "And I sure am." With that, he revved the car to six thousand RPMs. The engine screamed, and the wheels whined.

"Do you want some?" He took his hand off mine and gave me a piece of green Freshen Up gum. "I love the exploding gel center." His roguish look made his eyes light up. With his summer tan against his pearly white smile, he was even more good-looking than ever. "Ready for some fun now? You have no idea what 400 with four on the floor can do. But, hell, you're about to find out." He kissed my wrist. It throbbed.

He swerved right into an empty gravel parking lot, popped his clutch, and did a couple of donuts, fishtailing his car. "Hold on, baby. Here we go." Jay cranked the wheel left and punched the gas, making the car roar and spin in circles. A burnt-rubber smell filled the car. I laughed for the first time in a long time. "If you don't smell the tires, it's a sissy peel out and doesn't count. How do you like me now?" Optimism twinkled across his face.

My heart answered. I smooched his cheek.

He touched where I'd kissed him.

Jay completed his last donut, and the Trans Am slid to a stop. He floored the car out of the lot onto the center drag and headed south down Main Street, speeding to the other end of town. The humid spring night air drifted through the car as he clicked on Bob Seger's *Stranger in Town*'s eight-track. The first song, "Hollywood Nights," played.

She had been born with a face that would let her get her way
He saw that face and he lost all control
He had lost all control

Jay rotated his leg effortlessly, steering the car with his knee and sweeping his fingers across my cheek. "I've wanted to touch your face again since my eighth-grade birthday party. You know that, don't you?"

"I know you've always made me feel pretty." I reached for the back of my hair.

"You should always feel that way." He downshifted to second and skidded right into the Dairy Freeze parking lot. The tires whistled. "How do you like me now?"

"A lot. I like you a lot."

After putting the car in park at the Dairy Freeze, he took both my hands.

"I just started here and love it. The owner, Mrs. Hopper, works hard, and the food's my favorite."

"Mrs. Hopper's dedicated to the Dairy Freeze." A flicker of emotion crossed his face. "I started eating here when I was seven. I'd call in my food order and bike down to pick it up."

"At seven?"

He flashed me his rockstar smile. "I'm just full of surprises now, aren't I?"

"That seems kinda young to get on your bike and get dinner on your own."

"Yeah, it was. My parents were at the American Legion—ya know, the place where the adults drink too much. If I got hungry, I called in my order. Mrs. Hopper said, 'Jaybird, I'll put it on your tab and have dinner ready. But be careful crossing Main.'"

"She's impressive." I pressed his hand. "But you are, too. You've been through a lot."

"You too, Sum. Sixth grade Field Day. I watched you run and win that armful of awards." He traced my chin with his thumb. "I always looked for you."

"I hope you didn't hear Mom yell at me." I squeezed his hand with my fingers. "'Nobody cares about your stupid awards,' she said. And she was just getting started."

Jay's voice dropped an octave. "That stings." He raised my hand and kissed it.

"I always think the next time, Mom's words won't hurt. But

they do." I sighed. A comfortable silence rested between us. "You had it hard, too."

"Nothing seems hard if I'm talking to you. Maybe it's your eyes. I get sucked in by them."

We stared at each other. He shifted his face toward me. *He's going to kiss me.* "UH-OH! I just remembered I have to be at Lexie's by midnight." I swung my head around to his dashboard. "What time is it?"

He pointed his finger at his car clock. "11:40. We can just pretend we didn't see."

"I'd love to, but I don't want to get Lexie in trouble." I leaned toward him. "What a bummer. Time's just flown by tonight. It's twenty minutes to Lexie's house, so we'd better go." I kissed him on the cheek again. "But you've been just what the doctor ordered. Really."

"Dr. Jay, at your service." He laughed. "And not the basketball player."

"No, for sure, not the basketball player." We laughed in unison.

"Best part of my day, Sum. Seeing you. The best part of tonight? Being with you again. Hell, babe, the best part of summer."

"You know just what to say to make a girl feel special," I whispered as he entwined his fingers through mine.

When we pulled into Lexie's driveway, all the lights were off except the back deck porch lantern. Jay reached out his hand, and I put mine in his. "I'd a helluva time. A blast." His tone grew affectionate as he walked me to the door. "You know that, don't you?"

"I had a blast, too," I said before we stopped under the light. "I don't think I've laughed so much in a long time."

He cocked his head and examined me like a priceless art piece. I met his gaze. He took his hand and gently brushed my lips with his thumb, and then pressed his lips on that exact spot with a long kiss.

"I've waited for this moment for a long, long time." He positioned his hand on the back of my head and brushed his lips across mine, lightly at first. Our mouths opened, and he gently kissed me. I returned his kiss, and then we forcefully rolled our tongues together. His mint flavor remained on my lips.

I opened my eyes. His were on me.

"Now, that's the taste of perfection, Sum."

He gave me a peck on the lips and smoothed away a wisp of hair from my face. Then, he kissed me again, and again, and again as the warm July air whirled around us.

"It's late, Jay. Lexie might be worried."

"Okay, babe. One more kiss, and then I'll go."

Two hours later, we were still kissing each other goodnight. The sweet scent of satisfaction lingered in the air.

"It has to be one o'clock by now." I touched him on the arm. "Your dad will be so worried."

"My dad's in bed. Dead to the world."

"Oh, dear, a car." I pointed to Lexie's driveway.

"How did he find me?"

With his headlights shining and his motor running, Jay's dad sprang like a lion from his vehicle, leaving the door ajar. "You little shit, get in that TA of yours and get home," he shouted from the driveway. "Right now!"

"This goodbye will be continued." Jay ignored his dad and gave me a peck on the lips. "Count on it. I'll call you tomorrow." He anchored his eyes to mine. "I'm crazy about you, Sum. Always have been. Always will be."

When I got to Lexie's room, she was fast asleep. Her digital clock radio read 2:10. I smiled at the glow-in-the-dark numbers. *So much for one more kiss goodnight.*

Three glorious Jay-filled months later, Katie left for Emporia State University after my grandparents paid for the college of her choice. I shuffled out to Katie's car to say goodbye.

Since she'd been partying with Mom, Katie and I barely spoke, but knowing she'd no longer live at home, my eyes seemed to sweat. Katie's presence buffered Mom's mood swings. I'd never known life without her. She'd always been there. I coughed up a piece of grit stuck in my throat as she got into her Maverick. I was a little girl again with soap in my hair. "How am I going to make it without you?"

"Don't you know by now, what you do doesn't matter? Mom's just how she is—don't let her bother you." With that, Katie sped her yellow car down our gravel driveway, blowing a dusty gravel storm behind her.

August turned into September, then September into October, and it was my turn to host the cheerleaders for the home football game dinner. The night before, the downstairs hall carpeting squished between my toes when the septic tank overflowed, soaking the carpet. I had to tiptoe down the middle of the hall to avoid getting my feet wet. With the mildew stink, I'd have to make sure the girls didn't go to my room.

After school, Jay headed to football, and I met the squad for practice before they followed me home. I didn't have a chance to help Mom clean, shop, or prepare dinner. I pulled my ear lobe while I chatted with half of the girls who rode with me. *What will Mom's mood be?*

Pulling into the driveway, I waited for the other half of the squad to arrive. "What an incredible house," one of the girls said as we trooped past our back patio.

In a fringed suede tan skirt and a tight black turtleneck for a backdrop for her large diamond necklace, Mom's winsome personality met us at the sliding door. "Welcome, girls. I'm thrilled you're here." She greeted every girl, repeating their name and looking them in the eye. "Come, sit down. Dinner's ready." The girls couldn't stop staring at my glamour girl mother with her flawless makeup, striking beauty, and professional hospitality.

"Yum." I kissed Mom on the cheek, not wanting to smear her lipstick. "Something smells delicious."

The great room's heavenly aroma of company casserole competed with a baked-bread fragrance. Faint background music played on the stereo; silver flatware, china plates, and crystal glasses sparkled on the table. Mom even bought colas.

Salads waited on our plates with the silverware wrapped in white linen napkins. "Please, make yourself at home." Her leather, black high-heeled boots hugged her black tights and clicked as she strode across the tile floor to serve dinner. Mom was the hostess, waitress, and cook in the restaurant of my dreams.

Devouring the meal, the squad chit-chatted around the glass-top table while Mom served her glorious chocolate delight dessert. With a mouth full of the fluffy crust and swirled pudding whipped cream, one cheerleader glanced sideways at me. "You're so lucky to have such a pretty mother."

Mom curtsied as if on cue.

Before we filed out of the sliding glass door, I thanked Mom. "I appreciate you working so hard," I gushed, "everything was awesome." *Why can't Mom always be like this? At least she's not mean all the time. Or would it be easier if she were?*

Within the week, the perfect woman who made dinner for my cheerleading squad disappeared. Day by day, Mom's drinking and drugs spiraled her down to a more depressed addict who barely made it out of bed. Throughout the fall, winter, and spring, Doc's Houdini disappearing act left Mom unable to cope. Then, finally, after one of his lengthier absences, he appeared without explanation.

With a burst of stamina, Mom sent Braxton and me to the store. Once we returned, she'd transformed into her supermodel self with a bright fuchsia-and-purple leather patched jumpsuit. She'd moved the bong and various pill bottles to her bedroom.

As I ate her rapidly created scrumptious chicken tetrazzini dinner, I slid my finger across the cool, thick glass of the table where I'd counseled a plastered and drugged-out mother the night before.

All at once, Doc shifted in his seat. "You're a carbon copy of Georgie."

I studied my fingers. *I'll never be her.*

When Doc left the table, Mom pulled me aside. "Fluff your hair for Doc." Bobbing her head, she continued, "Just put it on for him, will you?"

I did my best, but after what Doc did to Katie, I just as soon scratched his eyes out as to "put it on for him."

Twenty-four hours later, the jingle of the Dairy Freeze door signaled an incoming customer. Doc emerged in my line—an enemy in the camp. With its familiar salty potato aroma, my workplace made me thankful for the privilege of serving the best soft-serve ice cream cones in town. No matter what happened at my house, I was normal if I could just make it to work, school, or track. But my two worlds collided when Doc appeared with a pained, tight-lipped scowl and approached my order window. Double vision blurred me. "What can I get you?"

Despite how he treated Mom, she loved her husband. I took two steps back from his saddle-scented leather belt. "I need to talk to you—outside." His wrinkled face and monotone voice made him appear older than his forty-five years.

"I'm off in a couple of minutes." I gave him a blank stare. "I'll clock out and meet you at your truck."

Doc nodded slightly and shuffled away. I pulled down my stretchy shirt to cover my waist and tight denim jeans, dug my long, pink nails into my arms, and twisted the flesh. *He's never come to my workplace. He won't spook me.*

"Is something wrong with Braxton?" I asked after I got outside. "Mom?"

"Georgie's fine," he said, with stale, smoky coffee breath. "The problem's you." His weather-beaten, tanned face with its neatly trimmed mustache showed no emotion.

Me? Doc's the train wreck.

"You're the cause of all your mother's and my problems." Spit sprayed from his mouth. I pivoted away. *What?* Big Summer couldn't form the right words, and Little Summer couldn't speak at all. *What did I ever do except try to get along?*

"You need to get out. Tonight."

He emphasized the last word in such a detached manner that he could have been giving me his dinner order. I choked back the barf in my mouth.

"What?" *Who'll take care of Mom? Clean the house? Take care of Braxton?* I crossed my arms. "I don't know what to say."

"That's your problem." His sour, scrunched-up face remained stoic, but his blue eyes flashed black as night. "Isn't it?"

I clutched my belt loops for balance. My old enemy, dizziness, appeared. *What's Doc saying?* I cracked my knuckles one by one. *Don't let Doc see you panic.* I started hiccuping.

"Don't look at me like that." He moved closer, showing his top set of yellowish teeth. "You're the nefarious one."

I never know what you mean.

Although I daydreamed about leaving the ranch house, the familiar was safer than the unknown, and getting forced out by

Doc, of all people, didn't seem right. Somewhere, concealed deep within my spirit, a voice screamed, "Finally, you get to be free." *Mom's right. I'm selfish. No! Doc kicking me out is a gift from God.*

It's Doc's fault.

I'm not to blame.

I didn't fail.

But where would I live?

I always wanted to move to Dad's, but recently his rocky marriage didn't look good. I also didn't want to leave my high school, cheerleading squad, or track team, but most of all, I didn't want to leave Jay. We'd just celebrated our eleven-month anniversary.

Back and forth, the trees swayed in the April sunshine. *I smell spring. That's a good sign.* I held my breath to stop hiccupping. Doc's nasally voice brought me back to the Dairy Freeze.

"Now, get to it." He never made eye contact. "Be out by tonight, then."

"Wait!" My words skipped. "Wait a minute! Where will I go?"

Turning around, he lifted his arm by his ear, showing me the back of his hand before climbing into his truck. Then he hung a right on Highway 56 toward our house—his house, not mine anymore. At sixteen, with a math test tomorrow, I was homeless.

PART II

CHAPTER 16

THE GETAWAY

April 1979
Junior Year
Gardner, Kansas

I focused on Doc's truck until it disappeared. *That sucks!* The mango glow on the horizon reminded me that the sun would rise tomorrow. *But where will I sleep tonight?* Strong Summer stood toe to toe with Doc, but now Little Summer gagged with fear and worry.

I gotta get to the restroom before I become unglued. Dashing across the parking lot, I opened the bathroom door and sniffed the snot bubbling down my upper lip. After locking the latch, I clamped my tongue between my chattering teeth, holding onto the side of the sink. *I won't pass out. I won't hit myself. Doc will not win.* I tried to blow my nose, but nothing came out. *Now I can't breathe.* My whimpers turned to sobs.

"Where will I live?" I repeated to the shaking reflection in the mirror. "Dad's? No, not with his marriage problems. Katie's? No, since she turned druggie, I can't trust her. Grammy's? No, we've never been as close since Mom and Dad divorced. Grandmother Mema's? No, she still favors Katie. Jay's? Don't I wish! Lexie's? No, I wouldn't want to be a burden. My car? No, too embarrassing. Where, then?"

The Dairy Freeze mirror had no answer. Backing up against the wall, I shook my hands in front of my eyes, using my forearms to wipe away fresh tears.

Mom must know Doc kicked me out. She's probably already taken his side. She always does. *At least I get to leave the ranch house. Maybe this's my ticket to freedom.*

But freedom to where? *Plink!* Dropping to the bathroom floor, I rolled onto my knees and leaned over my thighs. *Plink!* I need a place to live. *Plink!* Annoyed by the sink's constant drip, I reached to tighten the leaky faucet handle. *But where will I live?* I licked my lips.

Wait! Greg! He'd told me I could stay at his aunt and uncle's house. But what about Jay? He'd dive in front of a semi for me, but what could he do? He had enough pressure from his parents' drinking. Only Greg could help—but at the mention of Greg's name, Jay ignited like a jack-in-the-box; he despised that I'd ever been with Greg. How would I tell Jay that I was living with Greg's relatives—if they would even still have me?

I spun around from the mirror, unrolled toilet paper, dabbed my eyes, and stopped my tears. I felt my back pocket for change, jogged to the parking lot payphone, and used a dime to call Greg. He answered on the second ring.

"Hi, Greg." I fanned my face. "Is that option to live with your relatives still behind door number one?" I stretched my sore calves from the track workout on the rickety blue bench. The rusted hinges squeaked while I gave Greg the skinny on Doc. "I'm so embarrassed." My voice cracked.

"Don't be embarrassed, Summer," Greg said. "Of course, Doc kicked you out—he's a war criminal and belongs in The Hague. Let me talk to Dad. Find you an exit ramp. Call me in thirty."

"Thanks, Greg." I sniffed. "How can I thank you?"

"You don't have to. I want to help. Besides, how can you keep clocking those sub-minute 440s without a home?"

A half-hour later, I called back. Greg answered on the first ring. "Doc's done strong-arming you. I brokered the deal without a full-court press." He chuckled. "I'm glad you're finally part of the family. You'll love Aunt Anne and Uncle Mike."

"What a relief. I ... I admit. I'm rattled." I scratched off splintered particles from the wood bench sticking to my leg, "Thank you so much! I'll be there by 8:30." I faltered, struggling for words. "I'll never forget this."

"I'm your Good Samaritan, Summer." He paused. "Just know, if I had your life, the white-coat people with the butterfly nets would be looking for me."

I laughed slightly before hanging up the phone and then pushed through the employee door. The well-oiled machine of the Dairy Freeze hummed on as usual. Inhaling the salty grease aroma of the deep fryer, I waved goodbye to the cook, who flipped patties on the grill. Picking up my purse, I headed back to the pay phone and slipped another dime from my back pocket to call Jay.

"Hey, babe." I mustered up a cheerful greeting.

"Something's wrong. I can tell." Simply hearing his voice made me feel better.

"Mom and Doc are just being their usual. You know."

"Crap! Can't they give you a break? Are you home?"

"No." I sniffled.

"Where are you, Sum?"

"The Dairy Freeze."

"I'll be right there."

I hung up the phone and headed to my car. *I'll make myself look like I've not been crying. Then I'll feel better.*

Rifling through my purse to find my brush and makeup, I used my rearview mirror to fix my messy hair, added eyeliner and mascara to my red-rimmed eyes and smoothed beige foundation over my blotchy, splotchy face. The moment my mirror revealed a miraculous transformation, Jay's '76 Trans Am turned right into the front Dairy Freeze entrance. *Not a second to spare.* He circled to the other side of the U-shaped parking lot.

Waving at the silver car, I rolled down my window as Jay swerved beside me. My heart zigzagged as I applied strawberry gloss over my lips.

He sauntered up to my open car window. The Dairy Freeze sign blinked behind him.

What'll Jay say about living with Greg's relatives?

"How's the hottest chick in school?" He leaned in and kissed me. His gum tasted minty.

Hope smiled at me. "Hi, handsome." I swallowed a sob.

He leaned against the car with an easy-going attitude as if he had all the time in the world. "Let's blow this clambake, get dinner at Pizza Hut, and you can tell me all about it."

"I can't eat." I lowered my eyes.

"You? Not hungry?" Jay touched my face through the window. He circled the car and got into the passenger side. "What happened?"

I pressed my chin into his shoulder, and the waterworks started again. With the toilet paper I'd stuffed in my pocket, I wiped off the recently applied mascara running down my face. Then, between gulps, I explained the situation. "I wanted to kick Doc in the back of the knee, waving me away like that."

"That chaps my ass Doc gave you the double middle finger. I'd like to beat the crap out of him." Jay stroked my hair. "But I'm going to lay low and be here for you instead."

"Man, even if Doc didn't kick me out, I couldn't live in that house anymore." My voice was scratchy, and my body ached. Jay swept a strand of my hair back from my forehead. "Doc blamed me. How's their crazy marriage my fault?"

"Oh, babe." He smoothed my eyebrows with his fingers. His brown eyes drooped. "I've just got to kick his slimy ass."

I attempted a smile. "I love you for that, but it won't help." I looked Jay square in the eye. "And I don't want you to kick Greg's ass either." Jay's eyebrows straightened, and his head slightly jolted. "I need to tell you something you won't like."

He started to say something but hesitated. "Tell me."

"I'm going to live with Greg's aunt and uncle. We set it up sophomore year after Mom's fall. About thirty minutes ago, Greg told me their spare bedroom was mine."

"You called him first?" Jay's mouth dropped open. He blinked his eyes. His tone was measured. "I should kick Greg's ass right now. He's always hitting on you, thinking I'm not looking. And now, you—staying with his relatives?"

I reached for his arm. "They have such a close-knit extended family." I bit my thumb, nibbling off the skin. "I know it'll be hard for you if I'm around Greg."

"Hard doesn't even begin ... " Jay's teeth clenched. Perspiration beads burst onto his forehead. "Screw it. I don't give a rip!"

Without looking at me, he got out of the car. I found him leaning against my hatchback. I hustled to my Nova's smooth silver bumper and sat beside him. He stared ahead. A couple of minutes later, he dipped his face toward mine.

"Maybe Greg's just using his relatives to worm his way back into your life. He's still got it bad for you. I see the way he stares at you. I did the same when you were with him." He rested his forehead in his hands. "Besides the aunt and uncle deal, he's never done right by you."

I twirled his dark hair on the back of his collar with my fingers. "I know this is difficult. I get it."

He lifted his head. "I know you do."

I took Jay's hand. "But I'm hanging on by a thread here, and if you leave angry, it feels like Mom ignoring me." I sniffed three short breaths. He weaved his hand around mine as I burrowed into his side. "It's a lot to accept, I know. Living with Greg's family. You're right. He'll be around me more, but what can I do? Why are his relatives even letting me live there? Who does that?"

Jay popped his palm against his forehead. "Oh, Sum, I'm such a doofus—worrying about how this affects me instead of thinking about you. You just got kicked out of your house." He smothered me with a hug. "I'm so sorry," Jay said in a low tone, pausing between each syllable.

"When you dismiss me, it ... it ... " I flopped on his shoulder, jabbering in his ear. Tears of makeup streamed onto his shirt. "It hurts. I don't know why I'm so sensitive. I'd rather you call me ugly than walk away."

"How could I ever do that?"

"Oh, I know you don't think I'm ugly, but leaving like that feels the same."

"That was crummy of me." With the end of his white shirt, he wiped the watery foundation off my face. "We'll always work things out. I'm just a jealous jerk. Greg being around you—it ... makes me ... selfish." The tips of our noses touched. "I only want to love on you."

"Oh, Jay, I know." I buried myself back into his arms. "You're the only one who sees Little Summer's real side and still loves me."

"Ya got that right." He touched my hair. "Your tears make your eyes even greener, Sum." He stood and drew me tight. "It's frickin' awesome Greg's relatives are helping. But if he even looks at you wrong, I'm beatin' the shit out of him. Now, when do we rescue your stuff from the ranch house?"

"Soon." I kissed him on the cheek. "Lexie will help. I'll call her. I also need to call Dad."

"You do that, and I'll get you an ice cream cone. I don't want your low-fuel light blinking."

"Smart man." I smiled at Jay. Our eyes held. "What would I do without you?"

"You're never going to have to find out. We've got this, babe."

Digging in my jeans pocket for another dime, I called Lexie and asked her to meet us at the Dairy Freeze. I used my last dime for the operator and reversed the charges—the clink of the ten cents flushed through the payphone's thick silver change compartment. I scooped out the coin from the shiny oval container.

The operator identified herself. "Collect Call from Summer," I said. The call would annoy Dad. Mom was right; Dad was tight. When Mom gossiped, there was always a shred of truth.

Dad accepted the long-distance charges, and without taking a breath, I told him about Doc and living with Greg's relatives. "I'll send you half the child support if you're sure. I'll never give your mother another penny." *So, why's he keeping the rest of the money?* "But why live with them?"

"What choice do I have, Dad?"

"You could live with me."

Seconds on the telephone transmitted a lifetime of regret through Southwestern Bell's phone cable: Dad leaving me with Mom. Dad not rescuing me from her house. Dad not making his second marriage work.

"I appreciate you always respecting my opinion even if we disagreed, allowing me to talk to you about everything." I stood up on my tippy-toes. Was I a prodigal daughter by not returning to the father I hadn't lived with since I was four? The father I was thankful for, but from whom I'd always needed more. The father who forged me into the person I was, but now, it wasn't Dad I wanted. It was Jay. "I can't live with you." My tongue raced back and forth on my swollen bottom lip. "I don't want to change schools and move an hour away."

"I guess that's right."

"I love you, Dad. I'll call tomorrow." I wiped my eyes and ran back to Jay.

"What did he say?" Jay handed me the cone, and I licked off the cool, fluffy top, letting the rich milk taste fill the void in my stomach. Jay's thumb brushed my lips, wiping off the dripping ice cream. "I hope he was understanding."

"He was ... sorta. He agreed to send me half of the child support. I'm not sure why not all, but I didn't ask. So at least I'll finally have money. Not only will I not take any from Greg's family, but I'll also see if they'll let me pay them." I massaged my temples. "It's a lot. Moving into a house without even knowing the people." I finished my treat and lay my head on Jay's shoulder. "But it's better than living at either Mom or Dad's, where I always feel responsible for their problems—especially now with Dad drinking so much."

"I get tired just watching you give at the expense of yourself." Jay paused, excitement filling his eyes. "You should stay at my house." He put his arm around me. "I'm serious."

"Wow, that's sweet, but I can't move in with you. We're only juniors. Plus, with your parent's partying, one more person might push your family to the max."

Pain rearranged his laid-back expression. I moved closer to him. "Oh, babe, I don't judge your parents and their excessive drinking. Are you kidding?" I nestled into his side. "Alcohol is no family's friend."

"Don't we both know it?"

Just then, a gray Ford pickup truck parked beside my car. "Lexie!"

She poked her head out of her window. "Hello, Sunshine. Time to breathe. Help has arrived." Lexie shook her head. "Georgie scares me, and that should scare you. That's why I'm here."

"Thanks for dropping everything."

"Of course I did." She got out of her truck. "We share a brain."

"That's the truth." I whirled around to hug her.

"That's why I know your queen-of-chaos mom expects you to jump and ask how high on the way up." Lexie nodded. "Getting kicked out is the best thing to happen to you."

"I need to hear that. I'm sick of being one breath away from a breakdown. But I know I'll be the bad guy for leaving."

"Of course. She'll make you responsible for Doc—the problem she created. I'm glad not to have to watch you be her dime-store trinket anymore."

Jay nodded in agreement.

"You've seen it all, Lex." My friend, since seventh grade, identified what others missed.

"Yes, I have. But enough about her. How are you?"

I played with my bangs, remembering when Lexie cut my hair before eighth-grade graduation because Mom wouldn't take me to the hairdresser. "With you two here, I'm good."

"You always are." Lexie ruffled through her purse and pulled out a pen and paper. "But getting out of that ranch house will make you better. And it'll help your budget, too. With the insane .59-cent gas prices, you'll be rich not having to drive into town." She handed me the supplies. "Now, start writing what you need."

"You know how I love lists." I started scribbling down items.

"Yes, I do. I also know Georgie's a nasty cold sore."

"That's funny."

"It's true, and we'll stay five steps ahead. Everything requires—"

"Planning," Lexie and I said in unison.

Jay turned his head from Lexie to me in awe.

"So, how much time do we have to get your stuff, Sunshine?" She swung her truck keys. "I sure don't want to deal with Georgie's BS tonight."

"Me, either." I took a deep breath and put the list in my pocket. "Mom and Doc's recurring counseling appointments right now. I know because Mom slotted me to go tonight."

"Dodged that bullet, didn't you?"

"Yes, and it buys us about an hour."

"Then, let's go!" Jay headed to his car and yelled, "We're burning daylight."

Minutes later, with convoy precision, the Trans Am, Nova, and Ford sped to my former house. Jay led the way; I was on his tail, and Lexie trailed behind.

Darkness fell under a creamy celestial circle suspended in the air., illuminating the attractive ranch house. My white knuckles gripped the steering wheel, turning right into the driveway. Neither Mom nor her place was what they appeared to be; they were what I pretended they were.

Tailgating Jay's car, I ground gravel down the driveway. Jay stopped by the garage, and I jammed my car behind his, leaving a lane for Lexie. Jay approached my vehicle. I stuck my head out my window, getting a whiff of the dried horse manure.

"Sum, you getting kicked out is freakin' miserable." Jay aimed his hand high in the sky. "But that full moon up there's a good sign."

"You're right."

Lexie's turned into the driveway, so Jay opened my door, and the two of us met her at her truck. Then we hurried up the driveway to the back of the house. The shaft of light guided us along the pebble path to the back door of the charcoal-black house. Mom never locked the door. I didn't even own a key.

Jay opened the sliding glass door and found a light switch. "Let's get your stuff and haul ass out of here."

"We should have forty-five minutes before they return."

"Let's not cut this even close." Lexie held three oversized trash bags. As if on cue, a high-pitched barking started. "Those yipping coyotes are us," Lexie said, handing us a trash bag. "A wild band of animals rescuing one of our herd."

Tears welled up in my eyes. "Jay, Lexie, you're the best friends ever."

"We love you, babe, and wouldn't have—"

"Let's cut the sentimental crap and get to work." Lexie pointed to my pocket. "When your mom returns, I don't plan to be here."

I pulled out my list, and we hurried down the basement stairs, stopping near the bathroom. An emptiness sounded through the house, and a musty odor rippled through the air. "I hope I can read my messy writing." I crinkled the paper in my hand. "Medals, awards, clothes, books, track shoes, and bathroom stuff. I'll start here," I said, pointing to the restroom. "You guys go to my room."

As I hurried through the doorway, I knocked over an open bottle of lavender bath splash. I bent over, tipped the bottle upward, and loaded my shampoo, round brush, blow dryer, and Lexie's hot rollers. The herb fragrance saturated the room with a dream-like atmosphere.

Back in my room, Jay and Lexie lugged armfuls of school clothes from my closet and drawers and stuffed them into two of the bags. I plucked my awards, certificates, and track medals off the wall and grabbed my alarm clock, jewelry box, and letterman's jacket. They toppled unevenly among the toiletries I'd just placed in my trash bag. Jay gathered up my schoolbooks.

"Your mom sure splurges on designer brands." Lexie examined an outfit's tag before dropping it in the bag.

"You're right, Lex. I can always be thankful for that."

"Even if you didn't have food." Lexie shook her head. "I'll toss all your shoes in my bag."

"Thanks. There aren't too many." I stretched sideways, grabbing photos of Jay and me from the wall.

"Don't touch that first drawer, Jay," Lexie ordered. "I'll get her underwear." He hung his head with a hangdog look. "Trade me, Jay. You get the shoes."

We got it all in one trip, loading two trash bags in Jay's car, one in Lexie's truck, and stashing my schoolbooks and coats in my Nova.

"Wait! I forgot to write notes to Mom and Braxtie. And give him his new sketch pad."

"I'll go back with you." Jay offered, grabbing my hand.

"I need to do this myself."

I kissed his fingers before I wandered back into the silent house, pausing at the sliding door near where Mom had fallen. *Why can't I remember the rest of that night?*

After running downstairs, I lay flat on my bedroom carpet and swiped my arm under my bed. *Bingo!* I yanked out the sketch pad from my secret hiding place. I wanted to surprise Braxton once I decorated it. *Too late for that.*

In my nightstand drawer, I snatched up a lonely blue ballpoint pen and drew a heart by my baby brother's name. Right underneath it, I added a note.

Sweet Braxtie, I have to leave. Doc kicked me out. Come and visit! Nothing will change! I'll always be here for you. I'll call. I love you!!!!!!! Sum.

I pressed so hard that part of the pen crumbled. I tore out a page of Braxton's notebook, holding the pen together as I wrote another note.

Dear Mom, Doc came to the Dairy Freeze and kicked me out. He told me I was the reason for all your problems and had to be gone tonight. I am leaving so you two can be happy. I love you, Summer.

I guess I'm still trying to be the perfect daughter.

A terrified truth scratched its way to the surface: I won't be the perfect daughter anymore.

I was bleeding blue. The pen leaked all over my fingers. Mom wouldn't want me to ruin her bath towel, so with toilet paper, I blotted out the ink and, with a swish, flushed it down the toilet. In the trash can, I threw away the damaged pen.

With Braxton's sketchbook snuggly under my elbow, I climbed the stairs, left Mom's note on the kitchen counter near the vodka bottle, and tucked Braxton's sketchbook under his pillow on his unmade bed.

Jay and Lexie stood by the open sliding door. Jay held out his hand. "How ya doing?"

"A dozen ways at once."

"Just a regular day for you, Sum."

"Yes!" Lexie said. "But let's get out of here."

I checked my list. "My spikes!"

"Georgie will spike you if she finds you here. So, let's not bump up against time."

"They're just over there." Pointing to the garage, I called back, "There's a method to my madness." I shot back inside and flung open the utility room door. As I snatched my track shoes from the garage floor, they slid down my arm with long red streaks but didn't break the skin.

A minute later, I stepped over the patio steps. Reality captured me. "When Braxton gets home, he won't find me."

"It's not your fault." Jay's voice boomed with authority. "Doc threw you out. You can't save Braxton. Save yourself, Sum."

"I can't move." I closed my eyes. *Moms are supposed to love their kids. She's why I have to do this.*

"Breathe, Summer. If Georgie finds us here, she'll get that gun. Then it'll get ugly." Lexie lifted her shoulders, making her look taller. "Your mom's house is like an itchy bra. Time to trash it and get another one."

"You're right."

Lexie grabbed one arm, and Jay, wide-eyed from the bra comment, shut the slider, looping my other arm into his.

"Headlights!" Lexie signaled toward the road. Her voice rose like a coyote's howl. "Georgie! Let's get the hell out of Dodge!"

"Meet at the Dairy Freeze." Jay hollered. "Go!"

We dropped our arms and sprinted to the driveway. Jay peeled out first, tires spinning on the gravel driveway. I got a whiff of the burning rubber dust flying as I waited for Lexie to take off before I jumped into my car. Lexie stayed on Jay's bumper, and I followed, turning left out of the driveway just in time to miss Doc's truck veering toward me.

Once I turned right on Highway 56, I passed Lexie, gunning my gas pedal to keep up with Jay's lead foot. He was airborne. My Nova couldn't beat Jay's Trans Am, but I didn't let him out of sight. The car's engine rumbled while the night air whipped through my open window.

Jay was standing beside his vehicle when I swerved into the Dairy Freeze parking stall. I bolted to him.

"Sum, we got out of there just in time."

"By some miracle." I lifted both fists in midair. He kissed my forehead. "What's next for you? Skywriting?"

Lexie steered into the spot by us and got out of her truck. "Talk about too close for comfort. My heart's pumping enough blood for the three of us."

"Freakin' A!" Jay wiped imaginary sweat off his brow. "Your mom had to know that was us."

"She knew."

"Georgie pretends to be stupid, but she's anything but." Lexie nodded. "I'm sick of anticipating your mom's every move, but I'm surprised she didn't chase us."

"She wouldn't give me the satisfaction of showing she cared."

"That's why you're gone."

Jay sandwiched his hands over mine. "Take the win, babe."

"I will. Thanks for getting me through this." We huddled together and hugged. "Let's check this night off the list and go to Mike and Anne's."

Lexie and I followed Jay the block over to their house. Every bit of the homeless ragamuffin I appeared to be, I stood motionless with my two best friends under the bright porch lights and rang the long-chimed doorbell. We each carried one trash bag, but Jay had taken the largest. As he repositioned the heavy sack over his back, my track medals split the plastic bottom and clattered on the cement steps. Without a word, Jay, Lexie, and I bent over and gathered the awards and everything else that had fallen through the hole. At the cool touch of my medals, I bit back tears.

Suddenly, with great fanfare, Greg's Uncle Mike swung the door wide open. "Get on in here!"

The three of us stood up. Six-four with a scrawny, extra-large build and a fuzzy beard, his thunderous personality welcomed us.

"Hello," Jay said. "How are you?"

"Better than I deserve to be. Meet my wife, Anne. She's the boss," he announced as Jay, with herculean strength, scooped up all three bags. Lexie and I trailed him through their front door. Remnants of their pork chop dinner lingered in their cozy, white house.

"I'll just drop these in Summer's room."

"It's right off the dining room." Anne pointed across the kitchen to an open door. Anne's short, slim body, graying, curly hair, and no-nonsense attitude perfectly complemented Mike's cheerful temperament.

"She'll be comfortable in the bigger room with the queen bed." Anne was all business. "I've also added hangers in the closet and cleared out the dresser drawers. And there's a towel, a washrag, and clean sheets on the bed."

"Oh, you've thought of everything." I put my hand on her shoulder. "Thank you. It's perfect."

Lexie made conversation with Mike as Anne and I followed Jay to my new room. She made sure I knew where everything was. "Tomorrow, we'll get to know each other better."

Soon after, she and her husband excused themselves to their upstairs bedroom.

Once Jay, Lexie, and I said goodbye, I headed to the bathroom to wash my face, questioning the childlike reflection in the mirror. *What have I done?*

CHAPTER 17

THE SIGHTING

April 1979
Junior Year
Gardner, Kansas

The following morning at school, concern was all over Jay's face as he paced in front of my locker, scanning the hall. I playfully bumped into him from behind, and he spun around, letting his hands fall heavy over my shoulders.

"How'd it go last night?" He sniffed my hair. "Mmm, you smell like strawberries."

"It was easier than I expected." I lifted my spiral notebook and sneaked a quick kiss. "But I had a dream that I was screaming underwater. Someone I couldn't see was dragging me down."

"Oh, girl, I just want to make those nightmares go away." He ran his fingers through my hair. "I hope your morning was better.'

"It was. Anne left early for work. Mike stayed in bed, and I had a bowl of cereal. Since I wasn't starving, the smell of the cafeteria's cinnamon sheet cake didn't give me that sick feeling."

"Whoa, imagine that."

"Exactly! And I collapsed in bed last night after studying for our math test."

He grinned sheepishly, revealing guilty dimples.

"What? You didn't study?"

"Well, nuts! I was busy helping the cutest girl in school move."

"Ha! Then we'd better study at lunch." I jabbed his waist with my elbow.

"Easy-peasy-lemon-squeezy," Jay whispered in my ear. "I mean-lemme-squeeze-yee." He slapped his leg. "Sorry! Couldn't resist."

"You're a hoot." I blew him a kiss.

"Don't start something you can't finish." He pulled me to him, giving me a tender peck on the lips. "Seriously, how are you?"

"Better than I thought I'd be." I straightened his shirt collar with my free hand, making it lay flat. "I even found lunch money in my pocket."

"That's great, Sum." He yawned. "I didn't sleep a wink worrying about you."

"You're so good to me." I leaned into his right side. "Makes me feel all lit up inside." I twirled around with a wannabe dance move and waved my hands. "The party has started. You like?"

"Not like—love." His eyes fishtailed over me. "They're my favorite." He pointed to my rhinestone denim skintight jeans. "Lacing up the front and back like that." He tipped his head. "Yeah!"

"I knew I'd feel better if I dressed up." I swatted his hand from my butt and slapped him on the back. "What am I going to do with you?"

"I've got a lot of ideas." A crooked grin stretched ear to ear. "You're rockin' my world." He studied me. "You're a freakin' star even coming to school."

"I love school. And wasn't going to let douchebag Doc win. He's such a ... " I tapped my temple. "What's your mom's word when someone's over-the-top selfish?"

"Ass?"

I gave him a fake smile. "Pleased with yourself?" I tilted my head with mock irritation.

"Just kidding—narcissist." He grinned without showing his teeth.

"That's it. Just don't make me spell it."

Jay exploded with hilarity. "Mom tells me I'm egregiously uncouth."

"Don't make me use that in a sentence."

Jay laughed harder. "Don't tell Meg—I mean, Mom—that I actually use her vocabulary words."

"You know what I think?"

"What? Cut me, hit me, Mick." Jay skimmed his lips across my forehead as he said the famous movie line. "Call me Rocky. I can take it."

"I know you can." With my hip, I knocked him in the butt. Jay and I'd watched *Rocky* at Overland Park's Glendale movie theater. He loved to quote Sylvester Stallone's Rocky Balboa character and imitate the sincere boxer.

"Your mom's always on your team. Remember her poems before every home game? With her curved calligraphy."

"Ya, I love taking you there before the football games." He sighed, grief filling his eyes. "Mom's such a different person when she's sober and not d-drunk."

"I know, babe." I fiddled with the hair that covered Jay's ear. "Those royal blue posters show her love."

As if on cue, Jay recited one of Meg's former poems:

"Jaybird's great! Jaybird's great!
His spiral will not be late
He's destined to a certain fate
Winning state in '78!"

"Impressive!" I clapped and tried to whistle. "Both you and Meg."

Jay put his hands up Rocky Balboa style. "You're right. Mom's always rooting for me."

A comfortable silence stretched between us. "I'm just glad you're joking after last night." Hand in hand, Jay escorted me to my first period.

"Well, I didn't miss Mom banging on the floor this morning."

"I guess not." He cast an adoring glance and nuzzled his body by mine as we lingered nearby my classroom. "I'll meet you at the flagpole to walk to English."

My first two periods flew by, and in no time, I waited by the

American flag. It proudly waved in the wind as Jay appeared. He laced his fingers around mine. "Ready?"

"You know it." The current high school's crumbling buildings forced Junior English into dingy, dilapidated second-floor rooms above the nearby elementary school. "This's my favorite time of day, Jay, traipsing to class with you."

The sweet, fresh-cut grass by the elementary playground filled my nose as we rounded the sidewalk corner. Jay and I swung our hands in a steady cadence, strolling along the chain-link fence separating us from the school kids at recess.

"I can't wait to buy lunch." While I tried to tickle his chin, a young boy flashed past the swings, appearing on the other side of the fence. "B ... Brax." My breath caught cold and hard. I released Jay's hand and clutched his shoulder. *Braxton!* I'd forgotten that his elementary recess coincided with our passing period to English. Jay and I saw him almost every day. *I can't breathe!*

Shock stained Braxton's face stark red. He launched himself at the fence, which separated us. "Uh, um ... w ... w ... we got your notes last night." His upper lip trembled in the early-spring sunlight. His eyelids opened and shut as his chin indented, spasming in rapid succession. "When'll you be home?" He pushed his fingers slightly through the fence, tears falling from his eyes onto his sneakers.

"Braxtie," I silently mouthed. My chest seemed to rip from within. I couldn't speak. "Braxtie," I mumbled under my breath. *I want to hug away your hurt. Tell you I'll be back. But that's a lie.* I clasped his pinky and ring finger through the fence, touching his palm. It was sweaty. "I'm so sorry. I'll always be here for you." A spasming sensation gripped my head with bone-crushing reverberation. "I never wanted to leave you."

He folded his hunched shoulders forward while I scrunched my hand into my jeans pocket. My fingertips touched the wadded-up dollar bills. I inched the money to the surface and thrust it into Braxton's shaking hand through the fence.

He toed the ground with downcast eyes and removed his fingers from the wire mesh. "But when are you coming back?" he said, pausing between every syllable.

"Braxton, Braxton!" Mascara tears stung my eyes. I shook my head. "I don't know if I'll ever be back."

His body winced as his eyes pleaded, "Please, come home." He didn't wait for a reply. Instead, he turned and sprinted away, slogging through the sea of students.

"What kind of a sister am I?" I collapsed into Jay. "I forgot about my baby brother."

"You're a helluva sister." Jay steadied me with his hand.

"I failed him, and I'm never going to get over it."

"No, you didn't." Jay lifted my chin with his right hand and wiped away my tears with his left. "You had no choice. That asshole kicked you out. It's not your fault."

"Oh, Jay, oh, Jay!" I tucked myself into his outstretched arms. "I'm so ... so ... I just don't know."

"You're trembling, Sum. I'm here," he whispered in my ear as his breath warmed the back of my neck. "We'll make it up to him."

Tears streamed down my face. I'd left Braxton, and he would suffer. No matter how much I tried to care for him, it would never be the same. And nothing could change that. A shadow of shame tempted me to throw myself on the sidewalk, but I didn't want to make us late for English.

"Doc did this." Jay shifted in front of me. "It's on him." Black dots faded my mind in and out. I fought not to pass out until Jay grabbed my face and moved my eyes in front of his. "Sum, look at me. I'm right."

"I know you are. I'm expecting something of myself I'd never expect of anyone else." Jay embraced me, leaving no space between us. "But by leaving Braxton, I abandon part of myself."

"But you couldn't stay."

"I know."

"I'll kick Doc's ass. Just say the word."

"You're just trying to distract me and cheer me up. I love you for that." I dropped my mouth near his ear. "Don't kick his ass. I'll do it the next time I see him. And I'm just tough enough."

"Don't I know it?"

I managed a weary smile. "I'm trying to let it go. But I'm not really the let-it-go type."

"Ya got that right."

"You don't have to agree so fast." I laughed despite myself. "I know it's Doc's fault. I just wish that made me feel better."

Like a recurring migraine, Zoe appeared out of nowhere with Chloe, passing us on their way to English. Jay and I stopped talking.

"Heard about you getting kicked out." Her sing-song saccharine sympathy fell flat on the sidewalk. She took a couple of steps, walking backward without making eye contact. "Hope you're not too traumatized." She jerked back around, disappearing into the distance with her shimmering, shoulder-length, blunt bob-cut hair swinging happily from side to side.

"Well," I said, rolling my eyes. "Some things never change. That's Zoe for you. How'd she know?"

"Small town," Jay answered. "Everyone knows everything about everyone."

Mom must've called Zoe's mom after reading my note.

Minutes later, close behind Zoe and her two-girl band, Jay ushered me into English class with his hand between my shoulder blades. As the bell buzzed, I fell into my seat, and Jay lowered himself into the chair next to me. With its wobbly desks, painted-shut windows, and light hardwood floors, the makeshift classroom of barebones decor included only a blackboard on wheels and a box of chalk.

I breathed in the freshly polished floor and slinked into my seat, sneezing three times. Shafts of light cast a yellow tint from the three large windows and blinded me as our teacher, bookish Mr. Roberts, wrote a quotation on the board. Medium height with a narrow face and tar-black hair, he tapped letters on the chalkboard. Golden particles floated throughout the air and drifted to the floor when he scribbled words, wiping the excess powder from his hands onto his blue trousers. A dusty cardboard scent filled the air as Mr. Roberts read:

"'In the midst of winter, I found there was, within me, an invincible summer.' *Albert Camus.*"

After the teacher said something about the class's next novel being by the same author, he continued, "I'm reciting the quotation again. Observe my pointer stick. I'll hover over every word.

I'm Socrates and praying that one of you, by some miracle, is my Plato."

Pay attention, Summer. You don't want to get behind.

Balancing the novels like a waiter with too many plates, Mr. Roberts handed out *The Stranger*, a French book translated into English. Jay thumbed through it and exclaimed, "Finally! Camus wrote a short book we can finish."

"For Pete's sake, Jay. Don't call the author by the American pronunciation: Cam-us. It's French. It's French—*Cam-moo*—like the cow." Mr. Robets's good-natured, gray-blue eyes rested on Jay.

Jay's deep, cheerful voice forged a smile that tugged at the corners of his mouth.

"Well, since Jay can pronounce the author's name, we'll continue class," the teacher said as he picked up *The Stranger* and shuffled through it. "Today, students, we'll be discussing the author. For tomorrow, read the first hundred pages."

On the side of the room, a student's waving hand caught the teacher's attention. Jay turned his head toward me. "You just need to run the clock out of this day." His compassionate eyes made me teary. "You can do this."

Mr. Roberts kept talking. I forced myself to listen. The teacher's words turned into white noise in a long, dark tunnel. I couldn't keep my eyes open.

Pressure on my foot brought me back to English. Jay's leg was across the aisle, and his foot was resting on my sandal. My head tottered across my desk. Jay mouthed, "You okay?"

I gave him a thumbs-up. But I wasn't. I was sleepwalking through English.

The teacher roamed up and down the line of desks.

What's he saying? Pay attention. It's something about the author going to battle. Jay put my notebook on my desk and handed me a pencil. "Thanks." My voice was low, like a prayer. A static hum replaced the teacher's voice as the white noise started again.

Is he talking about World War I?

Mom's house was World War III, and I left Braxton there. *Alone!* I acted like I was taking notes on the teacher's lecture, but I shaded hearts around Braxton's name.

Jay's foot slid under my sandal. From the corner of my eye, Mr.

Robert's stood over my desk. "What's Albert Camus's quotation mean, Summer?"

The room grew silent. All eyes were on me. The sun's glare from the windows highlighted the board. I glanced away from Zoe's smirk and scanned the quotation.

"Did you want to add something?" The teacher rested the pointer stick by his side.

I slanted my head and rubbed the side of my neck, skimming my tongue back and forth on my lip. I repeated the quotation.

"In the midst of winter, I found there was, within me, an invincible summer." Albert Camus

"I've seen that quote before. I remember it—it's got my name, Summer." My cluttered mind cleared with textbook clarity. "It means that no matter what happens—even during 'winter,' the harsh and painful parts of life, we can somehow redeem those difficult times into a sunny and satisfying 'summer' if we refuse to give up."

Zoe's eyes rolled into the back of her head as Jay threw up his hands and clapped. "That's my girl! She's an 'Invincible Summer.'" Some of the class snickered.

"Splendid, Summer." Mr. Roberts returned to the front of the class and clanked his pointer tip on his desk. "I didn't know you were listening."

"Helluva answer." Jay gushed once we shot out to the sidewalk. "How'd you do that?"

"I know that quote from somewhere."

"Ya think?" His eyes beamed. "You're a freakin' genius."

"Oh, Jay." With my fingers, I combed his feathered bangs. "You think I walk on water."

"Of course I do." He high-fived me. "Don't you?"

"Yes!" I snapped my fingers. "No! I don't walk on water. I don't even know for sure where I've seen that quote. But years ago, I think someone gave me a note with it, and it might be in my diary, glued on a page there. I did that with a lot of greeting cards."

"Did we get it from the ranch house last night?"

"No. I forgot. My diary's hidden under my other twin bed." I dawdled by Jay's side. "It's a Pepto-Bismol pink leather book with Diary written across it. I can't believe I didn't grab it. Somehow, I have to find a way to rescue it." I slumped by his side, thankful for his shoulder. "I can't think about it now. I'm so frazzled that I'm surprised I can even complete a sentence."

At that instant, a tiny voice squeaked, "Thanks for lunch." Jay and I spun around to see Braxton wave, turn, and run away, his straight brown hair sticking out over his ears.

"He was trailing us. We usually don't see him on the way back from English." Jay looked in Braxton's direction. "That's a good sign."

After school, a rapid chorus of *clunk, clunk, clunk* echoed up and down the halls. Lockers shut with speedy precision as eager students sprang into action, pushing and prodding through any open lane to get out of school.

Jay shifted on the balls of his feet by his locker until he spotted me. Then, with his hand stretched out, he met me at the trophy case.

"Look, Jay, this year's first-place League Meet track trophy is front and center." I flicked my shimmery, pink fingernails on the glass. "And behind it is our cheerleading spirit stick from last summer's camp. We'll win another one this year if I'm elected head cheerleader and have anything to say about it."

Jay's eyes illuminated with pride. "My girlfriend's such a badass."

"Not really. I just like to win." I used Jay's shoulders as a launch pad and jumped over his head. "We vote on the head cheerleader in two weeks. I want to be in charge of the squad."

"You will be." Jay hooked his elbow around mine, and we herded with the other students toward the exit. "I know it."

"How?"

He drew me in closer. "Even when you ditched me freshman and sophomore year, I knew what you were doing. You've been a cheerleader every year and deserve to be the head honcho."

"Your confidence inspires me." I flipped my hands in the air, feigning shock. "But it appears you've been watching me."

Jay's dimples simultaneously indented his cheeks. "Take it as a compliment."

"You're an awesome boyfriend." I hit him in the shoulder. "So,

I'll give you a 'Get out of Jail Free Card.' Come on. Cough it up. You've been stalking me."

"Oh, that stings." He stopped short. "Hit me again, right here." He pointed to his lips.

"You think if you flash that cute smile, you can get away with anything." I wagged my finger in his face.

"You've got my number now." With a chuckle, he sat back on his heels.

"It's a good thing you're so fun-loving." I smacked his shoulder again for good measure. "This time, I'll let it go. Since you walked me off the ledge a million times today."

"I'm so relieved." He grabbed me by the waist. "I don't want to be in the doghouse once I get home."

"Home?" I put both hands over my mouth. "I don't have one." I blew out a long breath of air. "Why am I okay, one minute, and the next, waiting for a windowless van to whisk me away?"

"Think about your day. I give you an A." He removed a tangle of stray hair from my face. "Let's meet after track and my football meeting. I'll follow you to Mike and Anne's."

"Thanks, Jay. Then I won't have to go alone."

"I'll swing by the girls' locker room—say 4:30?"

"Yes." I sagged against him. Tears sprang out of nowhere. "Thank you. I'm just afraid to go to my new, new ... What do I even call it?"

"Home, Sum. You call it home."

CHAPTER 18

PROM

April 1979 – May 1979
Junior Year
Gardner, Kansas

After track practice, I showered in the girls' locker room, dressed in my sparkly jeans, and grabbed my stuff. Then, without looking, I burst out the door straight into Jay, almost slipping on the gym's glossy floor. "I'm a mess with a capital M," I said.

"Let's do this. Rip off the bandage. I'll follow you to Mike and Anne's." Jay flashed his down-home smile. "No drag racing, though, Sum."

Since dating Jay, we often raced to the ranch house. His car was faster, so the only way to win was to get a quicker start and take the lead. That way, he couldn't pass me once Main Street's four lanes narrowed into Highway 56's two.

"I love when my Nova beats your Trans Am." I kissed him on the forehead before we tromped through chattering students and free-throw shooters to the student parking lot. Under the heavy April cloud cover, we lingered by my car. "Today feels like it's lasted a year. You've been a lifesaver."

He hugged me and took my books. "I'll give you five minutes, then ring the bell. After that, let's eat at Pizza Hut. With my house only two blocks away, I'm at your beck and call."

I nodded more confidently than I felt and opened my door—*Jay's right. I need to check going to Mike and Anne's off my list.* I drove the half-mile and parked in front of their Leave-It-to-Beaver-looking house. Jay's Trans Am shadowed me like a pace car, pulling up behind me. Glancing over my shoulder, I signaled a thumbs-up, inhaling the springtime floral scent.

With my leather purse slung over my shoulder, I hopped the steps and stood like a solicitor on the porch. A continuous row of perfectly trimmed evergreen bushes looped around the house underneath the black shuttered windows. Dryness spread throughout my throat. *How is it that I'm living with strangers?*

Without any warning, Mike swung open the door.

I flinched.

"Hello, Summer." His boisterous voice was a welcome friend. "Come take a load off your feet, check under the hood, and kick the tires." I followed him through the door like playing a part in an *After School Movie Special.* "I'm going to sit here," he said, sinking into his worn, leather recliner, "and you there." He pointed to the burgundy loveseat.

"How are you, Mike?"

"Super good, but I'll get better."

I sat down on the comfy couch and smiled. "You're funny."

"Funny-looking, maybe." He leaned his recliner parallel to the floor. "Anne works at the post office in Kansas City and gets home late," he said, offering me a Brach's candy orange slice from his half-eaten bag.

I took one. "Thanks." I sucked off the sugar from the coated candy treat.

"My brother says he's never had an athlete with so much speed who works so hard. And you're talented enough for a University of Kansas track scholarship."

"He's a great coach." I put my hand over my heart. "He's been good to me. And you and Anne, too." I choked up. "Thank you so much for tak—"

"Now, now. Let's not go into that," Mike said with an iambic pentameter rhythm. "Anne and I are happy you're here."

"I am, too. And I want to pay you."

"There'll be none of that."

The doorbell chimed.

"Who might that be?" Mike popped up from his chair, his wayward gray hair worse for the wear. "You tell Jay to come on in here."

I leaped for the door.

"Look who I found." I pulled Jay over to Mike. "This riffraff was on your doorstep."

"Hello again." Jay shook his hand. "I think you put in the electricity for our pool pump."

"That would've been me." Mike sank back into his recliner. "But I work as little as possible."

"That's the way to do it." Jay settled on the loveseat, taking my spot. "Did Sum tell you about her track meet? Four golds again."

"You're my favorite fan, Jay." I lifted my books from him and turned toward my new room. "I'll be right back."

"You're going somewhere fast," Mike said when I returned. "And I'm cracking myself up."

Jay laughed while I yanked him up from the loveseat. "I'm taking Sum to dinner."

"Good." Mike handed me a key. "Use this. Anne and I'll be in the rack early."

Jay and I headed outside. After he opened my door, I slid into the passenger seat. He leaned over until his nose almost touched mine. I breathed in his warm, minty smell. "I can't wait to kiss you."

"Not in front of their house."

"I'll take a raincheck. And on more than just a kiss." Jay's eyes crinkled as he pecked my cheek. "I've hounded you day and night for almost a year, but remember prom's in three weeks. Near our anniversary. But who's counting the days."

"You are."

He winked. "Ya think?" Jay's Trans Am howled to life and screamed down the street. He turned left, squealing his tires onto Main Street toward Pizza Hut.

Moving into Anne and Mike's was a double-edged sword. The first week, I cried from missing Braxton but appreciated the ease of my new home. The following week, I cried from Mom's lack of concern but welcomed the break from her. By week three, I cried from wanting my diary until I realized I had no money for a prom dress.

I phoned Dad every Sunday night to chat about school and track. "At the end of the week, I'll send your monthly hundred-and-twenty-five-dollar child-support check."

I didn't tell him that the first one was long gone.

Once I hung up, I called Lexie, complaining about my money woes. "I just got my tax refund," she said. "Filed early. It's yours, Sunshine." She had constant cash from making $2.90 minimum wage at a nearby town's Kmart. "Let's go tootin' around prom shopping tomorrow."

After track the next day, Lexie and I tore to Oak Park Mall and bought Gunne Sax prom gowns. She chose a long, white lace Victorian masterpiece with a low-cut neck, which fit her like a glove. My soft baby blue full-length gown shimmered with matching ribbons, hugging my waist and rustling when I moved.

"As soon as I get Dad's money, we'll square up," I said as Lexie paid for our dresses. I hugged the garment bag with my prized purchase. Lexie was my fairy godmother, and I got to go to the ball.

"I'm not worried." She smiled. "I know you're on a shoestring budget."

We took our packages and threaded through the crowded mall, finding Lexie's truck in the parking lot. "How are you doing at Mike and Anne's?" she asked.

"Great! It's like flipping on a normal switch."

"What a relief," Lexie said as she started the engine. "Have you heard from Georgie?"

"Not a peep."

"No surprise." Lexie took the off-ramp for I-35 south. "You shouldn't have to deal with that. No one should."

"Living in that house scraped off layers of skin." I gave Lexie a piece of gum and put one in my mouth. "The worst part is I still want my diary from there."

"How about Katie?"

"I ... I thought about calling her at college to see if she could nab it." I blew a bubble. "But everything changed after she started the drug thing with Mom."

"No kidding." Lexie turned to me. "You know I like Katie, but you're smart to give her some space."

"You're always right on the money, Lexie." I reached over and touched her elbow.

"Of course I am. We share a brain." She laughed. "And this Saturday, 10:00 a.m. sharp—be at my house. We'll eke out every spot of sun and get some color for prom."

"Perfect! I'll have Jay pick me up at 4:00, so we can stop by his house for prom pics." My insides churned. "Remember, I'm spending the night with you if anyone asks. Mike and Anne are letting me take care of myself. I even called the school office when I overslept last week."

"You're glowy just talking about it." She fluttered her lashes. "I'm sure Jay's over the moon. I'll run interference for you."

Thirty minutes later, we turned into Mike and Anne's driveway. Jay's car waited on the curb.

Lexie laughed. "There's Romeo now."

"Romeo thinks it's been a long-ass time coming." I reached down and scratched the back of my ankle. "I just can't wrap my mind around sleeping with him. I'll need your antenna to decide if I go through with it."

"We'll flop around all damn day and analyze the situation."

"You're a riot," I said, grabbing my things, running across the front yard, and plopping into Jay's Trans Am.

For months, I'd been making excuses not to have sex with Jay. It's not that I didn't want to, but I wanted to be a good girl. A year earlier, after a painful period of severe cramps that Tylenol with codeine couldn't kick, Mom took me to her OB-GYN. He put me on birth control pills. *I love Jay, and prom's close to our anniversary. It's meant to be. I think.*

Jay's voice pulled me back to his car. He pointed to the garment bag. "Do I get a sneak peek?"

"No way! Get out!" I slapped his hand away from the gown. "You'll see it once I think you can handle it."

Jay burst out laughing.

"Lexie wanted to take it, but I'm not letting it out of my sight." I readjusted the dress on my lap. "She's covering for me. Saying I'm spending the night." I chewed my inner cheek. The reality of telling Jay I'd sleep with him made me doubt my decision. "Your brother's booking the hotel, so he'll know, but make sure no one else does. Especially not Timmy. He thinks he's your best friend, but so does every one of your football buds." Balls of chewed skin dotted the inside of my mouth. "Since it's close to our year celebration this weekend, it's a go. If you're game."

"Oh, I'm game." He smiled, showing all his teeth.

"I'm sure you are, and I think I am, too. Just don't tell your buddies, or we'll be back to playing it by ear."

"Mum's the word." He hugged me so tight I struggled to breathe. "I didn't just fall off the turnip truck, Summer Michelle."

"Don't call me that." I pushed him away and folded my arms across my chest. "Whenever I was in trouble, Mom called me Summer. But if I was really going to get it, she called me Summer Michelle." I closed my eyes and stretched my tongue over my bottom lip.

I didn't have to open them to see Jay's face. The weight of his stare made me look. His expression was tender. "Change your mind at any time, babe." He gave me a reassuring nod. His eyes never left mine. "It won't make me love you any less."

I've held out a lifetime—almost a year. I uncrossed my arms and leafed my fingers through his hair. "I'm ninety-nine percent sure it's a date."

Saturday arrived before I knew it, and right at 4:00, Jay picked me up at Lexie's. "You look like a goddess. And you smell sexy-sweet. Like spicy vanilla."

"It's my Charlie perfume." I swished my slinky dress, showing off my maroon Nina spiked heels.

Jay started his Trans Am, but before he put it in gear, he leaned over the center console and stuck his tongue in the tiny crevices of my left ear. Hollywood handsome in his dark navy suit and matching light blue ruffled shirt, he wagged his head, flashed a satisfied grin, and sped down the country road.

In no time, we were at his house. Meg welcomed me as if I

was the best thing to happen to her son. Her silky, brownish-black bob cut and red lipstick set off her straight, white teeth. She fluttered about, helping Jay pin on my baby blue rose corsage covered in white baby's breath. I didn't need any help attaching Jay's blue-tipped white carnation boutonnière before Meg made us pose for enough pictures to fill a hundred photo albums.

"The TA's waitin'. Gotta go, Mom." Jay ushered me outside with Meg still snapping photos. Jay opened my car door.

"Thanks! See you tomorrow at your birthday brunch. Remember, I'm staying at big bro's tonight." He got in on his side. Our secret plans for the night rode along with us as he turned right on Main Street. "How about all those pictures? Meg's so—"

"You mean 'Mom.'" I blew him a kiss. "You're such a hooligan."

"You have no idea." He lifted his eyebrows. "But you're about to find out." He hit the steering wheel with a laugh.

What if he tells his buds? I'm still not sure about it. He'll be so disappointed, and I'll see it on his face. No. Tonight's the night. I think. We've already planned it. At least, Jay planned it.

"You're such a comedian." I punched his bicep. "Let's split dinner."

"Nope."

"Be careful. I might just have to injure you."

"Don't make promises you can't keep."

"But you always pay for everything."

"Whatever."

"That's probably smart on your part. I still owe Lexie for my dress."

"And what a dress it is. I can't take my eyes off of you." He gaped at me. "You're just too good to be true."

I smoothed out my swooping layered gown and made a high-pitched giggle. "I'm glad you like it. I wore it, especially for you. But really, the country club's so expensive." I massaged his right ring finger as he drove. "Even if your family are members."

"Oh, Sum. Dad pays." He laughed low and long. "Courtesy of the bank."

"What?"

"What did you think happened when I signed the bill? They go straight to Dad. He's always been generous."

"Just like you."

I leaned into his shoulder and nibbled on his ear. Jay stroked my hand as we exited I-35 for 435 until he had to shift to take the country club exit.

"You know you're hot. Smokin' hot."

"You're just looking forward to tonight. I'm sure it's all about the dance and not sex."

He raised his eyebrows. "Oh, it's about the dance for sure." The buttery sun dipped low into the twilight while he swerved into Brookridge Country Club's parking lot adjacent to the green verdant golf course. Jay lightly kissed me on the lips. "I'd have run to Overland Park just to be with you tonight. And I'm not even a runner."

We made our way to the entrance and strolled across the lobby. Jay and I struck quite a contrast in our prom attire to the other forty-something country club diners as the hostess led us under an elegant chandelier, seating us at an intimate corner booth.

We sat across from each other and right away ordered drinks. I ran my fingertip over the white linen tablecloth and put my matching napkin in my lap. Soon after, the waitress brought us Dr Peppers and filled our crystal water glasses.

"Yum!" Jay smiled and sniffed the sizzling filet mignon served at a nearby booth. "Now that's what I'm talking about. I'm so ready for a steak." He clamped his hand across the table over mine. "Does that look good?"

I raised my eyebrows and nodded.

The waitress returned, and Jay ordered filet mignons, baked potatoes, salads, and orange sherbet.

"Remember, no butter on my potato."

"What?" He drew patterns on my wrist. "I thought you liked it."

"Oh, I love it."

Jay angled his head in confusion.

"I can't eat it. Growing up, Mom said it was only for adults."

He rested his hand over mine and lowered his voice an octave. "Eat as much butter as you want, Sum."

The waitress brought us our tossed salads, and we scarfed them down and then gorged ourselves on the piping hot bread. Minutes later, she reappeared with the rest of our meal. I placed a bite of the juicy, tender meat in my mouth. "I was just teasing." I batted my heavily made-up eyes. "I know you can handle my prom dress."

Jay burst out laughing, almost choking on his steak.

"Thanks for the courtesy laugh." I opened the ketchup and shook half the bottle onto my plate. "You're my E-ticket boyfriend."

"What's that?"

"It means you're one in a million." He pointed to himself as if questioning my comment. "Yes, you. It's a Disneyland expression."

At that instant, the sea of ketchup I'd just gushed on my plate reminded me of Mom's bloody face. With her eyes closed, her mannequin-like mouth poured out a crimson pool of blood. I brushed away the imaginary warm liquid that trickled down my arm. My fork fell from my fingers and clanged on the white bone china dinner plate.

Jay's voice snapped me back to the restaurant. "You're swaying side to side, babe." He leaned across the table and ran his finger over my neck. "And you've got a rash of red streaks."

"I'm okay." I fanned my face. "I just got an image of Mom's bloody fall. I never even think about it except to wonder why I don't remember what happened after I put her head in my lap."

"That's a helluva thing to carry." His voice was a whisper. He eased into the booth seat by me. "Pump the brakes on that memory, Sum."

Grasping my water glass, I took a big gulp and scooched closer to Jay. "The room's spinning. The same thing happened when my Oil of Olay bottle shattered, and I slashed my finger." I lifted my pinky.

Jay gently traced his finger over the white scar. "I'm fighting not to be barking mad at Georgie." He eliminated any space between us.

"It's not a big deal," I said. "I'm not even dizzy anymore."

"What's your dad say about it?"

"He's so preoccupied that I don't tell him much anymore. But if I did, he'd say to pull myself up by the bootstraps." We started eating again. "I look forward to our weekly calls. They're not as difficult as they were at first. I disappointed him by not living there, but he has enough problems with his marriage up a creek."

"I've always liked your dad." Jay rubbed my knee. "He's a good guy. A banker like my dad."

"And a football player."

"Like me." Jay chuckled. "Ya gotta love it."

"Sitting together during the Chiefs games at Arrowhead, Dad tried to convince me to be the first girl in Kansas on a boy's football team. I sidelined that fast."

Jay finished off his Dr Pepper. "I would've dug that."

"I wanted to be a cheerleader instead."

"Mighty benevolent of him to let you do what you wanted." Delight creased Jay's forehead as he mimicked my shocked expression at his impressive word choice. He cut a large hunk of steak. "You know it's Meg, I mean, Mom. She's got me on the word-a-week plan."

"I love Meg with her advanced vocabulary."

"I'd probably learn more of her words if she always acted like she did tonight." I placed my hand on his back, nodding with understanding.

In our booth, resembling Siamese twins, we cheered in unison when the waitress appeared and slid our sherbet in front of us. I spooned down the sugary dessert and kissed Jay, leaving some syrupy orange cream on his lips.

"Mmm!" Jay shot me a crooked smile and signed the bill, lifting my palm off the table. "Let's bail." He slid me out of the booth and put his arm around my shoulder.

Promenading out of the country club, Jay opened the double doors. We resembled proper first-class members but enjoyed the pleasure of third-class merriment. Under the clear night, I snuggled into his secure embrace just as a white light crossed the sky, leaving a long tail. Jay pointed to the heavens.

"That makes this night perfect." Leaning against his car, Jay touched my hair. I grabbed his face and gave him a minute-long kiss.

"Now, that's what I'm talking about. I've been dying for that all night."

❧

Junior prom dazzled in a nearby hotel five miles from the country club. As Jay and I entered the "Stairway to Heaven" themed ballroom, he winked at me. Light blue butcher paper, silver streamers, and glued crepe paper with cotton ball clouds decorated makeshift dividers around a large spinning disco ball hanging in the middle of the dance floor. Under the revolving, mirrored sphere, there was a sandy-colored tangled ladder. Jay and I took photos beneath the floral-scented white gazebo adorned with fresh flowers and stringed lights. Rumor had it that Timmy and Zoe got booted out for sneaking in vodka to spike the punch at the refreshment table. At least, that was the story. They may have just been no-shows.

After getting our prom picture, Jay and I hit the dance floor. A couple of fast dances later, Led Zeppelin's theme song turned the dance floor into one long, slow dance. "You're glowing."

While the background music played, Jay kissed my fingers and nuzzled me into his chest. "There's no one in the world I'd rather be with."

For half the song, we swayed together in harmony. Then, nestling my head on the level part of his shoulder, I flattened myself against him. A backdraft of heat ignited my body. I arched into him to get a whiff of his musky scent. A warm, tingling sensation spread through me.

The flashing disco ball strobe light spotlighted colored patterns on the dim-lit dance floor.

Hot orange. Hot red. Hot orange-red. Hot orange. Hot red. Hot orange-red.

I raised my head. Jay's gaze was on me. I gave him an off-the-shoulder smile. "Let's go."

"I thought you'd never ask." He swept his fingers across my lips and pulled me into him. "This's been worth the wait." Then, with his arm in the curve of my back, we exited the dance floor without saying a word.

❧

Glued to each other the next morning, Jay and I met his family back at the country club to celebrate Meg's forty-fifth birthday. Jay's dad waited outside the double doors. While the three of us made our way to our reserved table where Meg waited, Jay's brother crept up behind us.

With an unruly, Cheshire cat grin, Jay tossed his brother the hotel key so that he could check us out. As the key sailed midair from Jay to his brother, Jay's dad's blank expression flashed from awareness to hilarity.

I twirled a strand of hair, swallowing the taste of awkwardness that followed me to the lunch table to honor Meg's special day. *At least Jay's dad didn't say anything.* I wiggled my burning nose and turned to greet Jay's mom. *I don't regret my decision. I trust Jay. He'll never hurt me.*

CHAPTER 19

ENGLISH CLASS

May 1979
Junior Year
Gardner, Kansas

"Why's Mom not calling?" I wriggled my hand free from Jay's palm. "Last week, I mailed her a letter with my phone number." I fidgeted with my hair. "I should know what makes her tick, but she's tricky. I'm still trying to wrap my head around why she said nothing after Doc kicked me out."

Jay shook his head in disbelief.

"Why didn't she stand up to him? Boot his ugly ass out. Instead, she only cares about herself. I'm choking back vomit."

Jay slanted his eyes and growled.

"Steam's coming out your nose. I love how you get revved up." I shrank beside him and kissed his folded brow. "Thanks for being on my team."

"I'm always on Team Sum." He inclined his head to me. "Always."

"I need it," I said, rubbing my eyes. "I caught my toe putting on my jeans this morning and almost fell. And that's not the half of it." I picked up a rock to toss in the street but dropped it. "My legs are itchy from washing my jeans with too much detergent. Mom always did the laundry."

Jay held out his hand; I rested mine in his.

"I'm so frayed I don't even know my name. I'm on a guilt trip, panicking about blowing it and being that selfish girl Mom accuses me of."

"You're not selfish, Sum." Jay squeezed my hand. "You're being gnarly hard on yourself."

"You're right. But four weeks and not even one chirp from her." Jay and I turned onto the uneven sidewalk near the elementary school. Under the misty May morning, a canopy of tattered clouds gathered into a line of on-deck storms. "Why does it hurt so much? Why do I care?"

"Because she's your mom."

"You're right again." I pointed to the playground in the distance. "And still no Braxton since the first day when I told him I wasn't coming home. I've thought about calling him, but I don't want Mom to answer, and I sure don't want to drive by the house and see Doc."

"Last night, after I dropped you off, I did donuts through Doc's clinic parking lot."

I looked up at Jay and scrunched my nose. "You didn't have to see him, did you?"

"No, but I might have screamed some bad words at him."

"I love you for that," I said, kissing his cheek. "I just worry about Braxton."

"He'll come around, Sum." Jay raised his pointer finger in the air. "Maybe Georgie's keeping him home."

"Probably so." I took two unsteady steps backward. "To make matters worse, I don't know how to get my diary, or even if that 'Invincible Summer' quote's in there. How did I even remember it?" I shrugged my shoulders. "It's not like I'm at the library every day looking up famous sayings or something and then writing them in my diary."

Jay looped his arm through mine as I babbled on, hanging onto his bicep. His muscles flinched in corded knots.

"I just can't believe I left my diary at the ranch house. Trying to get it from Mom would be like dying from a thousand paper cuts. And I thought about asking Katie, but that's not a good idea." The overcast gray drizzle matched my mood. A light layer of condensation coated the sidewalk, giving me a whiff of its earthy scent. I curled my lips, making them disappear into my mouth. "I just want my diary. I'm like a rubber band ready to snap."

"You're not going to snap, Sum."

"Maybe I won't snap, but that diary's mine, and I want it back. *Ahhh!* But I can't figure out how or how to make Mom and Braxton talk to me." I stopped on the sidewalk and pivoted in front of Jay. "Maybe that's the reason I'm half a bubble off." I itched my arm. "Mike and Anne are super nice, and I'm thankful there's no drama, but I'm on my own, still not really in control of anything. And I can't try any harder." My forehead knitted together. "Maybe I can sneak into the ranch house and steal my diary."

Jay opened his mouth to speak and then closed it. "I know it's desperate," I admitted.

"Ya think?" He arched one eyebrow. "Let me steal it for you."

"You'd do that, wouldn't you?" I dropped my chin and kissed his cheek. "I know you would, but the diary's not that big of a deal." Tears sprang to my eyes. "The big deal is missing Braxton. And Mom not even caring."

"Oh, babe. It's all so wrong." His slow, low tone comforted me. "Just freakin' nuts."

"Thanks. I know." I flung myself under his arm. "And it's nuts that I've not heard one word from Grandmother Mema either. I'd call her, but she'd believe Mom's word over mine about how things went down. I feel like throwing a fit." I raised my voice. "It's Little Summer's fault."

Jay was silent for a moment. "Nah, Sum." He nudged me in jest. "Don't blame your spunky self."

"But she's so needy," I said.

"Nope." Jay slipped his arms around me. "She's feisty. She's my girl."

We fell into a peaceful silence, rounding the corner for the final turn to our English class's entrance. Jay rested his nose by my ear. "Ya know your silky prom gown made your eyes turn an ocean shade of green." His hot breath hovered around my face as he slid his hand under the back of my shirt, touching the bare skin between my shoulder blades. "I'll never forget that night."

"I won't either." I shaped his bangs. "Ever."

From across the playground, an elementary school boy barreled toward us. His exaggerated leg movements in gray cotton slacks made him appear to run in slow motion even though he was moving fast. Medium overgrown brown hair tugged on his navy rain jacket under his white button-down shirt and collar. The fragrance of bubble gum filled the sidewalk when Braxton met us at the point where the elementary fence and playground ended. Tucked under his arm was my Pepto-Bismol pink diary.

Jay's mouth dropped open. Slack-jaw disbelief filled my face.

"Braxton!" I belted out. "That's it!" I jumped up and down and ran in circles around Jay. "How did you know I wanted this?"

"I heard you talking about it the first day you left home." He blushed, casting a rosy hue across his face. "Last night, I decided to find it."

"Oh, thank you! You don't know what this means. I'm so relieved." I grabbed the fence and found his finger. "You're the best brother in the whole world."

"Braxton, meet us at the end of the sidewalk. The diary's too large to jam through the chain links." Jay said, pointing to the gate near the old high school building that housed the top-floor English classes. In a flickering flash, my brother disappeared.

Jay and I trucked to the end of the playground, and Braxton handed me the leather-bound book. I hugged him and gently wiped the sleep crusties out of his cornflower-blue eyes. He half-smiled before his feet pitter-pattered out of earshot over the blacktop.

"Thanks, Braxtie!" I shouted, hiding my diary under my spiral. "You're my angel."

A blinding flash of a golden white sheen lit up the sky with a crack of lightning as a surge of wind swerved through the playground. Multiple booming thunderclaps followed soon after.

Jay and I stampeded for class, dodging large drops of freezing water while we bustled toward the door. Just as the bell buzzed, we trudged over the English classroom threshold. Shaking off the rain, we took our seats. Although it was May, the heater's iron-hot odor burned throughout the classroom.

Unaffected by the two soaking students, Mr. Roberts started his lecture with a slight snort. "Since the class finished *The Stranger*," he explained right after the bell stopped, "you'll spend the entire period writing a personal narrative—a story in the first person." He scanned the class for understanding. "Since the protagonist, Meursault, limits his account to his thoughts and perceptions, you'll gird yourself to do the same by remembering that powerful writing isn't written. It's rewritten." The teacher wandered around the room while he gave directions.

"What's a protagonist?" Jay whispered.

"The main character," I murmured back without looking at him.

"What's first person?"

"Just use I."

"Summer, do you have a question?" Mr. Roberts appeared at my desk. "Or are you a Renaissance woman trying to be the teacher?"

"No." I pulled down my shirt and shook my head.

Just then, another adult peeked into the class and stepped back into the hall. Mr. Roberts rested his hand on the door frame and swung back into the room. "Talk about what you're going to write with your neighbor."

"Man, I can't believe I just got you in trouble."

"No, you saved my ass. I couldn't hold two thoughts together walking here." I held up my diary. "And you helped me get this."

Our teacher returned. "Okay, back to the narratives. No light-weight ones." The rain droned on like a broken record, beating in sheets against the window as it competed with the teacher. "Understand Camus wrote *The Stranger* from a dark place. A place of sorrow. Grief." He paused for effect. "Write about a crisis of conscience you've experienced in your brief sixteen years—or just make something up. It's due tomorrow—the start of class." He paused to make sure the students understood. "No skimpy stories. I expect stellar ones after reading Camus's tip-top literature. Don't tank your grade. If you're lost like the Donner Party was, just ask for directions."

Flipping through my diary's pages, I pretended to be paying attention as my diary's sloppy, cursive writing fanned before my eyes. Over the years, I'd skipped sheets between the journal entries and glued greeting cards into the book. But Camus's quotation wasn't there.

A noiseless figure emerged by my desk. "Summer?"

I leaned forward, slipping my diary under my spiral, then turned sideways.

The teacher gave me a paralyzing frown. "Do you know more about Camus than I do?" Glancing forward with his hands clasped behind him, he craned his neck before me.

Mom's words haunted me. "Summer's always been a problem."

With pin-drop silence, all eyes focused on me. Jay slid his foot by mine as my face flushed and then grew pale. "N-no."

Why do Mom's words still have power over me? So what if I make a mistake?

"The storm seems to have found you off your game." Mr. Robert's blank expression formed a thin line on his lips, and he returned to the front of the room. "Now, class, start writing. Camus was the last word in absurdity. Dig deep and model his out-of-the-box prose. It's a long shot, but you might write a life-changing piece."

Jay gave me a thumbs-up.

Blinking away tears, I gave Jay a sluggish smile and hunkered down in my chair, pulling out the diary. I missed the quote during the first pass-through. It was toward the end of the journal. A Crayola rainbow-construction-paper card with designer, purple calligraphy writing displayed Camus's quotation.

"In the midst of winter, I found there was, within me, an invincible summer."

The card was from an eighth-grade Kansas Leadership Program. I'd won a scholarship to the summer camp and met Barb, a compassionate counselor who left the homemade note on my bunk.

I opened the card.

Summer, in your eyes, something told me, "Here is one of these gentle people who radiate beauty simply by living." Maybe it will help to know I care. Barb

Filled with purpose, I started writing. The students' scratching pencils faded into background noise. Memories from my past tugged deep from within, pushing the scenes to the surface.

The Accident

by Summer Stevens

I tried so hard to be perfect. By the time our grandfather clock clanged seven chimes, I'd already taken the steps two at a time. Once Mom stomped her foot on the floor to summon me to the top level, I knew better than to dilly-dally.

I dropped my pencil after a coppery taste formed in my mouth. A recent memory needled my mind.

Anne had rushed home to make dinner during my second week at Greg's relatives. Before I moved in, she and Mike had never made a big deal about eating. On the cutting board, she frantically chopped potatoes. The knife had slipped and sliced her finger, causing cherry-red blood to spill over the countertop.

Whirling hot blackness had swept over me, so I steadied myself on the kitchen door frame. An image of Mom's face gushing red, gooey goop from her mouth came into view. Blinking ivory dots floated near my eyes.

"Hey, kid." Anne had waited for a beat. "You're white as a sheet. I'll be fine. I'll go wrap this and be right back."

"I'll clean up the mess," I'd said. "Then I'll whip up the best-mashed potatoes, set the table, and clean the kitchen, too."

Anne making dinner is too much. I won't put that on her. Jay always wants to take me out, so I'll eat with him.

She had returned with her finger wrapped, and we had chatted while I peeled potatoes. "Kid, you've got your color back."

"I love that you call me 'kid.'" I never knew why she called me kid, but it wouldn't matter what she called me. I just appreciated her kindness.

"Then, kid, I'm so glad you're here."

"I'm so thankful to live with you."

Mr. Roberts's voice transported me back to English. "You've been writing for ten minutes. If nothing's on your paper, it's time to panic."

I started writing again.

Thud! In slow motion, Mom's body free-fell through the air past the desk chair and face-planted without any break in her fall onto the same kitchen tile I'd earlier cleaned.

The tick-tock of the grandfather clock shattered the sickening stillness.

I charged to Mom, flipped her over, and in one movement, scooped up her head and cradled it in my lap. Ruby-red, ketchup-like blood slowly poured out of Mom's mouth and nose. Her eyes never opened.

I've got to call Zoe's mom! Dragging my mother, I scooted my butt over to the dangling telephone. Once my fingers touched the cord, I pulled the receiver to me. But how will I dial? What'll I do with Mom?

I started to weep. I tried to hold her with one hand and stretch my other toward the desk, but it was too high. I gingerly placed Mom's head on the ground, stood up, and speed-dialed Zoe's mom. "I think Mom's dead. She's bleeding all over the floor. Please hurry!"

"Don't worry," she assured me. "I'm on my way."

I hung up the phone and held Mom's head on my lap again. Days before, in health class, I learned that when people pass out, they may swallow their tongue. I fished under Mom's teeth with my pointer finger until I found it. What do I do with this slippery, wet thing now? It slid out of my hand, leaving a warm, sticky substance all over my fingers.

As Elvis's voice repeated, "Moody Blue," I kissed Mom's cool, gray forehead and milky-white cheeks. While I rocked her motionless body on my tender knee, the grandfather clock began to chime. I'm covered in blood. The antique clock chimed again.

It's all my fault.

The clock chimed a third time.

Why did I wish Mom dead? I didn't mean it!

Something like thin ice cracked under heavy footsteps. I heard my voice shout toward the sliding glass door. The spinning kitchen went black.

Buzz! The sound of the bell made me jump out of my skin. "Class's over," Mr. Roberts said. "You might have to take a canoe to your next one."

"My hand feels like it's going to fall off," I said to Jay, shaking my fingers.

"I'm not surprised. You wrote the entire period." Jay leaned over and whispered in my ear. "Way to not let Mr. Roberts piss you off." Jay rose from his chair and pulled me to my feet.

"He wants a gritty story," I sighed, "so he's getting a gritty story."

"Serves him right. He was crummy. Just crummy."

"I deserved what I got. Since Doc kicked me out, I've barely been able to concentrate." I touched my lip, tasting metal in my mouth. "My lip is split from the inside out." *How did I do that?*

"Let's get the hell out of here." He pried my fingers off my pencil and placed my books on his, guiding me outside.

Hours later, following track practice, Jay huddled around me at the drinking fountain. I couldn't get the cool liquid down fast enough. I'd just jogged off the track with my sweatshirt around my waist. My wind-weary ponytail fell over my shoulders.

"I love your natural look." Jay brushed off the water I'd splashed on my face. "It's frickin' awesome."

"You're pretty easy to please." I used my t-shirt to wipe off the sweat on my forehead.

Bending over, he pecked my lips. "Let's get away and talk." He led me up the gym stairs and over the girl's locker room to the bleachers. The crisp blue-and-white seats of our school's colors fumed with fresh paint. "What'd you write about in English that made you chew your lip bloody?"

"Mom's fall about sixteen months ago." I twisted my hair. "I don't remember what happened after her bloody head was in my lap."

"I can't believe what you've been through." He grimaced. "It's dark."

Soft light from the gym windows cast beams throughout the bleachers.

"At least the rain stopped." Jay twirled my ponytail in his fingers. "The sun's hitting your hair just right, Sum. It looks like you have gold strands in it."

"That makes up for the miserable English class." I kissed him on his right dimple. "And at least I've got my diary." I waved my newfound pink treasure. "Maybe the rest of Mom's accident is in here."

Jay rubbed my earlobe between his thumb and index finger. "Remember, no matter what, you're not responsible."

"But I feel like I am." I swatted off the salty sweat that had started drying on my arms.

"You've got to know," Jay said, "that your mom put you in a no-win situation."

"Did she?" I scooted next to him on the bleachers. "I know she started drinking, doing drugs, and fell. That's true. But maybe I did something horrible. I just don't remember." I yanked my sweatshirt off my waist, balled it up in my lap, and smoothed it across my knees. Bending toward him with half-closed lids, I asked. "What if I caused the accident?"

Jay squeezed me into him.

"Even before then, she treated me like dirt," I said, putting my hands on his cheeks. "Why?"

"I don't know, Sum. I wish I did." He slowly shook his head. "But I know you're a freakin' star for a daughter."

"My mind knows the truth. Not that I am faultless." I gulped a breath of air. "But I've tried my best, so why can't I shake off her cruel words?"

"You're fast, Sum, but no one could outrun those." He grazed his bottom lip with his front teeth. "I should read the diary with you tonight. I wish I didn't have that crappy family dinner I have to go to with Meg—I mean, Mom and Dad."

"You need to leave now, or you'll be late." I hung my arm over his neck. "You say goodbye first."

"No, you say it first." He threw his hands up. "Forget it! I'm not going."

"No! It'll be a fun family night. We'll compare notes tomorrow." I swept my hand through his silky, dark bangs, giving him a long hug. "You know you have Meg's shiny hair."

"You mean *Mom*." He broke into a deep, guttural chortle.

"Whatever."

"Wait!" His voice had an edge of amusement. "You're using my line again against me."

I put my hand over my mouth and laughed.

"Whatever." He paused. "Just go easy with the diary. You've already been through a lot. Don't push your memory too hard."

"I probably will." I hugged the diary. "I just have to remember what happened. And you know how I am when I put my mind to something."

"Oh, I know." He raised his eyebrows and moved his lips to my ear. "But it may just be too much."

I stared at the gym ceiling. "That's what I'm afraid of."

CHAPTER 20

JAY'S PLACE

May 1979
Junior Year
Gardner, Kansas

The following morning, Jay was waiting in the school lot with his back resting against the passenger-side door of his Trans Am. I stopped my car next to his and rolled down my window.

He uncrossed his feet, leaned over, and touched my chin.

"Quick, get in. I've got so much to tell you." I motioned to the parking area. "Zoe's slinking around the cars, and I don't want her to eavesdrop." I turned off my ignition and hurdled over the console to the passenger side.

"I got home too late to call." He plopped into my driver's seat. His voice caught with emotion. "That's why I'm here early."

We exchanged glances. "Great minds think alike." I wrangled his face next to mine and kissed his cheeks all over. Then I slid my tongue down his throat and gave him a real kiss.

"Whoa, girl! You're speaking my language."

"We speak the same language."

He outlined my lips with his thumb. "Now, what about the diary?"

The corners of my mouth sank. "It was a bust." I brandished my pink journal. "It started in eighth grade and lasted until the part about Mom's fall that I already remember. Here's the final entry."

September 16, 1977

Dear Diary,

I woke up in a cold, dark sweat. Last night I said horrible things before Mom passed out from vodka and drugs. She broke her fall with her face. The last thing I remember was her bloody head in my lap. I have no memory after that. Somehow I ended up in bed, but now I'm afraid to go upstairs. Maybe Mom's really hurt. Or dead. I don't know if I can tell my new boyfriend, Greg. He has such a perfect family. How could he understand? I've only let him see Mom's nice side. And Lexie's visiting her mom for the rest of the week. I would tell Jay, but he's dating Zoe.

Jay slanted one eye at me. "No wonder you didn't write about the rest of Georgie's accident. Greg doesn't know his ass from a hole in the ground." Jay jingled the keys out of the ignition and handed them to me.

"Or because I was traumatized about you being with Zoe." I gave him an emphatic nod. "Now put that in your pipe and smoke it."

Jay rested his hand on my shoulder. "I was never into Zoe. It was always you."

"Oh, I know, Jay." I pecked him on the cheek. "I'm just mad that I didn't write more. Why? Why didn't I at least tell what happened?"

"It was too much, Sum." His eyes turned tender. "Remember, you're not responsible for Georgie's fall."

"My brain tells me I am." Absent-mindedly, I repeatedly wound my shirt's enormous designer button until it popped off. "Crud." I tossed it in my ashtray.

"You have a steel trap for a mind."

"But it hasn't helped me remember, and I've tried." I thumped my manicured nails on the dashboard with a ratatat. "And you know how hard I try."

"At everything," Jay said. "Even last week, balancing that ten-cent mistake in your checking account."

"You're right. I give until it hurts, then feel guilty I can't give more." I dabbed under my eyes with the length of my forefingers, catching the tears before they fell. "You were spot on about Little Summer. She's spunky. I love my inner little-girl self."

"Me, too."

"Little Summer had a lot to tell. She's easy to spot—lots of exclamation marks."

"Of course. Little Summer's a frickin' fullback."

"Love the football comparison." I straightened the white collar of his short-sleeved shirt with the royal blue horizontal stripe. "You know just what I need." He climbed out, circled the car, and opened my door. I jumped out and leaned against his chest. "I don't want to browbeat you with my diary disappointment."

"Oh, browbeat me." Jay pressed his palms into my shoulders and massaged them. "Pleeease." He snatched my fingers, and hand in hand, we tromped across the gravel parking lot between rows of vehicles organized like a drive-in movie theater.

Once we entered the double-door entrance, Zoe followed shortly behind us.

After school, Jay and I met at the girl's locker room door.

"Sum, I forgot to invite you over tonight." Passion flashed in his eyes.

"Are you trying to get some lovin'?"

Jay thundered his deep, husky chuckle, making his dimples shake. "Always, but no. Mom and Dad are making dinner. They're not at the American Legion."

"I love hearing you laugh." I put my fingers on the dents in his cheeks. "Sounds great. I'll tell Mike and Anne."

"You're enjoying living there." Jay's face grew serious. "I'm so thankful they've made your life rockin' easy."

"Yes, when I think about us dropping off my stuff a month ago…" I licked my lips. "Can we talk truth, Jay?"

"Don't we always?"

"Yes, I guess we do." I paused. "Here's the deal: Even with all the sobbing because Doc kicked me out, it was a gift. I still feel guilty leaving Braxton, but it's a new life only worrying only about myself." I stood on my tiptoes, kissing his forehead. "I'll be late for practice, so I better let you go to the weight room."

"Don't let me keep you." He gave me the side-eye. "But let's make it clear: you're not letting me go—you're going."

"Hahaha!" I hit him on the chest. He boomeranged me back for a quick kiss and stuck his tongue down my throat. "How do you like me now?"

"Whatever," I mocked. He gave me a pleased look. "Tonight, Jay, I'm going to whoop you upside the head." I trotted away toward the outside door.

"Don't make promises ya can't keep," he yelled behind me.

The hot air was heavy, silencing the chirping birds as I stepped onto the dirt track. Inhaling the black licorice aroma from the weeds feathered throughout the grassy midfield, I released a long breath.

Running was my confidence. Dad never wanted me to feel disappointed if I lost.

"Don't take it to heart if you don't always win," he repeated. "There'll always be someone with more speed." Still, I could train harder and run faster than most girls.

After an easy warm-up jog, I practiced the starting blocks with Coach and handoffs with my relay team. While jogging my cool-down mile, the fiery sun beat through my shirt, causing a ribbon of sweat to trickle down my chest.

Greg sneaked behind me once I rounded my last curve, tapping me on the shoulder. During practice, a gaggle of girls grouped around him. As valedictorian, he was off to KU to play basketball. Since I'd moved in with his relatives, we'd barely seen each other. "Hey, Summer. Wait, I'll cool down with you."

I slowed to a walk.

"I could've watched you run all day." He flashed his self-assured smile. "You know Mike and Anne love you living there."

"They're wonderful people, Greg."

He gave me a double take. "Your tanned face and sun-streaked hair remind me of our summer together."

I wiped the sweat off my forehead and tightened my light brown ponytail. The week before, Lexie and I lit our tresses with lemon juice. "I'm so grateful for you helping—"

"Summer." Greg zigzagged his thumb down my arm and

draped his hand over my shoulder. "You know I was glad to tee up their place for you."

I tilted away.

"I'd have been a gutless wonder, going nowhere fast if I'd done nothing." Greg examined my hands. "You still have your long fingernails. I love how they clicked when we practiced free throws." He pointed at my outfit. "That's quite a get-up you got going there."

Because of the sweltering May day, I'd rolled up my clingy tank top, tucked it into my bra, and wore itty-bitty jogging shorts. "What? Oh, yes. It's so hot. You could fry an egg on the sidewalk."

He nodded his approval. "You've got a bee buzzing around that good-looking ass of yours." I stretched my neck to look and stepped aside as he swatted it away.

Did he just say I have a good-looking ass? I shifted from my left foot to my right and glanced toward the gym. *Jay'll be leaving the weight room with a perfect view.* "I'd better go. I'm so thirsty. It's painful."

"Good luck at State on Saturday."

"Thanks," I hollered back.

I scrambled to the water fountain by the gym's side door, gulping down freezing mouthfuls of water as fast as I could, letting the refreshing liquid chase away my cottonmouth. After I stood up, a massive brain freeze gripped me.

So did Jay's eyes. "Do you have anything to say?" A tendon pulsed in his neck.

"Oh, you saw Greg."

"I saw him touching your ass." His nostrils flared. "I should beat the shit out of him."

"Slurp that back." I stepped eye to eye with Jay. "You don't have a dog in this fight. There is no fight. I live with his relatives. He made it happen. I'm not about Greg. I'm about you."

"I'd rather play football with a broken finger—he held up his slanted, swollen knuckle as evidence—"than see him grab your ass like that. He needs to keep his frickin' hands to himself."

"Jay, it was a bee." I rearranged his bangs with my pinky. "He's a normal guy. I take no offense."

"But I do. I don't trust him."

"Well, you probably shouldn't." I twirled my hand in his. "But I always have a plan, and it's to be your girl."

"Sorry for sulking, Sum." He hung his head. "I just lose control when it comes to Greg."

"I get it. But if, with a finger broken in three places, you can rip off your cast and star in the last game of the season, you the man! And can do anything."

Fifteen minutes later, after showering, I zipped to the drugstore to buy chocolates. Then I lead-footed it home, changed clothes, and sped to Jay's place.

He met me at the front door and snagged me into his arms. Sweet-smelling honeysuckle inched up the trellis under the porch's wrought-iron welcome sign.

I took two steps backward and modeled my new outfit, sliding my palms into the pockets of my low-waisted jeans. "I saved all my money to buy these Calvin Klein's."

"Freakin' A." Tiny muscles around Jay's mouth shuddered with excitement. "I can't take my eyes off you." He flipped the door shut with his heel.

With my worn leather purse slung over my shoulder, I balanced the candy, depositing it on the foyer table. "What'll Meg think?"

"When you rock a pair of jeans like that"—he curled his fingers around mine and pinned me into the front door—"she'll understand. I've got to kiss you."

"What am I going to do with you?"

"Oh, I can think of a lot." He winked. "A lot."

He leaned into me and tightened his grip around me in a full-body press, depositing a smooth, patient kiss on my lips.

An electric tension tingled throughout my body. I ducked under him, smoothed down my top, and snatched back my candy.

Jay's hand rested on my skin, where my shirt wasn't long enough to cover my waist, guiding me to the mahogany table. Getting a whiff of the smoky barbeque beans, I drooled from hunger.

Meg looked up from her state-of-the-art kitchen. Behind her hung a framed poem written in her flawless calligraphy bordered by an illustrated seagull. "Are those Russell Stover candies for us?"

"Oh, yes." I handed her the box.

"Chocolate turtles! My favorite." She got out a small silver platter. "Jaybird, open them for a centerpiece."

"My mom also loves them."

"How delightful, Summer." Meg's eyes opened wide. "I've got something for you."

"For me?" I turned and pointed to the framed picture hanging on the wall. "You copied that poem and drew the bird, didn't you?"

Meg nodded.

As if on cue, Jay recited from memory:

"Dreams"

Hold fast to dreams
For if dreams die
Life is a broken-winged bird
That cannot fly.

Hold fast to dreams
For when dreams go
Life is a barren field
Frozen with snow.

"I love that poem by Robert Louis Stevenson." An ornery grin covered Jay's face.

"By Langston Hughes, Jaybird." Meg corrected him. "Not Robert Louis Stevenson."

"Whatever." Jay winked at me.

"You're such a scooter, misquoting the author of my favorite poem." Meg's red lipstick and painted nails set off her olive skin. "And you distracted me. I'll be right back."

Meg disappeared down the long hall off the living room toward the bedrooms. Returning in record time, she handed me *The Thorn Birds* by Colleen McCullough.

"You will enjoy this epic novel. It's melancholy but well-written."

"Thanks so much. School's almost over, and then we go to cheer camp, but I'll finish it by July."

"No hurry." She touched my elbow. "Keep it as long as you like." She returned to prepare dinner.

Jay pulled out a kitchen chair for me and dropped into another one. I leafed through the paperback and started reading the prologue.

"Look, Jay. It's the Langston Hughes's poem that you just recited." I held up the bookmark. "How can Meg print like that?"

Jay flipped it out of my hand. "She gets all her talent from me." He beamed at his mom. "Let's turn on some Eagles."

"Remember, Jay, when that group of us saw them at Arrowhead Stadium? Linda Ronstadt sang 'Desperado.'" I put the bookmark back in the book.

"Of course I do. I never missed a bleep of what you were doing." I inched my chair closer, resting my foot over his. "And you're bleeping worth it."

Meg's mouth turned upward while she uncovered the platter of patties. "C'mon. Let's go to the family room."

An orange-tinged sunset streamed through the large windows as Jay led me past the sleek black grand piano into one of the matching leather cranberry couches. After he turned on the turntable, he sank next to me.

On his way out to the grill, Jay's dad passed us, displaying his ground chuck hamburger creations. "Summer, how many burgers do you want? I have enough to feed our small town here."

"If you're sure, I'd love two."

He considered this for a minute. "This ain't my first rodeo. There's no spittin' way you can eat two of my beefy patties. But I'd like to see you try," he guffawed, making his silver hair shake with laughter before disappearing across the room and out the back patio slider.

I grabbed Jay's chin, staring at him eye to eye. "You know I'll eat them both."

"Oh, I have no doubt." Jay sprawled himself over me. "My money's on you."

"Hotel California" started playing.

"You know, Jay, at Mom's, I was a 'prisoner of my own device.'"

"*Was*, Sum, *was* a prisoner." He nudged me with his knee as

Meg powered on her KitchenAid mixer. When it stopped, she came to the couch, stirring the bowl of chocolate frosting. "Thank you for helping Jaybird at school, Summer."

Jay popped up and dragged his finger through the frosting. "Yum, Mom," he said, pointing to himself with his chocolatey finger, "but ya know, I'm the one tutoring my girlfriend." He scooped out another finger full of frosting before Meg shook her head and returned to the kitchen.

"Before it gets too dark, Sum, I've got to show you my pool project." Jay tugged me across the family room to the back door, but I stalled once a shadow materialized on the other side. I gritted my teeth, digging both feet into the plush, white carpet. Grayish black spots with vivid pink streaks distorted my vision, and a watery taste formed in my mouth.

"What is it?" He questioned. "Your face's white."

"I'm fighting not to pass out. Your slider reminds me of the ranch house. It's … it's so creepy. But … I … I don't know why."

"I'm here." He huddled me into his chest.

The woozy feeling disappeared. "Strange. Now I'm fine." I slipped my hand into his, and we trailed past his dad's charbroiled cheeseburgers sizzling on the patio BBQ. I took a deep breath and nodded. "Really. Show me your project."

ZZZZ! I bounced off Jay. The whip sound reverberated throughout the backyard. "'Another mosquito bites the dust,'" he said before he clicked on the lights. The extra-long kidney-sized pool and deck had a built-in stone grill and kitchen. "Check out what I've rigged up." Some sort of machine with a medical hose hung by the pool.

"I wouldn't touch that with a ten-foot pole."

"Smart." His mouth puckered. "I plug this extra-long hose into the compressor." He bebopped over to show me. "And put this other end in my mouth. Then, I never come up for air."

"Impressive." I raised my hand in a touchdown motion. "Even if it looks kinda scary."

"I plan on a lot of pool time with you this summer." He drew me close and licked my ear.

"Shush! I don't want Meg to hear us from the kitchen window. Let's help her finish dinner."

Once we ate, Jay and I cleared the table, and I thanked his parents.

"My best compliment," Jay's dad said before his son escorted me out the front door, "you devouring both those burgers. Even with your slim frame. Jay says you're a track badass, and you're going to clean house at State."

I smiled. "Thank you. Dinner was delicious."

"Hold on!" Jay hollered. "I'll follow you home. I've got a new eight-track." He turned toward the house. "I'll be back later, Mom, once Sum listens to my tape."

In all her old-world elegance, Meg appeared at the front steps. "Now, don't be too late, Jaybird." She waved. "School's tomorrow."

"I won't." He blinked innocently. "Don't worry."

When we got to Mike and Anne's, I parked my Nova and slid into Jay's passenger seat. We rolled down our windows. The berry scent from the front yard mulberry tree hovered in the car. "I wanted you to enjoy the Trans Am before Dad trades it."

"Oh, we've had fun making the tires smoke." I clapped my hands. "At least a thousand times."

"Don't I know it! Dad warned me the TA was gone if I burned through another clutch." Jay drove to our favorite make-out place: a nearby dead-end street.

"I didn't listen, and now it's good as traded."

"Are you upset?"

"No, I'll like what he gets. He always does right by me."

"He loves you so much." I adjusted his t-shirt. "And your mom adores you. So, you better get back home before they miss you."

"Sum … " His tone turned serious. "They started drinking by the time I backed out of the driveway. They won't even know I'm gone." Darkness dimmed his handsome face. I circled the top of his hand with my fingertips, then kissed the spot.

"I have something for you." A shaft of the crescent moonlight illuminated his changed countenance. "I thought you'd like my Elvis's eight-track purchase." He slid the tape into his car player. Elvis's voice cycled through several songs before "Moody Blue."

Well, it's hard to be a gambler
Bettin' on the number

That changes every time
Well, you think you're gonna win
Think she's givin' in

"What's wrong, Sum? Red streaks are all over your neck." He brushed my hair back from my face.

I plugged my ears with my thumbs as waves of gray weaved into my mind. *Why had I ever wished Mom dead?* My eyelids locked shut. A thread of a memory unraveled from deep within the wells of the forgotten night Mom fell. A wisp of a recollection ricocheted off my unconscious memory. A clock chimed. The ranch's slider emerged with barren blackness, rustling rocks, and familiar footsteps.

"Babe, I'm here." Jay hoisted himself into the passenger seat and spiraled me onto his lap. "You're freezing." He stroked my cheeks. "But your face is burning up."

"Jay! Jay!" All sounds faded away except my deep, panting breaths. "That's … That's the Elvis 45 record that played during Mom's face-plant."

I was fifteen again. Alone in the house with Mom after Doc departed. Headlights appeared on the road. They turned into the driveway. A car door slammed. *Crunch. Crunch. Crunch.*

"Someone's coming." I gulped for air and collapsed onto Jay's chest. I heaved as if I'd just finished the 440. I slumped beneath his shoulder. "I'm dizzy. There are footsteps on the rocks."

"Who is it, Sum?" He placed his hands on my head.

"It m-m-must be Zoe's mom. That's who I called. But I waited. And waited."

Something like thin ice cracked under heavy footsteps. "Some-one's there. Outside the slider." I clung to Jay. "I can't look."

"I'm with you." I inhaled the heat of his breath on my face. "You can do this."

"The car's going dark."

"You'll never be free if you don't force yourself to remember," Jay said. "This won't beat you."

I forced my eyes open, lifting them to his. "No, Mom will not win."

The door of my memory cracked open, allowing brightness to

shine through the long hallway of my mind. I flipped a limp Mom over on her back and snuggled her hemorrhaging face onto my crisscrossed legs. With her eyes shut, dense, scarlet-red, pasty blood gushed from her open mouth and nose all over the floor. It dribbled down my arm and fingers. Seconds crawled along while the record player repeated the 45 of Elvis's "Moody Blue." I teetered toward unconsciousness—hanging on for relief. "The path's stones are crunching. Someone's here."

"Is it Zoe's mom?" Jay tangled his hands around my hair and pulled my ear to his lips. "Little Summer can tell."

"I don't know! I don't know!" My child-like voice turned trance-like. "But the slider's open."

"Who is it?" Jay questioned.

I swung my head from side to side. "It's … it's … " Time passed backward.

"You're breathing so fast, Sum."

A dark shape loomed out the patio through the slider. In the kitchen light, the form of a man, chest out, restless black eyes, and a sour, scrunched-up face came into focus. The smell of hate hung over the kitchen. After a long pause, a primal scream shot out of my mouth. "'No, Doc!'"

"Oh, Sum! He can't hurt you anymore."

"But Doc's hurting Mom. She's on my lap, and he's slapping her. *Is he trying to wake her up?*" I thrashed into the fetal position. "Blood's spurting everywhere." I coughed under Jay's arm. "Doc's pulling my hair. Draggin' me away from Mom. Through the puddles on the kitchen floor. I've got to protect her. Now Doc's hitting me. Make him stop!"

"I'm here." He tensed his grip around my body.

"The blood's warm. Heavy." I wriggled back and forth against Jay. "It's smeared all over me."

"You already survived this."

"He's swinging Mom's motionless body over his shoulder. And yelling, 'Clean this bloody mess up.' It smells like Windex. There are not enough paper towels. They're all dripping with red." I sneezed three times. "Now, he's smiling. An angry smile. 'This's all your fault. Because of you, I have to help Georgie. Take her to my clinic.' He's flicking his wrist backward over his head, waving me away. Dismissing me. 'Don't turn your back on me, Doc!'"

"What a wimpy, weakling wuss."

"'Go to bed, Miss Perfect Summer. Don't you think you've done enough damage for one night?' He left out the slider. Never looking back."

"I can't believe that frickin' loser blamed you." Jay ripped his shirt over his head and wiped the perspiration off my face. "You're drenched, and you never sweat."

"He said it was all my fault, Jay."

"He's a jackass, making you feel guilty like that."

And I did feel guilty because I was furious."

"Of course, you were"

"But … but … I said mean things to Mom. I remember, Jay! I remember!"

"'*Summer, I have a whole bunch of pills and might just take all of them —right now—and you'll never see me again.*'"

"'*Don't take the pills!*'"

"'*I'll do what I want, Summer Michelle. But you'll never live with your dad even if I'm gone. I'll kill you first. He'll never have you. Bar none!*'"

"'*You don't mean that.*'"

"'*Yes, I do, baby. Yes. I do.*'"

"*You're psycho, Mom. Just plain psycho.*"

"Oh, Jay! Mom's eyes were spooky dark but ghostly white, too." I tried to swallow but gagged instead. "After that, I ran downstairs and locked myself in the bathroom."

"Oh, babe." Jay crushed me into his arms. The touch of his skin was my heartbeat to reality.

"You're brave, Sum. A warrior." He smoothed his hand over mine. "Do you know that?"

"I know till I don't." I attempted a smile. "And this is where my memory returns. I hid for an hour. That's when Mom must've taken all those drugs, then she fell, and I woke up in bed." My words were monotone. "The next morning, I tiptoed into her bedroom. She looked like Rocky once Apollo got through with him. Mom stayed in her room for a while and then was doing laundry again."

"Did you ever ask her about it?"

"No." My voice was faint.

"At least she's all right," Jay said.

"Exactly." I shivered. "If she had died after I said those terrible things, how would I have lived with myself? I felt bad enough that she had to replace her front teeth."

"But, Sum, if you hadn't gone upstairs, you wouldn't have been there to turn her over. You saved her."

"I've never thought about that."

"She'd have suffocated in her own blood."

"You're right."

"You're such an awesome daughter. Your mom is so luck—"

"No, Jay! I'm horrible!" I dug my nails into his arm. "There's more. More."

"What? What happened?"

"Mom's face has no emotion. She won't talk. She's just staring at me with those eerie eyes. 'Don't ignore me! Freeze me out! I hate you!'"

"You're here with me, babe. She can't hurt you."

"But she turned away, has her back to me, Jay."

"'*Why won't you look at me, Mom? Why don't you love me? I wish I'd never been born. I always know what you want from me, but it's too much, and I feel guilty if I don't obey. I can't do it anymore. You can't have my life. Take all those pills. I hope you die!*'"

"'*Believe you, me. I just might. Then you'll be sorry. That'd be just what you get for ruining everything.*'"

"I'm here!" Jay wrapped his arms around my convulsing body. "I'm here."

"Help! Can't—" I choked without air. "Can't … "

"Sum!" He forced me to look up. "Take a deep breath. Through your nose, out your mouth, like after a race. You're a track star. It's over. Finally."

I followed his instructions and pretended to be recovering from a 440 dash. "I-I'm okay, now." Air filled my lungs, and I involuntarily yawned, burying my head back into his shoulder. "Oh, Jay! I can't believe I thought those things, much less said them."

"Oh, Sum. I'd have said much worse."

"You would've?"

"Oh, yeah." He stroked my damp hair. "Somehow, you ran through the walls that night."

"It's true, something superhuman helped me, but now I just want to wash my eyes clean from those scary images." I nodded. "Spit them away."

"Let's do it." Jay interweaved his hands into mine, pointing them to the bright beam under the lone streetlight. "On three. Ready? Wait for the drumroll, then let's spit those memories right over there." He beat our hands on the dashboard. *Tap! Tap! Tap!* "One, two, three."

On three, the two of us spit out the passenger side window.

"Fricken' A." Moisture coated his eyes. "You're freakin' awesome. You don't even spit like a girl."

"You're just blowing smoke up my dress." I smiled weakly, tapping him on the nose.

"Now that's my idea of something." He slipped from under me and hauled himself back over the stick shift.

"I must have weighed a ton."

"You weigh nothing." He put his soggy shirt back on and paused. "You okay?"

"Because of you." I smoothed out his shirt. "But sometimes it feels like I'll never be free."

Jay's speech slowed, and he cocked his head toward me. "One race at a time, babe." His soft eyes met mine. "One race at a time."

CHAPTER 21

MEG

May 1979 – September 1979
Junior and Senior Year
Gardner, Kansas

"On your marks," the race official commanded the sprinters.
Squatting in my royal blue-and-white spandex outfit, I placed my fingers flat on the track and shook my right foot, positioning it into the starting block. I followed suit with my left and then backed into the blocks. Brushing off the reddish-orange tartan track particles, I set my hands behind the starting line. The spring sunlight warmed my head, and a brisk breeze blew through my light-brown pigtails.

Forty-eight hours after Jay helped me remember the rest of Mom's accident, I arrived in Wichita on pins and needles for the Kansas State Championship Track Meet. Earlier in the competition, without enough pure speed for the 100-yard dash, I was happy to make the finals even if I didn't medal.

An hour ticked by before my 440-relay placed third. Then, with two hours to rest, I blazed through the 440-yard dash, winning gold, setting a state record, and dreaming about a full-ride scholarship to The University of Kansas.

"Set." Runners froze into their starting positions. With my butt high, I contorted into a crouched position, leaning forward, ready for my favorite and last race: the 220-yard dash. As my silver "S" necklace dangled under my chin, the crack of the gun's smoky smell signaled the start of the race.

My hamstrings burst from the blocks, accelerating me around the curve into first place down the straightaway. My pendant swung across my tightening chest as I dug deep within for snatches of air to catch my second wind. Despite my rubbery legs, numb arms, and tired jaw, I edged out my competition for gold with a record pace.

Jay and I celebrated at the Dairy Freeze a day later. "I'm sorry I couldn't watch my girl kick ass at State." Jay turned over my two gold medals and one bronze. "Way to set two records." He kinked his neck to the side. "It really pissed me off. Dad made me trade cars yesterday. He was petrified the Cutless 442 Coupe would be gone."

"You were there in spirit." We sat in his new car with the familiar fast-food aroma and munched double cheeseburgers and fries. "But I still missed you." I swallowed and leaned over, giving him a salty kiss. "You're my best cheerleader. I can't wait to be yours for football this fall." I patted the passenger side white door. "I love the black stripe. Snazzy wheels, too. What's the year?"

"It's a '77. The sport rims are different from the TAs but just as cool." I gave him a high ten and readjusted myself, knees to my chest.

"After annihilating the competition, you seem kinda down, like you need some TLC."

"Don't I know it? Dad kinda freaked me out at State."

"Why?" Jay took a swig of his Dr Pepper.

"Maybe it's his divorce." I looked at my hands. "I don't know. To use his own words, 'He plays it close to the vest.' But I think it's because he's drinking a lot."

"What makes you think that?"

"When I spent the night with him before he drove me to State, his kitchen trash can overflowed with empty beer cans and scotch bottles."

"That's rough, babe." Jay took a handful of fries and stuffed them into my mouth.

I gulped my drink and chewed enough to talk. "I want him to

be happy, date again and remarry. But his drinking's such a bummer," I said. "Remember after prom, your football dinner?"

"Mmm ... prom and that slinky, blue dress." He bent over and sucked my bottom lip.

"That makes everything better." I grazed his forehead with my lips. "Anyway, I thought it would be a good time to check on Dad." I turned my nose up. "Did I already tell you this?"

"I don't mind hearing it again."

"I hate repeating myself." I shook my head. "Well, I didn't tell you this part. After work, he came home from his successful high-paying VP bank job and got wasted."

"You just described my dad." With a guilty look, Jay shrugged his shoulders. "I guess I'm sorta like them. I love when we party. Tracks over, so I'm stoked we can drink together again."

"I like partying with you but never want to be my parents." My palm bumped my eyebrow. "Dad didn't think I knew his large, plastic cup was full of Scotch." I lunged into Jay's lap. "Thanks for letting me vent. You're just what I needed."

~

A couple of days later, Jay and I entered the sidewalk by the elementary school. "Look, Sum, here comes your brother."

Braxton waved across the playground, dodging an incoming rubber ball. Despite his brand-new jeans and bright red striped shirt, he was a poster boy for neglect, with his rumpled hair uncombed and his yellow teeth unbrushed. Shoes untied, he stumbled toward us like an adorable puppy and stuck his right thumb and finger through the fence to touch mine.

"Mom wants you to call." He tipped his head toward me. "Says you need to see her counselor." He freed his fingers and ran away.

"Braxton is Mom's messenger boy, but has he eaten today?" I closed my eyes. "It makes me want to barf."

At last, school was over. I rushed home to phone Mom. *She finally wants to talk. I'm not a jilted prom date anymore.* Braxton answered. "She's not here."

He's lying. I always covered for Mom when she ducked the telephone and made me say that she wasn't home. "I don't want to lie, Mom," I used to argue. "Can't I just say you're not available?"

"Don't cross me, Little Miss Know-It-All. Get off your high horse and do what I say."

The dread in Braxton's voice snapped me back to the phone call. "Mom's just … just …."

"You don't have to fib," I told him. "I'll call back."

"Okay." Braxton's voice was weak as water. "She's taking a bath."

"Thanks, Braxtie." A sob shook me. *I miss him so much.* "It's so great to hear your voice."

"Gotta go."

"I know."

Fifteen minutes passed, so I called again. Mom answered. "Meet me tomorrow to see my psychiatrist."

"You sound horrible."

"How should I sound? How could you just leave like that?"

"What could I do?" My words rose with each syllable. "Doc kicked me out. Did you even know?"

"I know you're lying. He said you just left." She let out a sigh. "Why bring that up anyway? I'll pick you up tomorrow at 4:00 at Pizza Hut." The receiver clicked dead.

I called Jay and then Dad.

"It's okay, Dad." I rocked back and forth, my feet making indentations in the carpet. "It'll just be a couple of hours. Mom says the therapist wants to meet me, and that's a big deal because he usually just doles out medicine."

"Watch the gifts. That's the beginning of the end. She'll get her hooks back into you. A leopard doesn't change its spots in her upside-down world of 2+2=5."

The following day after school, I stopped by Jay's before meeting Mom. "I'll be fine," I assured him. "What can she do?"

"A lot." He rocked me like a hammock, murmuring in my ear, "Stay alive. You're jumping back into the snake pit."

"I'd rather be having dinner with you."

"Then do it." Jay swooped me up in his arms and twirled me around. "Why can she just snap her fingers and Shazam? You jump."

"I wish I knew," I said as he set me back on my feet. "Even with all that's happened, I'm still excited to see her."

I took off for Pizza Hut on the edge of town and found Mom waiting in her red Corvette and holding up a new outfit and matching sandals. *I love her taste in clothes.*

"Go try them on in the bathroom. Right now, or we'll be late." I shut off my engine, slamming the door on Dad's warning.

A few minutes later, I returned to her waiting in the car. "The outfit's fantastic, but I think the sandals—don't get me wrong, I love them—might be a little big."

"Are you sure?" Annoyance stretched across her face. "Just wear them. You look fabulous."

I put my head down. "M-maybe you're right."

I tossed my old outfit in my Nova and opened Mom's Corvette, and she started the car. "You just left." Mom's lips puckered into her little girl's voice. It sounded funny in her red leather pants but seemed appropriate with the cat face plastered on the front of her shirt and the feline's tail on the back. "And you really hurt my feelings."

"What should I have done?" I twisted my "S" necklace. "Doc kicked me out. And for over a month, you never called."

"I didn't know."

"But Braxton said you found the note explaining everything. And I mailed you my new number." *She believes her lies.*

"I've been busy. Doc's back. Our counseling's working." Her aqua eyes were a symphony of perfection. "But you wouldn't know. You moved in with that awful couple."

"You mean Mike and Anne—the saints who took me in?"

"Let's just go from here." She gave me the once-over. "You look dynamite in that outfit. Good thing you don't have Zoe's giraffe neck. She even walks like one."

"Zoe's a mean girl but doesn't have a giraffe neck." I applied lip gloss. "Did you know last weekend I set two state records?"

"Oh! Oh! I forgot to tell you. I started running."

"That's great, Mom."

Thirty minutes later, we meandered through the atrium's swaying trees and cascading waterfall ahead of arriving at the psychiatrist's door. "This swanky doctor usually doesn't take clients, but he's making an exception. Zoe's mom put it all together," Mom said before he welcomed us into his menthol-scented, dark-paneled office.

"This is my A-honor roll, track-star daughter," Mom announced while we sank onto the doctor's leather couch. "But she's always bugged."

What?

"To borrow Shakespeare: 'The lady doth protest too much, methinks.'" The short, fifty-something man with cropped chestnut hair and thick tortoiseshell glasses ignored Mom. Instead, he turned toward me. "I can read the writing on the wall. Tell me about Doc."

"I don't think he treats Mom right." I blinked my eyes to stop the waterworks.

The psychiatrist cocked his head with understanding and waddled over to me, handing me a box of Kleenex. "How?"

"Mom allows Doc complete control. He knows she's desperate for him to stay home, so he leaves. She drinks to forget. That makes her insecure. Then Doc treats her worse. The pattern repeats. It's hard to watch." I dabbed my eyes with a tissue. "I don't like Doc. But I love Mom."

"Bravo!" He lit the pipe in his mouth and freed a hazy cloud of smoke. "You're too young for Don Quixote, but your mom is tilting at windmills, trying to make Doc change. You see this because you're more self-actualized than she, overcoming the Four Horsemen of your family's apocalypse."

I don't understand what he's saying, but he seems to understand me.

"No wonder I pay you so much an hour." Mom threw back her head and laughed. "You're sharp as a tack."

"Thank you, Georgie. Your compliments are flattering." He pulled the pipe out of his mouth and set it down. "Your daughter was right to throw down the gauntlet and leave." He nudged his glasses up his round nose. "She's the perfect case study of divorced children. Fast becoming a mini-adult, she's the by-product of her adult conversations. But, unfortunately, this maturity is the price of her childhood. Your daughter's the only one who knows what's happening. You pull her in only to push her away, thus making her feel responsible."

"I adore her. She's always been smart. Strong."

Why's Mom not embarrassed that the doctor agrees with me? I glanced back and forth.

"Much more like me than her dad." Mom gawked at him like a schoolgirl.

What? Now, I'm like her.

The psychiatrist scratched his silvered, bristly beard and pivoted to me. "You don't need to return. How you've managed to be so well-adjusted, I don't know. You've cheerfully defied the odds despite your contingent of obstacles." He turned toward me. "Do you have any questions?"

Where do I start? My memories from Mom's accident. Trying to be perfect. Feeling insecure when I disappoint people.

"No, I'm good." *Mom wouldn't want me to talk about myself.*

"Final point: All roads lead to Rome." The therapist bent forward. "Or, in your case, Summer, all roads lead to Georgie. Give her back her nervous sorrow, and you're free." He stood up. "Once you two take off, I'll round up the usual suspects."

He laughed before his fat fingers closed the door. *I don't understand everything he said, but I'm glad I came.* My emotions jumbled together. *What do I do with these feelings now?* I scratched my elbow, putting them out of my mind.

On the way home, Mom gushed, "I can't believe how much he liked you. I always knew you were something else. I love you so much."

"Thanks, Mom." *It's hard to enjoy Mom's attention when I'm only as good as the last thing I've done.* "I wonder what Jay's doing?"

Mom's voice pitched with a slight inflection. "He's probably with a gorgeous girl."

Why would she say that?

"Watch him, Summer." She turned her head toward me and said, "The apple didn't fall far from the tree."

"What do you mean?" We were almost at Pizza Hut.

"His parents are complete drunks. Alcoholics."

"Jay's not like that." *But you are.*

"Don't be so sure. He'll let you down."

"He's not much of a drinker." I lied, squirming in the bucket seat.

Silence ticked loudly until Mom blurted out, "At least you got my long waist." She shook her head in disgust. "It'd have been a crying shame if one of those dwarfed short ones ruined your fabulous figure."

Why does my mother say those things?

Mom didn't call the following day or the next, and by the end of the week, our junior year had ended.

On the first Monday of summer break, Jay took me to get my wisdom teeth removed. Even though I never wore Mom's sandals again, I rubbed the blister's scar on my foot as he drove to Overland Park. Dad met us at the oral surgeon's office to get my four impacted teeth removed, paying the three-hundred-dollar bill with my July and August allowance.

Once the elderly nurse ushered me into the surgery room, Dad left. I chewed my fingernails. *Why's Dad making Jay take care of me?* The doctor finished the procedure, and the same nurse guided me into the waiting room. Through the haze of heavy drugs, I vaulted using a cheerleading stunt into Jay's arms; he closed them around me. I rubbed his back. "Your muscles are enormous!"

Then I completed a perfect dismount with a dramatic dance. When Jay finally captured me, I belted, "I love you."

He put his finger over his lips, so I mouthed, "I love you."

Then, quick as a cat, Jay captured my teetering, wiry body, flopped me over his shoulder, and carried me to his car before I passed out.

"I can't believe Dad confiscated all my summer money," I said after Jay changed the blood-soaked gauze packs from my mouth. My head felt like knitting needles had stabbed it.

"I can help there."

I'm flat broke. My new $2.35-an-hour lifeguard pay will not cut it either. How will I buy my class ring, senior pictures, and cheer uniforms? I can't ask Mom or Dad for money, so I'll have to spend less.

"No, I'm good with money, Jay, but thanks," I mumbled and fell asleep on his couch.

Once my teeth healed, I started my lifeguarding job at the city pool. Braxton turned up by my chair. My ten-year-old brother strutted around the pool, acting like Mr. Popular, whose horde of friends had just left, but I was his only friend. Braxton didn't tan well and didn't even like the water. Still, he spent the day with me. Later that night, Jay and I took him to the drive-in.

"Katie flunked out of college," Braxton told us. "She's switching schools."

"What a bummer, Braxtie. I haven't seen her since I started lifeguarding."

Grandmother Mema will foot the bill for Katie's new college. But I better get that track scholarship because she won't pay for mine. "How's Mom?"

Braxton looked straight ahead. "She spends most days sleeping on the couch."

"We love you being with us. Plan on a movie a week, Braxtie." I ruffled his hair. "Just not next week. I leave for camp tomorrow."

After we dropped Braxton at the ranch house, Jay drove slowly back to town. "Pack me away in your camp bags, Sum." His head hung low. "I'm going to count the seconds until you return."

"Me, too." I twirled his hair while he drove.

Bright and early Monday morning, the cheerleading squad drove twenty-five minutes to Baker University for four days of showcasing our routines. The private, prestigious liberal arts school in Baldwin enjoyed leafy green grounds and New England-style brick buildings.

"Okay, this gymnasium's full of screaming girls who want to take home a spirit stick," I said to the squad on the last day of camp. "As head, I'll do everything to continue our three-year streak and take home another spirit stick for our school's trophy case. And since we just gave the performance of our lives, we've got it in the bag."

During the night, there was a disturbance by a gang of drunken boys who stormed the campus.

One of those boys repeatedly hollered, "Summer!" in the center of campus, imitating the original *Rocky* movie.

A staff member pulled me aside the following morning to ask if I knew who'd shouted my name. I shook my head, but my face tightened like a snare drum. We didn't take home a spirit stick.

I let the squad down. It's on their faces. Mom's sixth sense knew Jay drank too much.

When I arrived home, Jay waited in Mike and Anne's driveway.

"Hi, babe. How was camp?"

"You're on my list." With one hand on my hip, I waggled my finger at him. "Don't 'babe' me. Don't even try it."

He gave me his charming, deer-in-the-headlights look.

"Screaming for me like Rocky did for Adrian? On Baker's campus? Really? We saw that movie together, remember? You imitate Sylvester Stallone all the time."

He said nothing.

"This isn't a movie, Jay. It's our life. I can't have a life where I'm in love with a drunk. Not after my parents. And I won't talk about yours."

Jay spoke for the first time, scrunching up his nose. "I blew it."

"Stop while you're behind." I had Jay on the witness stand. "You were selfish. Perfect! Now I sound like Mom." I stomped my feet. "I'll never be my mom."

"I wasn't trying to be selfish," he said. I'd cut him to the core. "I thought you'd feel special hearing your name in front of all the cheerleaders. And I missed you. We'd never been away from each other that long."

"You're right," I agreed. "We're always together." The pain on Jay's face tugged at my heart.

"Sum, let's hop in the car and talk."

We got into his Cutlass and drove to the Dairy Freeze.

"Jay, since track ended, I've only drunk enough for people not to question why I'm not drinking." I looked down, putting my hand like a visor over my hairline. "I've seen enough alcohol and drugs to last a lifetime. You know I never want to take drugs and might not even drink anymore."

He parked near the payphone.

"I finally stopped slapping myself, but now I want to slap you. What were you thinking?"

"I wasn't. We all got wasted, and I let Timmy and the guys convince me to go. It was a stupid idea all the way around." He pointed to his face. "Go ahead. Slap me right here. It'll make me feel better."

"You wouldn't hurt a fly, Jay." My voice dropped. "But what do I tell my squad?" I paused to get a breath. "I don't even really care about the stupid spirit stick, but I care about you drinking too much."

"It won't happen again," Jay said, covering both of my hands with his. "I promise, Sum."

"Are you sure?" I snapped my hands back. "Life is about hard work and not just partying and football. You have a great personality, but I don't always want to have to ride your ass."

"I love when you trash-talk me." He chuckled. "No, really. You sound like Mom."

"I love Meg. And I love you, but you've always been a handful."

"I am a handful." His face jiggled with laughter. "Ya got that right."

"I can never stay mad at you for long."

He shifted a strand of hair out of my eyes.

I put my head near his. "I've got to get to work. We don't want one thing to lead to the other."

"Oh, let's do," he said with an open-lipped grin, "let one thing lead to another."

I kissed him on the lips. "I'm sorry I freaked out about the spirit stick. I wanted to win one my senior year, just like being Homecoming Queen. Kinda shallow, I know. But I can't lie to you."

"Don't ever lie to me." He sighed with relief. "Even though you didn't get your spirit stick, I have no doubt you'll be Homecoming queen."

The first Saturday after the spirit stick fight, Jay and I stayed away from his partying buddies and timed it just right during his parent's absence to take advantage of the empty house. The second week, we repeated the pattern, so by the third Saturday, on a clear, warm, late June night, when Jay picked me up, he had a Cheshire cat grin on his face.

"Where are Meg and your dad tonight, you naughty boy?"

"They're at the annual Country Club Summer BBQ Bash." He raised his eyebrows. "And won't be home until late."

"Say no more." I batted my lashes. "It's a date."

Ring! Ring! Ring! "I don't care who's calling." Jay lifted his head as we were making out on the family room couch. "I'm sure not answering it." Jay set his jaw. "If it's important, they'll call back."

At 9:30 p.m., the doorbell rang.

We hadn't moved.

"Mmm ... I hate to stop, but I better get that. Don't even breathe. I'll be right back." Jay raised his pointer finger. "You can count on it."

"Man, I'm sorry about your mom," Timmy muttered to Jay.

I bounced off the sofa, smoothed my matted hair with my hand, and ran to Jay. Timmy's burly body leaned against the front door. He scratched his sandy blond hair and lifted his downcast gray-blue eyes, refusing to look at Jay. "Your dad called mine. He couldn't get you on the phone."

Jay shot me a glance. "What's wrong with Mom?"

I clutched Jay's hand. It was ice cold.

"I don't know," Timmy answered. "You're supposed to follow me to the hospital."

"You'll come, right?" Jay turned to me and asked.

"You know it."

Jay got his wallet and keys, and we headed for his Cutlass.

After parking the car, hand in hand, Jay and I sprinted toward Suburban Medical Center. The hospital's impeccable landscaping and expensive brick buildings felt more like a hotel than a hospital. Racing by the flags waving in the wind, we entered the circular-covered lobby to find Meg's room.

Days later, we learned that a deer had hopped into the road while Jay's dad was driving home from the country club. He tried to swerve but still hit it. Somehow Meg fell out of the family's pickup.

Questions circulated around town: Were Jay's dad and mom arguing? Were they drunk? Did Jay's dad see the deer? Was there even a deer? Did Jay's dad push her, or did she jump?

Ugly rumors refused to be silenced. I didn't listen or let anyone repeat them. I never found out what happened. Maybe Jay did. I didn't ask. It may have mattered to some, but not to me. The only thing that mattered was Meg. She was in a coma.

I'll be there for you, Jay, just like you were for me.

The following week, Jay and I got on each side of Meg's hospital bed and cheerfully chatted with her even though she didn't speak. His mom never responded but squeezed Jay's hand as he tenderly stroked her shiny, dark hair.

"Meg, your fingernails are so long," I said over her still body when Jay's voice cracked. She squeezed my hand, and I sniffed the hospital's disinfectant odor through my tears. "When you leave, they'll look like you've been at a salon." Meg's high cheekbones framed her closed eyes and mute mouth.

Jay and I stayed positive with our optimistic personalities, week after week, clinging to hope that soon she'd be better. "It's like Camus's quote," I told Jay when we left the hospital from our Saturday visit. "Your mom's in the winter of her injury. But soon, summer's coming, and she'll walk out of here. If she can squeeze our hands, she must be getting better."

But Meg didn't get better. Even though her cuts and bruises healed from her late spring injury, her brain didn't. Spring turned into summer, and summer disappeared into early fall, cluttering the hospital's grounds with colorful autumn hues. Amidst a backdrop of windblown leaves and barren trees, the naked landscape foreshadowed the coming bleak winter.

During our next visit, Jay and I were on each side of Meg's hospital bed while a janitor sterilized the back counters. Blurry black dots hijacked my vision, making my fuzzy head heavy.

Before I knew it, Jay whooshed over me on the ground. "Sum! Are you okay?"

"Absolutely!" I popped back up and swished spit around the paper taste in my mouth. "I'm good." I took a deep breath. "That cleaner reminded me of Mom's face plant. At least I haven't had any other flashbacks."

The following Saturday, on a cool September morning, Jay stood with a weighed-down heart at the foot of Meg's hospital bed. Without speaking, I inched my way to him, keeping my arms at my side, and gently rested my head on the curve of his neck. We stood motionless for a few minutes, then he raised his arm and wrapped it around my shoulder.

Finally, I left the room to give Jay time alone with his mom.

When I returned, he was gone. I found him around the corner, leaning back against the wall, resting his face in his hands.

Soon after, Meg started slipping away the night before Jay's birthday. Jay's dad told the doctor, "Tomorrow, my son turns seventeen. Do everything you can to keep his mom going." The following night at 1:00 a.m., Jay's mom passed peacefully with Jay, his dad, and his brother at her bedside.

Now it was my turn to comfort Jay. His football team helped, too. They taped Meg's name on their helmets. *I'll be Jay's rock like he was mine.*

Once the funeral was over, we headed to Jay's house. In the sky, swollen clouds of darkness competed with the sun, trying to break through the forest of moisture. The gray hovering mist seemed to know the woman of the house would never return.

Although the sun gave a valiant effort to shine, tiny raindrops pinged into a steady drizzle. At the reception, Jay and I comforted relatives and consoled his dad. Then, when Jay's father wanted to speak with Jay alone, I wandered toward the front yard's oversized oak tree.

Sooner than I expected, Jay strolled out the front door. He leaned forward and bent down, picking up a tawny leaf from the front steps. Then, lowering his eyes and fixing them on me, he tilted his head toward his Cutlass. I met his gaze and slightly lifted my chin, meeting him in the driveway. We got into his car and drove away.

Once Jay dropped me off at home, he staggered back to his car with uncharacteristic depression.

Feeling the weight of Jay's grief, I opened Mike and Anne's door. They were already in bed. I headed straight to my room. Meg's half-read *The Thorn Birds* book lay on my nightstand by my king-sized bed with the sky-blue quilted bedspread and matching shams.

I opened the book and thumbed through it: Meg's calligraphy bookmark drifted down to my bedspread.

"Dreams"
by Langston Hughes

Hold fast to dreams
For if dreams die
Life is a broken-winged bird
That cannot fly.

Hold fast to dreams
For when dreams go
Life is a barren field
Frozen with snow.

Meg, with her fierce love for her family; Meg, the broken-winged bird whose dreams died too young; Meg, whose home would now be forever frozen with snow, was gone.

Oh, Meg, I'm so sad.

I returned the book to my table and got into the shower, letting the hot water wash away my tears. I cried for Jay and the loss of his mom. I cried for Meg and the loss of her family. I cried for myself and fear of being unable to help Jay.

After turning off my bedside lamp, I lay wide awake. I flattened the pillow over my stomach, staring up at the ceiling. A lone tear slid down my ear onto my shoulder. I put the pillow over my head.

What'll happen to Jay without his mom?

CHAPTER 22

HOMECOMING

October 1979
Senior Year
Gardner, Kansas

"Lexie and I both made Homecoming court!" With my hands on his shoulders, I used Jay as a springboard, jumping up and down. Immediately after school, I read the list posted by the hall office. "Zoe and Chloe are the other senior attendants." I fixed Jay's hair with my fingers. "Good for them, but let's hope they keep their horns hidden."

Jay spun me around by the waist. "You rock, Sum."

He set me back on my feet, and I danced down the hall, pulling him beside me. "All four of us senior girls date football players, and since only the team votes, any one of us could be queen," I said as Jay accompanied me to cheer practice before hitting the weight room.

A couple of seconds later, I chased him around the corner. "But you're the cutest football player of all." I kissed him on the cheek. "I've known that since cheering for you during sixth-grade pee-wee football." I tilted my mouth near his ear. "If I'm not queen, though, it better be Lexie. Not Zoe."

That night, I phoned Mom to tell her the exciting news. "I have the most fabulous Homecoming outfit, Summer. Wear it, and you'll be queen for sure." I twirled the phone cord in my fingers. *Dad says Mom's gifts have strings. And since the team votes before the game, her outfit doesn't matter.* "Come home and try it on."

"Thanks! I'll let you know. Homecoming's an eternity of two weeks away."

Unfortunately, my packed schedule didn't distract me from every five minutes imagining, "And your 1979 Homecoming Queen is—Summer Stevens."

Still, life went on as usual, so prior to the first Friday home football game, Jay's dad grilled beefy BBQ cheeseburgers. Jay tried to act excited, but a dreary stillness whittled away the time until we left for the game.

"I'm sorry, Sum." Jay's dull eyes darted all over the road driving to the stadium. "These home games make me miss Mom."

"Of course they do, babe."

Jay parked underneath a tree with thick orange leaves seemingly dipped in red paint and opened my car door. I squeezed him tight before he said goodbye.

I stole a look back at him. Wandering through the bright floodlights, he turned into the football field's locker room while the band's pregame show serenaded the stands with a cacophony of drums and cymbals. The overhead speakers harmonized Queen's "We Will Rock You."

My pleated cheerleading outfit flared up as I spun back around, so I smoothed my skirt over my royal blue tights and jogged to the gym, breathing in the crisp autumn scent. The cheer squad made space for me in their warm-up circle formation. After stretching, I slid into the splits, and something like a paper tearing crinkled through my right hamstring.

I jumped up as if someone had just yelled fire and shook my right leg. There was a slight throbbing in the area that attached my glute to the hamstring, but I gradually glided back down into the splits and sprang up again, sprinting in place.

I'm not in pain, so I must be okay.

Later that night, cheering at the game, Jay and I made eye contact. My leg didn't bother me, so I put the strange incident aside.

The next weekend, I drove to the ranch house to check out

Mom's fancy designer velvet suit and raw silk blouse. Thankful for her generosity and the opportunity to see Braxton, I still panicked about seeing Doc, so I took my secret weapon: Jay. Since Meg's shocking accident, Jay and I spent every waking moment together.

When I told Dad that Mom had offered me her emerald-green outfit, there was a lull in the conversation. "Put a pin in it, Summer. Think about it. It's a Trojan Horse." But I was in a pickle with no budget and Dad not offering any. I didn't even have ten cents to spare.

I filed those thoughts away once Braxton rushed to meet us. I hurled myself out of the car toward my baby brother. My right hamstring tweaked, so I shook my leg as if preparing for a race before smothering Braxton with a hug until he turned blue. I inhaled his gum's fruity smell and ruffled his cowlick.

"You always hug him like that, don't you?" Jay asked, watching me smooth Braxton's hair. "What a smile—both of yours."

I nodded my head, turning the corner toward the house. Mom stood at the slider. Even with her hot pink lipstick and powder blue signature eye shadow, she couldn't hide she was loaded. "Marvelous! You're here. Quick! You're going to die over my outfit!"

In no time, I modeled it for Jay. His eyes popped out of his face. "Sold!" I said, smiling at him.

We got ready to go, and Mom followed us to the door. "Braxton, Katie, and I will be at the game." Jay opened the glass sliding door and stepped down the cement steps onto the patio. "And maybe Doc."

I hugged her. "I haven't seen Katie in forever. How's she doing?"

"Not good." Mom's smile disappeared. "She's partying at college number two. How she got started doing that, I'll never know."

I bit my tongue. *How can Mom say that with a straight face?*

Jay put his hand on my back. "We better go, Sum," he urged, draping my Homecoming clothes over his shoulder.

"You're right, Jay." I turned to Mom. "I just love the outfit. Thanks! It's more than I could've expected."

"You'll be queen." Mom trailed behind us. "I saw Zoe's outfit. Her long legs and short waist make her look like an ostrich."

Jay's mouth fell open.

"Sheesh, Mom! Zoe's a cute girl. We've got to give her that. Even if she stabs you in the back every chance she gets."

"Eww!" Mom's voice went high. "So touchy. You must be scared about her being queen."

What do I say to that?

Like clockwork, I turned to Braxton and squished him into my arms, tousling his hair before hopping into Jay's car.

"That's some get-up," Jay said as he drove back to town. "You're a freakin' brick house."

I thought about Homecoming a million times a day until Friday, and then I was so excited I couldn't think at all.

After school, I beelined home, distracting myself by organizing my sock drawer before getting ready. Finally, I took a shower, blow-dried my hair, and used hot rollers to thicken it. I matched sparkly green eyeshadow and thick liner with extra mascara to make my eyes pop.

Dressed and ready with full makeup, and teased-out hair, my spicy perfume filled the car as I drove to school. Before I met the other attendants in the cafeteria to take our places on the Homecoming platform, I trekked down to the bright orange lockers at the end of the hall for the math homework that I'd forgotten to grab earlier in the day.

Zoe found me swinging open my locker. She wore a purple velvet suit with a cream silk blouse that complemented her updo of ringlets. Mom told me she'd gone to Overland Park to have her hair and makeup done, and it showed.

"You look like a beauty pageant winner," I said, gesturing with my math book. "I've got a test on Monday."

"You're the queen, Summer. You won. I just had to tell you."

I bunched my eyebrows together in confusion.

"You shouldn't be surprised. Jay's quarterback and team captain. Of course, the football team chose you."

"Thanks for the vote of confidence." I balanced my book under my arm, shut the door with my elbow, and rotated to face Zoe. "But you must be mistaken."

"And you must be fake. No one can be as bubbly as you." Zoe shook her head, but not a strand of hair moved. "Just kidding. But not about being queen. I saw the roses with your name in Mr. Roberts's room."

Zoe was tight with Mr. Roberts. Not only did he teach English, but he also taught Yearbook and Newspaper and seemed omniscient, knowing everything about everyone.

She fired her shimmering smile. "So happy for you, Summer." She leaned forward and hugged me, book and all. "Don't tell anyone I told you." With that, she toddled back down the hall.

A pinball frenzy beat in my stomach, but I wouldn't let Zoe's hoopla throw me off, even though my favorite perfume soured in the air. My mind refused to believe Zoe's announcement, but my heart was another matter. She reminded me of Mom. *I don't trust her, but I want to.*

I headed back to the cafeteria and found Lexie. "You're gorgeous." She wore a light gray suit with a white-and-salmon-striped blouse. My bestie's eyes flickered with delight. She'd also hot-rolled her hair; it was a thick, wavy work of art. "Let's go do this."

A rosy hue hung over the stadium and the surrounding thick, fall-colored trees. Oily popcorn popped from the concession stand while the Homecoming procession climbed the stairs to the elevated stage in the swaying bleachers. Queen's "We Are the Champions" blared out the speakers for background music.

"So, I've been thinking," I said to Lexie as we sat side by side. "We're *I Love Lucy*'s Ethel and Lucy; our moms are the factory bosses. Just when we think we have their issues wrapped up, their problems speed up the conveyor belt, and their lives throw us off balance."

Lexie faced me. "I stopped stuffing myself sick with Mom's crap long ago. She won't be here."

A hilarious vision of Lexie and me cramming chocolates in our mouths made me grin. "My mom will. If it gets ugly, tackle me, and put me out of my misery." She bowed.

With Lexie's never-ending entertainment, the first half of the football game ended before I realized Mom had not appeared. Without time to think about it, I followed Zoe, Chloe, and Lexie, who trailed the underclass attendants. Our fathers waited in convertibles, inviting us to enter our coach as ladies-in-waiting. My father tailgated Lexie's dad, chauffeuring me around the track as I sat on the seat's backrest of the borrowed baby blue Cadillac. The harvest moon smiled down on Jay in his number-sixteen jersey as he looped his arm in mine and escorted me to the mid-field crowning stage near Lexie.

Mom's a no-show. I'm so disappointed.

"Look out, Sunshine! Strong headwinds ahead. Georgie's weaving in and out of people ahead of Katie and Braxton." Lexie's lips barely moved. "She got some 'splaining to do.'"

She's bombed. I'll be queen and force her to notice me.

"Catch your breath, Summer." Lexie leaned near me. "You're wide-eyed and pale."

Braxton and Katie jostled through the crowd to keep Mom in sight and rounded the corner of the concession stand after her. My brother and sister caught her elbows just as she stumbled into the grandstands. I fiddled with my fingers.

As the last convertible drove off our small town's spotty greenish grassy field and out the dilapidated fence, the bleachers in the stands didn't have one seat to spare. Our school hosted another sold-out Friday night of magic with bullhorns tinkling in the wind.

Thump! Ring! Pop! The drum majorette blowing her whistle led the band's booming drums as the ensemble of flag spinners, twirling batons, and drill team members paraded down the field performing our school's fight song. The atmosphere of celebration ricocheted throughout my body. When the announcer's voice came over the loudspeakers, I tried to chuck Zoe's words, but they stuck in my mind. "You're the queen, Summer."

"Ladies and gentlemen and football fans alike: And your 1979 Homecoming Queen is … "

Gleaming, golden-haired Zoe's name sounded over the speakers, so Timmy crowned her queen. At my involuntary wince, Jay's rock-hard arm tightened around mine. I was paper-doll still, hanging on to him like bait on a hook, but I refused to surrender to enlarged eyes or an open mouth. Zoe wouldn't know she fooled me. There would be no dustup. Instead, I'd drive out of this ditch with a genuine, skin-stretched smile plastered on my face.

Why did I listen to my lifelong nemesis?

I released Jay's arm and took my place on the float. The senior princesses flanked Zoe, our new queen. "Congratulations," I said. She put her fingers on her mauve cheeks, making her eyes twinkle, and turned her back.

It seemed like a year until the final game buzzer released me from my Homecoming prison. "I can't believe I didn't even get to sit near you," Lexie said as she stepped off the platform. "Here comes your man. Tell him congrats on the win."

Jay jogged up and yanked off his helmet—hair drenched, perspiration inching down his face. I bounded off the float, and he smothered me into his arms.

"Dang, girl, you're a freakin' beauty. Where's your family?"

"Oh, they all left at halftime." I strangled out the words while he guided me into the emptying field. "I'm so thankful you're here."

"Oh, Sum. That hurts."

"At least Katie came up after the crowning. She told me Braxtie was with Mom, and they had to get home before Mom passed out. I didn't realize how much I'd missed my sister. We promised to get together and catch up. Dad also left around then."

If I'd won, maybe they'd have stayed.

"That's crappy."

"Them leaving didn't make me mad, but I'm furious for believing Zoe."

"Believing Zoe for what?" He gave me a long, salty kiss. "I love swapping spit with you."

"I should say swapping spit's disgusting, Jay. But I've always dug it."

"That's just one of the things I love about you." He pulled me into him. "You should've been the queen."

"I'm yours forever for saying that." He gave me another tasty kiss. "I'll give you the lowdown at Pizza Hut. I don't want anyone to overhear."

"I look forward to it," Jay said as he took my arm, and we strolled across the edge of the field.

"Then we'll sing "Kumbaya" and stuff ourselves with Canadian bacon pizza," I said, snuggling under his arms. A tremor of satisfaction pulsed throughout my body. "My favorite place is with you." I swept his sweaty bangs off his forehead.

"This is where you belong."

"You played such a great game." I stopped and put my hands on his chin. "Meg would be so impressed with your two touchdowns."

"I miss Mom."

"I know." I wedged myself into his shoulders. "I wish I could take away your loss."

"You are." He drew me tight. "You are."

We crossed the field in the comfortable silence of the afterglow covering the stadium.

"Sum, what does "Kumbaya" even mean, anyway?"

"I don't know. We sang it at that camp when I got the 'Invincible Summer' card from the counselor. I think it means 'being happy.'"

"Well, babe, you make me happy." Jay stopped and lifted his helmet to the sky. "Look. That moon's freakin' awesome." He shivered in the cool night as his sweat started to dry. "I noticed it throughout the game. I could stay here with you and look at it forever."

"Me, too, Jay." We started walking again toward my Nova. My pink Candie's sank into the white daisies, and lime-green grass sprinkled throughout the infield. A soft mint aroma filled the air.

"I dig that moonlight reflecting your hair," Jay said as I unlocked my car. He brushed a strand of it from my face. "I'll shower quickly and pick you up at Mike and Anne's."

"I'll be ready in a hot minute." I gave him a long smooch on the lips.

He patted the top of my nose. "I'll be scheming for more of that."

Thirty minutes later, Jay and I waited for our pizza in a tiny booth for two with a red vinyl tablecloth. He folded me into his side on the matching seat cushion. "I'm sorry I couldn't pull off making you queen." The scent of baked mozzarella and pizza dough floated through my nostrils as the murmur of high schoolers got louder once more teenagers arrived. Jay put a quarter into the mini jukebox at our table, and Bob Seger entertained us. "Timmy had a lot of guys vote for Zoe, but many guys voted for you, too."

"It's not your fault." Tears stung my eyes. *Why do I always take things so personally?* "I'm sorta lost in space here. I just wish Lexie were crowned and not Zoe. She's such a vicious girl—to everyone but you. She must have known she was queen when she told me I was."

"What?" Jay squinted. "She told you what?"

With one breath, I gave him the skinny on the whole story.

Jay heard our number and retrieved the pizza. "That's really bitchy," he said, returning to his seat. "You're royalty. She's not."

"That makes me feel like a queen." I blinked away a tear. "The hard thing is that I can't cry." Comforted by the warmth of his leg touching mine, I scrunched even closer to the side of his quad.

"Why?" Confusion crossed his forehead. "What do you mean?"

"If I cry, I'll be splotchy with swollen eyes." I straightened back my shoulders. "And ruin our Homecoming pics. Zoe won't take those away." I sniffed a sob. "But why did I believe her?"

"You always see the best in everybody. And she's had it out for you since the beginning."

"Don't I know it?" I took two slices of pizza and sank my teeth into a thick bite of the buttery, crunchy crust. "Because of you, Jay."

"Me? What do you mean?" He gobbled half a piece of pizza with one bite and pointed at himself. A long string of mozzarella cheese hung from his lips.

"She'd crawl naked through a sewer to get you back." I took my napkin and snatched the cheese from Jay's face.

"Whoa!" He looked unconvinced. "What about Timmy?"

"Why do you think Zoe's dating your best friend? I gulped my Dr Pepper. "For info on you! And after Meg died, didn't she give you a boatload of football pics she took for the yearbook? Eleven by fourteen glossies?"

He scratched his right eyebrow. "Well, yeah."

"I rest my case. Our relationship tortures the poor girl. But I won't have bloodshot eyes from crying. No way. I won't give her that."

His eyes filled with admiration. "That's what I love about you. You're tough as nails even if you get a bummer deal."

"Zoe got the bummer deal." Our thighs stuck to each other in the cramped booth. "I got the guy." I turned my head and gently kissed him, tasting tomato sauce, then trapped his bottom lip between mine in a long, slow suction motion.

"Let's blow this clambake and get out of here." Jay tossed some dollars on the table for a tip and nabbed my hand. "I've got something in the car for you."

When we got to his Cutlass, Jay popped in Bad Company's *Straight Shooter* eight-track, and our favorite song started to play.

"I wish I could give you the sun and the moon, as the song says, but you'll have to settle for this." Jay pulled out a ring box. His large, gold senior ring with our cobalt blue school color stone shined in the middle of our class emblem.

"Oh, Jay!" I moved my finger over every inch of the ring. "Who cares if our pictures look like I've been crying? I love it."

"I have one more thing." His eyes twinkled with mischief. "Close your eyes."

"What? What are you up to now?" His shoulders brushed mine as he leaned into the back seat. "I can't keep my eyes shut anymore."

"I'm almost ready." He brushed back up against my shoulder while getting in his seat again.

"Open them, now." He chuckled his joyful, contagious laugh louder and louder.

I cracked an eye open a smidgin. "You seem very pleased with yourself."

Jay handed me a homemade cobalt blue-and-white perfectly painted spirit stick with thin blue and white ribbons perfectly tied around the ends. The spirit stick read:

**Awarded to SUMMER STEVENS,
the Best Badass Cheerleader EVER!**

On the other side, it said:

**Awarded to SUMMER STEVENS, the Best-Looking
Cheerleader with the Best-Looking Ass EVER!**

"Since elementary school, you've always been good to me." A

lone tear slipped down my cheek. "The spirit stick reminds me of your sixth-grade birthday party. I was so desperate to go but didn't have a present. Mom wouldn't buy one, so I riffled through our eight-track tapes and found Elton John's *Goodbye Yellow Brick Road,* but it had a spot on it."

"I wouldn't have cared about a present." He smoothed away my tears.

"But I did." Putting the spirit stick in my lap, I popped each of my fingers. "I had to wrap it in aluminum foil because we had no wrapping paper. So, when you started opening it at the party, I could barely keep my eyes open. Do you remember?"

"I only remember diggin' you were there." He leaned over and made a sucking sound on the nape of my neck. "I always had it bad for you."

"Well, I had it bad for you, too—especially after what you did." I pressed my hand into his and held them up. "You waved the tape over your head and cheered, 'Oh, Elton John—my favorite,' covering the grease stain with your thumb."

The following night, once the Homecoming dance ended, Jay and I sat waiting for our friends to arrive at his house. "Come sit by me." He waved me over from the kitchen to his cranberry couch in front of the crackling fireplace. A smoldering mound of logs broke into pieces, filling the family room with a wood-smoke smell.

"Right here." He patted the oversized, soft cushion next to him. "And then don't move a muscle."

"I can't wait to see our Homecoming pics. You looked so handsome tonight, and Zoe did not beat me. My eyes were not puffy." I curled up on the couch beside him. "The dance was a blast. Your house bash will be, too. What time does your dad's liquor cabinet open?"

"A half hour before the dance." Jay's eye flickered.

My jaw dropped. "How did I miss that you're hammered?" *I don't plan on drinking one drop tonight.* "You need a swift kick in the ass if you've been drinking since then. I hope your dad's okay with that."

"Oh, he doesn't care. He's more out of it than ever these days."

I scooted away from Jay and crossed my feet, but he parachuted his body, pillowing his head onto my green, velvet lap. "You're a brat," I scolded.

He answered by tightening the muscles in his cheeks, deepening his dimples. "Mmm. And you're on my bingo card tonight." He lifted his head and nibbled on my ear.

"Oh, I see how it is." Jay dropped his head, and I combed my hand through his hair. He found my hand and pressed the tips of my fingers.

Meg's only been gone a month. Jay needs time to mourn. Then he'll stop drinking so much. But what if he doesn't?

I don't have a plan, and I always have a plan.

CHAPTER 23

GOODBYE

October 1979 – July 1980
Senior Year
Gardner, Kansas

I called Mom to see if she was feeling better the following morning.

"Oh, I got up early and feel fantastic."

How can she drink so much and not be hung over?

"Wearing my outfit made you look like a billion bucks, but you sure can't make that mop of hair look good to save your life."

But I got your hair. I wrapped the phone cord around my hand, unable to form a thought, much less words.

"Summer? Are you there?"

"Yes, but why say that, Mom?" I finally piped up. "Homecoming was painful. Zoe didn't do me any favors by lying about me being queen."

"Zoe might be a bitch, but at least she's not sensitive. No one wants to be around that." There was a slight inflection in Mom's tone. I braced myself. "Homecoming was karma, baby. Serves you right for moving out."

"What?" I pushed away my breakfast cereal. "Doc kicked me out. I didn't leave." I started eating again, but the milk tasted spoiled.

"Oh! I forgot," Mom gasped. "Zoe and her mom are coming over." Mom changed her tone. "But listen! Mother and Daddy want you to visit. They've invited you for Thanksgiving."

"I haven't been there in what seems like years, but I guess it's only been seven months."

"Gotta go! Zoe's here." The phone clicked.

A month later, when turkey day rolled around, I drove Mom and Braxton to my grandparent's house. Katie was with her boyfriend. Doc was MIA, but not before he doled out heavy narcotics for Mom from his animal clinic. He'd been doing it for years. She popped pill after pill. "My back and stomach hurt. I don't think I'll live much longer," she complained. "You don't know how sick I really am."

"You're only thirty-eight."

"But I look so old!" She pulled down the overhead mirror and ran a finger over an invisible wrinkle. "I'm getting a facelift and a boob job soon. Then a tummy tuck. Don't tell a soul. Katie says I need them. She's dumb as a board, but she's right about this." Mom pointed to the back seat. "Braxton's grounded for a month. He's been taking off with the car."

"Katie's smart and would never tell you to get plastic surgery." In the rearview mirror, I winked at my brother. "And Braxton's never done anything wrong in his life."

He smiled and nodded.

Two hours later, we arrived at my grandparents. Once Grandfather watched us drive up the long drive, his steel-blue eyes met us at the door. Although it was out of season, he'd bought strawberries from a greenhouse. Standing at the sink, Grandmother Mema and I fell into a rhythm of washing and cutting them. *Why won't my hand stop shaking?* I sucked in a long breath of the sweet, fruity smell. "I guess you've heard about me moving out."

"Yes, but we're glad you're here."

"I hope you know I still want to be part of the family."

She faced me, putting down her knife. "Grandfather and I understand there is more to the story than what we have been told."

"Thank you." I touched her elbow. "That means the world." She picked up her knife to cut strawberries again.

"Your mom said you're considering the University of Kansas. Grandfather's elated you may attend his alma mater. He was a full-back and kicker. Back then, players wore leather helmets."

"Cool! I remember hearing that." I washed another strawberry but resisted popping it into my mouth. Grandmother Mema might think it unsanitary.

"He's a loyal football fan, so you can watch the Jayhawks with him. He attends every home game. Even if they lose, he says, 'At least the band's always good.'"

"It'd be awesome to go to a game with him." *I hope he doesn't change his mind.* "KU's my first choice for college. I'm chomping at the bit to run for them. They've been in contact with Coach. It appears I've got all my ducks in a row for a scholarship letter during spring track."

"Both of you are athletes." She eyed me with appreciation. "He was also in a fraternity. Do you want to join a sorority?"

"I'd love to, but I don't know anything about them."

"I was a Gamma Phi Beta at Oklahoma University."

"Then I'll try to be that."

"No, Pi Beta Phi fraternity is better. The Greek system uses fraternity as a synonym with sorority." She stopped cutting straw-berries and got her purse from the table. "Georgina, your mom's namesake, was a Pi Beta Phi—Pi Phi for short—at The University of Kansas. If you pledge her sorority house, I'll give you her twelve-diamond arrow. She would be elated if she were alive. My friends will also write you letters of recommendation."

My mouth dropped open. "Wow! That'd be incredible." *I don't understand what it all means, but I'm thankful she cares.*

"Before college starts, I'll buy your dorm bedding." She pulled two crisp ten-dollar bills from her wallet and put them in my straw-berry-stained hand. "And college clothes, but in the meantime, here's some spending money." *Twenty bucks might as well be a thousand.*

"Thank you!" I hugged her, but not too tightly. "That'll be so helpful getting those things checked off."

"Remember, Summer"—her voice changed to a teacher's tone —"do not end a sentence with a preposition."

I nodded as if I understood.

On the last day of vacation, Grandfather made his famous

Lipton Onion Soup cheeseburgers and crusty cheese twice-baked potatoes. Before dinner, Grandmother Mema handed me a stack of thank you notes I'd written her throughout the years. Red ink-slashed marks covered them.

"I've corrected your grammar and punctuation."

"Thanks." I crammed down the burger, but it was like swallowing rocks. The meat tasted rotten.

The drive back took forever. After dropping off Braxton and Mom, I hustled to Jay's. We'd made plans to meet, but he wasn't there. Since Meg's death, Jay had started taking me home at midnight and drinking with Timmy and his football buds. I liked them, but I didn't trust them.

I left a note on Jay's door, "You must've forgotten our date. See you tomorrow."

At 2:00 a.m., a rustling under my window woke me up. I got dressed and tiptoed out to the driveway. Jay stood with stooped shoulders by his Cutlass.

"You smell like a liquor cabinet. How's partying late at night going to bring Meg back? I'm grasping at straws here on how to help you." I paced back and forth in the yard. "What's your excuse?"

"Sir, no excuse, sir." Jay imitated the war movies he loved to watch. Then dropped his chin. "I don't know why I'm drinking so much."

"I don't know either, but it's not attractive." I stormed up the steps and spun back around. "This behavior will destroy you. Destroy us. Don't be another race, I have to run." I opened the front door and crept to my room, hurling myself catty-corner across my bed.

The next morning, Mike and Anne had already left for church when Jay's car rolled into the driveway. I met him on the porch steps and waved him inside. He plodded into the living room, pitching his head forward as he propped his elbows on his thighs.

Then, with red, swollen eyes, he handed me a folded yellow legal paper and mouthed, "I love you."

I crossed the room, jerked the paper out of his hand, and opened the letter:

Sum,

I'm very sorry I've been partying with my friends late at night. I've tried really hard, but I'm still kinda bummed out about Mom and am sputtering out of control. I don't know how I could expect you to understand if I don't say anything. Even if I was upset a little, I had no right to be out carousing late with my friends because you've been doing so much for me lately, and it's about time I give A LOT back. AGAIN!!!! I'm VERY SORRY! SOOOOOOOOOOO much. I love you!

Much Much, Much, Much, Much, Much Love, Jay

P.S. I could never lose you.

I refolded the letter into a tidy little box and leaped into Jay's lap.

"I don't blame you for being freakin' irate." Using his thumbs, he swept my feathered bangs to the side. "I'll do better."

Jay stopped the midnight partying but not the excessive drinking.

"I need a beer," Jay slurred. The weekly Saturday night open bar bash Jay hosted at his house was in full swing. With a spurt of energy, he jumped up, put his arms around me, and leaned into me. My shoulders were the matching puzzle piece to his. We held our embrace, slow dancing until he dipped me back and pulled me close, curling his tongue into my mouth. His whiskey breath tasted hot as he pressed me into the fridge door. Once his shoulders hulked over me, he picked me up from the waist and spun me around the kitchen, almost dropping me.

"You're such a rebel, but I forgive you because of those cute dimples." I nibbled on his ear. "You're totally wasted."

"Guilty." He tilted his weight back into me, and we bopped around the kitchen until we started to fall. "Whoa, Summer, it's a good thing I have such a bitchin' girlfriend. You're strong enough to carry me."

"Let's hope it never comes to that." Finally, we made our way back to the couch.

Zoe rushed through the room and out the back slider. Timmy followed. Since Zoe's Homecoming stunt, I hadn't uttered a single syllable to her and tried to avoid her after she'd arrived with Timmy. "Gross. I think Zoe just threw up."

Jay didn't hear me. His eyes were closed; his head cradled my lap.

My drinking days just ended. I want this track season to be my best ever.

Track started in a month, but my leg still ached. The problem wasn't in the belly of the hamstring. It was under my butt and the connector of the hamstring. It didn't hurt during cheerleading, tennis, or cross country, but I pulled up lame when I sprinted. The original sharp pain turned into a dull, constant throbbing. Coach didn't know how to help. Finally, Dad sent me to a doctor who said to rest, use heat, and it would be fine by track season.

During the first day of practice, an earthy swell of warm sun signaled spring had sprung, making my leg feel better. On the second day, it seemed healed, and by the third day, stepping over the red blossoms that ran alongside the track, my leg felt new.

But sharp pain forced me to the dirt once I accelerated from a steady run to an all-out sprint. I got up, brushing brown particles off my knee. *It's like the nightmare when you forget to study for a test, and then you remember in the dream you need to study, but still forget to do it.*

Jay was supportive, but he didn't know how to help. Desperate and out of other leads, I begrudgingly asked Doc for help. He still had the revolving-door-husband policy and gave me a topical veterinarian gel. While I lived at Mom's, Doc tried to force animal antibiotics on me. I never took his illegal drugs; he wasn't a doctor, but I attempted his miracle cure. The side effects gave me garlic breath but didn't help my injury.

Since I couldn't run without hurting my leg, I helped my team. Then, at regionals, carrying a teammate's sweats, I overheard a runner saying, "Summer holds state records and used to be super fast, even winning four gold medals here last year."

Hiding under the bleachers, I squatted forward and bent my face down. "God, why don't you love me?" I sniffed three times, trying to stop the tears, but finally wept bitterly. "Please, God! Don't take track from me. It's all I have."

The following Monday, during practice, Coach found me. "KU called." His face was grim. "Since you're hurt, they can't give you that scholarship, but they want you to walk on and try to make the team. Let's hope your leg heals by then."

You just kissed your scholarship goodbye, Summer. Will Dad pay for college? Mom won't. Grandmother Mema's extra gifts won't cut it, either.

That night when Jay and I ate cheeseburgers at the Dairy Freeze, the smell made me want to vomit. I tore my sandwich into pieces and crinkled the wrapper, crumpling it into a ball. I tossed it in the trash.

"What's up, Sum?" Jay did a double-take. "You're always hungry."

"I don't know." I shook my head. "The cheeseburger tastes funny." I pulled my fries out of the white to-go bag. "I'll eat these. They taste good."

Throwing away my dinner started a pattern of pitching most of my food. As a result, I lost ten pounds, making my slender frame look sickly. Then, Coach gave me a novel about a girl with anorexia. I didn't know what that was, but I couldn't deny that the main character and I had similar food habits.

"The good news is," I answered Jay after he confronted me about not eating, "it's saving me a ton of money. I've been flat broke for what seems like since I was born."

"Oh, babe." He looked like I'd shot him out of a cannon.

In our royal blue caps and gowns, the senior class sat alphabetically in the gym, ready to be called to the stage for high school graduation. I was nowhere near Jay or Lexie, but as luck would not have it, Zoe plopped next to me.

"Summer! We get to sit next to each other!" She tapped the seat by her. "Your mom told me your dress was expensive."

I nodded, took my seat, and stayed silent.

Mom, Katie, Braxton, Doc, Mike, Anne, and Dad sat in the audience. Dad and Mom hadn't spoken one word to each other since the Junior Olympic track time trial, and graduation was no different. All my life, their refusal to get along tainted every important life event.

Before the class strutted across the stage for our diplomas, the commencement program consisted of a blur of announcements, awards, and speeches. Distracted by being hungry, I jumped hearing my name. "Summer Stevens, you've made history. The Most Inspirational Athlete goes to a female for the first time in Gardner-Edgerton High School history. Summer, come get your award."

Jay hollered my name loud enough for the whole gym to hear.

In my acceptance speech, Big Summer started strong, thanking Coach for all he'd done athletically and personally. I wanted to publicly acknowledge him for finding me a place to live when Doc kicked me out. But Little Summer took over, and the sobbing started. I groaned and lumbered off the stage before someone had to carry me off.

"I humiliated myself," I whispered to Jay once graduation ended.

"Nah. You just showed your love for Coach." He took my hand. "I'm so frickin' proud of my girl. Let's celebrate your award this Saturday night at the country club."

"I look forward to it. Tonight's graduation party's going to be just plain weird. Mom said she wouldn't attend Mike and Anne's for cake, so Katie's bringing Braxton, and Dad's coming alone. But how can I complain? You don't have Meg."

A couple of days later, Jay and I had our private party. Once dinner was almost over, Jay put his fork down. "Sum, babe, you gotta eat more. You want to eat. It's in your eyes, but you don't."

I rolled my ankle as he talked. I'd started carrying food with me but not touching it.

"Like tonight, you only had a salad without dressing, but then you ate the whole bread bowl." His brows wrinkled with worry. "You cannonball straight into every problem, so you know your lack of eating can't be good, right?"

"You're right. I'm sick at the sight of food and don't like feeling full, but I constantly think about what I'll eat. I don't know what's wrong." I leaned across the table and kissed his cheek. "For some reason, though, your dinner's lookin' mighty good."

"Now we're cooking with gas!" Jay sliced off a hunk of his filet mignon.

"Mom's got her foot on my neck, trying to sell me on moving home." I chewed Jay's tender steak. "She's a slick used car salesman who can make sticking a fork in your eye sound appealing."

Jay gave me a thumbs down. "Not a good idea."

"Exactly, unless I want to rip all my hair out. I'm staying at Mike and Anne's until I leave for KU. Since I didn't get my track scholarship, Dad's paying KU's tuition, books, and room and board."

"That's great, Sum."

"It's a miracle."

"And I'll only be forty minutes away at Baker in Baldwin City."

"What? Not calling it Baldwin, but the actual name, Baldwin City?"

"Impressed? I hope! I'm trying to make up for my Rocky impression from your cheer camp. Can't believe that's where I'm going to school." He smiled and traced his finger over my lips. "I leave mid-August for football. At least we'll still be close."

After Jay's country club steak, I made myself eat small meals. By July, I was eating somewhat like my old self and had regained most of my weight. Sitting in my lifeguard chair, I planned my Dairy Freeze dinner.

I'll get a double cheeseburger, large fries, and a chocolate shake. I'll bet Jay gets the same.

I wrapped my whistle around my pointer finger with the expertise of a second-year guard as the sultry weather blew the withered sun-crisp flowers into dingy ground cover. I kept my eyes peeled for Braxton, who was a no-show. He'd spent most of the summer at the pool, sitting by my lifeguard chair.

Why doesn't Braxton have any friends? He doesn't like sports or school. He only enjoys chasing butterflies and drawing buildings. At almost twelve, he has only me. How's he going to survive life?

At last, I changed into my sparkly jeans and said goodbye to

Mr. Joseph, who, during the summer, ran the town pool. "Where are you and Jay off to on this sweltering late July night?"

"Dinner and the drive-in." I got my keys out of my purse.

"Watch out for those vicious lightning bugs." He pushed his black glasses up his nose. "They're one of the ten plagues of this unseasonably hot summer."

Parking on the backside of the Dairy Freeze's parking lot, I applied mascara, eyeliner, and strawberry lip gloss while the lightning bugs created an extravagant light show against the dewy twilight of purple-pink, swirly clouds.

"Hi, Summer." Zoe's voice was a squeaking clarinet. She perched herself near my car window, adjusting her mid-back golden tresses. Wearing glitzy tight jeans, authentic pink cowboy boots, and a matching hat, she looked like a Long & Silky shampoo model. Heavy black eyeliner enhanced her navy eyes, and her low-cut shirt complimented her figure.

"What do you want?"

"Two minutes." She wiped her eyes. "It's about Jay."

"After Homecoming, why would I trust you?" I tapped my temple. "You're smoking something strong if you think I'm listening."

"I thought you were the queen." She put her palms in the air and tilted her head toward me. "I did."

"Do you think I can't walk and chew gum?" I gave my horn a quick toot. "You're a liar! GO! Get the hell away from my car!"

"I guess Jay hasn't told you. Has he?" She leaned in my window, her baby powder smell filling my car. "I don't want to rub your face in it."

"Jay and I tell each other everything."

"You're smokin' something even stronger if you believe that." Zoe didn't bat an eyelash. "You've fallen asleep at the switch. I'm only telling 'cause I care."

"Right!" In a frenzy, I started rolling up my window but stopped halfway. "Lexie says you're a toxic layer cake." In record time, I shut the window the rest of the way.

"You're so gullible and naive, Summer." She clucked her tongue. "After Jay drops you off, he's smoking pot with his football team," Zoe shouted through my closed window loud enough for the whole Dairy Freeze to hear. "Bet you're surprised. And to boot, Jay also told them you two are doing it."

I swayed my head back and forth, trying to digest her words that repeated in my mind.

"I knew you'd want to know." She tossed her hair. It fell perfectly back in place.

Zoe's car left the fast-food restaurant as Jay's Cutlass circled the lot and parked beside me. I rolled my car window down. "Hop in, Jay," I said in a monotone, trying to smile.

I can't feel my face. What if Zoe's right?

"Your tapping foot tells me I'm in trouble." The last glimmer of dusk radiated through the car, catching the concern in Jay's eyes. "Let me have it. Cut me, Mick."

"Don't *Rocky* me, but hold onto your hat." He sat shotgun. A calm rage came over me. "Zoe ratted you out. She should know, dating Timmy."

"What?" Jay's smile turned to terror. "What did she say?"

"I thought your side hustle of sneaking out was over. I had no idea you were still getting high with your stoner buddies." I swung my "S" necklace back and forth. "We've never lied to each other."

Jay's lips moved without uttering a word. Then, finally, he looked at me, attempting to talk. "I ... I ... I only smoked pot once," he said, touching his forehead.

"Good try." My heel beat with betrayal. "It's easier to lie if you don't look me in the eye. Stop playing me for a fool."

"You're right. I'm drinking from a fire hose here." A vacant sorrow gripped his eyes. He rolled his tongue over his upper lip. "I haven't smoked pot as much as the guys, but I've smoked a bunch. I didn't tell you since you hate drugs. I knew you'd be mad."

"Usually, when I'm mad, I want to kick your ass, tell you it belongs in a sling." I rubbed my eyes. "But now I just feel stupid. And you've never made me feel that way." I looked at my sandals and picked off my pink fingernail polish. "We're only seventeen. So maybe it's not fair to put my expectations on you. But you're the only person I've ever trusted."

His face fell. "You can trust me."

"No, Jay. I can't." I lowered my eyes. "I need someone, something I can depend on."

"After what you've been through, I don't blame you." He tried to put his hand on my shoulder. I pulled away.

"I feel like your mother instead of your girlfriend." I shook my head. "And I don't like it. I'm out."

"Please don't die on this hill." His eyes pleaded. "I wasn't thinking, just being a too-cool little shit. Forgive me."

"Oh, I forgive you, Jay. That's the rub. But I'm about to have a mental breakdown here."

"We'll get past this, Sum."

"How? There's more."

"More?" Jay closed his eyes.

"Telling your football buddies we're sleeping together? How could you?"

Jay rammed his hand through his hair.

I started crying. "I don't even have the strength to be mad." I raced my "S" necklace across my chest at a record pace. "Zoe's some freakin' Eddie Haskell. Friends with Mom, as she spreads juicy gossip all over town, except her info's true."

"Don't look at me like that." He wiped away a tear. "Your face goes crooked in pain when you talk about your mom. I never want to do that to you. I colossally blew it." With his right hand, he brushed a stray hair from my face.

"Why, Jay? Why be the big man? Telling your buds you've been getting a piece?" I slunk down in my seat. "I want to know, and don't give me some flimsy excuse."

"I'm up against the ropes here, but I've got nothing else. So, I'll tell you." He blinked his eyes. "I needed the guys to know I got to sleep with you since that's what they all wanted."

"Is that supposed to be a compliment?" I shrunk my nose. "Make me feel better?"

"I just couldn't stop myself from braggin'." Jay exhaled a ragged breath. "How can I make this right?"

"I don't know. I don't. I'm holding on for dear life here." My words were paper thin. "I need space. You need to go now."

Head down, Jay got out. I started my car and pulled out of the Dairy Freeze parking lot.

After I drove down Main Street through the town's new streetlight, I screamed at the top of my lungs.

CHAPTER 24

THE SWEET PRINCE

July 1980 – December 1980
Freshman Year of College
Gardner, Kansas and Lawrence, Kansas

Once I drove away from Jay at the Dairy Freeze, I fought the urge to swing a U-ey back to him. *But he lied. How can I trust him?* The minutes turned into days, and the days turned into a week as I hid in my house. *I'm afraid I'll see him but afraid I won't.*

"You can quit being half-alive," Lexie called me with her daily Jay update. "He's gone. Bailed early for Baker."

College can't come soon enough for me!

Weeks later, it was finally my turn to leave for KU. The day before the big move, I called Mom. "What's cooking?" Neither of my parents volunteered to take me, but Katie did. Mom smacked her gum faster than she talked. "Tomorrow, Katie'll be there at 9:00 a.m. sharp. She's thrilled. Don't make her wait."

"My Nova's loaded and ready to go."

After I hung up the phone, I zipped to The Downtowner restaurant, swung open the door, and handed the cashier a five-dollar bill. "I've got a debt to pay."

The waitress craned her neck in confusion.

"Just take the money and make me feel better."

It seems like yesterday I dined and ditched that lunch check during freshman year.

The next morning, Katie appeared at Mike and Anne's, and we loaded her car with my new bedding and clothes from Grandmother Mema. "Here's a gift from Mom." I examined the backpack in wonderment. "She said it's the newest thing."

"Awesome! Mom always knows what's in." We nodded in agreement before departing for the University of Kansas.

I trailed Katie the forty-five-minute drive to Lawrence, Kansas, never letting her Maverick out of my sight. Then, finally, she turned onto Jayhawk Boulevard, KU's main thoroughfare.

Snuggled between the sprawling flatlands of the Sunflower State, the campus's rolling hills resembled an Ivy League school. Once we made a right onto 11th Street to Gertrude Sellards Pearson (GSP) Hall, my misery from missing Jay faded.

Katie and I unloaded my things, and we met Elissa, my roommate. I forced myself to stop staring at her. With waist-length wavy blonde hair, hazel eyes, and a sincere smile, her glamor could have graced the cover of *Seventeen* magazine.

"We're on our way to Smoke House," I said in an attempt to make friends, "wanna come?"

"Thank you for the invite, but my parents and I just ate there." She pointed to her textbook. "I'm getting a head start on memorizing body parts for anatomy class. It'll pay off exponentially. Premed's going to keep me on my toes."

"Pre-med. Impressive." I gave her a thumbs-up. "I'm going to study business. Math seems to kick my butt, but somehow, I'll manage."

Elissa hung on my every syllable as if she were listening with her eyes. "Math's easy for me. I'll tutor you."

"Wow! That'd be so helpful. And I'll treat you to Smoke House."

"I'd love that." Elissa grabbed her book. "Go by the front desk and get a coupon for the best BBQ in town. And take Jayhawk Boulevard to see if Tan Man's still at Wescoe Hall. Before my parents left, we spotted him."

"Who's he?"

"A guy who runs around campus shirtless. Even though the mythical Jayhawk is our mascot, I hear this Tan Man is, too."

"That's so funny. I'm from a small Kansas town, but I guess I'm not in Kansas anymore." We hugged as if we'd known each other forever.

Katie and I got in my car and shut our doors, but I paused before starting the engine. "Who gets hair like that? Well, I guess you do, Katie." I laughed. "But Elissa's sure got personality to spare."

Thirty minutes later, the baked brisket aroma hovered over our table, so I asked Katie for a bite of her sandwich. It was my first meat since Jay's country club steak. "Yum," I said, savoring the tangy sauce and smoky beef flavor.

"Have more." Katie offered.

"That's okay. I love the salty taste of these." I stretched a Suzy-Q fry around my finger. "Lunch is my treat. Dad's footing the bill for college. I could never afford the $358.00 a semester for tuition —$719 for a whole year!"

"I thought he would."

"I'm so relieved." I dipped my fries in excessive ketchup. "I've got to earn all my spending money, so tomorrow, I'm applying for a job."

"I just got one since I'm not returning to school." Katie shook her head. "I'm done partying with Mom."

"Oh, Katie!" I heaved a heavy, grateful sigh. "I'm so thankful you dodged that bullet."

The first three months of college fell into a predictable pattern. Since KU's prerequisite fall classes were more demanding than high school, studying with Elissa filled my nights. She helped me with my biology and math. Working at the student union hijacked my weekends, and walking on KU's track team took my afternoons. During the off-season long-distance training regiment, my injured leg held together. I'd never run forty miles a week before, and my feet paid the price. All except my big toenails fell off.

If Jay appeared in my mind, my crowded schedule chased him away.

When Thanksgiving rolled around, I decided to stay on campus. Grandmother Mema and Grandfather were traveling, Katie was with her boyfriend, Dad was with his new girlfriend, and Mike and Anne had already done too much for me.

By Friday, I missed Braxton, so I called home.

Mom answered. "It's about time you quit bumbling around and cared about somebody but yourself. Get home, now." Mom's voice burbled through my dorm room's phone. "Braxton's just shot himself. He's been smoking pot. Stealing drugs. Narcotics from Doc's clinic. How can he do this to me?"

"B ... B ... Braxtie?" My mouth filled with a bloody, zinc taste.

"I can't talk." *Click!*

An hour later, my car's tires crunched the velvety snow blowing sideways down the long ranch house driveway. A scarlet-blood moon with copper streaks framed the foreboding house. Wintery air tore through my coat, blinding my eyes as my powdery footprints marked a path to the slider. Before I stepped through the door, I inhaled the smell of winter.

Mom lay sprawled out on the blue couch. "What in God's green earth took you so long?" Sitting on the sofa's edge, I leaned closer to hear her.

"He's downstairs, asking for you." Dark circles drooped under her eyes. "I've been flat on my back since it happened."

Making my way to the door, I descended the stairs to the family room. Braxton's clear blue eyes and chiseled good looks made me doubt Mom's drug suspicion. He looked like a youth model on the orange sectional, except he was bandaged and wearing a sling.

"Oh, Braxtie!"

He said nothing.

I tucked the sketchbook I'd brought under his hand and kissed his forehead. "Draw me a masterpiece."

"Maybe later." His voice was bland.

"You're not yourself." I rested my hand on his button-down shirt that matched his eyes.

He smoothed his lips together.

"Hey, buddy, what's wrong?" I hugged his good shoulder.

"What would I do without you? What were you thinking with that stupid gun?"

"Just trying to scare Mom. That pistol's always under the towels."

Footsteps came down the stairs.

"Hi, Doc."

He tipped his head in my direction. "Your brother's chest wound only skimmed the surface." *Doc's talking like Braxton's not here.* "Somehow, he only has a small pneumothorax: a collapsed lung. So, they sent him home to recuperate." With that, Doc tramped back upstairs.

Doc's not the same man Mom married the first time. Instead of a hot-headed drunk, he's now a cool and reserved one.

"Mom said you were into drugs." I swung my "S" necklace back and forth. Braxton wouldn't look me in the eye. "Smoking pot and stealing even worse stuff from Doc's clinic."

"Mom exaggerates." Braxton's nose crinkled. "And you know it."

I nodded. *I can't deny that.*

"She's trying to control me. But she can't. I'm almost a teenager." He patted my knee. "You know how she likes to control."

"She does." I studied him. "But when did you become so savvy? You've hardly said two words your entire life, and now you have Mom analyzed to a tee?"

"I've always known," Braxton said with a biting look. "Even if I never said anything."

"Well, good for you, little brother. But don't ever do drugs. They're like playing Russian Roulette." Agitation crossed his face. "They're not your friend." I coughed. The air seemed to be full of dust.

"I'd never do drugs." Braxton looked me square in the eye.

Is he lying? "I love you so much, Braxtie." I tousled his thick brown cowlick through my fingers. "I'm just down the hall if you need me."

A stowaway thought lodged into my mind as I made my way to my old room. *I'll never see my baby brother again.* The silent walls mocked my foolish thinking.

Driving like a Daytona 500 winner, my Nova skidded to a stop in front of

The Downtowner restaurant. The hostess pointed up the stairs. I took them two at a time.

Braxton! His back was to me in the diner's booth. But he was safe. Crack! *Just then, a whip-like gunshot filled the air. I released the Monarch butterfly from the cage I carried.*

I woke up with a jolt from my bizarre dream, bolting for the downstairs sectional. *Braxton? He's gone.*

The stairs creaked from footsteps. "Braxton?" *Oh, please, please be Braxton.* "That better be you."

In front of the downstairs slider, an image emerged. *Doc!* His voice sounded from across the room. "The police just called." Doc's face had a flat affect, and his eyes were emotionless. "In the middle of the night, your brother stole your mother's Corvette and drove to the town's swimming pool. He rigged the car with carbon monoxide," Doc said in a detached manner. "Drugs were everywhere. He left a note. Your brother committed suicide. Your mom and I are meeting the police."

My face puffed up, and I turned to the wall. "Wha … " I mouthed. Time suspended around me. "What?"

Wracking wails shook me. A crescendo of screams like a howler monkey escaped from my mouth.

Out of nowhere, Mom's poodle appeared, licking my leg. My mother's voice called from the top of the stairs, "Miss Pooh, come here. Now." The ground slipped out from under me.

All sounds faded away except the grandfather clock's four chimes. I rested my elbows on my thighs, leaning over my knees, gasping shriveled breaths. Piercing physical pain expanded throughout my body. I clung to the rim of the coffee table, holding on with every ounce of my strength. When the room stopped spinning, I snuggled under Braxton's covers on the couch and scribbled a poem in his sketchbook.

After sixty minutes of the clock's tick-tock consistency, Mom's sobs rang throughout the ranch house. Once she got downstairs, I hugged her. She pulled away. She'd stopped crying, but her eyes were still red.

"I'm only a sister, but for you to lose a son like this. I can't imagine."

She stopped crying. "What'd Braxton say last night?"

"Not much," I said. Mom moved away from me behind the couch. "I told him I was worried about him using drugs."

"What did he say?"

"He told me he wasn't doing drugs."

Mom's eyes flashed icy and hard. "You should've known he was lying."

An involuntary shudder rattled my body. "He was pretty convincing." I dabbed my eyes. "He was."

"You!" She charged around the sectional toward me. "You were the last person to see Braxton alive."

"I know. I had this terrible feeling that I'd never see him again."

"Then why did you leave him alone?" She stabbed her pointer finger into my chest. "Why?"

"It was just a random thought." I backed away. "How … How could I have known? How could anybody?" I stretched my arms to the back of my head.

"Don't go there." She turned on her heels and ran screaming up the stairs.

I'm not blaming Mom for Braxton killing himself. So, why's she blaming me? I tried to take a deep breath, but a suffocated sob broke free.

I threw on my sweats, hoodie, and tennies and escaped into the dark through the downstairs slider. I didn't look back. I just started running. Mom's accusations ran along with me through the blustery snow as the sunrise crept up the horizon.

When I returned, dawn's light filtered into the downstairs family room. I snuggled back under Braxton's blanket. Doc reappeared and handed me a piece of paper. Written on a page of Braxton's new sketchpad was his suicide note:

"I'm not a baby, and I'm not afraid to die. I just wonder what it feels like. And what happens then."

Later that day, I called Lexie and told her the news. "The funeral and reception are this Tuesday. Zoe's mom's planning the whole thing. Please invite everyone."

How can Braxton be dead? I can't believe this is happening.

The next day I tried to comfort Mom. "I wrote something for Braxtie's funeral. He'd want me to read it." I held up his sketchbook and started speaking:

"My Little Brother–November 1980. Relentless tears. I guess I'm trying to figure out why, little brother, why you left."

"Doc! Doc!" Mom's shrieks rebounded in the stairwell as she fled upstairs. "Summer's attacking me."

The entire time before the funeral, Mom replayed Elvis's "Amazing Grace." It somehow got me through the minutes, hours, and days. Then, at last, the family shuffled into the church for Braxton's service. I shifted in the pew between Katie and Grandmother Mema, staring blankly at the blurred faces in the audience. None of the pastor's words made sense until he said my name.

Katie elbowed me. I stumbled to the rickety podium with red-rimmed pupils and folded and refolded my poem.

Outside, a horn honked, and a slender ray of light radiated through the stained-glass window. I opened my mouth. Only a chirp came out. Not a muscle in my body moved. *Oh, no! It's going to be the Most Inspirational Speech all over again.* My heart pounded through my sweater as my eighteen years passed before me. Finally, I squared my shoulders and opened my mouth again.

My Little Brother – November 1980

Relentless tears. I guess I'm trying to figure out why, little brother, why you left. It must get easier. It has to get easier, but the crying continues.

I can't believe you're gone. I already miss our laughter, our talks, your voice. Why couldn't you share your pain? Did I fail you? Do you miss me? I miss you, my little brother. Life was so hard. Did you ever really have a chance? Why did I make it, and you didn't?

You must be at peace now, chasing butterflies through the diamond dust on the streets of gold. Jesus understands your heartache like no other.

You're Shakespeare's Hamlet, little brother. "Good night, sweet prince, and flights of angels sing thee to thy rest." But I'll miss you forever, my little brother!

Finishing reading Braxton's poem, I put my hand over my

heart and returned to my seat. For the first time, being on stage wasn't about me. Instead, it was about my brother.

Once I sat down, Zoe stood up and sang, "It Is Well with My Soul." The pastor prayed, the family filed out of the church, and I followed Katie to her car through the melted brown, slushy mud. The milky clouds stretched above the morning mist. "Nice job on the poem."

"Thanks," I said, pulling a washcloth from my purse and pressing it over my eyes, soaking up the hot tears; tissues weren't enough anymore. "Grandmother Mema said suicide's selfish because it causes others to suffer. She's probably right. But I, for one, don't have the heart to be angry. Braxtie suffered so much."

Katie nodded.

I returned to the ranch house, and soon after, Lexie found me organizing food for visitors.

"Hello, Goldilocks. Your poem was just right. For a sec, I worried about you up there."

"I worried about myself, too. Especially being around Zoe." We exchanged uneasy glances.

"You knew she'd sing since her Mom planned the funeral."

"I know," I said. "At least she's got an angelic voice."

"Go figure." Lexie rolled her eyes. "Zoe's usually the house guest that won't leave. But she told me that she'd be a no-show today."

"Hallelujah!" I held up my fists Rocky-Balboa style. "Thank you, Lexie, for being here. Mom hasn't uttered one syllable to me."

"Nothing new." Lexie opened a pack of Starburst, giving me the pink one. It tasted like strawberries. "Georgie stays close at a distance."

I nodded as we prepared the food on the kitchen island. "I feel for Mom. Losing Braxtie. But why's she blaming me?" I rotated my wrists, cracking them. "And avoiding me like the plague."

"Your mom flips everything around to be your fault. I'd like to tell her a thing or two." Lexie's upper lip rippled. "She manufactures crisis after crisis, but Braxton's death is a real one. So don't do her clean-up on aisle seven."

"I love how you get it." I massaged my calf with my foot.

"Of course, I get it, Summer. We share a brain."

I smiled for the first time since Braxton died.

"I also get that every time Georgie opens her mouth,"—Lexie looked around to make sure no one heard—"she's lying about you."

"I wish I could Windex my mind from all the mean things she's said. Why does she say them?"

"You hold up a mirror, and she doesn't like her reflection. She accuses you of being what she is. We could analyze her forever, but it might kill us." Staring over my head, Lexie put her hand on my shoulder. "Okay, Sunshine. Lay low or fling the hospitality door open wide. Jay just sauntered up the patio steps."

From the corner of my eye, his shiny dark hair came into focus. I edged toward the slider, but Jay met me halfway, and we hugged. Our embrace lasted just a little longer than it should have.

"I should kick your ass," I said, "all the way back to the Dairy Freeze, but I'm just going to talk you to death. The good news is I talk fast."

"Oh, yeah!" He laughed his deep, throaty chuckle. "I know." He sidled up next to me.

"I'll take that as a win."

"Take the win, Sum." His face grew serious. "You don't need to kick my ass. I took myself to the woodshed after you drove away that day."

"You deserved it, Jay. You lost the game. Didn't even make it on the field."

Jay's pupils expanded, and his voice spiked high. "Oh, I just wanna play, Coach. Pleeease, lemme on the field."

We chuckled so loud that Mom turned to look. *I can't believe I'm laughing.*

"That's just what I needed, Jay. To laugh my head off."

"Head?" His eyebrows arched.

"Ass. Laugh my ass off, but I'm trying to clean up my mouth."

"I like when you say ass."

"I'm sure you do." I paused so long that Jay shifted back and forth. "Don't ever lie to me again."

"I won't, Sum." He covered his hand over mine. "I've learned my lesson."

My voice softened. "I sure hope so."

"You must be torn up about Braxton. How can I help?"

I lowered my eyes and then looked up. Jay stared at me. "You already have." I put two fingers on his lips. "It's shocking that I can even complete a sentence after Braxton's suicide. But, no matter what I go through, you always seem to make it easier."

"You're a warrior, Sum. Always have been." He studied my face. "Look up 'warrior' in the dictionary, and you'll be there waving."

"You've always been my biggest cheerleader."

"And always will be, too. Just keep talking, Sum. I missed hearing your voice."

"That's funny. I just thought that." I smiled and whispered in his ear, "Don't go anywhere."

I made my way to Lexie and turned back to Jay. He cocked his head toward the porch. I lifted my chin slightly. "Make excuses for me, Lex."

"Go," she paused for effect, "follow the yellow brick road."

Jay disappeared out the sliding glass door, and I trailed him. No words were needed. We knew what we were thinking. We got in his Cutlass and drove away.

When I returned, Lexie met me at the door. "I thought you'd been raptured."

"Thanks for covering for me. Some things never change."

"That's the truth?" She laughed. "Here's what you missed: Doc smells like an ashtray, and your mom like a bottle of vodka. Katie and your grandparents have already left. Others are leaving, too."

"Thanks. I'll take over from here. Fill you in later."

As if on cue, the grandfather clock struck five times. The winds switched, and Mom was on my side again. "Have fun with Jay?"

"Yes, I did."

The winter's sun shone through the sliding glass door illuminating Doc, the ever-faithful husband for an audience. The instant he closed the door on the last guest, his smarmy smile appeared. Then, scooping up the vodka bottle, he said to Mom, "I'll get you a glass."

With the dexterity of the skilled animal surgeon he was, he poured Mom a drink. "I'm going to jettison out for a pack of smokes," he said, his saggy eyes devoid of emotion.

Once he served Mom her drink, he made his way to the slider, turning back to us sitting at the glass-top kitchen table. He nodded and, with a monotone, announced, "I'll be right back." Not fast, not slow, but with the steady promise of freedom, his boot heels clicked the porch for the final time.

Good riddance! Don't let the door hit you in the ass on the way out. You won't be back. Braxton's gone, and now, so are you.

"He's gone for good, Mom. I feel it."

"You're street smart, Summer. Maybe it's time. But he's still the sexiest man ever born." A single tear slid down her face. "And the only man I've ever loved."

"I'm sorry, Mom. I am." I touched her hand. *Should I confront her about the night of her accident?* Before I knew it, the words spilled out. "I wish I'd asked Doc about the night you fell." I took a deep breath. "Zoe's mom said she'd come, but Doc showed up instead. And blamed me."

"Doc never liked you. Always liked Katie better."

"That didn't go so well for her."

"What do you mean?"

"Nothing. Just that I didn't like him either." I tried to continue, but the words wouldn't form. Finally, I bent my head and asked, "Did you take all those pills that night of your accident to kill yourself because I said those mean things?"

"Not at all. You just lose count of how many you've taken. I don't even remember the accident, you saying mean things, or taking the pills." Mom touched my hand. "But I know I'd have died without you."

CHAPTER 25

JAY

December 1980
Freshman Year of College
Gardner, Kansas and Lawrence, Kansas

The Sunday following Braxton's funeral, Mom asked me to go to Zoe's mom's church. The Pentecostal service was like a *Saturday Night Live* skit, spoofing charismatic Christians flailing their arms and speaking in funny languages. Both of my grandmothers' churches were as quiet as this one was loud.

The animated worship distracted me until the minister's words spoke straight to my heart. "I'm not here to tickle your ears. I'm here to tell you the truth, and the truth will set you free," the shaggy-haired young man in jeans and a peace t-shirt preached. "You don't have to earn it. Just tell Jesus you love him and are sorry for your sins. Then invite Him to take the steering wheel of your life. God's not mad at you. He's mad for you."

Since I first saw You, Jesus, in your old bathrobe at Grammy's church, I loved You. I'm sorry I've lied, stolen, and wished Mom dead.

The pastor continued, "You don't have to perform for Jesus's approval."

What? Not perform? I'm Yours, Jesus! Where do I sign up? I'm sick of trying to be perfect.

"Now lift your arms if you made Jesus your Savior and best friend."

I don't want to do that in front of strangers. With a will of their own, my hands shot straight up and waved wildly in the air like I was back in Miss Stiglic's class. Instantaneously, an electrical impulse of invisible light tingled inside my toes, transmitting streaking vibrations throughout my body, finally fizzling out my ten fingers.

After I returned to my seat, Mom and I said goodbye before I got into my car and returned to Lawrence for school. She didn't mention the church service.

Returning to my dorm room, I told Elissa about Braxton. "It's so painful." She handed me a Kleenex. I grasped it with both hands and dabbed my eyes. "Let's just chat about Rush instead. It'll distract me."

Since Braxton's death, I'd blown my nose raw. I said, "I guess a thousand girls are trying to get into twelve sorority houses."

Sitting on Elissa's bed, she nodded. "It's all everyone's talking about."

"I'd love to pledge Pi Phi. It'd make Grandmother Mema ecstatic."

"Pi Phi's my first choice, too." She sighed. "I think it's everyone's."

When we turned out the lights, I silently talked to Jesus. "Even though I slept with Jay only five days ago, no more sex." *Why do I think that? Somehow, I just know sex is not right anymore. How will I break it to him? I can't think about it now.* I curled up under my bedspread and fell asleep.

Meg's silky black hair bordered her pleading eyes. "You need to tell Jaybird about Jesus." She gripped my arm. "Please!"

I argued that I didn't even know much about Jesus. That I'd just made Him my Savior hours before. "That doesn't matter. He'll listen to you, Summer. Only you. And I want him in Heaven with me." Meg's emphatic eyes seemed to laser through me, so I nodded. Then, at once, a celestial smile illuminated her face.

I sprang up in bed. The clock read 3:07 a.m. Time seemed to click backward until morning arrived. As dawn disappeared, I called Jay's dorm room before I talked myself out of it. I almost hung up, but something about Meg's desperation made me wait for him to answer.

"Sorry to wake you up, Jay. But I need to see you."

That night after football practice, Jay drove to Lawrence and met me at an off-campus Wendy's. He paid. He always did. He ordered a single. I got a frosty and fries.

We brought the food to a booth in the back of the red and yellow fast-food restaurant. The familiar Dairy Freeze aroma and seeing Jay made it feel like home. We sat side by side like we used to back at Pizza Hut. I scooped a large spoonful of the creamy chocolate shake into my mouth, and it dissolved down my throat. "Thanks for driving the thirty minutes here."

"Happy to, babe." A sly look formed on his lips. "It's usually forty, though."

"But you were coming to see me."

"That's why it only took twenty," he said without missing a beat.

"Aren't you the clever one?"

"This ain't my first rodeo. Anytime you call me, you know I'll come." He chuckled, unwrapping his cheeseburger. "I smell what you're cooking. And dang, I like it." He looked me straight in the eye. "A lot."

God, give me the courage to tell Jay no more sex. "I don't think you're ready for what I'm going to hit you with," I said, remembering his soft lips on mine. "I may not be either."

"Before you tell me your news, don't forget you were a great sister." He added ketchup to his cheeseburger. "How are you doing with Braxton?"

"So-so. Throughout the day, I forget he's gone. Then I remember." I looked down at my fries. "It hurts even to say his name. Your coming to the memorial helped."

A Cheshire cat grin covered Jay's face.

My cheeks flushed at the memory. We exchanged a long look.

"I was so stoked, Sum, to see you … And … Ya know, I'm just going to leave it at that."

"Smart man." I blew out a breath. "Mom and I went to church before I returned to school."

"Good for you."

"I need to tell you what happened there, or I'll lose my nerve." He was chewing his Wendy's single. I struggled to find my voice. "I've … I've become a Christian, so now I'm a 'reborn virgin.'"

Jay squinted his eyes at me and stopped chewing.

"I know this sounds strange since we just slept together."

His face turned gray. In slow motion, Jay resumed chewing and then swallowed by bumping his fist on his chest. He dropped his cheeseburger, wrinkled his eyebrows, and rubbed his chin. "What? Uh, oh, okay?"

"You must think I'm nuts." I burst out laughing. "Telling you, of all people, that I'm a 'reborn virgin.'"

"Babe, I'm trying to process what I'm hearing." There was a long pause. "Uh … ooooooooookayy. Summer, what in the hell has happened to you?"

"You're too kind to make me feel stupid."

"I'm completely lost here." He exhaled a long breath. "What does this mean?"

A seriousness came over my voice. "I want to do it God's way, so I've given my life to Jesus. I don't want to sleep with anyone again until I'm married. Does that make sense?"

"It does, but not really." He pinched his eyes shut and then opened them wide. "I'm trying to wrap my mind around what you're saying." There was no judgment in his voice. "I can't say I agree, but I'll try to be glad. I think." He paused and cocked his head. "That's crazy, though, giving up sex. I can't imagine not having a physical relationship with you."

"It seems strange to me, too." I couldn't look at him. "From the moment we first met, we were physical mag—"

"Magnets," he said with a knowing smile. "Just being near you makes me want you." He slowly shook his head. "I can't live with no more loving. I just couldn't do it."

He's right. I'm not sure I can either, but if I don't stand my ground, I'll be sleeping with him again—and fast. "Tell me how you really feel, Jay."

"Don't get me started."

"I don't know how to explain it, but even though I know so little about God, I want to obey Him. Please Him." I paused. "And I don't want to be like Mom, always needing a man. I want something more. God is it."

"Sum, you could never be your mom."

"You always know what to say." I used my fingers under my eyes to dam up my tears. "You think I won't miss the physical part of our relationship? I just want to be okay."

"You're more than okay."

"Only because of you." I lowered my voice, inclining my head toward him. "You've been my crutch."

"You're the strongest person I know." He touched my hand.

"Oh, Jay! I almost forgot the real reason I asked you to meet me."

"There's more?" He moved his hand and wiped his forehead. "I'm not sure I can take more."

"I know, Jay, but I have to tell you about the dream I had last night about Meg."

"Mom?"

I nodded and told him how she demanded I tell him about Jesus. "I don't understand what it means, but you must know. Meg loved you so much." I blinked. "Maybe it's her way to tell you she misses you. I don't know. It freaked me out."

"Well, I'm pretty freaked out right now." Jay touched his eye.

"You should be."

"I'm just relieved to see you again." He smiled. "You've always helped me not miss Mom so much. I feel guilty that sometimes I'm angry she's gone."

"Of course, you're angry. The whole thing was so tragic."

His eyes grew red around the edges. He closed them for a minute and then reopened them. "You ready to go?"

Leaving the restaurant, Jay stopped midstep and turned to say something but didn't. Finally, we stood by our cars. "So, where do we go from here?"

There was a lull in the conversation. "I need more from life than just partying. You need more, too." I twirled my "S" necklace. "That's why you left me to smoke pot with your football buds. Jesus is our chance," I said, bending my head slightly and placing my hand on his shoulder, "to do it differently, Jay. Do it God's way."

Jay's eyes turned indifferent. As a football player, he would be a big man on campus. That meant he would be about the physical; I would be about the spiritual. He would be about the world; I would be about Jesus. He would be about partying; I would be about praying.

"What about you?" I asked. "Where are you with God?" He stared blankly at me. "What He's done for me, He'll do for you."

"I don't know what to say, Sum." His voice was even. "I mean it. It's been hard watching you feel crappy."

"You always make me feel better." He reached for my hand, but I moved it away. "I'm trying to figure this Jesus thing out. I want to attend church and learn what it means to be a Christian. Go with me. He'll help us. I don't want to beg, Jay. But I'm kinda begging."

He said nothing.

I want Jesus for Jaybird as much as I need breath. An interwoven knot of physical and emotional yearning tore at my gut—for all we'd been through, the heartache we'd survived, and how much I loved him. How much he loved me. Tears burned my eyes.

"Please don't cry, Sum."

"Never feel sorry for me. It'll hurt worse." I looked away. "I hate being needy, but I don't want to lose you."

"And I don't want to lose you. But you told me never to lie to you. And this Jesus thing … I can't wrap my mind around it. It's just … just not for me." He gave me a wistful smile. "But I'm happy you've found something."

I squeezed my eyes shut, trying to make my tears go away.

It was as if an invisible spiritual door closed between us. With all our history, we could never let each other go completely. We cared too deeply. The reality was that Jay was the same person, but I'd changed. He didn't understand. I didn't understand either. But the time came to say goodbye.

I hugged him. "I'll always love you, Jay. You know that."

"Oh, Sum." He brushed his hands over my cheeks. "You'll never be out of my life for good. I promise you that. If you ever need me, I'm just a phone call away."

With that, my best friend, the only person I felt truly loved me, got into his car and drove away.

CHAPTER 26

THE UNIVERSITY OF KANSAS

December 1980 – April 1981
Freshman Year of College
Lawrence, Kansas

"Can this be what you wanted, God?" My words were a tripwire, making me cry even harder. "I'm struggling here." Snot trickled out of my nose, and I wiped it with the sleeve of my KU sweatshirt.

Under a thick cloud cover, I crept out of the Wendy's parking lot like a grandma. A car honked and zoomed around me. I followed it onto Jayhawk Boulevard and drove past the campus's brownstone buildings and campanile clock tower. The bell's musical serenades jarred me out of my malaise just in time to turn into GSP's parking lot.

Minutes later, I lumbered down the cobblestone path to my dorm's front desk. "Do you have a phone book?"

The upperclassman on duty handed me the telephone directory. Leafing through the musky-smelling yellow pages, I searched for a nearby church, scribbled down the address, and stuffed it in my pocket. Then I returned to my room, passing the dorm's student kitchen. The stinky smell of recently zapped broccoli in the newest microwave contraption drifted out to the hall. A girl sat at the table eating hunks of veggies like potato chips.

Once I got to my door, Elissa swung it wide open. "We're all devastated about Braxton, so the girls on the floor made this." On the wall hung a poster board with individual sympathy notes in different colored markers used as a border for Albert Camus's quote: "In the midst of winter, I found there was, within me, an invincible summer."

"Ooh! Thank you." My voice cracked. I put my wrist over my lips. "This … this quote means so much to me. How did you know?"

"You embody the quotation, Summer. And with your name, I knew you'd love it."

"I do!" I sniffed. The inside of my nose was raw. "Jay and I broke up again." My voice faltered.

"Oh, you're getting it from all sides. I see it in your eyes." She got me a tissue. "In class, I learned that when researchers analyzed emotional tears, they found stress and pain hormones in them, theorizing that crying flushes out toxins."

"At this point, I must be zilch for toxins."

She nodded. "Do you know the cure for crying?"

I raised my shoulders.

"Joe's Donuts." Elissa grabbed her purse. "My treat. Let's go!"

Years before, glazed donuts made me sick at the horse shows, but this time, they comforted me. *It's funny that donuts taste good, even if sometimes other food doesn't.*

Before I knew it, Sunday arrived. I was still weepy, but every day I cried a little less. It was clumsy going to church by myself, so I sneaked into the empty back pew and scooted over the one-piece red velvet cushion to the middle section. Somewhere along the way, I'd memorized John 3:16 but didn't understand what it meant. I wanted to know intellectually what I'd experienced emotionally.

With the scent of polished wood and a rough-hewn cross as the backdrop, an older man with positive energy and wire-rimmed glasses explained that God's Son, Jesus, died on the cross for humanity, and His death allowed us to forgive others.

"Jesus is the secret decoder ring you wanted as a kid. He's got all the answers." The pastor scanned the audience and grinned. "Well, maybe that's what your parents wanted. With this college-aged congregation, I'm off a generation. I'm so old that King David could have given me slingshot lessons."

The audience chuckled. "Because of Jesus's sinless sacrifice and choosing to die for your sins, He has the power to help you forgive," the pastor continued. "You're His beloved. He's caught your tears with his fingers and stored them in a bottle."

He must need a swimming pool for mine.

"Jesus died for the damaged people who've hurt you, and armed with His love, He'll help you show them mercy. God is close to the brokenhearted and saves those crushed in spirit."

Then He must be sitting right by me.

The pastor asked who we needed to forgive. "Remember, they may not deserve it, but that's what Jesus did for you, so when you forgive others, you release yourself from the injustice of their sin." The pastor wore compassion on his face like the cardigan on his shoulders. "This frees you from harboring unforgiveness, which holds you hostage in a self-made prison."

Mom!

"Summer, don't try to quiet what you know is right," God said to my heart.

"The Lord's specialty is healing soul wounds." The pastor concluded, "But first, forgive yourself. Jesus's blood declares you 'not guilty.'"

Can I be off the hook just like that? I closed my eyes and bowed, pleading in silent, slow motion as if I were the only one in the sanctuary.

"You are a treasure, Summer." God's voice said. "Believe it."

Forgive me for wanting Mom dead? I didn't want that. I only wanted her love. Braxton's toothy smile appeared. Tears dropped from my eyes, so I dabbed my knuckles on my face, spreading the moisture over my skin like lotion. My fingers touched my lips. *Oh, Jesus, please help me forgive myself for not saving Braxton.* I raised my eyes to the cross.

"You did what you could, Summer," God said. "Do you hold life and death in your hands?"

I soaked up the sobbing with my sweater's edge. The scent of baked bread filled the air.

"You'll never be totally free from Braxton's death, but I'll help you get through it. But stop."

It's the same voice when I almost crashed who said, "Stop! Stop the car!"

"Stop being so hard on yourself."

But Mom doesn't love me, so I must be too much for her.

"You're not too much for me," God spoke again. "Don't apologize for how I made you. I created you exuberantly. Those who really know you, love you."

The voice I knew to be Jesus continued, "I loved you enough to die for you." A knot of guilt partially unraveled somewhere deep within.

Thank you, Jesus! Please forgive me under the bleachers for saying you didn't love me. I know you do. A fatigued serenity consoled me.

Once the pastor's voice spiked with authority, I almost jumped out of my skin. "Remember the people you've offended and apologize. Don't have amnesia about any good they've done. The greatest gift Jesus can give is changing people to be more like Him. Don't wait. Forgive and be free." He closed the service with a prayer.

I didn't understand how God, Jesus, or the Holy Spirit fit together as One—but if the Lord wanted me to do something, I'd do it fast before I changed my mind. *Will Mom listen? That's the $64,000-dollar question.* I raced through the church doors and into the light rain's fresh air.

Stepping one toe into my empty dorm room, I dove onto my bed, dialing the ranch house's phone number. *I need to call Mom before Elissa returns.* Sweat spread under my arms. After five rings, I pulled the phone away from my ear. *I guess I didn't hear you right, God. Whew! I don't have to apologize.*

"Hello?" Mom's voice answered right before I almost hung up.

"Mom!" I swiveled the receiver back to my ear. "I owe you an apology. When I was young, I wished you were dead. I was wrong. Please, forgive me."

"What? You sound mentally ill. What's wrong with you? Get help. See a counselor. Call me if you're better."

Silence crackled through the phone. "I'm just trying to say sorr—"

"Well, um … " Mom's high-pitched voice was far away. "I guess that's okay."

"No, it's not. God's bringing up all these things—"

"Do you have paper clips for brains, Summer Michelle? Your apology isn't helpful. You're a 'do to deal with' now, aren't you?"

"If a 'do' is an energetic personality, then yes, I'm a 'do.'" I busted up. "I'm only laughing because we're finally discussing my stressful childhood."

"Why bring that up now, Summer?" Mom's voice pitched high. "You're eighteen. Stop grandstanding." The phone seemed to go dead. I almost hung up. *I bet her eyes aren't blinking, and she'll say some-thing incredibly cruel.* "You just carry things on and on. I don't care about your apology."

Why can't she understand? "What should I do, then?"

"Stop running your mouth. Nobody wants to hear it, especially me." The phone crackled with silence. "At least you lived in a nice house and enjoyed my fresh vegetable garden. The kitchen always smelled like celery."

"What?" My mind skipped through scenes of my childhood. "You mean like Grammy's acre garden?" *Mom's rewritten history. And she believes her version.* "You grew no homegrown veggies, Mom. I forgive you for telling me things that aren't true, though."

"You what? Don't come home for Christmas. It's your fault. You made me uninvite you." She paused. "That's why no one loves you."

"Jesus loves me. And He doesn't expect me to be perfect." *Click!* The phone went dead, but I continued, "And He doesn't lie to me!"

I twirled the upturned phone, tilting back on the bed. My eyes widened to hold back the tears. I breathed through my nose three short sniffles and crawled under the covers.

I'll call Mom back. Make her listen.

I dialed. She didn't answer.

"Ahhh! Why did I just call Mom again?" I shouted. "Why do I still need her love?"

I fell out of bed, crawled to my running shoes, and stumbled out the door.

The sobbing started at KU's Campanile Hill and reverberated around Memorial Stadium, past the red-roof buildings. I tried to stop while passing students around campus but only cried harder.

Finally, after forty-five minutes, I bent over to catch my breath. I was exhausted, but my eyes were dry.

When I returned to my dorm room, classical music played while Elissa studied. "Can you believe Rush's starting this weekend, Summer? At least we'll know if we're in a sorority before break."

Where will I spend the holiday? Is it too risky to tell Elissa about Mom? "My mother told me not to come home for Christmas."

"Oh, Summer." She put her hand on my arm. "Come with me. It'll be nifty. My parents will love you."

"Will I be imposing?"

"Absolutely not. I'm not taking no for an answer."

Three days later, before Thursday's first ritzy Rush party, Mom phoned. "You've got to come home and get this outfit for the sorority parties. It's just to die for."

I won't confront her about hanging up on me. "I'm in a time crunch, Mom." *I always say yes to her gifts.*

"Then I'll have to give it to Katie."

"I'm sure she'll love it," I said.

"Even though you could make friends with a tree, don't treat those sorority girls like you can do. Mark my words. They won't like you."

Wham!

"Mother warned me, Summer, if you want to be in that highfalutin' sorority, you better put a muzzle on that mouth of yours."

Did Grandmother Mema say that? "Gotta go, Mom."

I put Mom's jabs behind me and attended day one of the four-day Sorority Rush parties. Pi Beta Phi was my first house, and I enjoyed the chitchat, skits, songs, and stories, feeling right at home with the gracious girls. That night I cut sorority houses that may have wanted me with dreams of Pi Phi deep inside.

Every day as a potential new pledge, I got a list of sorority houses still interested in me. For every round of parties, the sororities and rushees listed choices in order of preference. I just had to stay on Pi Beta Phi's list. They sure were on mine.

For the first two days, my Pi Phi bid card appeared like clockwork every morning until the final morning. Not only did I not have a Pi Phi card, but I had no card. I'd been dropped. Completely! By cutting houses that might have wanted me, I ended up an independent—pledging no Greek House. *Grandmother Mema will be so disappointed. Maybe Mom's right. I talk too much. No! I won't listen.*

Mom's lies tried to stick to me like a second skin.

I forced myself out of my dimly lit dorm room to the cafeteria. My Converse sneakers screeched on the waxed floor. The buttery French toast wafting from the grill made me hungry until I chewed the rubbery texture. It tasted like moldy cantaloupe. Once I returned to my room, I got down on my knees. "I can't fix getting dropped by the Pi Phis. God, will you help me?"

The Campanile clock tolled its chimes as the phone rang.

"Hi, Mom."

"What time will you be home for Christmas?"

"Pi Phi dropped me."

"Can't have it all, Summer. So, when'll you be arriving?"

You uninvited me. "I'm going to Elissa's." Mom slammed down the receiver. I didn't call her back.

Soon after our last final, Elissa and I road-tripped to her house. "In my economics class, they taught The Law of Diminishing Returns," I explained on the way to Overland Park. "I finally realize trying to please Mom with her unstable behavior costs me more emotional energy than what's beneficial."

"You've overcome so much, Summer." She tilted her head toward me. "You're finally at the top of your bottom."

"Thanks. Day by day, I'm less afraid to disappoint Mom. It's a start." I blew out a breath. "I'm bummed about Rush, but I'm thrilled you're a Pi Phi. They're lucky to have you. If anyone deserves the sorority of her choice, it's you."

"I wish you were in my pledge class."

Christmas feasts and holiday celebrations filled Elissa's home. Before I knew it, our two weeks were up. The freshman spring semester had begun.

~

"Summer! Summer!" Elissa woke me up after she returned from her Valentine's Day Pi Phi party.

"All of January, there were rumblings that Pi Beta Phi might have Open Rush—space for more pledges. They brought pizza and chocolates for tonight's chapter meeting and asked if we knew anyone who'd make a good sorority sister. I leaped out of my chair, yelling your name."

"What?" My mind just revved up a thousand MPH. "What does that mean?"

"It means that when the girls get to know you, they'll want you for a sorority sister." She tapped her fingers over her open mouth. "And I know a lot of active members. We all attended Shawnee Mission East High School together."

"That's a miracle." That night I dreamed I was free-falling off a ladder, but at the last rung, I flew parallel to the floor and then shot up, sailing across the ceiling.

Two Pi Beta Phi parties later, I got the bid card that had eluded me during regular Rush. I was a Pi Phi pledge. To be an active member, I just had to make my grades. That wouldn't be a problem. I hugged Elissa. "I know you did this for me. Everyone loves you, so the Pi Phi's love me, too. I'm flabbergasted but so grateful!" *Thank you, God, for making me a Pi Phi!*

"I'm happy to the bone for you, Summer. Let's celebrate at Smoke House tonight after my dissection class."

"Perfect! I've got a phone call to make."

"Grandmother Mema, you're not going to believe it." I held my breath. "I'm a Pi Beta Phi."

"Summer, dearest, I'm ecstatic." She paused a long beat. *Maybe she's not that excited.* "I've wanted to ask you something for some time now."

What could she want? My enthusiasm flattened.

In my silence, she continued. "When you were young, I justified treating you poorly because of my disdain for your father." She cleared her throat. "I was wrong. Will you forgive me?"

"Of course! Yes!" I said at once, blinking my tear-filled eyes. "I forgive you." Neurotransmitters in my brain lit up in rainbow colors. Her apology was worth more than all the gifts and trips I'd never received. "Your apology means everything."

"Thank you! I have a lot planned for us." She sniffled.

Oh, my! She's crying.

"We'll waste no time. Next summer, we'll go on an Alaskan

cruise. You also need a diamond ring like Katie's. So, during your first free weekend, come down. And bring your delightful room-mate, Elissa, too."

After we said goodbye, I called Mom. I hadn't phoned her since she hung up on me before Christmas. "Jesus somehow made me a Pi Phi."

"Don't bring Jesus up. When I took Katie to church, she told me to stay clear of you." Mom's voice shifted to a little girl's. "I've never thought you liked or cared about me. You were always so partial to Marvin, who never gave me a red cent."

Mom right. Dad's frugal. But why does she repeat his faults that I'm trying to forgive?

"I do love Dad, but I've always had enough love in my heart for the both of you."

"Why're you so angry, Summer?"

"I'm not angry, Mom." I crossed my arms. "But I can do angry if you want, and this ain't it."

"Don't say *ain't*." She clicked her tongue. "You've changed. What's happened to you?" *Click!*

It was then that I knew what I'd always known: no matter how perfect I tried to be, Mom couldn't love me the way I wanted. She was what my college English professor called "an unreliable narra-tor"—a character whose version of events can't be trusted.

While the receiver in my hand hummed a dead dial tone, Little Summer grew more realistic, accepting the truth about Mom. Big Summer, who'd always understood her, grew more humble. Finally, the two sides of my personality merged into my true self—not quite as strong as I appeared, but not as weak as I felt either, and although not completely healed, less desperate for Mom's love.

I don't have to feel bad that Mom's upset, and I don't have to stress about what Katie said. *If she even said that.*

I grabbed the phone from my rickety nightstand and inhaled the fresh-washed sheets under my snuggly covers. Katie answered on the fourth ring. "Mom just hung up on me."

"What's she mad about now?"

I kicked off my covers and rested my feet on them. "Almost three months ago, I asked for forgiveness for wanting her dead."

"You what?" Katie chuckled. "She must have flipped. You can't let her bother you. That's just the way she is."

"I knew you'd say that." My frustration with my sister returned. "But the snag is, Katie, you saying things like that feels similar to Mom's maliciousness." I rolled over onto my back, resting my head on my pillow sham.

"I don't understand."

"Of course, you don't. It's not your burden that I've always tried to do one more thing for Mom, hoping she'll be different." I sucked in a breath. "I know you don't mean it, but if you say 'don't let her bother you,' it reminds me of trying to please Mom's Pac-Man personality."

"What's a Pac-Man personality?"

"Oh, you know, that new video game where the round, yellow character gobbles up everything in its path. That's Mom. She always hurt my feelings, but for some reason, she didn't hurt yours."

"No, she didn't," Katie said nonchalantly. "Maybe because I lived with Grandmother Mema and Grandfather as a baby, and they met all my needs. I never considered Mom my mother."

"Well, Katie." I pulled my knees up to my chest. "I didn't have that luxury. I'm not mad, but let's call it the way it is. I'll own being too sensitive. But have you considered that your bad mood starts once Mom tries to control you? Anger and hurt are close cousins."

"I never thought about that."

"Well, think." My voice was shaky. "When you're with Mom, you're a Stepford daughter."

"You mean like that weird *Stepford Wives* movie where the women turn into robots?"

"Yes. For Mom, you have mindless obedience, and then you're snotty. Like after you did drugs with her."

Katie paused. "I was scummy to do that." Her voice faded. "And I'm sure it made me bitchy."

"Oh, Katie, I forgive you," I said. "I have my own deal with Mom—always trying to win, but really the win is not going ballistic when she provokes me."

"Since we were little, Summer, I've never understood you."

"But you always listened, even if I didn't understand myself." I laughed, tracing my "S" necklace with my finger. "Mom's the Stockholm Syndrome I learned about in psychology class when victims bond with their abuser. And justify their captor's maltreatment."

"That's confusing, too much to think about."

"I know." I shuddered. "Just like Mom telling me, you said she should stay away from me."

"What?" Katie's voice exploded in shock. "That's what she said you said."

"Trying to figure out Mom's like herding cats." Leaning back on my pillow, I stared at the ceiling. "A tricky cat at that. We can't let her divide us."

Through the phone, an understanding passed between us. "You're right about everything, Summer."

"Thanks, Katie. That means the world." I scratched my nose. "Did I tell you that Zoe's mom gave me a homemade lacy fabric photo album for graduation? I overheard Mom tell her that I didn't like it." I popped each one of my ten toes. "The next time I saw Zoe's mom, I told her I loved it."

"Did Mom find out?"

"Yes! She went berserk."

"That's Mom."

"I'm trying not to prostitute myself for her attention anymore. It's like a dog returning to its vomit."

"That's gross."

"I know. The good news is we are a team. If one knows, we both know." I unwrapped a piece of minty Freshen-up. The liquid melted in my mouth while I chewed the lumpy gum. "We must never allow ourselves to drift apart again."

"Yes, but how'd you get so smart?" Katie paused for a beat. "And know all this?"

"It must be from God." I smiled at the phone.

"But I'm the older sister, so I should be teaching you."

"Oh, no, Katie." I blinked. "You had a lot—" I hesitated. "As the older sister, you took such … such a hit for me … You were my protection … against … against … "

Neither one of us said a word. We both were thinking about Doc.

"He never touched me again once he returned." Katie's voice was sleepy. "And he never beat me again, either."

"He only slapped me during Mom's accident." I rubbed my forehead, swallowing my sudden scratchy throat. "Did you ever tell Mom what Doc did?"

"Yes, just a month ago. She acted like my best friend."

"That's Mom, Katie. She's over-the-top phenomenal, the person you'd call in an emergency—until she is the emergency. It'd be easier if she were difficult all the time. Then we'd know what to expect. Pavlov's dogs prove that."

"Who are Pavlov's dogs?"

"Oh, it's my psychology class again. The class's like therapy." I chuckled. "This experiment randomly rewarded dogs for good behavior, making them more obedient. They salivated for their next treat, just like Miss Pooh's mindless obedience. Of course, that's what Mom expects. But back to Pavlov's dogs, since Mom was fantastic sometimes, it kept us trying harder for her attention. Or, it did me. Doc hated me from the start, so I never tried with him. He liked you more. Not a benefit, though."

Katie's voice was low. "Mom told me Doc's dad beat and molested him. It doesn't make it right, but it makes sense."

I dropped the phone and quickly picked it back up. "Katie, this is a lot to take in, but I want to hear everything. Do you know why he disappeared all the time?"

"You mean you don't know?" Katie was startled.

"No, I never understood."

"Summer, he had a girlfriend in town at his clinic. I think he just married Mom again for her money."

"You mean Grandfather's money so that he could retire. That makes sense. And we continued being ragamuffins, living *The Lord of the Flies'* nightmare, raising ourselves."

"But we managed somehow." Katie's voice took on a light tone. "Even riding in the back of a truck cross-country to Disneyland."

"That's just what I was thinking." I sprung to my knees. "You know, Katie, you can do anything. Do you remember getting that gun out from under the towels in the linen closet?"

"Why did Mom keep a loaded pistol there? What was she thinking?"

"She wasn't. It had no case, no safety clip." I popped a bubble with my gum. "But you sure knew how to shoot when that car with no lights sped down our driveway at midnight. Looking like Jaclyn Smith of *Charlie's Angels*, you stood on our front steps and fired three shots up in the air. I've never seen a car back up so fast."

"I'd forgotten about that."

"Ahhhh! I should've never brought up that miserable gun." I shut my eyes. "What was I thinking? I wasn't. Braxton shooting himself and then killing himself. I feel terrible … losing him."

We both grew quiet.

Katie finally said, "You were good to him."

"That helps, Katie. Our precious baby brother." A drumline beat beneath my eyes. "He was such a neat kid. I miss him every single minute of every single day and will for the rest of my life."

"He loved you so much."

"Since the sympathy cards stopped, it just seems more brutal. Some days I just want to stay in bed." With my pillowcase, I wiped fresh tears from my eyes. I gazed out the window. The early March sunny day foreshadowed the better weather to come. "I keep waiting for him to call. He used to say, 'Oh, you're so boney.'" I wadded up my gum and tossed it in my trashcan. "I can't believe he's gone. Poor Mom."

"You're a doll, Summer, always thinking about everyone else. I should've been a better sister. But, instead, I was always getting you in trouble. Stealing stuff. That bar fight."

"What bar fight?"

"My birthday, remember? I flirted with that Overland Park guy, and he and his friend followed us to the Tumbleweed Bar, and they jumped Jay."

Jay? At the mention of his name, my heart lurched. "I haven't seen him since Wendy's after Braxton's funeral." *I hope he's happy.* "What was he thinking, trying to fight them?"

"Protecting you."

"At least those bar guys fled when Jay's dad appeared." I took a drink of water and sprayed it through my teeth back into my cup. "But how did Jay's dad know his son was out cold?"

"Someone in the bar must have called," Katie said.

"I can still see Jay's dad hauling him to the car, muttering with relief, 'C'mon, let's get your sorry ass home.'" I laughed. "Katie, I've always been thankful you're my sister."

"I've not supported you enough, Summer. But I will from here on out."

"That's all I've ever wanted." I bounced back on the wrinkled bed. "Katie! Come to KU next week. I'll invite the dorm floor to Smoke House. We'll go big or go home."

"You have the cutest personality, Summer. I'd love to visit."

We said goodbye, and I snapped the receiver back into place. The promise of peace played in my mind as I burst out of bed and cracked open my dorm window. An extravagant breeze blasted throughout the room. Below on a flowering bush, a pinkish-lilac blossom began to bloom, and surrounding the plant, a kaleidoscope of brightness lit the ground. A single two-tone orange coral Monarch butterfly rested comfortably on a milkweed plant.

Braxton! His butterfly. A message from him to encourage me. I raised my head toward the clear, open sky and blew Braxtie a kiss—remembering his crystal, sea-blue eyes. His voice spoke to me:

"Don't grieve anymore, Summer. I'm designing and building you a mansion in Heaven. Many years from now, we'll reunite. But on Earth, you'll live your life for the two of us. When I was young, I depended on you to make my life count, and now, I depend on you to keep my memory alive. I believe in you. I miss you, but I'd never leave Paradise. Since I was a baby, I watched you, admired you, and loved you. God made you fearless. He provided a Heavenly Host of guardians to guide and sustain you, whose purpose was always and forever—Saving Summer."

EPILOGUE

J ay. *Do I dare call? I hear his contagious laugh.* I talked myself out of it. The following day, I chewed my nails to the quick instead of picking up the phone. The next week, I threw my hands in the air and stopped resisting. I dialed Jay's dorm room.

He answered on the third ring. "Hello?"

Hearing his voice, I couldn't speak.

"Hello?" Jay said again.

"Can you meet at Wendy's?"

"Sum?" he said with one low, long syllable.

I started laughing. "What? Did you almost fall out of your chair? I can see your shocked eyes and lopsided smile through the phone."

"Nope. Not almost. I did just fall out of my chair."

"Sheesh! Peel yourself off the floor and be ready to drive a hundred miles per hour to make it to Lawrence in thirty minutes. Am I scaring you yet?"

"You've always scared me a little, but I'm lovin' the ride, rolling down the high."

"I'm calling BS on that." I laughed a high-pitched giggle. "You've never been afraid of me. You probably should've been, but you weren't."

Jay laughed his deep, throaty chuckle. "You know me so well."

"That's why I've just gotta fill you in on my life."

"I'd love to hear."

"If I tell, I may have to torture you."

"Ya promise?"

"I promise that if you look up 'fun' in the dictionary, Jay, you'll be waving from the page."

"You're right. But as your biggest cheerleader, I'll also be saying, don't worry, Sum. Jesus, your mom, or me being a punk football player will never mess up our connection. You can't shake me that easily. I'll see you at Wendy's in twenty minutes."

ACKNOWLEDGMENTS

"You will succeed in whatever you choose to do,
and light will shine on the road ahead of you" (Job 22:28). NLT

Thank you, Jo and your family, for allowing me to share Jack's sunny spirit; Missy, for calling me after reading every chapter; Lisa, for the years of making me laugh; Kiesa, for continually and cheerfully coming alongside me to make this book a reality; Elissa, for photographing and beautifying Bartie's butterfly; Jorge, my outstanding principal; Kerry, for offering constant feedback; Marie, for allowing me to read the story aloud; Fhatyma, Katie, Marnie, and Tracy, for your heart for Summer; Mia, Suzanne, Jeannie, Kristine, Judy, Laura, Susan, Gail, and Stephanie, for reading the story; Mr. Green and Roon, for making me look good; Debbie and Veronica, for your savvy promotional skills; Hillary, for your beautiful narration; Ben, Katy, and Holly, for your wisdom; Cindi, for the idea for Summer's story; Danna, Laura, and Sue, my BSF, church, and prayer groups; and my authentic students, for sharing their stories with me.

Finally, thank you to my fantastic family for supporting me as I disappeared for days on end to write *Saving Summer*.

ABOUT THE AUTHOR

Suzy Ryan is an author, educator, Ironman athlete, and SCAD survivor. After twenty-plus years of teaching bright-eyed enthusiastic pupils, tired-eyed apathetic ones, and everything in between, Suzy realized each and every student had a story to tell—some even as traumatic as her own.

Her debut novel, *Saving Summer,* was born out of a desire to offer a bridge of hope for students, encouraging them to see themselves as victors rather than victims. Awarded Valley Middle School's teacher of the year in 2020, Suzy now teaches 6th, 7th, and 8th grade English and Social Studies at Carlsbad Seaside Academy. A Kansas native turned California girl, she enjoys spending time with her husband and three adult children.

If you liked *Saving Summer*, please leave a review on Amazon and other platforms. You may also visit Suzy's website, suzyryan.com, for updates and special giveaways.

Thanks for having a heart for Summer—if you'd like to share your own story of resilience, Suzy would love to hear it.

Founder of Warrior Publishing, Suzy is available for speaking engagements and can be reached at:

savingsummerbestseller@gmail.com